# Rhapsody of Blood

## Volume Two – Reflections

# Books by Roz Kaveney

## Author

### Fiction

Rhapsody of Blood: Volume One – Rituals

### Non-Fiction

From Alien to The Matrix:
Reading Science Fiction Film

Teen Dreams:
Reading Teen Film and Television from "Heathers" to "Veronica Mars"

Superheroes!:
Capes and Crusaders in Comics and Films

### (with Jennifer Stoy)

Battlestar Galactica:
Investigating Flesh, Spirit, and Steel

Nip/Tuck:
Television That Gets Under Your Skin

## Editor

Tales From the Forbidden Planet

More Tales from the Forbidden Planet

Reading the Vampire Slayer:
The Complete, Unofficial Companion to "Buffy" and "Angel"

### with Mary Gentle

Villains!

### with Neil Gaiman, Mary Gentle & Alex Stewart

The Weerde Book One

The Weerde Book Two:
Book of the Ancients

# Rhapsody of Blood

## Volume Two – Reflections

A Novel of the Fantastic

## Roz Kaveney

**Plus One Press**
*San Francisco*

This is a work of fiction. All of the characters, organizations and events portrayed in this novel are either the products of the author's imagination or are used fictitiously.

Plus One Press

RHAPSODY OF BLOOD, VOLUME TWO – REFLECTIONS. Copyright © 2013 by Roz Kaveney. All rights reserved. Printed in the United States of America and the United Kingdom. For information, address Plus One Press, 2885 Golden Gate Avenue, San Francisco, California, 94118.

www.plusonepress.com

Book Design by Plus One Press

Cover artwork by Amacker Bullwinkle, copyright © 2013 by Plus One Press

Publisher's Cataloging-in-Publication Data available on request

ISBN-13: 978-0-9860085-7-3
ISBN-10: 0-9860085-7-5

2013913176

First Edition: November, 2013

10 9 8 7 6 5 4 3 2 1

*For my mother*

# Acknowledgements

My thanks are due to Deb and Jacqueline, my editors, without whom this would be a less smooth read than it is. Also to Deb in her other role as my publisher, along with Nic Grabien, and for putting me up/putting up with me last year on my book tour.

A team of people either listened to this or read chunks of it. Among these are Simon Field, Graham Kent, Lesley Arnold, Cel West, Zoe Stavri, Pat Cadigan and Angelica Tatam—my thanks to you all.

Shana Worthen and Simon Bradshaw gave me useful technical advice, but should not be held accountable for the way I misused it.

And Paule, as ever.

# Reflections

"Be assured that, when you look into the abyss,
the abyss looks also into you"
— *Nietzsche*




"It Doesn't Matter if You Want It Back, You've Given It Away"
— *Palmer*

# Swellegant

## Roraima 1995

"Best party ever," Caroline said, after changing into her seventeenth outfit of the evening. This one was a sort of homage to Zandra Rhodes, all flame-red and pleated ruffles.

Emma was finding the whole thing a bit remorseless and exhausting. Clearly, being returned to a biological age of twenty had not given her a twenty-year-old's capacity for all-night partying.

But she'd never enjoyed parties that much, even at twenty.

Still, it was nice to see Caroline enjoying herself, for once in a room where almost everybody could actually see her and talk to her. They should hang out in the magic community more, Emma supposed, and felt vaguely guilty that they hadn't ever done so much.

Then she felt herself yawning and went pink with embarrassment that Caroline might think she was bored.

Caroline floated over, sometimes making it a dance-step to the rhythm of the samba-band that Gustavo's little group of avant-gardistes had reconfigured themselves as.

"You need some nibbles, darling," she said. "You're looking fetchingly pale, which probably means you haven't eaten in hours. And you hardly touched your tea even though it did come from the Ritz. Go. Find snacks. Don't mind me—I'll be all right. Cute girls; cute boys; cuteness generally."

And off she floated, and within seconds was shimmying up against two of the House of Art whose armour had morphed back into backless sequinned gowns, yet still had something of the martial about them.

Emma followed her nose and found a small bar adjacent to Morgan's excessively vast and baroque ballroom where some sort of sprite was serving cocktails. There was a table there, with one chair at it, and a reserved ticket in her name.

The single plate didn't say "Eat Me" because it did not need to. It had a single small bagel on it, stuffed with cream cheese, smoked salmon and a single delicious sliver of dill-impregnated pickle.

The moment she finished that, the plate suddenly had three spring rolls—one of them was full of pork, one prawn and one duck—and a little bowl of dipping sauce.

"How does she know I don't want bean sprouts?" Emma asked herself, without caring much. There followed—each time faster than the eye could see, or perhaps at moments when Emma was simply away in the moment enjoying flavours—a bowl of pea-and-ham soup, a bowl of bhel puri tingling with tamarind, small brown-bread sandwiches full of crisp bacon and perfectly ripe avocado, a single perfect potato pancake with a dollop of sour cream, six grapes and a fragment of hard sharp cheese. And then a small chocolate cube that had something in it that made her feel awake and energetic again, something at once sweet and bitter and brutal fierce on the tongue.

A single glass of cold clear water and a thimble of the darkest stickiest coffee she had ever known brewed.

Emma found herself suspecting that this was not so much a meal as a job offer, or perhaps a proposition, and considered both briefly before thinking of all the men who had died for Morgan today. And waved away the second cup when it appeared lest the wonderful aftertastes in her mouth become ashes.

She decided not to go back to the party and headed away from the ballroom down dimly lit corridors. How often, after all, had she been given effective carte blanche to wander around the hidden palace of a great enchantress? Well, never, as such...

The corridor seemed to go on for miles ahead of her and every few yards there was another open door to some interesting or potentially dangerous room. A modern laboratory full of centrifuges and expensive looking microscopes; an equally brightly lit room full of benches and retorts and athanors, totally twenty-first century except for the dried blowfish hanging over one desk and the dried bat pinned through the heart to another.

And rooms and rooms of books—it was as if Morgan did not so much have a library, but a score or more of them, each dedicated to a particular area of her interests.

Somewhere up ahead there was a damp, earthy smell, almost as if Emma were heading out of the building and into the cloud forest outside it. Then she realized that what was ahead of her was not the outside, but a room, a single vast room, that brought the cloud forest into the building, and tamed it and domesticated it.

She wandered in, down carefully maintained brick paths between the trees and after a while—this thing went on for yards and yards—she came to a bench, and a small pool, in which there swam three tiny crocodiles, or would those be alligators?

Their beady little eyes watched her attentively and she felt like doing nothing so much as sitting down and watching them back. There was a sort of tiny focussed intelligence there that she found compelling...Then she realized that there was something behind the eyes, and behind the small minds of these crocodiles.

"Hello, Sobekh," she whispered, because it did not seem

appropriate to announce his presence aloud in someone else's place of power.

"Stay where you are"—his voice did not so much speak as slither in her mind—"and be very still. As I would." And suddenly she knew in her bones just how it is that the log you hardly notice can suddenly snap its jaws on you, how that shadow in the murky current can be your death, and all unnoticed.

She was still, and knew that she was not invisible, but still unseen.

The two gods bickered as they walked down the path like old friends or old lovers who have had such arguments time and again to the point where the relationship, the friendship, the flirtation, is the argument, the bickering, the game.

"I can assure you, Hekkat," said the Lord God Jehovah. "I am not bluffing; I am not double-bluffing. The young women do not work for me—I have never seen them before and was only even vaguely aware of their doings."

So much for omniscience, Emma thought.

"Obviously," Jehovah went on, "you are their secret employer, whatever you say. Their insolence, their unbecoming lust for each other—this is the sort of thing you revel in—and it is so typical of you to work through such people behind denials and deceits. Other people may have forgotten, but I fought your Kindly Ones."

"So you did," Morgan said with a grim cheerfulness in her voice, "and had the Huntress not been with you, that would have been the end of your story, and Star's too. And probably not for the better as things have turned out. I'd be proud to be the girls' employer, but I am pretty certain that, if I ever asked them, they would blush a little, shuffle their feet and be done with it."

Morgan sighed.

"I tried the smallest, the very smallest of seductions on young Emma a little while ago, and she shook it off in seconds. Quicker by far than you would have done when you were that young."

She paused, as if thinking.

4

"I still think she works for you," Morgan said. "One of your archangels was there the first day she did anything noteworthy, and they tell me he prophesied great things for her then and there. How could that be the case if he had not been prompted?"

"How indeed?" Jehovah said, and there was a thunder of disapproval behind his tone. "Afterwards, his colleagues put him to the test, gently but firmly, and he said that there had been a whispering in his ears that he took for my prompting, but was not. Neither the Son nor Ghost talked to him, or so they say, and the Metatron was singing to me that day, whose voice can be taken for mine. And Gabriel, who has more initiative than I would wish sometimes, was drilling battalions on the fields of Heaven in manoeuvres that demanded his full attention."

Morgan chittered her teeth at him.

"Yes, yes, it wasn't me. It wasn't anyone who worked for me. We were all doing something else at the time and looking in the opposite direction. We all get very tired of it all, Nameless. It's what you always say. Perhaps you should let me at the archangel; I'm sure I could get him to remember something."

"I sent him off," Jehovah said, "on a routine patrol, into shadow, and he has never come back."

"How convenient."

He started to bluster. "It's not all people who work for me that talk her up; it's a lot of the little powers."

"Yes, yes, that's true—dryads and such—they all seem to think she is some sort of Second Coming of who knows what."

"Where did they get that idea? If not from you."

"Not from me, I assure you, Nameless. I never spend time with a dryad if I can avoid it. Tiresome silly women always going on about their favourite trees."

Jehovah laughed. It was like a great bell.

"You actually went and talked to dryads about her. That's hours of eternal life you will spend eternity not making back. I remember, back when I was a young god, spending time with the cedars of

Lebanon; lovely girls to play with, but you have to get them to keep their mouths shut. Or they would have driven me mad."

He laughed again, nostalgic lust in his voice.

"Yes, I talked to them, and it did no good whatever."

Emma thought of Morgan trying to be nice to dryads and had to stifle a giggle.

"And now the girl is visibly one of the mighty. In her own strange way." Jehovah's voice mingled resentment, incredulity and awe.

Morgan laughed, briefly. "We were all like that, I suppose. In our early days. To our elders and betters."

"That was different; I mean, who was there, back then? Everyone was pretty much starting out. Even Mara was only, what, a couple of centuries older."

"Nameless, Nameless." Morgan really was talking to him as if he were her dim teenage brother. "Our elders and betters were around, if you went looking for them and weren't too proud to take instruction."

He clearly wasn't going to rise to that and there was an awkward silence.

Emma was conscious, not of holding her breath but of breathing so gently she almost felt faint.

"Well, if it isn't you she works for," he finally said, "just accepting that possibility for a second…"

"And it really isn't you either, is it? I know a lot of your tells and you really aren't lying, for once. I mean, who's left? Asgard moved off into shadow and you didn't leave much of Olympus; she's just not their style and I don't see any of the Indians being that devious, either."

"Could be the Adversary, I suppose."

"That doesn't even make paranoid sense. Until now, I wasn't even sure he existed. Maybe we just have to accept there is some player we've never heard of, and she works for them."

"I still think it's probably you."

"No, Nameless, you really don't believe that. Not any more.

6

Because, my dear, you are not stupid and are a realist. You know I am cleverer than you, and if I really were the girls' employer, I would have a better cover story for the fact than either accusing you or saying you don't know."

"Well," he grumbled "maybe saying that is your better cover story."

There was a silence that Emma knew was just Morgan fixing Jehovah with a withering glare.

"The interesting question"—Morgan had clearly decided to move on—"is whether she is important because everyone says she is, or the other way round. Or whether, at this point, she's got enough admirers among the mighty that it's as if she is being worshipped by them."

"You mean, she's becoming a sort of meta-god."

"Well," Morgan said, "that's what several of us are, at this point, anyway. I think. Especially Mara, for all that she denies being a god at all."

Jehovah made more grumbling noises and wandered off into the tropical shrubbery, not deigning to give Morgan's last point the dignity of a response.

It immediately became clear that either Morgan had always known Emma was there, or had noticed it at some point, because her next words were clearly not just a soliloquy.

"He really can't cope with very complex ideas, poor lamb. I'll explain it all to the Son next time I see him, and he'll find a way of hammering the point through Nameless' thick skull."

Morgan plonked herself down on the bench next to Emma, who took the opportunity to breathe out vigorously and then take a thoroughly welcome breath.

"Oh, and the little ones are called caymans." Morgan threw them some small scraps of what looked like chicken. "Hello, Sobekh."

His voice came out from under the water.

"Hail, Morgan that was Hekkat."

"Some of the mighty would resent trespassers. I, though, am sensible."

"I would not have been here if you had not permitted me. I am a weak old god who cannot force my way in anywhere any more."

After all, Emma thought, Morgan wouldn't have caymans in her arboretum if she didn't want to give the old guy a chance to turn up from time to time. And teach her protégées how to be very quiet.

"Sobekh," Morgan said. "I suppose I might as well ask. Have you any idea who it is that Emma and Caroline work for? You don't seem to have any purpose in life except to be well-informed."

"If you've any idea, I'd really like to know too." Caroline popped into existence, unusually without bothering to have changed out of the red outfit. "The Boss is perpetually flashing into my head and I still don't have the slightest idea. They just think at me—and I can't tell you male, female, old, young or anything. If you told me they were a whale, or a computer, I couldn't contradict you. Or maybe that's just a geas they put on me and I really know, but don't know I know. Or something."

Sobekh looked up at them from the pool with four beady sets of eyes and chuckled.

"Oh, I've tried. Believe me. A Japanese tourist went for a swim in the Dead Sea and forgot to take his watch off—I manifested out of the strap just so that I could ask the Lord of Salt. He's an old being, older than anyone we know, and there isn't much he doesn't know."

"So?" Morgan was clearly not in the mood to hear gossip.

"He doesn't know anything. Nothing at all. He spent most of my audience grilling me about you, Emma, because he clearly knows very little about you, either, which is odd."

"Odd?"

"He's fascinated by new players, always was. But somehow he knows almost nothing about you, less than most people. It's as if someone is keeping his attention off you."

"So," Emma said, "the Boss is someone with the mystic power to cloud gods' minds, that either no one has ever heard of, or that they've forgotten about. I bet you two think the Boss's true name is just on the tip of your tongue, if only you could forget to try and remember it…"

The chance to tease two of the mighty was too good not to take, especially since she was pointing out to them something that was almost certainly true.

"So, maybe, evil after all." Morgan sounded almost petulant.

Sobekh chuckled again. "Morgan, so typical that you would assume someone is evil, just because they are even better at games with minds than you are…"

He snorted his amusement one more time and then, suddenly, the four small reptiles darted under the water and were gone, and him with them. Morgan turned to Emma and Caroline.

"What must you think of me? I'm forgetting my duties as your hostess. Emma's seen quite a lot of the rooms already, so, Caroline, what would you like to see?"

It was a splendid piece of manipulation—Emma thought—for someone finally to remember that Caroline wasn't just an appendage. It did Morgan credit, of course, for kindness, politeness and smarts blended wonderfully together.

"Actually," Caroline said, "I bet someone who's as much of a patron of the arts as you are has wonderful things to show us." She glowered sexily at Emma. "I've had quite enough music tonight. So you can come traipse round a gallery. You do have a gallery, don't you, Enchantress?"

Morgan looked slightly abashed. "Oh, not something someone like you would take all that seriously. It's just a few things I've picked up down the years—there's the odd piece that people tell me has merit, but—ah, well—I specialize."

For an awful ten minutes, as Morgan led them down a hidden staircase that appeared in one of the larger trees, and round corners that seemed to defy geometry, Emma worried that she was about to show them some sort of awful magic porn collection. Elder gods in embarrassing intertwinings.

Actually, though, she could see why Morgan was both slightly blushing and showing off something she was secretly very proud of.

The long discreetly lit room was full of paintings, and sculptures and photographs, and they only had one, very recognizable subject.

Caroline was scurrying back and forth as fast as only a ghost can, not knowing where to look next because there was so much. She plucked at Emma's arm.

"Look, sweetie, it's a Delacroix. I love Delacroix and I've never seen it before."

It was a bit like Liberty leading the people, except that the woman had both breasts covered, and was shorter and darker, and the crowd were dressed differently.

"I liked his other one," Morgan said, "and so I asked him to paint this for me. After all, she was actually there, at the Hotel de Ville."

There was a Donatello Pieta, with an armed woman resting her hand on Mary's shoulder.

There was what looked like a Hokusai print, with an armed woman surrounded by swords.

There were images from Greece and Egypt and Mexico—and they were all her.

"It's not a gallery," Emma said. "It's a shrine. You really do love the Huntress—I thought Jehovah was just teasing."

Morgan shrugged. "Thousands of years. And for most of them she wouldn't even speak to me. Now, well, we're polite."

Emma reached out a tentative hand and the old lovely goddess took it in a firm clasp that turned into a hug.

"Thank you," Morgan said. "I don't ever ask for kindness, but, well…"

Emma knew anything she could say directly would be the wrong thing, so she went with the safe obvious remark. "After all, she did save my life…I'd like to meet her again, sometime, and show her that it wasn't just some random victim she saved."

Morgan laughed and a mood was, probably thankfully, broken. "Thank whoever that none of us is afflicted with false modesty."

Caroline was staring at something less spectacular than the actual art in the room, but framed and lit with equal care, a faded snapshot of Mara seated at a cafe table with two coffee cups and a bottle of something, and a large heavy-featured man listening to her.

"Isn't that…?" Emma asked.

"It is indeed," Morgan smiled a grim smile. "He was in the most terrible of trouble some few years later and called on me for help—and he knew that it was a fee I would regard as worth my trouble, that clever, bad man…"

"I wonder,"—and there was real fascination in Caroline's voice—"what those two could possibly have had to talk about."

# Age of Reason

Aleister Crowley giggled.

"So Plato got it wrong. Madame Blavatsky got it wrong."

"I told them so," I said. "But neither of them listened." I sipped my coffee and made a face because it was stone cold. "But Atlantis is a story, as much as a set of facts, and some stories are just too important to people for the truth to have a chance of winning."

He looked at me with eagerness. "And Jesus? Is he one of those stories?"

"I'm not sure you get to hear young Josh's story," I said. "But no, he was a better man than you can imagine. The best man I ever knew. Without an equal."

"So who ran him close?"

"Not people who go around starting religions, at any rate. That tends to be bad for the character."

"And you're going to tell me that the modern age is utterly

12

degenerate and there are no good men any more, woe is us?"

Crowley gestured and the waiter brought me another espresso. I smiled at both of them and at the memories that suddenly came to mind.

"Not at all. Three of the best mortals I've ever met I knew a mere century or so ago, along with a ghost, and an immortal who has become one of my few friends. Now there's a story. Massacres, escapes, duels, monsters."

"By all means."

"A story from which you will learn something about the importance of silence, the passage of time and the fate of magicians foolish enough to cross me."

"I would expect no less," said Aleister Crowley.

I sipped at my coffee, which I had already finished, and lifted the flask of liqueur which was empty.

Without my saying a word, or even staring at him in reproach, Crowley snapped his fingers and both were replaced with gratifying speed. The waiters gave him looks of hatred, and averted their eyes from me, which is as I would wish.

"Take heed then. It was two hundred years ago, give or take, in Paris. On the eve of the feast of Saint Bartholomew…"

I allow myself few luxuries, but, every few months, sleep is one.

Not dreaming, mind, only the fitful sleep of a dog at the hearth, because dreaming would be not a luxury but a weakness, a path for enemies into my heart. And what would I dream of? Gods and monsters are the work that comes to my hands, and fair women, the sisters and loves of my heart, are what waits for me at journey's end, when work is done. I have memory, and no need of dreaming.

So, dreamless, I awoke to moonlight and the clanging of the tocsin and the clash of arms and a screaming chant of "God Wills It," not in the street outside alone, but on the stairs beyond my room.

The children of the man in whose house I slept were screaming. I

13

take no care for the casual violence of men and women, but the terror of children? I retain a distaste for it. I have seen too many dead or tortured children not to sorrow for each one as if it were one I had borne in anguish.

Mother to none, I protect the weak against the strong.

Rousing, and seizing my weapons, I passed through shadow to the room below mine, where my landlord and his family slept. And found two men in ill-scoured armour pinioning him, while another tore his wife's linen shift and a fourth held a knife to his young son's throat.

The two smaller girls held each other, where they lay in a far corner of the room, and a doll cradled between them, and shrieked still.

A priest—or at least a man in a black robe—was tearing pages from a small leatherbound book.

I came out of shadow, and, with a quick grasp and twist of the hand that was not holding my lance, broke the arm that was holding the knife, then, leaving that man where he lay gasping, struck down the one so desirous of rape that he did not turn when I arrived.

I held the point of my lance to the priest's throat. "Who disturbs my sleep?" I asked.

"Loyal servants of the King, and of God's Holy Catholic Church," said the priest, with the cold arrogance of men whose daily work is other people's misery.

It was as if he thought himself safe from me. I longed to beat that security from him, but thought it better to stay as calm as I could.

"As are we all, I am sure. Yet you disturb my sleep, and the king's peace."

"There is no peace," he said. "We come to kill those who would disturb it."

"A fat old man?" I said. "And his wife and small children? I see no rebels here."

"Protestants," he said, holding up the ravaged book, which had a plain cross embossed in its leather.

14

"Your point?" I jabbed him a little harder with my own.

"The wedding," he gasped. "It is a plot. They come to Paris under the guise of peace, so we kill them before they rip away the mask."

"Ah," I said, and turned the lance in my hand to clout him unconscious with its haft.

The distraught mother did her best to pull her torn dress together and started to wail and pray.

I turned to the two men who still held my landlord, and whose hands were still on him, and not on their swords. "If I were you," I told them, not unkindly, "I would leave. I have no particular relish for the shedding of blood."

One of them reached for his sword and I pierced the muscle of his upper arm, where he had left the straps of his rerebrace loose.

"Nor any reluctance to shed it," I continued, as he squealed with pain.

The other loosened his grip, and my landlord broke free, and rushed to comfort his wife where she lay sobbing on the old feather bed on which the family slept.

The would-be rapist came back to himself, squinting and groaning; the man with the broken arm helped him to his feet. I looked at them sternly as I returned my lance to its sling on my back. "Take your priest, and leave. Leave in peace, God's and the king's."

The unwounded man spat at my feet. "We'll be back, Calvinist whore, and burn this house about your ears. As God and the King decree."

Then he pulled a knife from his belt and hurled it at the two young girls.

I seized it from the air by its hilt as it passed me, walked over and rammed it through his open mouth into the wood of the bedroom door. "As you wish," I said as he choked on blood, then slumped in death. Men of violence have such obvious tells.

I turned to the others. "Now go," I said. "And leave your weapons."

The priest was still half conscious. I forced him to his feet, then from the room behind the others as they left, and threw him after them down the stairs. Which left a corpse to dispose of, but everything to its time and place.

I turned to my landlord and his family. "They, or those like them, will return. We should not be here."

"Are you an Angel of the Lord?" the son asked.

I have no particular time for angels, an ill disciplined rabble Jehovah values too highly, but the child meant well.

There were shouts in the lower room, and a clash of swordplay, followed by a thud, a cry and the slamming of the outer door. There followed a clatter of heavy boots on the stairs and a young man's voice shouted, "Uncle Jacques!"

My landlord smiled. "In here, Gaston."

Three young men, dressed in once-elegant black clothes that had the dust and stains of combat on them, burst into the room, their drawn swords bloody. Their leader, who had a thin line of hair above his lip, looked with interest at the corpse that hung from the door as it swung behind them.

"My lodger." My landlord's gesture explained both me and the corpse.

"My thanks," said the young man, with an overly decorative bow and flourish of his hat. "Jacques is my favourite and richest uncle." He looked me up and down, appraisingly, and I stared fiercely at him until he turned his eyes away. "So you are the mysterious lodger," he went on. "I never quite believed Uncle Jacques when he said that someone lived in the attic room."

"She saved us all," said the boy. "She is a warrior of the Lord. Or an angel."

"No," I said. "Merely a good neighbour."

Gaston had left one of his friends downstairs to lug the bodies of the priest and his bullies out of the way; I still held my hand over the eyes of one of the young girls as we passed by, and her mother held the other's face against her breast.

16

Children learn so much about the harshness of the world as it is; I do what I can to help them survive that knowledge and sometimes can shield them from it, as well as from the world.

The young boy looked at the bodies in delighted wonder. Too much delight, but it was not to be helped.

"Do you plan to leave Paris?" I asked Gaston.

A solid plan is only a partial shield for mortal flesh, yet most who find themselves in cities caught up in blood and riot have none, and perish for it. Myself, I never plan, but I can see how some might consider this a fault, the pride of the strong.

"I have a wagon piled with wood." He gestured. "See, outside. Wood that can serve both as hiding place for those who need it, and as a moving rampart for those of us who will defend it."

He pulled out, and flourished, a horse pistol, black with brass fittings dulled with lampblack, and I noticed that his companions had almost as many of the new guns in their belts as they did knives and swords. "Will you ride with us, mademoiselle?" he offered, with a gallantry that was not impersonal. I ignored it.

"I have other errands this night." I glanced up and down the street—dark and silent, heavy with sleep. The sounds of our battle had not travelled past Jacques' front door. Good. "I have conversations to have with the men of power who awoke this fury."

"The boy said you were an angel..." Gaston said.

"I am not. I am one of the powers of this world, for good and ill. Bloodshed in the name of God and gods—it is my business to make enquiries. You need know no more."

"What is your name?" Gaston asked.

I smiled, because he knew it already. "I am the Huntress."

Protestant or not, he crossed himself. "In the name of God," he murmured, "and of Jesus Christ, his son..."

I cut him off. "Your god is no concern of mine. What men have made of young Josh concerns me somewhat, but is not my task this night."

And, as his men helped the children and their parents in among

17

the artfully piled wood on the wagon, I left their sight. They had as good a chance as any that night, and more than most.

I passed as quickly as I could through streets that ran with gore so deep that even in the darkness of shadow they stained my sandaled feet and bare calves a black that was darker than shadow. Even hidden in shadow, I saw more than I wanted of knives against throats, and slit bellies, and of pistols held so as to shatter the frail skulls of pretty women into a rose of brain and bloody bone. I saw plump burghers made to run a gauntlet of staves with nails in them and crawl to the finish because their child's life was the prize, a prize snatched from them at the last with a curse and a cracking of bone. I saw old women held against an inn door by bravos, ravaged by a score, and yet manage to tear with their broken teeth at the face of the last man in line.

I saw a hundred times things that I might have stopped or avenged, and each of those hundred times, I had no time.

I cannot count or tell such nightmares. I have seen too many, and I am not hardened but I cannot save them all. I would if I could, but I need to be where the one who draws endless life and power from each severed artery or smashed bone is coming into new life, because, if I do not, there will be a hundred more dead for each I stop to save.

Which is why, at such times, I run through torchlit streets raging and weeping and slashing with my lance and sword at those men of blood who stand in my way, and yet cannot pause to see if they fall.

I came at last to the home of the House of Valois, across the Seine and down to the foot of the towers of the Louvre, to the new palace that stood in the shadow of those towers, the place of luxury that stood where the lime kilns had been, to Catherine's palace of the Tuileries, the place of lace and silver plate at the heart of the blooddream that was St. Bartholomew's Eve.

The throne room smelled of spilled wine and of piss in corners, but not of magic. It was empty except for a lackey sleeping in a chair by the door, a cudgel loosely clutched in his hand and crumbs of cheese and bread about his mouth and on his livery.

Downstairs, in the kitchens, most of the servants were snoring drunkenly, their heads lying on the tables among the crusts of last week's pies. Ignoring all else, a cook was stuffing dried figs into tiny bird carcases, and placing them on a single vast gridiron. A woman baker was standing over a vast bowl of dough in ferment. The only rituals here were those of food.

A quick sweep of the library showed few books of interest to me. There was a hidden cupboard of grimoires that I smelled out instantly, and stove in with a kick, but nothing more inside than philtres and toxins—or, more rightly, concoctions that could serve as either at a pinch but would be more useful as purges and clysters.

As I neared the chapel my ear caught a high chanting, but it was only a Te Deum. I have known those who praised Jehovah with one hand and worked the Rituals with another, but not efficaciously in either case. I sighed; I had hoped for a chance to soothe my rage by killing those it is my work to kill, but here they were—not workers of dark magic, merely rulers who think statecraft subsists in sacrificing their subjects to their whims.

At the door of the chapel were armed men, with pikes and swords and muskets. I counted them as naught, and left them to lie where they had stood against me. Most of them would live, for all that I cared.

As I burst through the door, the choir faltered in its singing and fled in a rustle of robes and a clatter of dropped prayerbooks; yet the congregation hardly stirred, and only for a second or so.

I had not met these men before, but I had seen their portraits, or their heads on statues and coins—the dregs of the Valois.

King Charles leaned in his chair, as one who sought comfort and rest, yet the muscles of his face were those of a man twisting in misery. His right hand told beads while his left stroked the silken hair of a lapdog that yapped as I entered the room, then cowered and whined as it caught my scent. Its urine suddenly splattered his scarlet shoes and pooled on the floor at his feet.

I had seen his mother once before, when she was a young girl in her father's duchy of Florence. She had been quite lovely then, a nose so long and thin that it might have been a fault balanced by high arched brows and cheekbones of a size just to hint at strength, to keep her from the merely insipid.

Widowhood and regency had not agreed with her; there were lines around her mouth that spoke of pain endured that had become too readily an excuse for the exercise of casual brutal power. She was the controlling force in this room, but there was no stink of magic on her, just the stale scent of too many lavender infused pastries.

At her feet, her younger sons played dice with their perfumed boys and with women whose breasts were barely covered by black veiling and ivory crosses The princes wore rubies on their fingers and in their ears and had perfect oval faces, spoiled by white face paint and a failure to shave that night. And they giggled as they played.

Charles half-rose when he saw me, and then slumped in his chair as one who had long expected death to come for him. He turned to his mother. "All this, and still they come to kill me. Guards –" he cried, and broke off as he saw the men who lay beyond the door.

He looked at me in panicked entreaty. "It was not me," he pleaded, and pointed to his mother. "It was her, and the House of Lorraine, that decided it."

"Calm yourself, cousin Charles." The speaker was an ugly bearded man in black clothes who sat in a less ornate chair off to the side of the chapel, a beautiful redhead in a dark velvet gown holding his hands as one who would protect him from all harm. "Calm yourself. My former co-religionists were not men to send a half-naked girl to kill you—they believe far too much in decorum and dignity. And honour, which is why they are dead."

He half-rose and looked across at me, and smiled. His eyes were friendly and deep, his nose twisted and too big for his face. "This is a visitor rarer than any assassin," he said. "Forgive our manners, mademoiselle."

"Who is she?" yawned one of the youths from the floor. "And why

20

does she have the skin of a Turk, and why is she half-dressed in leather?"

"You neglected your lessons," said the ugly man, his accent that of the South.

"Just who are you?" Catherine spoke for the first time. "Your face is familiar to me. From Florence. But you are far too young…"

"She is one under authority," said the ugly man. "And not to be trifled with."

"Under no authority," I told them. "Save duty."

He looked at me intently. "I know why you are here. And in justice to my cousins here, the family of my new wife, however much I detest them, I must say that you are wrong."

"No," I said. "That was the reason I came, and, as you say, I had guessed wrong. But, as you also see, I remain. I have my tasks, my duty, and sometimes, somewhat, I meddle nonetheless in other matters. Because it pleases me, and because this king's breaking of his own peace woke me from my sleep, and I awoke angry."

I strode forward, struck the whining lapdog from the King's knee and took by the ear His August Majesty, Charles Valois of France, and pulled him behind me whimpering into shadow.

The light of early dawn was almost blotted out by the stinging grey smoke of burning houses and the blacker stinking fume of burned flesh. As I dragged him through the reddened mire of the streets, the King coughed and choked as one just saved from drowning, and then coughed again, deep coughs that tore at him like weasels.

The streets were full of bodies, the living and the dead. Many of the killers had dropped exhausted from the endless slaying, and lay snoring where they had fallen, their hands red to the elbow, the childlike smiles on their faces of those who knew what they had done and saw that it was good.

I could have killed them where they lay, but did not; my anger had dulled from its earlier brightness into that slow smoulder which might at any time flare into white rage.

"See your loyal subjects at their rest." I reached up and held his head between my hands so that he could not look away.

Then I took my left hand away a second and pointed to two small children who lay, their heads stove in with the hilts of swords, in the lap of a woman whose arms had been hacked off, and left to bleed out, and still, in death, cradled her dead children, and said again, "See your loyal subjects at their rest."

"They would have grown to be rebels, like all Protestants." He spoke with the slow rhythm of a child repeating a lesson.

"I could kill all kings who slay their subjects," I returned, "lest they grow to be gods. Yet I do not, because I am just."

"I am King,"—his voice still had an arrogance to it I was minded to remove—"and God alone can judge a King."

"And that is the thought that is in my mind." I did not want to separate the children from their mother, but I needed their corpses for what I would do next. "Take up the children," and I pushed him a little towards them.

He stood there as one not used to taking instruction, and so I instructed him, a little, in ways to which Kings are not used. Then I helped him raise himself from the filth in which he lay, his clothes stained by the blood of the innocent, and by his own as well.

"Take up the children." This time I did not brook any refusal.

He was a strong enough man, but he shuddered as he picked up their light dead flesh, and as their broken heads lolled where he cradled them. I have seen how men train their dogs not to kill chickens, with a dead bird tied around their necks, until it rots, and all the dog can taste or smell for days is that decay. And this too was the thought that was in my mind. My thought as to this King, and my thought also as to his God.

I took him by the ear again, and led him through shadow ten paces, and then ten paces more. On the twentieth pace he stumbled, and thus it was that Charles, King of France, sprawled in his filth and in the blood and brains of innocents, staining the floor of diamond, pearl and crystal that lies before the golden throne of Jehovah.

22

"Glory, glory," sang saints and seraphs and cherubs and powers and dominions, in the endless ranks that tiered down from where we stood and then somehow upwards again, and round, like the theatres of the Greeks or London and yet a sphere of concord and harmony, and then, as they saw me, the choir of saints and the angelic orders stuttered to a discord and then to a halt.

The impostor who shares Jehovah's throne fled from my sight as I once bade him to in words that brooked no argument, and that damnable white bird fluttered to the highest canopy. My hand itched for its throat, though I knew it was not for my wringing.

I had not seen Jehovah since the Aztec business. We were no closer to being friends.

"This wretch," I told him, "is the King of France. He orders the death of innocents. Deaths that you order too."

"I gave no such orders." But Jehovah could not meet my eyes, or look at the dead children.

"Yet men disturbed my sleep with bloody intentions and a cry of 'God Wills It'."

Jehovah sat silent. Charles sobbed where he lay, blinded by the light and terrified to soiling himself, as the living so often are by that sight they claim most to want to see, that sight for which they lie, and kill, and damn their neighbour.

"You have to understand my position," I said. "I tolerate you and your angels and their bullying of harmless little nature gods and psychopomps. I dislike the way you and Lucifer herd the dead into your tidy kingdoms, but I let it be."

"We serve the same cause," Jehovah said.

"Sometimes I wonder," I said. "Sometimes I wonder whether you, and Lucifer, have broken with that cause."

"We have not."

"I tolerated the power plays. And the splits, and the crusades. Because the first thousand years of a project are always messy."

He shrugged.

"Wars of religion. They just go on and on. All this 'glory, glory' is

one thing, but then there is the blood, the endless blood of children."
I looked at him and summoned that white rage. "Swear to me. Swear
that you do not feed on the blood and death of those slain in your
name. Swear it, or I will tear this throne and this heaven about your
ears and leave you a gutted corpse in its chryselephantine wreckage.
And then make an end of the Hell of Lucifer."

Jehovah sat on his throne as if turned to stone, and stared at me
as if he had never seen me before.

He does rage, as well. But it is one of the lessons I taught him. He
reached out a hand as if to cast some bolt at me. I ran up the steps
of his throne, light as a court dancer, and buffeted him once, and
twice, about the ears.

"None of that, boy," I said. "For our old friendship, swear."

He stared at me, and I stared back at him, for a long instant.

"I swear it," he said, after too long a pause. "Is that enough?"

"It is enough," I said. And feared as I said it that I should have
asked for more, yet I could not see how. "Beware of your
worshippers," I went on. "I have seen wars of faith, and watched
men kill and die for you and your many names. Beware lest they,
killing in your name, change you by slow degrees to a Baal or a
Moloch who welcomes that blood, to that which we fight. Beware
lest your worshippers find your distaste for that blood an affront,
and seek other gods."

Charles lay, still sobbing. "This is all madness and delusion," he
cried out. "God, why have you forsaken me? Jesus, why have you
forsaken me?"

"There your god sits," I snapped. "And disowns you as no servant
of his. As to the other, you are not worthy to speak his name."

Jehovah made as if to speak. "Nor are you," I cut him off, as I
stepped from his throne and seized the sobbing King again.

The two broken children still lay before the throne of Jehovah,
but, as I stepped away, one of the lower, more loutish sort of angel
strode up, and somehow they, and the filth Charles had left where
he lay, were gone.

Jehovah gestured and two small souls appeared where their bodies had lain, and with them their mother, and with them the man I had left hanging from a door and one of the guards from Charles' palace.

"Glory, glory," they sang to their God. In harmony.

"It is not all blood and misery," Jehovah said.

I had no more words for him, nor even my spittle for the steps of his throne. And was gone from that place in a step and another step, and took Charles from the heaven of Jehovah to the chapel of his palace.

"Glory, glory," he chanted, and then giggled and then sobbed and then screamed. Then fell into the silence of one who might not speak again, or might say words that would blast the hearer.

His mother sat there still and as she saw her son broken in mind, her bright eyes dulled. The taller of his painted brothers rose from his dicing and stirred the crying King with an elegant foot.

"Oh dear." He looked at me with amusement. "I always told him that he should never play with rough girls." And laughed aloud.

The ugly man rose from where he and his wife sat, walked across and stroked the mad King's head gently, not troubling that his long hair was soiled with blood, tears and gutter filth.

"Poor Charles," he said. "Alas, I find myself forgiving him." He gestured to the elegant fop at his side. "He will be king, and someday perhaps so will I."

"That day will never come." The dandy spoke with a steel in his voice that I had not heard before. "I will kill you first, Henri."

"Alas, Henri," the ugly man shrugged. "Who can say what fate will bring? Charles rose from his bed and bath yesterday morning a king and a sane man and not yet guilty of the blood of half a city. And now he does not even rule himself. And is stained inside and out. And will never be clean or sane again."

The dandy stepped back, not as one in fear, but as one learning respect.

"Mademoiselle," said the ugly Henri, the King of Navarre. "I think that concludes your business here." He bowed to me.

There are few men who can dismiss me, but when they do, I know them. I touched my forehead, in a gesture of salute, and was gone from that palace, and in a stride more, gone from the smoke and blood and mud of Paris. If only for a while.

Henri of Navarre was the only one of them that was worth a damn, and he died with a Jesuit dagger in his guts.

His cousins were a worthless crowd, and his children and grandchildren more of the same—all velvet, ermine, and a stench of piss and sorcery in the corridors. And then they built Versailles, which was more of the same, only with more fountains and more mirrors.

It seemed as if every few years, when I really needed to be taking a look at castration cults in Muscovy, or giant women witch-finders in Dahomey, I would find myself back at their Court, wandering around backstairs and peering through spy-holes at some over-dressed ninny trying to do the Ritual With A Pigeon And Two Mirrors. Which is hard to get right, and only works if you concentrate, but is the sort of thing people try who will one day decide to try the Rituals of Blood.

You don't know it, Crowley? I thought you were supposed to be a dangerous magus. What are they teaching them in the schools these days?

Take a pigeon and place it between two mirrors, so that the angle of the mirrors means it catches sight, each time it moves its head, of movement on the other side, and so constantly moves its head back and forth until it is entirely confused or tranced. Then slit its throat.

What do you mean, you don't see what that gets you except the makings of pigeon pie?

It's a metaphor for human life, you silly man. Distracted from imminent death by passing shows that are merely one's own shadow. So, if you take the trouble to baptise the pigeon first in the name of your enemy, it is quite a nifty little death curse.

Of course, you have to know your enemy's name, which is always a bit more complicated than people think.

No, not just true names, which are one of those things people and dragons keep in eggs on islands like hearts. The names that are what people call themselves in their minds. He may be Lodovicus Rex Francorum to you, but in his mind he is Baby Squidgy which is what his wetnurse called him, or That Useless Boy, which is what he heard the Cardinal say when he failed to construe a passage from Tacitus properly.

And often as not, the pigeon is smarter than you think, and gets scared, which means feathers and shit everywhere.

After Henri though, and especially after the English King, magic was safer than murder, because the King would always pay assassins more than even his brother could afford. Cutthroats always break their contracts, always inform against their employer—it's in their rulebook somewhere.

Well, yes, of course unless they're Jesuits or something. Obviously.

I got quite worried about the Fourteenth himself. I've known people who wandered round making everyone think they were the Sun before and it often ends badly. You have half the court prancing around dressed in gold, and the other half watching through emerald lorgnettes, and you don't stop waiting for the killing to start just because, as a matter of fact on this occasion, it never does.

I'd been there when the Third had Guise killed, which no one was expecting. The little flowers in their silks and Guise stalking past in black velvet with hatred in his eyes and suddenly half of them had daggers in his back.

"I had forgotten he was so tall," the Third said, and clapped his hands for more dancing. Kin-slaying is a powerful magic, and I held my breath, but it was merely politics, that time. And a killing that was the one good thing that the painted Henri ever managed to do in his long giggling life.

Politics and dancing—the two went together, and they spent the wealth of a kingdom on festivals at which the one masqueraded as the other, with cloth of gold, and Lully's music and a stench of death everywhere. That stench hung over each and every one of those festivals and it was usually only the smell of the peasants who had starved paying for them, but this time it felt like something even worse. Worse than peasant children who have choked on grass.

I needn't have worried, as it happened. Louis got obsessed with the widow Scarron, and she was the sort of woman who Jehovah relies on to police the world for him, unpaid.

Suddenly not so much gold brocade and bared breasts as priests everywhere and white lace at every throat and the rattling of rosaries even in the quieter corners of balls. And war. No more orgies, no more pretty boys. Just people marching off to the Netherlands and coming back limping and scarred.

The king was old and dying and suddenly the English, who liked barbarous poets and chopping their kings' heads off, were winning battles as if the Middle Ages were come again. The natural order was shaking, which always turns people's thoughts to magic.

I had my own problems.

The grander the court, the more flunkies there are to stop you in corridors and ask what you are doing there. I mean, I can't be in shadow the whole time, because it makes it hard to spy on people properly if you are a side-step away from the reality in which they are whispering to each other or some dark god.

I found myself having to waste power on glamours and shields, just to do my job. I don't know what came over the world, but suddenly a supernatural being could no longer dress as she chose without someone criticising her. Even at the court of Heliogabalus, or the Chin Emperor, I could turn up dressed in a plain strip of draped leather with a quiver of weapons and swords and spears strapped across my back and the arbiters of elegance would be too busy being terrified I knew their secret to start criticising.

I am a serious person, with serious work to do, but somehow it still stings if someone who ought to be shivering under her stays whispers behind her fan that you are obviously some provincial little nobody whose dressmaker should be whipped. Yet I am always conscious that every fraction of power I use is power that was stolen from the dead by gods I killed, and I hated using the plundered lives of eviscerated babies to make me look like some powdered and patched demoiselle.

I could, of course, have used actual money, if I regarded my work as some tradesman would. If the punishment of Gods and Men of Blood were something I calculated in books of accounts.

Item, gown studded with pearls and feather mask for attending Milord de Rohan's Sabbat. Item, tea service of engraved silver for the entertainment of informants. Item, town house in the style of Palladio and servants to curl my hair and patents of nobility. Paid for, no doubt, out of the many chests of gold and silver I have stolen from under blood-stained altars and invested at compound interest for seven thousand years.

I think not.

And how to balance the other side? Item, one chapel of anthropophagous lapsed Jansenists slain where they prayed. How do you reckon up such things? By the harm they did, or the harm they would have done had I not stopped them?

So in those days the English and the Germans and the Dutch and even the Swedes were catching French manners like the pox. I had to go to the Slavic lands just to get away from bows and cuffs and perfume. And even there Tall Peter was making them cut off their beards and wash occasionally.

And there would be shamans biting off lips and fingers at the edge of Tartary and barons playing chess with their serfs for pieces in Saint Petersburg and all of it would demand my attention. For an hour or so at least.

Then, back in France, the old king died, and the new king was already old when he was a young king, and everyone changed partners in the dance of politics, and all of the people were different and all of them were the same. The lace and the gold and the dancing and the stench.

One day, I was walking around the Marais, minding my own business, when I heard the scuffing sound of boots going into ribs from up a back alley. So I stopped minding my own business, because three against one is never something I am happy with, and three lackeys in green livery were beating a young man in red, and one of them had a wicked little knife out and at the very least someone was going to lose an eye.

All I had to do was say "Hey!" and they dropped him and ran as if I were the entire Paris Watch. So I did not have to waste any power on saving him.

He was a horse-faced youngish man with ink stains on his fingers and a habit, as I rapidly learned, of talking about himself as if he were the most important person I would ever meet, which, I have to say, I seriously doubted even at the beginning. But he did not deserve to be left cold and stiff up some alley where they would pile soiled hay on him.

"What was her name?" I asked, because these things are usually about some woman men think they are in love with.

He smirked at me in a truly irritating fashion. "Erato, I suppose. I wrote a ballad to his mistress, but it was merely a literary exercise." He paused, and said, "Erato is the muse of lyric poetry."

"Actually," I told him, "she was originally the muse in charge of the song of triumph they sang when they tore men's legs off. Those girls were all a lot more fun before Apollo calmed them down."

"I see," he said. "You are a deluded young woman as well as an exhibitionistic one."

I quite understood how people might want to beat him up in public. I summoned just enough of my power for a proper glare.

"Impressive," he said. "I could get you an audition with the Comédie, if you like. Though you'd have to dress better. You are darker than they like, but paint would take care of that."

When I declined to answer, he bowed elegantly, turned his back and stalked away. It had become an age in which it was progressively harder to inspire awe and terror.

I met him again a few months later in a coffee house in London. It was so convenient, not having to go all the way to the Turkish lands, just to drink the stuff, even if it did mean I had to use glamour to stay inconspicuous. Coffee, though, was not my main reason for being there. I was following a blood trail that the sharpness of coffee could not suppress.

"My god," he said to his companions. "There she is right now."

He walked over to my table. "Glad to see you took my advice about the costume; you scrub up quite nicely. I believe Mr. Cibber is looking for a leading lady, if you'd like an introduction."

"I'm not an actress."

"Well, my dear young woman, you are certainly not a lady. If you are not an actress, where does that leave you, hmm?" He considered me, and shook his head. "But no. If you were a girl from one of the whipping houses, you would be a little more pliant. And yet, not a madwoman, because your gaze is steady and your hand firm. Interesting."

He paused again. "And you have presence, I must admit. And knives in your hair... Yet I refuse to believe that ancient goddesses exist, let alone that they sit around reading news-sheets and drinking coffee."

"I'm not a goddess." I must have said it with some degree of vigour, because he stepped back and a number of the place's other clients looked at us.

As he stepped back, a couple of large men with battered faces, whose flaking leather coats were not those of the fashionable world, seized him by the shoulders and rushed him to the door. His friends, or at least his companions, turned their backs as smoothly as if they were parts of a clock's mechanism. Invisibility is a skill I have devoted centuries to learning, yet some people find themselves mastering it in a second.

I followed him and his captors into the street, and up the twisted alley where black and white cats were yowling and rats looked up with momentary interest before returning to their nameless meals. One of the men was slapping the young Frenchman in a slow soft beat that would gradually leave him unconscious and bleeding, while the other trampled his delicately shod feet with steel shoes.

It was the early phase of a standard interrogation that had not changed since the reign of the Old Queen a century and more earlier.

"He is a very annoying young man," I said as I came up to them. "Somehow I seem always to come upon him being beaten in alleys."

"This is none of your concern, Miss," the less scarred of the two told me. "He is a Frenchie, and a murderer and very probably a spy."

"He has been busy," I said, "and yet? Are you sure?"

"Tiger said there was a Frenchie involved." He had the dull bored voice of a not very intelligent man taking orders he does not understand very well. "And this was the first Frenchie we found. We've been looking for this killer since last winter, when the deaths started."

"And yet," because such men sometimes pay attention when someone contradicts them who has the authority to do so, "I saw this man being beaten in Paris a mere month ago. As I say, he makes a habit of it."

This man though was not one of the ones who listen, the first time. "It's all the same to me. One Frenchie is the same as another. We should beat each of them as often as possible, to encourage them all to go away. Same as with Papists."

His victim looked up with a spark of interest through the pain. "You know, that's almost a very witty remark. Beat one to encourage the others—there's something there. How strange to hear wit from the scum of the street."

He really was not helping himself.

"I very much doubt," I raised my voice a little to make the point, "that this silly little dandy is your killer."

"And who might you be, Miss?" said a much larger and more battered looking man who had followed us up the alley. He had the tawny skin of a man who had spent much time in other lands.

"Someone you would do well to pay attention to." The young Frenchman bowed to him, seeing someone who might be more

32

intelligent and might let him go. "I am not your killer, and time spent beating me is time your killer spends laughing at you." Which was well said.

A watchman lit a lantern at the corner of the alley, and launched into his singsong, "Six of the clock, and all's..."

"That will do," the larger man snapped. "Hop it."

"Sorry, sir," stuttered the watchman in frightened deference and scurried off on his rounds.

"Mr. Brown." I remembered him vaguely. "We would do well, I think, to talk to Mr. Wild, or perhaps, if you would be so kind, to the Master of Coin."

I am not especially interested in the mayfly agencies of human states, and yet a certain acquaintance with their petty hierarchies is at times a skill as useful as walking through shadow.

After all, as you know, the world of state secrets has some few things in common with the world of mysteries and rituals. Anyone may turn out to be part of either, or indeed both, and the oddest people turn out to be colleagues—the world's greatest savant and London's lord of thieves and beggars, for example.

What, you did not know Sir Isaac Newton ran Walpole's intelligence system for him? Next you'll be telling me you did not know Newton was an alchemist.

Well, of course you knew that; I know you are not completely stupid. Or ill-informed. Why else did they put him in charge of the Mint?

Though I had thought that, given your own background... Of course everyone knows. If you had not been working for the British all along, they would have hanged you in the last war for working for the Germans.

You fool nobody. Overacting is always a mistake—like telling the Zeppelins to bomb your aged aunt. That is just, well, obvious. But what do I know? I learned tradecraft from Sennacherib, when the height of cleverness was tattooing messages on the shaven pates of slaves.

"Mr Wild, alas," Brown's voice had regret in it, "was hanged for his crimes last year. I did not like the man, but he did great service."

"I had not heard of his death, I have been out of London. And the Master?"

"The Master ails. It is his great age." Brown added respect to his tone without losing the regret. "These killings are of especial interest to him, because he cannot see how they were done by the hand of man."

"That is perhaps because they were not."

"Yet the faces of the dead are chewed by human teeth, even though their guts are clawed out by some beast and their hearts pierced as if by a lance."

I had thought the blood trail of a kind I recognized.

"So—" the Frenchman was thinking aloud, but with more authority than many who are certain, "—it is a madman with a large dog and a lance. What could be simpler? You just have to wander the streets looking for such a man; even these fellows should be capable of that." He paused. "And when you catch him, you could take a cast of his bite, and check it against the wounds of the dead."

Brown regarded him with interest. "How do you explain the poison darts that fill the victims as if they were pincushions?"

The Frenchman shrugged. "In the Indies, as I am sure you know, the small brown folk shoot such darts from blowpipes. Obviously our murderer has a companion from those parts, as well as his dog, and his lance."

This was all very entertaining, but entirely beside the point. "Why," I asked, "did the Master tell you to look for a Frenchman?"

"Well," Brown said, "he said a servant of tyranny? And that usually means a Frog these days."

The Master's habit of thinking in the symbols of alchemy was obviously tipping over into dotage. That, or too much mercury in his laboratory. I had told him to beware of this when he was young and unknown.

34

"No." I too was thinking. "A servant, but not a human servant. Have some of the killings been in different places on the same night?"

I needed to know the worst.

"Yes," one of the scarred men volunteered. "Two girls were killed on their beats, and a watchman the same night."

"So." It was as bad as I had feared. "At least a brace then. And perhaps a pride."

I have always hated manticores. But not as much as the people who bring them into being; that takes a special cast of mind. To take a human mind and wreck it, and a human body and turn it into a beast, and then set it loose. There are some sins that call for a Hell deeper with anguish than is Lucifer's.

And then I spoke the name aloud. Brown knew what I was speaking of, and shuddered.

The young Frenchman looked at me askance. "I know that my madman is hard to credit. Insanity, though, is always possible, if improbable. And you are talking the language of mythology, the language of the impossible."

I smiled sweetly at him, and flickered out of glamour, and had my lance to his throat before he could say another word. "Mythology," I corrected him, "is a word clever men use to describe wisdom that they have forgotten." The lance was back in its sling as I spoke; I wished only to instruct him, not terrify him.

"How did you do that? Your clothes and hair changed for a moment as you moved, and you were faster than a snake with a rat."

"There are," I said, "things in this world that you do not know about. Ignorance is not a crime. Assuming you know everything that there is to be known is a folly. I am sure that you know things that I do not, and that perhaps you will be able to tell me some of them."

Actually, I doubted this—though the trick with the casts of the teeth was a clever idea—but, as an Italian once told me, you catch more flies with honey than with vinegar.

"I read about her, once," one of the men said. "The woman at my dame school taught us our letters with an old chapbook called The Roaring Girl of Jerusalem. She's hundreds of years old and kissing cousins with the Wandering Jew."

"I thought that was the Scarlet Woman dressed in the Sun and Moon," Brown said. "Which is something to do with keeping your alembics on a steady flame. Or that's what the Master said."

I had never before realized the real inconvenience to me of the growth of mass literacy.

"So," Brown went on, "that aside, what do we do about manticores?"

"Hunt them down with dogs," I said. "And take heavy losses. Or I could kill them for you. Except that the men who made them know how to make more, and they are what you need to catch."

"Well," Brown said. "We could try looking for more Frenchmen. This one seems a decent enough chap, but there must be some proper Frenchmen around here somewhere."

"I assure you, officer," the Frenchman said, "that no-one in France would meddle with such matters. Even if they are true and actual, such proceedings lack elegance and good sense; they are, as you would say, not à la mode." He bowed. "And it will be my pleasure to prove this to you and defend the honour of my nation. What monsters can stand for long against us?"

"And who are you?" I asked. I prefer to know the names of brave young men who are going to get themselves killed by my side, as my memory is the only memorial they are likely to have.

I was also impressed by a man who could ignore his crushed toes and his battered ribs, and be so courteous, so insightful and so very very annoying,

"I am Francois-Marie De Arouet," he said. "Known to connoisseurs of literature as Voltaire."

"That's quite a lot of names," said Tiger Brown. "Me and my men here, Jobbings and Clout, don't go by so many, and we get by."

"The important thing –" I paused to get their attention and

realised that I had it already. I sometimes forget that even the agencies of the state mostly live in a world where monsters, and women warriors from the deep past, are the stuff of tavern tales, not daily business. "The important thing to remember is that they have the darts all over their shoulders, and a sting like a scorpion. Let them close with you, and you are dead. Unless, that is, you are me. On the other hand, they are not the sort of monster that can survive a ball to the brain or a halberd in the guts."

Jobbings, or possibly Clout, said, "I'd wager good coin that my coat would stand up to any dart, Miss. The coats what we wear are good boiled leather that saw our granfers through the War. Armour of righteousness, Miss—boiled leather and the good old cause."

Seconds later, he proved himself. A form came bounding up the alley from the further end. Its claws clattered on the pavement and it stared at us with unseeing great blue eyes and swung its tail like a mace. It tried to claw Jobbings's guts out and found itself scrabbling on leather for a hold. Brown pulled a great horse pistol from a pocket in his coat and clapped it to the creature's red-haired head, and fired.

It fired a few of its darts from its shoulders and spined back as it died, but the darts fell spent before they could damage anything save the hem of Arouet's fussily draped red coat.

I walked over and pulled its head back, not minding the blood and brains on my hand, so that we could get a clear look in the lamplight at the face, human except for the extra rows of teeth which stretched the mouth in a fixed and horrid smile. It had the palest of white skin, with a few freckles and green-gray eyes. And it stank like a sewer rat.

I wiped my hands on its lustrous pelt and stepped back. "That was a lucky chance," I said. "They will not all be so easy to kill."

Clout or Jobbings stood up, his face ashen and his left ear hanging from his skull like a partly peeled apple. His coat, however, was impressively intact.

"Looks like a wild Irishman," Brown said. "I saw many faces like that as a young man at the Boyne."

"So," I said, "you have managed to kill one, but we need to find the others and find where they are being kept and where more are being made."

Arouet bounced up and down on the balls of his feet like a child dying to tell us his new good idea. "Is there a map of where the killings happened?"

Brown kicked the creature one more time to ensure it was truly dead and gestured us to follow him. "Mr Wild had a map," he said. "But it is in his business office, not his official office, so I'll thank you to keep quiet about anything you see there. He is dead, you see, but his business, like his work, goes on."

We walked further up the alley and then down an even tighter passageway and found ourselves inching between buildings so close together that the path we were walking was not one a fat man, or a very tall one, could have managed. The shoulders of the three agents scraped along the walls as they walked, bruising and flaking their leather coats still further.

We were in the city's secret places, a rookery beyond rookeries. And suddenly, we took a turn through a low door and were in a great room, where men in rags stood in patient lines at a table where they handed in farthings, and where young whores handed in, or collected, their powdered wigs from a row of hairstands, and where, in a far corner, four young men were practising walking on one leg with the other tied with leather straps as if it were a stump.

One of the whores made a sad face at the sight of Clout's, or Jobbings', torn ear and went to a drawer from which she pulled a needle, some thread and a small bottle of some spirit. She pecked him on the cheek and he smiled, then grimaced as she poured the spirit over his wound and commenced to stitch him back together.

She had clearly done this before—her stitches were deft—and she took as much care with this battered man as she would have done with one of her sisters in the trade.

"Mr Wild was King of the Beggars," Mr Brown said, "long before the Master tapped him to run our force. The Master has his little

38

jokes, you see, and it amused to him to have a second whom he could hang or burn whenever the mood struck him. As, last year, it did."

I looked at him with a question in my eyes though not yet on my lips.

Brown pulled a sad, but not very sad, face. "They caught him coining, Mr Wild. Richest man in London, and still labouring at coining. And he knew how down the Master is on coiners. I shall never understand the criminal mind, Miss, which is why the Master made me his number three. Because I may not understand criminals, but I can still hit them. Set a clever thief to catch thieves, the Master says, and an honest stupid man to put the hand of admonition on the thief's shoulder."

"This map, if it please you?" Arouet's voice had an edge of impatience. "And perhaps some rolls of thread, and some pins."

Brown led us to the map, spread out on a series of tables pushed end-to-end at the furthest corner of this great dark cavern of a room. "Lots of pins already. It's how he kept track of their beats and their pitches. Green pins for whores and brown for beggars and crazy Abraham men and blue for pickpockets, cutpurses and parish constables. The red pins are the dead."

The young whore cast off from her stitching of the wounded man and fetched more thread from the draw into which she put her bloody needle and the bottle of spirit.

Arouet looked smugly around at us. "None of you have any idea of what I am about to show you, do you?" he said, as if this were the best news he had had in years. "Watch, and learn."

He ran the black threads from one red pin to the next, round the circuit of the further ones and in an endless network of loops, like the web of a crazy spider. After a while, I started to see what he was doing.

"Here we have the outer limits of where the killings have taken place," he said. "And that would be a good line along which to draw the perimeter from which we move in. And look, there is a cluster there, by that church, and there by that warehouse, and there by the riverside. Wherever the creatures lair, they have to stalk out of their home and pace their way through the streets and alleys to get to where they kill and eat. And by joining up the kills—two hundred, good god, why did I not know of this already—we can see where their lair might be."

I had said without believing that he might be able to tell me something I did not know, but I could see that he was indeed doing so. I had never thought to find the unknown in such a way—this was an age of reason, perhaps, but it was also an age of sudden miraculous arrivals of knowledge.

"Now," he remarked, tying off the thread, "I'll wager Mr Wild was an efficient man who kept a record of every transaction he might make his profit on. And that his clerks continue to this day."

Brown walked across to another table where there lay great leather-bound books.

"Sometimes," he said, "when he was in his cups, Mr Wild said that he was Jonathan the Conqueror, and these were his doomsday books. And now they are all Miss Polly's. I suggested to the Master that we bring her into the work—she is as clever as her father—but he said it was no work for a woman, and that she is a person of immoral life."

"Ha!" A painted young woman with curled ringlets piled high on her head and her breasts barely contained in her green velvet bodice spoke up. I noticed, with interest, that she had managed an entry so soft that she nearly surprised even me. She had the confidence of someone who is in her own place and the delicacy of a dancer in one of Monsieur Lully's ballets. "That would be because your blessed Master is a codless eunuch whose idea of fun is sticking a needle in his eye. And he killed my da."

"That was the law, Miss Polly." The note of apology in Tiger Brown's voice almost, but not quite, outweighed his attempt to sound like the embodiment of justice. "Same as when they sent your Mackie for an indentured slave in Tobago."

"Law!" Her voice grew harsh and mocking. "I spit at the law. Law

40

is a whore anyone with copper change can buy, and then she turns and slits your throat for half a farthing. I wouldn't have had you admitted to my office, were it not that these killings cost me money, and needs must…Who's the French molly? And that girl who looks at me with frigger's eyes?"

She glanced at the table, looked more closely and scowled. "And what the bloody hell have you done to my map?"

Arouet bowed. "No sodomite I, but a poor slave trapped by the beauty of your gaze, Miss Wild. And the girl means nothing by it— she is either a madwoman or a goddess, I have not ascertained which, but I am sure she is no tribad."

There was an edge to his politeness—he was in her place, on her sufferance, and he hated it. He hated being beholden to a woman of no rank whatever, who pulled a mocking face at his routine gallantry as if she saw through every word to the arrogance beneath.

Every time he had nearly convinced me that he was a man of sense, Arouet managed to say something stupid, and worse, untrue. Worst of all, this man who could sound like a philosopher had all the petty prejudices of his class.

"And the map has been very useful. See there, we think that those patches where the skein is thickest are where the killers hide. Who owns those warehouses, there?"

"I do." Miss Wild pointed at the map repeatedly with a jabbing finger. "And there are no killers on my property. Or in that whorehouse there, also mine. And five other houses in the street."

She did not need to brag, but she fixed Arouet with a braggart's eye nonetheless.

"Polly," I turned my gaze full on her; I can be devilish charming when I can be bothered to be. "What exactly is in the warehouses?"

"Shit."

Arouet looked at her in genuine shock. Clearly the women he was used to would never say such a thing, even the whores, or at least would never say it in front of him.

She caught his expression and laughed at him. "Shit," she said again, "you lily-livered Froggie prude. Good London shit that the night-soil men collect and we store until the muck-spreaders or the Ordnance department have a need for it. Sooner or later, everyone needs to shit, and sooner or later everyone needs something made from it—even your damned saint of a Master needs it for his alchemy."

She spat, and a spittoon some feet away rang with it.

"We also collect piss for the bleach men," she said, "and pure, which is what we call dog turds, for the dyers. It's all money. And it doesn't stink."

Arouet looked even more shocked. "She just quoted Vespasian."

"No, I didn't." She looked him and laughed, as a women does who want to take down, a peg or two, a man who catches her eye. "Who's he? When he's at home."

"He was a Roman Emperor," I explained. "With one clever son and one crazy one. Which still put him ahead of the game as these things go." And then, because she was looking very bored, "Tell me about the nightsoil men."

She shrugged. "What's to tell? They drive around in carts, and they dig out cess-pits and cellars, and they smell of shit every single day of their lives. It's a job my da kept for people who really weren't any good at being thieves or beggars. They're good filthy lads with no plans of their own."

"My god," Arouet shuddered. "Imagine living next door to a warehouse full of ordure."

"Oh," Polly said with a certain air of superiority, "oh you sweet handsome innocent. Of course it's unpleasant for the neighbours. They sell up, and we buy up, and that is how one day I will buy Tobago and get back my Mackie."

And finally he looked at her properly and with respect. He was a man of feeling, after all, and he suddenly saw her as the heroine of her own romance.

"I've heard enough," Tiger Brown said, and I noticed with

amusement how silently and quickly Jobbings and the bleeding Clout positioned themselves for an arrest.

Polly put her fingers to her lips and whistled loudly; at once, two of the whores by the wigstands produced small pistols from inside powdered high wigs, and one of the beggars, who had been practising walking on a stump, was poised on a tabletop with four or five throwing knives ready in his right hand and one, in his raised left, aimed neatly at Tiger Brown's forehead.

I looked at him with a degree of scorn. "I am here to find monsters," I told him. "Not to watch you blunder around London arresting a series of innocent people. Miss Wild is a hardworking girl who is interested in making money, not monsters. Pay attention."

"Monsters?" Polly inquired, raising a perfect left eyebrow as elegantly as a court lady.

"I can hardly credit the evidence of my own eyes." Arouet was now all attentive to her, his voice confiding. "But yes, monsters. Lion body, human head, porcupine spines and the tail of a scorpion."

"And," I added, "from the stench of them, they travel around London in your carts."

Arouet looked interested, as one learning new things. "I had assumed that they were supposed to smell like that."

I spoke as one with experience in the matter. "No, the natural smell of a manticore is cinnamon and civet."

"Well ladida," Polly said and rolled her eyes at me. "Aren't we fancy?"

"If her warehouses are not where they are made,"—Arouet was thinking aloud again, but this time was doing so as part of an attempt to impress—"they ride back in the empty carts after deliveries have been made. So all we have to do is go to each of the manufactories in turn that they visit."

I sniffed the air. "Or we could wait here talking until the monsters come calling of their own accord."

Shit, cinnamon, civet. And hot iron, which meant something worse, and lavender and cut grass, which meant something I had not expected.

"Stand back," I said tersely. "I have rather more experience in these matters than you, and am considerably less frail."

The door by which we had entered burst open and the idiot predatory smiles of manticores filled it, mewing softly as evil kittens. With a whir and clatter, a harpy flew into the room and perched on one of its high shelves, constantly spewing its foam from the side of a mouth that protruded almost enough to be a muzzle or a beak

The young man with the knives poised himself for a throw but before he could move, the harpy laughed its cawing laugh and flicked its wing. Three iron feathers stood in his forearm and one in his throat. He fell choking on his own blood.

I noticed that Arouet had pulled a stiletto from somewhere and taken up the posture of a man who knew how to use it well. He stepped forward as if he desired to protect Miss Polly Wild, who had pulled out a brace of pistols from her clothing, and rested one on his shoulder as if to take better aim, while the side of the other gently caressed his cheek.

She was standing close to him, so very close. Danger clarifies some things.

The manticores drew aside and the one I had not expected drifted through them. I hate seraphs at the best of times, but if there is one thing worse than the sanctimonious chanting prigs and bully-boys that Jehovah has working for him, it is the ones who have left his service and become nasty-minded sadists for hire. And still have that insufferable smug grin, and the extra pairs of arms and wings.

Also, anyone who can afford to hire one is playing serious games. Bent seraphs are a calling card for the aristocracy of villainy.

It bowed to me, and held out a box inside which something scratched and whispered.

"I propose a deal." It spoke in the high sexless tenor they affect when not actually chanting. "If you surrender your weapons and come to talk to my principal, I will let these people live. And if you do not, I will have them all torn to pieces and then release this basilisk I seem to have with me. On 'Change, at noon. You will need to talk to my principal sooner or later, and we can make it a less bloody occasion than otherwise. If you prefer."

"And how," I said, "can I possibly trust you? I wouldn't trust a seraph that was working for Jehovah, let alone one of your corrupt breed."

It shrugged, a shimmer of feathers. "Ah, there, you, but not I, have a problem. I really don't care about dead people one way or another, whereas you have made saving them your life's work."

"My word is good," I said. "I will give it you, and hand over most of my weapons, if you reach into that box and throttle the basilisk. Then you will order the manticores to kill each other, here and now. I trust this is your principal's full complement of them."

"And the harpy?" it enquired.

"It is free to go as far as I am concerned."

"It had better fly far," Polly added. "A truce is a truce, but if it is anywhere a London pigeon can shit on it by tomorrow night, it will pay for Jem there. It did not need to kill him."

"It was its nature," said the seraph.

"Killing things that kill my men is mine." Polly's lips tightened as she spoke.

I looked at her saint's face, a perfect oval with a thin long nose like a perfect line down its centre. Any day is good to face my enemies that has such women in it, even if I am at no real risk, and they are not, as it happens, my type.

"Is there no other way?" Arouet asked. "You have met none of us before tonight. Yet you are offering yourself up for us as if we were your comrades in arms."

"You are," I said. "You all flit by me so mayfly fast that my loyalty is as firm to those I have known mere minutes as it is to those I have fought with for decades."

"It is," he said, with a touch of embarrassment at saying the words, "almost Christ-like."

"Josh knew that he was going to die. He was sweating with fear and he still stood and let them take him. I can assure you that I am not going to die, and I am not afraid—see, no sheen of sweat anywhere on me. There is no comparison, trust me."

Very carefully, so that no-one would see him as a threat, he pulled out the sword at his side, raised its hilt to his lips and kissed it. "I dedicate myself to your fight, mademoiselle, whether you live or die. You have shamed me by your loyalty. I shall always and everywhere wipe out evil."

Sincerity is always appealing in the young. I turned to the seraph, which had the cynical scornful expression with which such creatures always look on human drama.

"We have a deal," I said. "I need to see dead creatures before I stir further." I reached above my head and pulled my lance from its sling and offered it to the seraph, butt-end first. "You will care for it, or there will be an accounting when all things are done."

"Ah yes," the seraph said. Taking the box in one of its left hands and one of its right, it reached inside with the other pair. There was a hiss and a snap and the seraph winced a moment in pain—even such beings are inconvenienced by the bite of a basilisk, as you might be by a bee-sting or a mosquito—before twisting and another snap of a very different kind. The seraph placed the box on the ground and contemplated its wounded upper left hand. Its silver sheen was broken with a patch of sickly green that grew for a second, and festered, and then shrank away to nothing as the silver conquered it.

I turned to Polly. "Such creatures are not easily or safely disposed of."

"You joke," she laughed, but there was calculation in her eyes and no humour. "There is a man in Cimmery Axe who keeps them strung between hooks like partridges. This is London, Miss, where everything has its price and its place in a shop window. Shame really about these beasts. If we'd had notice, we could have had punters in and made a night of it. There's many a lordling who would cheerily bankrupt himself to bet on which of them would be the last standing. I never bet, but my money'd be on the brindled bitch with the dark eyes. What d'ya say, Tiger?"

The seraph cuffed the manticore nearest it so that it growled and

46

bared its teeth; then picked it up by the scruff of its still human neck and hurled it against another a few yards off. Dazed, it bit at the nearest throat and tasted the blood of its own kind, then staggered back, confused, with blood on its teeth. Its victim, not yet dead, slashed at it with a clawed paw. It dodged and knocked against a third, which turned and snarled—the second sensed a new enemy and swung its tail at it, failing to penetrate the thick quills on the shoulder, which rose raised up in anger.

I stepped through the door, handing two of my swords to the seraph as I went. "Polly," I said. "Shut the door. Monsters tearing into each other may be a grand sight, but not one worth dying for."

The door slammed behind me, and hardly a second too soon. Quills started to fly and manticores, stung with each other's poison, began to tear at their own flesh in their frenzy; I sidestepped from their way into shadow, and found the seraph waiting for me there.

"Our bargain is fulfilled," it said, "and you must come with me. To see my principal."

"I wouldn't miss meeting him for the world." And I added, in my mind, again, because I had few doubts that I knew who I was to meet, and that I had met him before.

In a few strides through shadow, we were out of the smoke and grime and stench of the City and along the river, which stank differently, of tidewater, sewage and rot. West past the gloom of Whitehall and the Abbey and out into the countryside, to a small village clustered round a new church and a few large houses. Lights were burning in the upper room of one of these.

"He stares at the stars, here," the seraph said conversationally. "Imagine. What humans will do to keep themselves from being bored."

"And yet, we find things out all the time."

"How sweet, and how sad. That you should still affect the notion of being one of them."

"Imagine," I told it, "how much danger you would be in at this second if I thought otherwise, if I believed myself some divinity with the right to crush all who offend me on a whim. Be glad, little seraph, that I am human, and dread the day when I change."

"Yet I have your weapons."

"I know," I said. "And what of it?"

We passed into the upper room where an old man with a hawk's face sat in his nightcap, a periwig lying discarded among the papers on his desk. It had been forty years since I saw him. Mortality rushes past us a day at a time and years go past and faces wither and minds turn from wisdom.

"I have the lance, Sir," the seraph said.

The old man's voice was firm and unquavering and he looked at me with envious hatred in his eyes. "Pass it to me."

I walked towards him. This would not take very long at all.

He took the lance and weighed it in his hands. "So many false gods have died on this," he said. "I thought to find it heavier to the hand."

"No," I said, "for then I could neither parry with it so well, nor throw it."

Quite suddenly, though hardly unexpectedly, he thrust at me with it. It halted a breath from my skin and he leaned on it with all his strength and it stood still as if stuck in oak. I reached down, took it from him and replaced it in its quiver.

I looked at the seraph. "My swords," I said.

It returned them. I chose to say nothing aloud of the ill grace and hesitation in its eyes. I looked into its eyes, though, with just a little of the power I keep in reserve until the feathers at the very tips of its wings started to smoulder.

"Leave us," said Sir Isaac Newton, and the seraph wavered like dust in sunlight and was gone.

"Are we done, Sir Isaac?" I asked. "And was this really necessary?"

"I grow old. And you are a blasphemous creature of the night who has lived too long."

"Deathlessness is my duty," I said. "You have done your work, and mine never ends."

"I was so sure," he said, almost to himself. "There is always a weakness in the stories. Every unnatural creature has its remedy of death. Yours had to be your weapons, that steal life from false gods and give it to you to squander that I would use accumulating godly knowledge."

"If you rely on stories," I said, "you might think so. And so many wizards and dragons do think so, and act accordingly. And thus find their deaths, in due course. I am a simple girl, with no such notions." I squatted by his chair and took him by the hand. "Was it necessary to kill two hundred people, and make monsters of so many others, just so that I would notice you again?"

He looked at me with scorn. "Whores and beggars died. And I made my manticores from rebels and papists who deserve no better than the rope and the gutting knife. What is the value of such people? I had hoped to solve the secrets of the universe, given time."

"Your time runs out." And for a moment I felt like Death with an hourglass and might have acted on that feeling.

"So, tell me, at least, before you kill me…" He had no fear of me and that softened me a second.

"Enough have died," I shrugged. "And what can I do to you that time has not?"

"Is the universe as I have shown it to be? A logical system built by God to show us the logic of His laws?"

He reached out and put his hand for reassurance, not on his Bible but on his Principia.

"Which laws would those be?" I asked. "Oh—'Thou shalt not kill'?" I laughed at his blank look. "I had people explain your work to me," I said, "because I remembered you as the young student playing dangerous games with the quintessence. Games you should have pursued, perhaps, if you wanted more time. And as far as I know, the universe is as you say it is—light splits as you say, and apples fall. I am grateful for the information, and I am sure Jehovah is too. He likes to know such things."

The pain in his face was greater than it would have been had I brought thumbscrews with me. "But he built…"

"No," I said. "He did not. Before he was, I am. And it was then as it is now. A chaos we struggle to know, with no maker's mark upon it. No sign of a beginning and no prospect of an end."

I reached for the papers on his desk. "What have you been about, you busy little man? More death warrants for men who served you? Or more laws of nature that I will not understand until someone talks me through them? Or more meddling with magic and alchemy?"

I moved to tear them across.

"No!" He spoke with a vigour that surprised me. "That is the crown of my life's work."

I looked at it. It was a heap of numbered verses from the bible, and lists of kings and battles and of lines drawn from the one to the other.

"We can know," his voice staggered, but the arrogance was still there, "everything that has happened in the last six thousand years since the beginning of creation. The Bible is revealed truth, but we can check it against known facts. And it all coheres. Glory to God in the Highest. It all coheres."

I found myself filled with elation, sadness and glee. I would break him yet, at least for a moment.

"You poor silly man. It does nothing of the kind. You say I have lived too long. You are right—too long for your silly system. When do you think the universe began?"

"About four thousand years before the birth of Our Lord." The quaver in his voice had not been there moments earlier.

I laughed aloud. "This night, you have held my spear in your hand. That spear was killing two thousand years before that—you felt its weight and commented on its lightness."

And I laughed again, in sheer vicious merriment. Like so many great criminals, he had chosen his own punishment, which was my laughter. "Go to bed, you foolish old man. Dream dreams of knowledge." And then I added, knowing it would sting him like one of his own beasts, "As a friend of mine once said to another friend of mine, go and sin no more."

I watched his face fall—I had thought him old before, and now I saw the decrepitude of an old man shamed and appalled.

"But, before you dream, I need to know a few things from you. Who taught you these things? The making of manticores was a secret I thought burned with the Museion, a small good to make up for the loss. And I had not known that any harpies still flew."

"The seraph came to me. An angel of the Lord."

"And taught you such things?"

"Darkness' weapons against darkness," he said. "That was the sermon it preached to me."

"You knew." I raised my voice and spoke with slow concentration. "After a while, you knew it was not a creature of Jehovah, but a servant of some other Master."

He looked at me in anguish and confusion. "Heaven help me, I had killed so many by then. I am damned for this, am I not?"

"I have no idea, nor care."

"It said…" He paused and then began again, struggling for exact words in his memory. "It said that it had been sent me by one who admired my work, and wished it to continue. My work on optics, it said, that in particular. And had I thought of mirrors as well as prisms?"

I should not have let the seraph go; it was my first clue in two centuries. But then, not so much a clue as a taunt. This old great man corrupted, and doubtless the seraph, were I to find it, would know little more than the message. Mirrors, but also the smoky fog of misdirection.

"Go to bed, old man. I will not destroy your papers as long as all is as you say." He looked at me defiantly, muttering prayers under his breath. "Take to your bed," I hissed, "before I tell you who sits at Jehovah's right hand, and who at his left. And what on a perch above his throne."

He shrank back—he would have clapped his hands over his ears had he the vital force to do more than flinch from the sight of me.

Later that morning, with the papers left as they had been, only more tidy, I was downstairs taking tea that the servants had brought me, when there came a knock at the living room door. Tiger Brown entered, twisting his hat in his hands, with Arouet and Polly at his side.

"Sir Isaac, your Master, is indisposed," I said. "But with his help, all is taken care of."

Brown sighed with relief. "I knew all would be well once he set his mind to it. And this long night of murder is over."

I noticed, with amusement, that Arouet and Polly were holding hands. Clearly, a long night, in which I had missed much.

"Is Sir Isaac awake?" Arouet asked hopefully. "I have longed to meet him."

I shook my head. "It has all been too much for him. He is indisposed."

Arouet looked disappointed, then looked at Polly, and consoled himself by putting his hands on her shoulders. Clearly they had talked much in my absence, at the very least.

"The creatures?" I asked.

"I sent them in a cart to the knacker's yard." Polly had the satisfied voice of one who has found profit in the evening. "There will not be a scrap or ounce of them left unused."

"They were human once," Arouet was playing the man of feeling to the hilt now.

"And were no longer now." Polly dismissed his sentiment, but stroked his hand. "And cost me money. Also, try explaining them to a churchwarden or a sexton. Best disposed of thoroughly."

"As you say," he shrugged.

The three of them turned to go. Polly turned back, dashed over and pecked me on the cheek, and placed her left hand firmly on my thigh. She whispered in my ear, "I know he done it."

"I can assure you," I said for the benefit of the others, while stroking her hand delicately out of their sight, "that the one responsible has paid and will pay for his crimes."

Polly pulled away and went once more to stand with Arouet. "I have a present for Sir Isaac, when he wakes."

She clapped her hands. Two of her men entered, weighed down with a heavy sack that clanked as they placed it on the carpet, and leaked blood.

"A small reminder from Polly Wild. Just the feathers. The bird is stuffed and roasted. No-one kills what is mine, and does not pay."

"I think," I said, "that Sir Isaac will not be rising from his bed any time soon. He is, after all, an old man in poor health."

"See that he is taken care of." Her tone had no compassion in it. "It would be a shame if he overexerted himself, and came to my city anytime soon."

"I am rarely in London,"—because I did not foresee any need for me to be there, with her in charge of it—"but when next I am, I shall check in on his health."

"See to it." She left me standing there, reflecting on the deeds and smallness of great men, and the quiet magnificence of strong women.

The Bishop of Rochester had an exceptionally irritating voice, a high whinny that was also indistinct, as if there were something holy about affecting speech impediments. It was his church voice—I had met him on another occasion, in a male brothel in Venice, and he spoke quite normally when playing at bezique. Even when he lost.

But here and now, his recitation of the liturgy crawled on my skin like lice. Putting up with such irritations was just another of the necessities of my work.

I had felt a quite distinctive twang in the universe as far away as the jungles of the Khmers, where something untoward was going on in a ruined temple full of long-dead snakelords. I had hurried to its source, which proved to be London. Again. Twice in a century; impressive.

53

I felt a certain obligation to try to give this one as much in the way of knowledge and thus choices as I had given the last one. No-one can say—you least of all, Crowley—that I do not play fair.

Who had the earlier one been? Well, who do you think? Yes, precisely, thank you. And of course the Stratford man wrote it all, except for the duff bits of "Pericles".

No, I don't care what you think about him; I was there on the first night of "Love's Labours Won". Best play I ever saw. He was very funny in it, too.

I headed for the Abbey—shadow has its currents and some of the strangest places are especially easy to get to—and found the service in full swing. Handel and more Handel.

Isaac was there, looking as I had seen him the first time we met in Cambridge, when I gave him a warning not unlike the one I gave you earlier. His old tired worn-out mortal body was on a gun carriage before the high altar and he was looking at it with incredulity and horror.

He looked at me as I arrived with the anxiousness of a hostage towards his rescuer, or a broken-winged bird to the cat that has not yet deigned to play at torture. I at least was someone he knew would have answers, even if they were not ones he would like.

"What has happened to me?" he said. "The Resurrection of the Body does not happen until the Apocalypse. Is this some particular damnation? I walk among men seen and unrecognized, and yet I am there, dead, as I remember myself. I hunger not, nor thirst, yet feel the satiety of one who has dined well. Especially since I have been in this place, watching my own exequies. With anthems by Mr. Handel."

"That fullness of what you still think of as your stomach," I said, "would be that secondary worship that men give to those who have served humanity. Know it well, and treasure it, because one day you will need it, and it will no longer be there."

He started to whisper and then, from the lack of reaction from those standing by us, realized that he did not have to. "Worship?" he repeated, in a voice at once thrilled and appalled.

"Here is the thing," I sighed. "You are now a god. Not a very important one, in the scheme of things, but one to whom I am going to have to talk seriously, given your late escapades. Which, as you see, were an entirely unnecessary set of sins. As unnecessary as your youthful games with the Quintessence. Godhood is the real Stone, not a spiritual exercise or trickery. You start with a clean slate as far as I am concerned, but I will be watching you. No human sacrifices in your name, and we will get along just fine. Otherwise, well, I don't have to give you the talk about my lance and swords."

He was not taking all this well. "And if I were you," I continued, "I would avoid Jehovah like a burned child dreads the flame. One of the few things in this world that you have always thought and which is still true, is that he is a jealous God. You are now his rival in business, his far weaker rival."

"Where shall I go?" he asked. "Where hide myself from His Wrath?"

"If I were you and had your interests, I would spend a century or two observing the motions of the planets. He really has not got used to the idea that there are whole other worlds out there. It's not as if you have a vast need for human company."

For the first time, he looked intrigued and not heartbroken. "On his last visit," he said, "the Astronomer Royal told me that Jupiter has three more moons. I was too tired to calculate what that means, how that system moves in perfect balance. And that damnable woman interrupted my studies with her demands and threats until I could hardly think. But now…"

I scanned the congregation. "You need to go, now," I told him.

Lucifer sat in the third row, very dapper in a scarlet periwig, and looking intently at his watch as if waiting for someone who was overdue. I pointed him out. "Avoid that man, if you ever see him. Avoid him as if he were the Devil himself, because actually, in your terms, he is."

Isaac glanced at him, took note and started to sink into the ground. I looked at him, questioningly.

"My quickest way," he said, "is via the Antipodes, is it not? When shall I return?"

"Give it a century or two. When we've got over our most recent disagreement, I will put in a word for you."

He sank into the paving stone of the Abbey's floor and was gone like a soap bubble. Suddenly he returned. "Hell," he said. "Am I merely taking myself to Hell by the most direct route?"

"No," I said. "It isn't really under the earth at all, and none of its gates is anywhere near here. One of the things about being a god is, you don't have to go there if you don't want to. Not that anyone does, really. I strongly advise against it. What I said about jealousy applies to Lucifer too. Stay away from them both if you want to last your first century."

The organ played some very tiresome voluntary as he disappeared for the second time. Still, anything was better than the twitterings of the Bishop.

Isaac was a bad man, in many ways, and probably more trouble than he was worth as a god. He was, though, a clever one, who knew things. The sort of person who would never be a trustworthy ally, but might, sometime, be a useful one. And, though it was a long way to go, at least I knew where he would be.

If, on the other hand, his involvement with the Lord of Smoke and Mirrors were less innocent than it seemed—I speak comparatively, of course—he would show up in my way sooner or later, and I would be entitled to regard his presence as evidence of guilt.

On the whole, I hoped him innocent. I could not see that the orbits of the moons of Jupiter would ever be any especial use to me, or humanity, but I had been wrong about such things before.

As I walked through the cloisters, I saw Arouet, with a small, a very small, man at his side. "No Polly?" I inquired.

Arouet smiled wryly and pointed across to the other side, where a veiled woman in black silk was having her hand kissed by someone who looked exceptionally important. Several other such men, in dark coats and expensive periwigs, stood waiting, as if for an audience.

"Alas," he said. "Our romance was brief. She says that she cannot now be seen to be involved with someone who might, after all, be a spy for the French."

"Now?"

"Now," he said, "that she has made her peace with the late Sir Isaac and has been appointed to his place. Not the Mint, of course, but his real place."

"Ah," I said. "Of course. He talked of a damnable female."

His small companion broke in. "You spoke to Sir Isaac before his death? When I heard he was dying, I sent him a copy of my epitaph for him," the dwarf went on. "I was wondering if he expressed an opinion."

I shrugged. "Not to me. But I am sure he admired it."

"What do you think of it?" he asked. "Nature and Nature's Laws lay all in Night/God said 'Let Newton Be,' And All was Light."

It was like most of the best poetry, elegantly formed and almost entirely untrue. I did not think it helpful to tell him so, or useful to encourage him in further conversation.

"Alexander," Arouet informed him, "the Huntress has no great interest in literary matters."

"She hunts, does she?" said Alexander.

"No," Arouet said. "She is the Huntress, which, as I understand it, means something quite other."

The dwarf called Alexander started at last to pay proper attention, and looked quite pale. Arouet returned to our first subject. "Mam'selle Wild sent to Tobago with an order of release, but her lover was already dead of gaol fever. Hence the black. I tried to console her, and harsh words were spoken." He shrugged. "I would say that I shall never love again, but it would almost certainly be untrue. I shall, however, avoid Englishwomen hereafter."

He bowed to me, as did his friend, less elegantly. And that was the last I saw of him for some fifty years.

Quite an enjoyable fifty years, as these things go. I spent a lot of it in North America, looking for traces of my enemy in places where he might have been, but was not, racing through empty woods under skies full of plump stupid birds, or on plains full of great shaggy beasts. The way you run through fields of almost grown wheat for the sheer pleasure of the run and the wistfulness of knowing that the harvest is coming. No, I don't have the Sight, not for that sort of thing, but I know people and I know that Wildernesses full of game become graveyards and then farmland. I saw it happen before, more than once.

I wandered the courts of Europe looking for charlatans and worse. Friedrich Wilhelm looked promising—collecting giants and flogging his son—but he was just a madman, nothing more. The son was a dangerous man, but not in a way that needed concern me, just someone who liked to push live soldiers around on the game-board of his mind for the sheer joy of the exercise.

I never took to the man. Once I saw him try to fluster an old kapellmeister who was visiting his son at the Prussian court. "Write me a six-part fugue on that," he would say, after pounding out some undistinguished melody, and the kapellmeister would just smile sweetly and comply. Later he sent the king a whole album of such fugues as if it had not been a whim but a serious request from one friend to another responded to with a friendly musical offering. I love that insolence which is called dumb, and knows that the world has moved on from kings that can just whip you when they feel like it.

Voltaire was there for a while, but not when I was. It ended less than well between him and Friedrich, or so I heard.

Oh, and there were wars, many of them started by young Friedrich. Some of them turned out to be important and some did not, and they interested me hardly at all. The habit of warfare appears engrained in humanity and there are more harmful ways of shedding blood, though not many.

Berlin was a college town, but one full of cold winds and professors whose lectures imitated eternity in duration, if not in substance. It was never a city where I went for relaxation.

Vienna—now, there was a city, once you got away from the court, which tried to be Versailles, in German. Winds blew through Vienna too, but they were winds that were warm and fertile with gossip. It was the heart of an empire, an empire so full of misunderstandings that its peoples had continually to talk to each other to make it work. To talk in Magyar, and German, and Wallachian, and Tosk, in Turkish and Slavonic and Italian, about trade and war, about prayers and gold.

There were small taverns at the edge of the Woods thick with the smoke of black tobacco and the dry reek of Pilsener beer where you could hear a different tongue at each table. There were restaurants where barons and field marshals discussed the profits of siege and the cost of peace and ate hot squabs in a cherry sauce even sweeter than their grass-scented Tokay. And there was a theatre cafe where the singers went to rest their voices from rehearsing and where the coffee was black as soot, bitter as death and fierce as a tiger.

It was owned by a tall thin man with hollows in his cheeks who laughed at his own jokes with the confidence of one whose flesh lay heavier on his bones. People paid to sit in his theatre to hear those jokes, though I never found him more than mildly amusing. Schikaneder sang though, in an earthy baritone as sweet as cherries, as wholesome and crisp as barley bread.

I was there the first time he sang his role as the birdcatcher. You know it? Of course, no-one that century had any idea what Egypt was actually like in its days of glory, so the whole play was peculiarly irritating to those of us who were actually there. The plot made no sense—first the priests were evil and then the girl's mother, who was, as far as I could see, younger than the girl by some three years, and had a better voice. Pretty enough songs though.

I have had experience of magic flutes, though, and the one in this play was nowhere near dangerous enough.

Jehovah was in one of the smaller boxes, beating time in an irritating manner, without any obvious angels in attendance. That's the thing about him, when you watch him unawares; he genuinely likes music, even when it isn't all about him, and pictures, that aren't of him and his toadies. He started off appreciating these things because it was part of pretending to be all-knowing and all-wise in front of his worshippers, and then he got a taste for it. It is one of the more charming things about him.

It meant he was in a good mood that night, so I wandered round between the acts and slipped quietly through the curtain and sat down with him.

"Mara." He spoke as if there was no bad blood between us. "I wouldn't have expected the opera to be…"

"It's not an opera," I said. "Opera is all steel and silk and straining. This is comfortable stuff you could play on a hurdy-gurdy."

Jehovah looked at me pityingly. "I went to Prague," he said. "I had been told it was a moral tale about the punishment of lust, but somehow the music made you feel the pity of it as well as the shame. He writes masses as well, they tell me."

I looked at him with a dawning suspicion. "Poor man," I said. "Not many more operas for him, then."

"The life of theatricals is short and filled with temptation," Jehovah said. "Sometimes, I need to be sure, really sure, that people who might be of service to me make the right choices in their lives."

The second act started and I made as to leave, but Jehovah patted the empty seat next to him, and poured me a glass of wine. I have no time for him, not any more, but that is no reason to be churlish. Down on the stage, the girl's mother threw a decorative tantrum, all roulades and trills.

"Remind you of anyone?" Jehovah whispered in my ear during the extended applause that followed the aria.

"No one in particular." Which was entirely untrue, as he knew it would be. He is never one to pass up what he thinks of as an advantage and one day someone will kill him for it.

"Of course,"—he really was not going to let this alone—"the pair of you really have kept up that ridiculous feud."

"What feud?" I turned to leave rather than talk to him about this.

"You and Hekkat." He reached out as one who knows he may have gone too far, as he had. "Morgan as she calls herself these days."

"Really? I hadn't heard." This was not entirely true, but I saw no reason to encourage him by rising to his teasing.

"She hardly kills anyone any more." He had obviously been bothering to keep track, which was itself interesting. "I'm not clear what magic she actually works beyond reputation and a capacity to drive people mad with desire. Never saw it myself, of course. Not my type; never was. Yours on the other hand, obviously."

I held my tongue, and he went on. "But, you know, all these operas with enchantresses in them, it's all her, you see. Poets and painters and musicians—they can't get enough of her. And she pays them, of course."

He was clearly aggrieved that there was some art in Europe that was not all about him. That is the trouble with tyrants; even when they have good taste, it gets caught up with their *amour propre*. Napoleon was the same.

"I've no intention of forgiving her past sins." I spoke emphatically. "But I am glad to hear that she is staying out of mischief. She could be far worse things than a patroness of the arts."

"So you really haven't seen her?" He sounded genuinely curious.

"We stay away from each other. I haven't heard anything about her for centuries."

"Oh," he said, "she's been around, like I say. Not so much lately, mind you. I used to see her at the opera all the time in London and Venice, a while back, but not recently. She doesn't seem to like the new fellows. Like this chap. Her loss, I'd say." He paused to consider, a look that might have been concern on his face. "You know, it's been really some years. Some Handel thing or other. Alcina, or some such. Must be forty years or more—hadn't kept track. Hope she's all right—there aren't many of us left from the old days."

I shrugged. "I'm sure she's fine. There are few beings in the world these days that could even inconvenience her, present company excluded."

It really was the rankest hypocrisy for him to wax nostalgic over a lost world of gods and heroes to which he personally had put a stop,

61

but he seems to think that talking charming nonsense to me is going to change things. I'm sure he thinks that one day I'll forgive him, or even start working for him.

In any case, his attention was already wandering back to the music. I finished the glass he had poured and left, quietly.

Some time later, when I was in Vienna again, I heard rumours that the musician had been poisoned by a rival. I doubted it—there is an admiration far more deadly than a rival's poison. Between people he admires and wants to own, and people he thinks are a threat, Jehovah does quite a nice line in quiet assassination. Lucifer too. Both of them are fond of poison, which is a point you would do well to consider, Crowley...

Well, of course he can send angels to smite people, just as Lucifer can open up the earth and swallow people down like the lecher in the opera, but mostly they don't. They haven't for a long time—they think that they can't afford to take the chance any more.

They hoard power, both of them. Just in case anything that happens in the world is part of some long plan that is not theirs. What happened in Mexico, what I learned there—I got angry, they got, well, scared. How else do you think Voltaire made it to an old age, in which he came back from exile? He took precautions for fifty years, of course—never slept in the same bed twice in a row except to break a pattern, always knew five exits from any room he spent time in, always used sheepgut to ward off the pox. There was a time when they would have razed a city to kill a man like that, but he knew that times had changed, that the bluff of lightning and brimstone was not what it had been. Someone had told him. I cannot think who that might have been.

The trouble is, telling him to take care of himself meant that he felt obliged to give the same warning to everyone who worked on the damned Encyclopaedia. And told them far too much else.

I don't think he told Rousseau, because he really did not like Rousseau. But then, who did?

I know I said I didn't see him for fifty years, but he was

interesting, and I kept track of his career. He was a clever man, you see, and they are always fun to watch.

I missed the day they brought him back to Paris and carried him shoulder high to the Academie. I've always been sorry I missed that because you don't often get to see someone have a day of perfect happiness in this world, let alone someone you rather like.

I heard of it, though, and travelled to Paris to congratulate him. And found him dying.

I entered the room from shadow and without being announced. His face on his deathbed was a sketch in angles and lines, hollows and deeper hollows, but his laugh was still that of the young man I had met in a Paris backstreet.

"Huntress. You find me indisposed, but at your service nonetheless."

"I am sorry."

He could not rise far from his pillow but managed a sort of bow nonetheless. "My dear, there is no need for polite lies between friends. You watch us all die and you pull a sad face because melancholy sets off your dark eyes and because you think that grief is a human thing you do well to practice."

I shrugged, because what he said was true. "Nonetheless, I am sorry. The world needs you."

"Ah," he said, "but I am tired of being needed. And there are others out there to do my work. I do not need to live forever. There is an attorney in Arras, they tell me, with ambitions to fight for justice."

He started coughing, deep coughs from the bottom of his soul. I fetched him the carafe of water and poured him a glass. "I would prefer brandy," he gasped. "But you are probably right."

Servants had heard him cough, and rushed back in, looking slovenly and half-asleep. At my look, he said, "They are not mine. They came with the house, as a loan, while I die." Then he added, "My dear, it would please me greatly if you would keep priests from entering that door."

"My pleasure."

"You see," he said, "I have already worked out the terms of my repentance. You can always find the right confessor if you shop around a little. I do not want to have to deal with Jesuits trying to get me to say more."

"You would hate it in Jehovah's Heaven."

"And the Hell of Lucifer?"

"Not so nice," I told him. "A sensible person would avoid both destinations entirely, if she can."

"And so?"

"There is a trick to it," I said. "I saw it done, but I cannot tell you how. As an immortal, with an endless task, I have no convenient way of finding out. Reach for the stars, and keep going."

"An eternity of night and solitude with lights in the distance. And time to think without interruption, without even the interruption of having to go piss." He looked dreamy for a second. "Not what I might have chosen, but hugely preferable to the alternatives on offer."

"Not solitude, necessarily. I sent Newton off in that direction some years back, and a whole host of Aztecs some years before that."

"Ah." Nice to contemplate occasional encounters, but space, as that superstitious dolt Pascal points out, is infinite."

"And yet I wander the world constantly meeting people in the most unlikely places," I said. "I sometimes think that there is a natural force that draws us together with those we are supposed to met, an affinity. Besides, Newton was heading for the moons of Jupiter, I believe, so at least you have somewhere to look for him. If you were to want to."

"I never did meet him properly," Voltaire said. "Something to consider."

And then he coughed some more and then some more again, until he seemed almost worn down to the point of that sleep which precedes death.

"I will leave you be, in a minute," I said. "And guard the door. There is, though, something I must know."

"Ask."

"I have noticed, down the years, that your close associates take precautions. The precautions I advised you to take, when we met in London. I saw Diderot once, sneaking from his room at night on tiptoe, to bed down in a stable, in the hay; and watched him a few days later, switching wineglasses on his dinner companion, with all the subtlety of a third-rate conjuror."

"I warned them to take precautions," he said. "I told them that some at least of what we wish to be unreal is real. Denying His existence is a good tactic, but poor strategy. He is worth no decent man's worship, but a sensible man's precautions."

I nodded. "Well and good. But what else did you tell them?"

"That magic is true, though not to be touched by the sane. Should I have left them defenceless?"

"And the Rituals?"

"I warned them of what to watch for in our enemies."

I winced. "I have been careful," he protested. "I only revealed this to good and honest men, and a few women no better than they should be, but too good for that. Only the defenders of ancient iniquity would ever stoop to such things."

He had roused himself to a passion that brought burning redness to his cheeks that faded as quickly as it rose up. He sank back among his pillows with a sigh of exhaustion.

"Polly," he murmured as he fell asleep. I stroked his forehead and then kissed it.

He was one of the best of men, and if he erred about the goodness of the sort of men he worked with, it was through nobility of soul. He thought himself a rake and cynic, but he loved people with the simplicity of a country priest.

The house was quiet those few days; from time to time, his plump middle-aged niece would bring in a cup of hot chocolate and sometimes he would rouse long enough to sip it. I kept away those priests he wished kept away and admitted those of his friends that he wished to see; a few days, which was all he needed of my time.

Apart from the priest to whom he made his pre-arranged confession, there was one he was intrigued enough to admit. A young seminarian tried to push past me and Voltaire bade me put him down from where I held him by his throat against the wall.

"Let him be, Huntress," Voltaire whispered from the bed. "He is here to gawk at me, not to pester me, I think."

I put the young priest down and he straightened the cloth round his neck where I had disturbed its neat white folds.

He was handsome but almost as gaunt as the dying man, that gauntness that comes from the endurance of constant physical pain. "I am no mere sightseer." He drew himself to his full height and limped across the room. "I wish to be a great man, and thought to take a lesson from the greatest Frenchman living."

"For that, you have my blessing, such as it is." Voltaire's voice implied that that would be very little. "But France and the world have need of great men, not great priests."

"With this foot,"—and the young man pointed to what, even encased in a heavy shoe, was clearly a mere wreck—"I can neither dance at court nor ride to battle. Yet I shall be of service, if I can."

Voltaire looked at me and I looked back at him; there was something in the young man's manner which amused him and was familiar enough to me.

"You will serve," I said, and Voltaire nodded agreement, "both France and yourself."

"Of course," the young man smiled. "All do so. You yourself,"—he looked at Voltaire—"though I cannot speak for your Moorish slavegirl."

"The Huntress is no Moor," Voltaire corrected him, "and no slave either, but the most disinterested being alive."

"Huntress, you say? Her of whom legends speak?" The seminarian nodded in respect, then smiled cynically. "Yet even she has that which she seeks. Pleasure, or revenge, or lost love, or the satisfaction of work well done."

I could not deny the truth of what he said, and Voltaire clapped limply. "Bravo! A triumph, young man. You have silenced us both. Perhaps you will do great things when you grow to man's estate, and if you cast the cassock aside, Monsieur...?"

"Talleyrand-Perigord." The young man's bow was more a flourish of personal style than any indication of deference.

"Two names is too many," Voltaire said. "There, I have given you advice to prosper by. Now leave us."

The young man nodded curtly to us both, and limped his way from the room. As so often happens, I thought little of him at the time, and was wrong.

Voltaire yawned. "After that brief excitement, I think I am ready to sleep again." And was snoring gently almost before the words were out of his mouth.

I paid him for a lifetime of wit and good works by ensuring that he died in peace as well as comfort. He said, at the end, "Let me die in peace," and I made sure of it. His soul slipped away in the night to wherever it went.

He did not, as I had hoped, receive the accolade of godhood from those who professed to love him. That the English managed that uncomplicated whole-hearted love of a great man twice in a hundred years, and the French never that I know of, speaks to national character.

They buried him in secret, out in Champagne, for fear of the Church. I guarded the grave for a few days, to be sure that no priest or magus disturbed him. The revolution moved him in the end, back to Paris and the Pantheon; later still, the pious had their way with his bones, thrown out as garbage and gone forever. Yet his heart remained, to be honoured; people talk of his intellect, but that was his core.

And I moved on, for I had neglected my work for all of a fortnight.

# Dead Names

## London, Oxford 1997

Neither of them could quite get the hang of search engines.

Caroline found them amazingly frustrating because she could peer at the screen over Emma's shoulder, and offer helpful suggestions, but could never actually use them for herself. And had to put up with Emma's terrible typing.

Emma just didn't like computers, she had decided. She could see that they were terribly useful, and that she was going to have to go on using them for the rest of her life, and that the Internet was just the most amazing thing ever. She really got that.

She didn't like them, though—it was sitting staring at a screen and having to type and not being any good at typing and getting a distinct impression that people with a different sort of clever were setting everything up to favour themselves and leave her behind in the dust.

It was especially frustrating when they were looking up something important.

"So," Caroline asked, "do we think he really jumped tragically off Beachy Head? And they didn't find his parked car, his shoes on the cliff and his note held down by stones for a whole two years?"

"Cover story, got to be."

"No body," they chorused.

"Comic book rules of death."

"Precisely."

"No body. Not dead."

Neither of them was snapping their fingers, but they both knew and loved the beat of these exchanges.

"Comic book death," Emma shouted.

"Beloved of all dodgy immortals."

"So, somewhere else, being evil, with a name with b, r, and n in it."

"Or maybe not."

"Love to have seen his face when a crack squad of Jehovah's best turned up in the quadrangle looking for him."

"Once you'd saved the world, he must have known that…"

"The jig was up and his hash was settled," they said in chorus and giggled like small girls who had done something exceptionally naughty.

Emma got up from her desk and walked over to the table some way away where she kept the coffee pot. She knew computers and drinks did not mix—she had learned this the expensive way. She was looking thoughtful.

"Would it have made any difference, if we'd told Jehovah before the opera?"

"He wouldn't have listened to you before you saved the universe." Caroline always knew the sensible argument to stop a woman feeling awkward. "Before that, it would have been, oh, really, little girl, now let the grownups talk; afterwards, it was all yes ma'am new sheriff in town."

"Well, yes, but maybe if I'd told him a little earlier than I did."

"Probably lots of disembowelled angels all over the quad. I don't

69

think lords of ultimate evil go quietly. As it is, he lost his current comfort zone. And that's a good thing."

Caroline was being remarkably calm and sensible about this, given that they were talking about the man who had organized her death. She wasn't even doing grim satisfaction, a look she had down to a t.

Emma said, picking up the tastefully black-edged bit of pasteboard that had arrived that morning. "I suppose the uncertainty as to whether he was actually dead is why they've left it so long before the memorial service."

"Hmm…Funeral of the most recent secret identity of the Lord of Ultimate Evil?" Suddenly Caroline was dressed in a cloak, with a fetching veil over her face. "You don't suppose," she hissed, "that it might be…A Trap?"

"Oh, very probably," Emma said. "But we don't have to go in mob-handed, after all. Not like Elodie's wedding. We just contact the Powers that be. He must know that—so either he has something really spectacular planned or he is taking our likely entourage into account."

She scurried her fingers round the keyboard. "I'm sure Jehovah doesn't use e-mail. But I know the House do, and I bet Morgan does."

Caroline shrugged. "I think the old boy expects people to pray to him if they want his attention."

"Oh really." Emma's tone was disgruntled. "As if we were civilians."

"I bet the funeral announcement is in the Times. I bet Jehovah reads the Times. Or has someone to look out useful cuttings for him." Caroline looked thoughtful a second. "Tell you who doesn't read the Times or e-mail," she offered. "The Huntress."

Emma found this so exciting that she nearly spilled her coffee trying to clap her hands without putting down the cup. "It would be cool to try to get her along."

"Yes, but Morgan…"

"You're right," Emma nodded. "We shouldn't meddle. We don't know the history. And we have no way of getting hold of her."

70

Caroline spaced out for a second in the way that usually meant an incoming message. "Boss says, really really not. And Mara shows up where she shows up. No accounting."

Emma checked the date on the pasteboard, and started bundling up her most funereal black outfit for the cleaners. The smears of ichor on it would never do at an official function, even if she did regard them as badges of honour.

The college chapel was full of dons and dignitaries and incognito powers. No one looked very sad—whether or not Browning had been the great instigator of dark rituals Emma thought, he had not been a particularly likable or inspired teacher. Nor had he been an easy colleague. And bad things tended to happen to Fellows of the College who crossed him. A Bursar who had questioned his port consumption had been found impaled on a church spire as far away as Banbury.

The more Emma eavesdropped, as she worked her way around the crowd waiting to take their seats, the more convinced she became that a guess based on a coincidence of letters, and his presence in a list, had been absolutely correct.

"He always talked of you." The emeritus Reader in Hittite was a doddery old gent with a lecherous eye and a wandering hand. "He said that you would have been his favourite pupil if you hadn't had that unfortunate breakdown in your second year, and changed subjects."

Emma stepped gently but firmly on his instep and his hand withdrew itself with lingering regret. "Do come to dinner sometime," he said. "We have a good cellar here—better now much of the best bits of it have been retrieved from his set."

Emma reflected that she was one of the few ex-members of the college who might well find herself in need of translations from the Hittite in the course of her working day, and nodded assent.

You usually know where you are supposed to sit at weddings. Emma tried, modestly, to sit among the academics and prestigious former pupils, but was firmly pointed by an usher to the other side. They weren't even pretending this was a purely civilian event. An urgent hand pulled at her wrist and when she looked down, it belonged to the faun.

"Didn't expect to see you here." Somehow he turned the remark into lechery.

"Nor I you." She was genuinely surprised. "If I'm right about him, the allegedly late Mr. Browning uprooted you from your time and place, and suborned renegade angels to kill you."

The faun looked shocked. "What, that nice old man? Scrambled eggs, sausage, bacon, two fried slice, two toast? Hades' droopy foreskin! I'd have expected a bigger tip if I'd known. And spat in his Earl Grey."

He turned to the shrouded figure to his left. "Did you know there was something fishy about him?"

"We always avoided him. He smelled of death." It was one of Sobekh's vulture demon friends, and its voice was like the slushy rattling of wet bones.

"You smell of death," the faun pointed out.

"He smelled of our death, and your death, and the death of everything. We just smell of the death of whatever we ate recently. It's different. You wouldn't understand."

Somehow, the wet rattling managed to convey deep distress and hurt. Emma had never really thought about carrion gods and where they stood on the whole good and evil spectrum; clearly, this old sad creature regarded Browning as its enemy.

After all, it had helped her once. And besides, cycle of life, she supposed.

Caroline sidled round the faun and planted a spectral kiss on the creature's terrible beak. Bless her, thought Emma, that means I don't have to do that, and she has no sense of smell.

The vulture and the faun shuffled up and Emma sat down beside them. Aisle seat, she noted, good for getaways.

Up in its ornate loft, the underpowered college organ wheezed its way through one of Bach's more forgettable chorales and the choristers shuffled their feet. The Master of the College, an elderly physicist who had discovered something important a long time ago, mumbled his way through an introduction. Much loved, distinguished, important political work that we can't talk about. Fund-raising from industry. Condolences from the Conservative leadership, but election imminent so no-one could be here.

"Honestly," Emma whispered to Caroline, "even if he'd been straightforwardly human, quite on the way to being a lord of evil in a non-magical sense."

A chorister screamed on an impossibly high note and the air changed. Everything was suddenly the colour of the grey stuff you scrape from between kitchen tiles and smelled of your own regret.

Everyone on the right-hand side of the chapel looked for a moment as if they were dead, and then several of them started to snore. The more excitable minor deities and creatures of terror gibbered and squalled and shouted in forgotten tongues—some of them trying cantrips and more of them simply swearing.

And above it all, laughter. Loud laughter, but not especially so.

A voice which came from the Master, but was clearly not his own. His eyes were closed and his jaw was moving like that of a puppet miming badly. His face was streaming sweat and snot and his cheeks twitched, as if he were in terrible pain.

Hearing it again, Emma was amazed that, when she had confronted Berin in Hollywood, she had not recognized Browning instantly. It just goes to show that context is all, she thought.

"No, I am not dead." His tone was almost conversational. "I am elsewhere with another name and another face and you will never find me until it is too late for everything that lives and much that is dead. The sleepers will awake, the ring of flesh will burst and all will be undone. Many of you have heard that before, when it was a secret, but now it is the simple truth that I speak aloud."

He paused.

"The pieces are in play, and there is nothing you can do."

Please don't make it a chess metaphor, Emma found herself hoping. I like my supervillains classier than that. She was suddenly sure that he was not going to kill anyone much today. He liked the idea of taking the world to doom and having as many people as possible watch him being clever.

Then she thought of the civilians, and realized that it would be typical of him to kill them to make a point.

She stood up because someone had to try to draw any fire he had in mind. Before she could speak, that laugh started again, this time more of a cheap snigger.

"Grandstanding again, Miss Emma Jones?"

"Half this chapel is occupied by defenceless civilians. You've mentioned wanting to kill me. I propose a trade."

That laugh again. "Tempting, but no. There are people here I'd rather kill than even you, you annoying child, and I will spare them today, on both sides of the chapel. Because I choose to. I have far better plans for all of you, you especially Miss Emma Jones. And your little ghost too."

"He avoided chess, at least, but he couldn't skip Oz, could he?" Caroline whispered.

Emma giggled. The laughter stopped, and the spell was broken. Colour returned and the civilians awoke and the noisy gods were still.

And the Master of the college dropped as if strings had been cut, groaned once and coughed once, and then spewed blood from his mouth and dripped it from his eyes and ears and nostrils. From the sudden terrible smell, he had voided more than the contents of his bowels.

The doors of the chapel were flung open, and bright daylight poured in. No, not just daylight, she realized as it stung her eyes, strong searchlights. Three men in hazmat suits marched up the centre aisle with a body bag. Behind them, another carried a folded stretcher on his left shoulder.

Sharpe followed them. He was clearly in charge of things—Emma was aware that these days he dealt with a lot more than just Art or even the Spook Squad, but they hadn't talked for a while. He was too busy sucking up to the next government, Tom had told her.

"I want this chapel cleared in an orderly fashion," said Sharpe. "Anti-virals will be available for those who need them in the further quadrangle." Then, in a less peremptory fashion, he added, "I am told by the Bursar that there will still be refreshments afterwards."

Emma was not surprised that the clearly panicky civilians let themselves be ushered out in an orderly though swift fashion by a small group of uniformed police. On her side, unexpectedly, the same was true—angels and goat-demons and wonderworkers, all acting as if they were suburban English people.

Sharpe walked up to Emma, and took her by the hand. "Miss Jones,"—he nodded to Caroline, even though he had no idea where she was—"Miss Smart. Well played."

"I did nothing. Of any use."

"My contacts told me that you distracted him for a few seconds. Always crucial at such times."

Emma found herself wondering precisely who Sharpe's contacts were in this context. Not, she suspected, his superiors in the Met, and what was a London copper doing running an operation in Oxford? Best not to know these things, she reflected, because you don't want them paying more attention to you than is needed.

He turned to direct the men with the body bag and the stretcher. Caroline looked across at it, and regretted it. "Eww, it's sloshing inside."

Which was why Emma had avoided looking too closely and took her chance to get as far away from it as possible, as quickly as was consistent with being managed by the ushering police.

Once in the sunlight, she pecked the faun on the cheek and decided to head out into the street to look for a taxi. She was not in the mood for canapes and explanations. Other people had had the same idea, it seemed. There was a queue some twenty people and beings long.

A goat-demon elbowed a bishop out of its way to get to the front of the queue and the driver in the lead cab shouted at him. "Oi,

Shabazett or whatever your name is, none of that. This is His Grace's cab, so hop it back into the queue."

The Bishop looked embarrassed. "I don't mind sharing. We both have trains to catch."

"That's most awfully kind," lisped the demon.

"Not at all." The Bishop shooed it into the other seat, deftly stopping its tail from being caught in the door when the irritated cabby slammed it. "Loved your paper on exorcism as colonialism."

Caroline looked flustered. "We're not going to get the next train; you might as well stay and network and eat."

Emma sighed. She really wasn't in the mood, but could see Caroline's point, Just then, a snappy little two-seater sports car pulled up along side her. Emma reflected that if a middle-aged man had been driving it, she would have engaged in cheap Freudianism, whereas...

"It's Emma, isn't it?" The driver was one of those blondes who have spent so much time doing sporty things in the sun of hotter countries that her skin had become like the soft comfortable brown leather of her saddles. "You won't remember me."

"Shit, shit, shit!" Caroline was clearly not happy. Emma had no idea who this woman was.

"We were up at the same time, but we didn't move in the same circles." The woman obviously expected to be remembered. "Have to say, love the work. You look just the same..."

It came to Emma suddenly: oh dear, this woman was one of Caroline's old chums, that Emma had always hated.

"Don't say anything," Caroline pleaded. "There's no point. He took all that. I never was."

The woman held a door open. "No thanks," Emma said. "I've got some thinking to do. I'll walk."

She couldn't do anything to cheer Caroline up, and her lover never wanted her to or asked her to. Things were as they were, and Caroline was dead and forgotten. Some things cannot be put right.

A few weeks later, Emma was sitting at her computer and Caroline was dancing around the living room, doing routines she'd copied from an American cheer-leader movie. Emma left her to it, periodically turning to watch and feel gently lecherous. She turned back to the screen and pasted into the top of the page the link she'd copied from an e-mail.

It really did help that Elodie's awful film about them both had acquired a cult following, what Emma gathered they called a fandom. And people wrote stories, and edited film-clips, and drew pictures—some of it was surprisingly good, and some of it…

Emma coughed and Caroline stopped what she was doing and drifted back. There on the screen was Caroline's face. She was happy and alive and wearing the red dress she was eaten in.

"How?" Her jaw had dropped.

"I got Elodie to ask all her little admirers to do photo research. For the sequel. And they just looked at fashion shoots and gossip columns from back then and found faces that looked right and she went through everything and she found a couple."

"But he erased me. By magic."

"And magic uses true names. As well we know. Unlike paparazzi." It had been Emma's idea, though Elodie had organized it all. "Look at the subtitle, 'the right hon Edward Smythe enjoys a joke with a friend.' Browning's magic used your name, and he wiped everything that had your name, but he couldn't take things that didn't."

She flicked to another site. "In Memoriam," it said. "Caroline Smart." And it had the same photo.

"But how?" Caroline was excited and happy and sad.

"Magic has rules," Emma told her quietly. "Magic killed you and erased you. But now you're better than magic. You're information."

They couldn't hug but, as much as they could, they embraced.

"He may think he has everything under control, and the end is coming. But maybe…"

# Worst Excesses

## London, Paris, the East 1794

It was an age of the making of nations and the fall of kings, but that was no concern of mine.

The British took lawyers and scholars to India to rule it for the Company, and the lawyers and scholars taught themselves languages that the Indians had half-forgotten and went rummaging in temple libraries for scraps of old knowledge. Parchments that had been left among decay and bones and spiders. I was there, watching from shadow at their shoulders, and all that they found there was the shadow of Gautama the Buddha, but had they searched elsewhere than they did, they might have found worse.

And I would have been there, to take precautions.

Rebels rose against the Spanish in the lands of the Inca and the Maya, and they had painted on their banners an image that they said was the Virgin Mother of their Lord. She stared out at the necessary little atrocities of rebellion and repression with the

78

arrogant stare of far other goddesses, ones that I remembered, even if their peoples no longer knew them. Nothing came of any of these struggles except the usual hangings. I watched to check that nothing quickened from the slaughter that was best left dead, and followed those stragglers that escaped to starve slowly in the deep woods and high hills. Just to be sure. So much of the time, my work is just to watch.

I found an Inquisitor in Granada, with a taste for finding heresy in the young and comely, and for confirming it with the breaking of their bones and the tearing of their flesh, and finding his own ecstasy in the wrecking of beauty and the burning of what remained. Such men are common, but this one noticed that the more he killed, the fewer white hairs there were in his tonsure, the less the veins and liver spots stood out in hands that shook less and had a firmer grip.

People do not even need to know of the Rituals to practice them.

His colleagues noticed him with jealous eyes and half-formed suspicions, but he renewed his asceticisms and fastings and vigils and they cast their suspicions elsewhere. Yet the more he starved and watched, his eyes grew brighter in the shadow of his cowl and his lips and cheeks more full and red.

They would have found and burned him in the end perhaps, or he would have grown so strong that he would have torn the Holy Office to shreds about him, but I have no patience for experiments and so did not wait to find which.

No, I did not break him on his own wheel or rack, or with his own thumbscrews. A clean thrust to the heart; what do you take me for? I kill and sometimes I delight in a kill, but that delight, like all other pleasures, leaves an aftertaste of guilt. I kill to protect the weak against the strong, not to take pleasure; if ever I forget that, I will be lost and damnable.

And this time was the time of one of my greatest failures, when I turned my eyes away from a great evil because I thought that the weak were being protected against the strong, that the weak had risen up against the strong in their own defence. And all of this was true, but it was not all of the truth.

I knew that much was happening in France, the tearing down of towers and the killing of a King, but I thought—may I be forgiven for thinking, though I know not by whom—I thought that it was just such another revolution as the English had had when they killed their stupid bone-head king, that man of blood, and many of their lords.

When, one September, the Paris militias went into prisons and killed harmless whores and old priests and random thieves, I thought it just a massacre, as Bartholomew's had been, and I hardened my heart. I had longed two centuries for the fall of that old order, and had stood back from the work nonetheless. I had hated Versailles and its mirrors and its fountains and all those who starved to make it shimmer, and had longed for it to burn, but had brought no flame there, for it was not a work for my hands. I had loved the man Voltaire and so trusted the men who banded together to finish the job of eliminating those evils he had fought. I should never trust, because the heart of man is wicked and works iniquity, and because a dying god once taught me to be thorough.

I was thorough, but not in France, where I should have been. I was being thorough in England.

The man Dashwood was ten years dead and his Club disbanded. His monks were scattered, dead in their graves or old in gentlemen's clubs dreaming of their wilder days over a second decanter of port. And it had all been mummery and theatre—rich men playing games of devil-worship to give themselves permission to fuck with abandon and Dashwood himself leading them on to excess, but no further.

But such groups in other ages have turned from debauch and manipulation to the Rituals, and I have to be thorough.

Dashwood's nephew Alderson had started a dining club at Oxford that he claimed was the Hellfires come again, and he called it the Phoenix. And I am thorough, and I have no great love for Phoenixes. Nor for any other things that rise up from death time

80

and time again—save for one, and she had not returned in an age. But in Alderson's time, the Phoenix was no more than a group of youths who drank until they puked and ate bad meat badly cooked and thought themselves very devils for doing so in Dashwood's name. They did not take pleasure with whores, or even with each other, and there was no whiff of magic to them.

Alderson moved on to other things, and Brasenose College let the club live on after his departure. For all I know, they meet still and spew beer and wine in corners of the room; in due course I tired of checking on them once they forgot the meaning of the club's name or what it boasted of rebirthing in flame.

In that year, though, I paid them my usual visit, watching them from shadow lest they think me a spirit and themselves important; and yet again they were just boys debauching themselves uninterestingly, an ill-cleaned skull with a black candle guttering in its brainpan and a dead bat, stiff with age and eaten by moths, hanging on a string from the ceiling the only concessions to the tradition they claimed to honour.

There was nothing for me here and I stepped out of shadow into the night merely to breathe the night air and feel the turf of a century-old lawn beneath my sandalled feet. A black-aproned servant stepped out of the shadows, carrying a tray, a small fat man with that particular flab that comes from living on other men's scraps.

"Mistress Mara?" he asked, with that orotund self-importance which is the only possession of the entirely powerless.

"No," I said, "neither good nor weak enough to rule or be ruled by any man. Mara, merely."

He handed me a card from the tray. It said, simply, *Two admirers of your work wish to draw a matter to your attention.*

I looked up from it at him. I could not tell whether the blankness of his look was stupidity or a mask over some profound knowledge of who I am and whom he served.

"Your carriage awaits." His voice was obsequious to a degree that might have been sarcasm. "As it has waited every night since the beginning of term. You have wealthy patrons."

"I have no need of patrons, or of a carriage." I tried again to read him. "Where are these friends that wish to speak to me?"

"At the other end of a carriage ride, I was told to tell you. A carriage with blinds."

I fear no one and sometimes it does not pay to be stubborn. "Show me."

At a side gate of the college, there stood a trim post-chaise. It was drawn not by a single horse merely, but by four, large black spirited beasts that champed and stamped and breathed out hot steam in the cold air of a night in early spring.

A coachman lolled half-asleep against its nearer wheel, a hat that had once been livery pulled down over his face and a muffler wrapping his neck.

"I can bring you refreshments for your journey," the college servant offered. "The young men have ordered far too much of the college port. Far too much of everything."

"I saw their meal," I shuddered. "I will take some drink, but none of the scorched roasts you English seem to think so tasty."

"I can bring you good English bread and cheese from the porters' pantry."

"That would be a kindness," I said.

I need no human food, but generosity is a virtue best rewarded with acceptance of it, and it had been too long since I had felt the hardness of breadcrust against my teeth and tongue, and the cheeses of the English have a simple salty bite in the mouth, and a pleasing crumble on the tongue. Alcohol does not affect me, but the rich purple taste of the fortified wine the English call port is a pleasant enough way of slaking thirst.

I climbed into the post-chaise, and relaxed into its padded seat. Taking the plate and bottle the porter brought me, I picked at the one and supped from the other, as the coach gathered speed, and raced away into the night.

There was little point to the blinds, since shortly the hoofbeats against the road had that particular resonance that comes from crossing a bridge, and I then felt the carriage turn left, so knew that we were heading for the London road. Some two hours later, we laboured up a steep hill and an hour after that, we drew up somewhere and changed horses with a speed that impressed me. Clearly all this had been arranged by someone with the power to buy or compel fast service.

Newton's successor had been Polly Wild, but that was long ago and I wondered idly how long she had lasted and who her successors had been; I take some vague note of such things, as I said, but this particular information had not come my way. I had not been interested enough to wonder why. Nor did I now, but took the luxury of a doze.

As the sun's rays sidled round the edges of the blinds, I heard the ringing of the City's bells; I cannot say that they woke me, for I had been at no more than the threshold of sleep, but they brought me to full alertness as the carriage left the comparative smoothness of a paved street for the sudden jounce of cobbles, and then drew to a halt.

I flung the door open, and found myself in a narrow courtyard between high buildings. I watched as one servant placed a set of steps where I could handily descend from the carriage and another unwound a strip of carpet that led me from the steps to an unassuming door in a wall with no obvious windows. There was an unneeded lantern at the side of the door, which one of them lit. They had the slow steady choreographed movements around me of men forewarned that I might be recklessly swift in my actions who had made allowance for this in advance.

I stepped through and into a room, or rather a set of rooms, that had been very different when last I'd seen them. They were still dominated by large tables that stretched back into the darkness and on which stood, not a simple map any more, but a relief, and not of the city merely but of the whole kingdom, the coasts of its neighbours and the seas between them. And I knew that the pins upon that map were no longer beggars and whores and ruffians, but regiments, ships of the line and the King's Intelligencers.

Where there had been tables stacked with the bound leather volumes that catalogued the Wilds' dealings, now stood bureaus with locked drawers, drawers big enough for the secrets of three kingdoms and an empire and for the ledgers that told of how those secrets were paid for.

But where once the rooms had been full of sweat and hustle, now they were silent save for the brute ticking of a man-height clock and the chink of cup against saucer on the small table in the far corner of the room I was in, where, small in a vast black leather armchair, Miss Polly Wild was taking her tea.

She was still dressed in black, as when I had last seen her, and was in no other way changed from that day some seventy years earlier. It was a simple mourning dress, picked out with pewter buttons and white lace at sleeves and high collar.

"Come and take some tea with me, 'Untress. Or I can have coffee brought if you would prefer it to break your fast."

Her voice had changed. She still spoke with the urgent tones of the London streets but now she chose it, had taken it from a quiverful of accents, and might, if she chose, in a second talk to me as if I were a duchess and she my peer. She gestured to a small chair by the wall.

"Make yourself comfortable. And do 'ave the coffee if you want, for I'm sure that the Bishop will want fresh when he arrives." She looked at me intently and caught the intensity of my stare. "Oh, don't worry about me. I've done naught that you need take care of."

I thought for a second, and then smiled my thinnest smile. "It was not just his post you pestered that old man for," I said.

"Silly old fool," she said. "All those poor Irish changed and dead and three fine whores as made me and Dad a mint of gelt, and that lovely knifeboy what I could have used in the work. And all the time it was there, sitting in his workshop, and him too lily-livered to sip it. Dark magics and bible-bashing, and the Elixir neglected in a dusty decanter."

I have seen the effects of Elixirs down the years. "But how could you know it would preserve you and not kill you?" I asked her.

"Because I didn't care," she said. "I sat and stared at it for months, I did, and started the work and it kept me busy until the men could come back from Tobago and say that my Mackie was dead. And so I did not care. I told Froggie Franky to go his way and told him it was the work, but I could have gone on having him and said he was my intelligencer. But I did not care and so I drank one day, and so here I am."

She took a sip of tea. "And my daughter drank it when she found the first grey hair, and she turned to stone, white marble stone, and her daughter drank it when she took a fever and she burned to ashes and smoke in a minute, and her daughter, her daughter is lost in Paris. Where she does the work, for me and England."

"And you expect me to help her?" I said. "And it is for that that you have brought me here? You could have saved your labour, much as I pity your losses." I got up to go.

"You've not heard out the Bishop," she said. "And my daughter, well, she weren't Mackie's."

I sat down again.

"She was Frankie's," Polly said, "and don't deny it. You were sweet on him, awful sweet, terrible girl-frigger though you be."

There was a cough from one of the further rooms, and the dragging of a lame foot.

"Here he is now," she said. "If you're going, say, so I don't have to ring for a new chair. Or you could give him your seat, of course, being as he is crippled, and a man of the cloth."

"Miss Wild has her little joke." It was a voice that I half-recognized. "I was a bishop for a while, but I found that it did not suit my aspirations."

The man who limped into the room was older and heavier on his broken foot, but I knew him at once. I nodded a greeting. "Monsieur Talleyrand."

He gave the half-smile of one who expected to be remembered by personages of importance, but was nonetheless gratified.

"Far as I'm concerned," Polly said, "you're the Bishop, because you're the only Bishop I know that I can rip the piss out of. Also, if you ain't a Bishop, you're a bloodthirsty Frog revolutionary kingslayer whom I should probably have slung into the hulks. You wouldn't like it in the hulks; they smell horrible at low tide."

He gave her a courtly bow, even though it cost him pain. I offered him my chair, and he waved a hand in polite refusal, standing up straighter than I would have thought possible. Clearly this was a man with no wish to be obliged. He flashed a sardonic smile in my direction and then turned back to Polly.

"I am grateful for your forbearance, mademoiselle. And you may call me Bishop if you will, but the Pope in Rome would disagree."

"And he has no fucking jurisdiction in this realm of England," she retorted. "That's in the 39 bleeding Articles, ain't it, so I can call you what I damn well please."

"You have detained me here these last few months," he said. "Your master Pitt wishes me gone, and I would wish to have an ocean between me and the Tribunal. The Huntress is here now, and I can say my piece to her, as you have wished, and then be gone."

"If you would be so kind," she said. "Bishop."

He turned back to me. "Huntress," he said. "I call you that because it is more honourable, as I understand it, than any mere human title." He paused, gathering his thoughts, and then went on. "Nonetheless, it is my humble opinion that you have neglected your responsibilities of late."

"There has been bloodshed," I said. "But that is common enough in times of unrest. Revolutionaries kill people and grow drunk on blood; it is the way of such men."

"Many of my former colleagues," he continued, "are as intoxicated by murder as you say, but the members of the Jacobin

Club—they are different. They combine a taste for slaughter with a desire to refashion God."

"They will not have much luck in that. He is unusually stubborn."

"I think," Talleyrand said, "that they wish to depose him, and kill him, as they did the king."

"And become gods themselves?"

"No," said Talleyrand. "They believe in democracy"—he said it as if it were a curseword and Polly reacted to it as if it were a bad smell—"and none of them would want the throne of Heaven. They think themselves too good for that. They wish to create their own God in their own image, a god that will kill for the common good. Sometimes they talk of Reason and sometimes of the Supreme Being. In all of this, they think of gods and goddesses that will do their bidding. I know these men. I worked with them while I could bear to. And before I truly knew them."

I sighed deeply, suddenly aware, so deeply aware that it was the closest to pain I had felt in an age—aware that I had made a mistake and that the legacy of my harmless advice to a man I liked was his advice to men he trusted, and that trust's betrayal.

"What are they like?" I had better know the worst.

"Saints with the logic of madmen," he told me. "Robespierre and Saint-Just—these are men who at the same time would lock up churches and arrest men for atheism, dandies who call for endless parades of death but would never let blood stain the lace on their cuffs."

There was a quiet anger in his voice, mingled with regret and self-contempt that he had not seen through his former allies sooner. It was this, as much as his words, that drew my attention—here was a serious man confessing his own criminal folly.

"They killed the King and Queen, harmless fools that they were. They killed many of my class who were brutes and rapists, and many who were not. And now the Revolution has turned on its own—they kill men who were once their brothers."

This gave me pause, because treachery to kin and those brothers in arms who are more than kin adds its own flavour to dark magic.

I looked at him and at Polly long and hard, and they looked back, clear and full. I saw much desire to manipulate me to their private ends, but no untruth whatever. I sighed. "I thank you, Monsieur Talleyrand."

"I can tell you more, if you wish."

I shook my head. "You have told me what I need to know. And I am sure you have briefed Miss Wild endlessly. She will be accompanying me, and can tell me whatever else I need to know, when I need her to tell me." I nodded his polite dismissal.

"I would help you if you needed me to," he said.

"I am sure. But there will, no doubt, be fights to the death and hairsbreadth escapes before this business is done, and you, your Grace, are lame in one foot."

He tossed his head proudly as if I had questioned his manhood. "I have killed my man." I sensed that all this was a matter of form—for him Paris was a trap, a lion's mouth he would not want to stick his head into a second time.

"I have no doubt of your courage, but a duel in the Bois is not a scuffle in a back alley. It is Miss Wild I would wish at my back at such a time; my regrets."

He made a gesture of protest, but when I looked firmly at him, his regret was ever more clearly a mask over relief that I expected nothing from him.

He nodded and turned to Polly. "I've not forgotten," she said. "The money for your travels is with my clerks."

"I would not wish you to think, mademoiselle, that I am a bought traitor. I ask for my expenses; no more."

"No, no," she agreed in bored tones. "You work for the real France against those who have betrayed and disfigured it, a fight in which you and I are allies today, who will return to traditional enmity tomorrow. And the labourer is worthy of his hire."

He limped from the room, a man incapable of shame. And in his case, that was a strength not to be dismissed. Once he had gone, she sat back in her chair, took a sip from her cup and then spat, genteelly, into her saucer, as if to rid her mouth of a taste. "Still a fucking traitor, for all of that."

"Traitors," I said, thinking of one in particular, "are usually men who serve more masters than one from an excessive desire to be useful."

Polly ignored my remark, and continued to fume. "Talking to me like he was a proper person," she said. "Fucking Judas."

I was in no mood to share with her the memories she had awoken. "How soon can you be ready to come with me to Paris? There is, in such matters, no time to be lost."

"I can't possibly clear my desk before this time next Tuesday," she said. "There's the cabinet papers to write and the King to talk to. And I have to get permission, obviously."

"I would have thought you above the permission of kings and statesmen."

"As I am," she said. "But there are Powers nonetheless to which I am answerable."

I tired of this. "We need to be in Paris. For the sake of your great granddaughter, and also of a world that has too many gods in it already." I reached to tug her into shadow and take her with me by main force, and found her immovable.

"And," she added as if she were politely ignoring my attempt at force, "we 'ave to go by carriage and ship for that I cannot walk in shadow. Much as I would find it convenient to do so and you are not the first to try to take me there or show me the ways, I cannot walk there. I am fixed here in the world of light, where travel is an unhandy thing that takes time and, like I said, permissions."

I was taken aback, simply because I am not used to having the universe gainsay my will.

Some three decades later, in a conversation just such as the one we are having, I talked to a man who claimed to be the magus Cornelius Agrippa about this; his opinion was that it was the elixir, that it had pinned her in the Real, too solid to move from it. But these are matters of speculation, Crowley.

At the time, I scowled, and then shrugged. "We still need to be in Paris."

"And so we shall," she said. "In due course and with attention to my duty. I am not free like you, 'Untress, and cannot flit around on my whims; I have responsibilities. Bide with me and we shall be there before you know it."

It amused me out of all ill-temper that one who had been immortal for what was, to me, the blink of an eye, should presume to lecture me on the virtue of patience.

"After all," she went on, "poor young Augusta is either dead or not dead as we speak, and will not be any less dead in a week's time if she has met with misfortune. Each minute that ticks past is one in which she might die—either we arrive in time to rescue her, or we arrive too late and avenge her; that remains true whether we arrive in a minute or a week."

"And the Jacobins' new gods?"

She shrugged. "Them's your business after all. We get there, we find them, you kill them, quick as like when you have a ferret round to clear the rats from the drains. I would not presume to tell you your trade, just as you will not lecture me about the necessities of mine."

I found myself corrected, by one who had authority to do so, and confess that I was impressed at what the brash girl I had met a mere seven decades earlier had made of herself. She talked of her dealings with Powers, but she was on the way to becoming herself the Power that she remains.

Impressed or not, we did not have a week to waste if half of what Talleyrand said was true. If we had to travel in the mundane world, that gave us even less time to fritter away.

"I will give you a day." I looked at her sternly and then laughed, because her ready agreement was that of a woman who had all along said one thing and been prepared to negotiate it down to another.

I do not play cards, but she is not one with whom I would care to sit at a casino table even if I had a taste for such things.

You have never heard of her? That hardly surprises me; I doubt that she ever deals with agents at your level any more.

I had nothing more important to do than to wait for her, and so that is what I did for several hours, as men in court livery and the dress of cavalry and marines and the rags of the gutter and the finery of whores came and went, and laid information, and were paid for their trouble in fresh minted golden guineas or battered copper pennies and ha'pennies and farthings.

Polly had learned her trade at her father's feet, and then taught herself things he never knew, and I was not bored as I waited, because it is always instructive to see men and women labour in their vocation. And I would not need be schooled in patience by one who had been a mayfly mortal girl until so recently.

She owned the works of Voltaire bound in green morocco leather, and there was much there that I had never before had the time to read. When she saw what I was reading, she made as if to speak but then thought better of it, and I knew that we both mourned his passing and the inheritance of knowledge that he had left to lesser men.

The hours of night came and went, and Mr Pitt called in and sat in Polly's best chair drinking her best port and cursing the Whigs until he became sodden enough to be carried home by the men she had for such errands. I cannot say that I had any opinion of the great man, because he chose, from discretion or insolence, to ignore me altogether, and Polly mostly, and addressed most of his comments to the invisible air.

And then the one for whose leave Polly waited came, borne into rooms almost too small for him in a gust that combined the stench of the gunpowder that has defeated so many enemy ships and the salt spray that beats upon cliffs and the coarse gently aromatic grasses that flourish on those cliffs and the blue cornflowers that grow among them.

91

He was, as I had surmised, the Lord of Cliffs and Narrow Seas, and, though we had never met before, we nodded to each other as if old friends, because that is the way of Powers with each other.

Like many such beings he was made up of the images—and, for all I know, the souls—of all those who have died defending the realms he guards, and he flickered as he stood, sometimes in the helmet and breastplate of the Romans who stood at the Saxon Shore and on the Wall, and sometimes in the blue-dyed nakedness of those who opposed the Romans when they came and sometimes the leathers and mail of those who came later. Sometimes he was an archer with the calluses that bowstrings wear, and sometimes a rag-clad sailor with the burned tattoo of powder on his cheeks and sometimes he had the fresh cheeks of the women and young boys who went as soldiers and sailors for love of their men and stayed for love of war.

"Lord," I addressed him.

"Huntress," he said. "We have never met, yet I have seen the signs of your passing through the realms I guard, and I cannot but thank you."

This was not said with perfect grace. Such wardens like to think that their guardianship is eternal and that it supersedes all other authority, and they are wrong. I passed into the British lands, and the Saxon lands, and the English lands, long before there was even one realm for him to guard, let alone the neighbours it acquired.

And I have killed in those lands beings that no mere guardian of borders could ever have coped with, beings that would have charred and blighted the lands he cherishes beyond mending. The Lion and the Unicorn were not always mere heraldry like the Red Dragon of Wales, but maddened lords of conflict that ate up both forests and souls wherever they passed, and that they have been forgotten into prettiness speaks well of the ability of the minds of men and women to scab over and heal themselves with lies.

The full measure of gratitude to me is something for which I hope, but which I never expect—some lip service to that measure was a pleasant enough surprise, and so I decided to be gracious in return.

"My Lord," I said. "Pressure of business has caused me to be remiss. When I have come to your realms, and often when I have left, I have done so in hot pursuit, without time to…"

He smiled the smile of one who has gotten a due that he did not expect, and waved my feigned concern away. "Tush, Huntress. Of course you have my permission to enter and leave at will, that goes without saying or your need to ask."

It also, I thought to myself, goes with your utter impotence to offer me let or bar, but, as so often, politeness consists of silence principally and merely. So I smiled, and nodded, politely, and so did he, and that was our business done.

"Miss Wild." He turned his gaze on her. "You wish to quit my service?"

With all of her other callers, even the man Pitt, she had been busy with her eyes or hands at the same time as she talked to them. She rose from her chair for him and stayed standing, even when he gestured her to sit down. He was a stern and magnificent master. And yet, from the softness in his tone as he talked to her, I saw that this being was perhaps her best friend in the whole world.

"Not quit," she said. "Never quit, my Lord, but to pursue the interests of the kingdom beyond its borders. I would help the Huntress destroy those who are the prey of her mission and the enemies of these realms. And I would save or avenge the life of your servant Augusta, my only remaining kin."

All of this she said in a voice and manner at once formal and deferential. Her hands, normally so busy—pointing her witticisms with a gesture, or tapping a table or chair arm in impatience—were still at her sides.

This was a being to whom she owed not allegiance only, but respect, and it was a respect that she felt deeply. Most of the time, even when dealing with the mighty, Polly was and is still the brash girl I remembered, dealing with equals as an equal, but not with the Lord.

It is, I suppose, not him merely, but that which he stands for. Polly feels that emotion called patriotism. I envy her that, in a way; it is a mission akin to my own but far less solitary, one she shares with thousands upon thousands of the living and the dead.

She curtseyed and kissed his ever-changing hand. He bowed and kissed her forehead, lord to vassal, master to servant, and also friend to friend. She handed him a great key, and he feigned reluctance to take it, for a second.

"I will entrust you with it again, if you return," he said.

"When I return," she corrected him.

"Just so," he said. And then they were done.

She clapped hands and relaxed into the woman I knew and said, "And now, my Lord, and you, 'Untress, let us take tea together, one last time, before our journey. 'Cause I doubt we shall taste it or strong ale once we set foot in Frogonia—coffee if we are lucky, and cheap red wine."

Tea was a new-fangled fashion in her youth, but one to which she had taken with delight, a delight that she felt unaffectedly decades later. Whenever I am tempted to think of her as a universal spider, whose intrigues bind your human world up in her great games of statecraft and dominion, I remember that she is also that endlessly young woman with that glee at simple pleasures, and I sigh and smile.

We sat an hour or so, sipping mediocre lapsang from fluted bone china, and exchanging those politenesses most appropriate on the eve of mortal danger for two of the three present, and then, in a flurry of wind and weather, the Lord of Cliffs and Narrow Seas was gone, without adieux.

Polly smiled indulgently as she looked after him, into the empty air. "He has his ways. He thinks of some errand, and away he goes, all business. That's how I like men to be." She did not add, "and women too," but between her and me, it needed no saying. She sat still and upright for a second, thinking of things undone and things still to do, and then turned to me. "I am uncommon grateful that you have waited for me this long day, 'Untress. For one as you, as

94

can girdle the world in a wink, it must be more tiresome than my fancy reaches."

I made a polite demurral, as insincere as it was needful.

"Still," she said, "since we have to travel by roads as go somewhere, rather than through the uncharted dark, at least I can fix so as we travel in some style."

She got up from her chair and walked behind a screen, a screen decoupaged with beauties of the day, duchesses and courtesans in their high hair and fripperies, and I mused some minutes on the light things with which men and woman fill their short lives.

She returned, having replaced the simple black mourning dress, with an elegant riding habit, fawn kid-skin breeches and a yellow jacket, jaunty as a schoolgirl let out of tutelage with money to spend.

I have seen less practical outfits on men and women at the start of adventures, and I noted with approval the two small pistols that sat snugly in pockets at her side and the vicious sharpness of the great pin that held her small round hat to hair that she had put up in a governess' bun.

She picked up a small portmanteau from beside her chair, smiled, "Off we go," and turned to walk to the door without bothering to see that I followed.

The carriage outside was the one in which I had arrived, save that this time its windows were not shuttered. She opened its door and climbed in, to find me already sprawled on the seat. I shifted to make room for her and noticed with amusement that she managed to sit so that no inch of her touched any inch of me.

"I may be the Huntress," I said. "But let us be clear, Miss Wild, that you are not my prey."

"Just so we're clear," she said. "We'll be spending a lot of time together."

"And have done already."

"That was different. There was folks around and we were in my chambers, where my rules apply."

I forebore to point out to her that in any human place, and most divine ones, I make my own rules, because in truth I am no seducer, nor wish to be. I have never understood those adventurers who mingle dalliance with their business.

"You misjudge me, Miss Wild. That I am a lover of women, is true; of women dead so long that even their dust is gone. One of those women is reborn, from time to time, and from time to time, we encounter and renew true vows made in a time beyond your imagining. And you are not she."

"I didn't mean –" she started, and I set a finger on her lips. And felt their softness as a moment of intimacy I would think of fondly in other times and climes.

"I notice beauty," I said, "and wit, and charm, and courage. All of which you have, and I treasure them in you. As in so many down the long dry years. But I am sworn, and never forsworn, save once in great heat and the greatest of need. And lovely as you are, you are not she. You need have no fear of me."

She relaxed, and smiled. "'Untress, I've been unfair. Unfair and unkind. My fear is of myself and my own imaginings. I loved my Mackie once, and he was deadly as a dark night in St Giles, and he was an eyeless kitten to you; for fifty years and more, I have thought of him, and of you, and those thoughts knot and tangle."

"As thoughts do," I agreed. "Which is why actions are simpler."

She nodded and sighed, and looked out of the window as our carriage rattled past the Monument and across Old London Bridge. And things change and pass, and where there had once been a raggletaggle of tumbledown houses and booths there was now a clear run through to the other side with the jump of the carriage wheels on the new stone of the centre span, and the noise of water rushing through the central piers with gravel and sand scouring the stone like an angry scullion.

I slumped in my seat and closed my eyes. "If we have to travel as mortal men do," I said, "I shall imitate them in one other thing, and sleep until our carriage ride ends."

"I am all of a maze," Polly said, "that one such as you still feels the need for sleep after all the ages of 'umankind."

"No need at all, but a simple human pleasure that I share when I can lest I forget it and lose one more human thing. Trust me, young Polly, it is in such small things that our salvation from godhood lies."

"Not so much of the young," she said. And then, in hushed and wondering tones, "What was it like then, 'Untress, in the olden days when the world were new and fresh?"

"It smelled of pine forests," I said, "Pine forests and the sweat of honest work on people that bathed rarely. Not, I think, to your taste. Nor to Monsieur Rousseau's if he had to endure it." And then I yawned, because when I set my mind to sleep, I can even manage to persuade myself that I tire. "Wake me at journey's end," I told her, and wrapped myself in the dark velvet of oblivion.

I woke to darkness with Polly's hand on my shoulder, salt stinging in my nose and on my lips, and the suck and draw of sea on shingle beating gently in my ears.

"I have a man, to the which I need to talk alone." Polly breathed in my ear, so softly none else might hear. "He is a silent one and a solitary, and takes no pleasure in the unusual or the sudden. He needs coaxing, like a trout in a stream or a pigeon at a window, with a gentle finger and a plentiful supply of breadcrumbs, these particular breadcrumbs being the kind that are gold and have writing upon them. Hence, I require that you sit here, quiet as if you were still asleep, only without the snoring, and do nothing to perturb him. For all that I am the King's High Lady of Intelligencers, when I needs a safe passage to Frogonia, I has to ask nicely."

It gladdened me that she, so newly come to power and to the possibility of eternity, was thus far still without that first flush of arrogance that makes the mighty think of mortals as mere, and there to serve us without demur. I have hopes for Polly as one of the friends who may last me down the years—so many are made immortal by the most harmless of means and then become spoiled, quite spoiled, as if they were monsters made by the Rituals. And some whom I once liked, I have had to remove from the scene, and others I avoid.

After a while, Polly came back to the carriage and removed a small brown valise from its secure niche above the seats.

"We've passage," she said. "Bought and paid for generous. The tide is turning, though, and we need to be swift aboard and out to sea if we are to land on the other side before Monsieur Pry gets the chance to see our sail white against the dawn."

I was at her side before she finished speaking, and moving sharply down the beach to where a small vessel just floated at the water's edge. We splashed through the last few yards and helpful hands pulled Polly aboard. I had no need of such and swung myself on deck as I had on a myriad other such small craft down the years, though few so trim and yare.

Something was out of its proper place here. The wood under my fingers had a slickness and give to it that belonged to no natural tree. I sniffed it carefully, and there was a hint of sulphur mingled with the sharpness of tar and paint. I wondered just how much Polly knew about the man she had hired.

I turned around to where he leaned against the mast, his eyes hooded as he watched the two dull-eyed young boys who were his crew stow Polly's valise neatly away and fuss her to a bench nailed to the deck, before weighing the boat's small anchor and pulling at the sails.

Sails which filled with wind suspiciously readily as the man against the mast pulled out a tin whistle and played what I recognized as a song from the Finnmark. He had a grim smile as he put the whistle back in the pocket of his sea-coat, and the wary eyes of a man who has more masters than one, and fears the lash of each of them.

The two boys were dressed in sea-gear that saltwater had rotted to rags and showed old scars beneath the tatters, whip-lines and rope-burns and bruises of cudgels. When his attention was elsewhere, they whispered to each other, or caught each other's eye and smiled.

The man's eyes grew warier as he saw me look at him and weigh him and his crew.

"You are the one they call the Huntress," he said. "She told me, but I know you from my grandfather's book of cunning."

"Your grandfather was a cunning man, then," I said. "But was he also wise?"

"Wise?" he repeated.

"Wise enough to have warned a foolish grandson that everything bought has to be paid for in one coin or another. Even the winds you whistle and a swift boat made from wood that once grew in Hell."

The boat gathered speed as if the waves had no purchase on it as the wind set fair to the South.

From her bench Polly spoke up, almost anxiously. "He came highly recommended, he did. My master the Lord and my master the King use him all the time." She had the grace to look embarrassed.

"Paid for it all is," he said. "Fair and square and handshook and done."

"Handshook."

"Handshook and bum-kissed. To Duke Lucifuge Rocofocale hisself, as sometimes needs cargo moved discreet, and needs that cargo more than any soul of mine."

"But not this night," I said.

"Not this night," he agreed. "You and her are my only cargo, and the shore of France the only haven I steer for."

"Just so we are clear—I have no particular yearning to visit the Hell of Lucifer this season, when I have business in Paris and none in Pandemonium."

"That's your business. And your own, just as mine is. To be minded by myself alone." He looked me in the eye with the insolent pride of all his kind. "Jeremiah Stagg, owner and master."

Owner and master of the boat, and of its crew if my guess was right.

I have no liking for such hedge wizards and windwhistlers and the like; they begin with making large profits from small magics, and draw conclusions from this that take them on a short journey into over-reaching. They suffer from the madness of thinking themselves clever, and more clever than powers that learned to rig a thimble when the world was young and even then wicked.

The same is often true of those men who have a taste for slaves. And those gods.

It is no business of mine how they choose to damn themselves, except when they bring themselves to my attention, whether through the Rituals, or by inconveniencing me.

As you, of course, Crowley, will never now do.

But for now, I watched him as he walked the deck of his ship like a cock on his kingdom of sawdust and dung.

One young boy scrambled up the mast quick as a Barbary ape, and not the quicker for a rope's end that flicked at him from his master's hand as he went. The other kept his hand on the tiller and seemed to do naught that needed correction, yet did not escape the back of his master's hand. Both boys looked at his back with an icy hatred not less disturbing for having so little intelligence in its glare.

"No need for that," Polly said, as he struck again.

"I do what I will with my own."

"And I have paid for your time with my own good British guineas," she returned. "And am minded against the sight of the whip when I am paying."

I looked at her with enquiry in my gaze.

"Sometimes," she answered, "sometimes I think of Mackie, who died as a slave among slaves. And my eyes will not weep for him, so my heart and will must answer instead."

This tenderness did her credit, though I do not now see her running the affairs of the realm she guards in such a spirit.

But that night the waves grew rough and the wind in our sails had a force that was more than Stagg had summoned, and I joined Polly on her bench that I might wrap a tarpaulin around us both to protect her travelling outfit from salt spray.

Stagg laughed at us as the wind tossed and matted his hair into elf-locks. "I take no ladies on my boat," he said, "for fear of such storms as I cannot yet manage. Perhaps, if this blow continues, I should toss one of you overboard to placate the lords of the sea."

I fixed him with my coldest stare. "Of all your acts of folly, that attempt would be the culmination and the last."

He swore at me then, and at Polly, calling us names of which bitch and cunt were the least particle.

"That is an ugly tongue you have there," Polly said.

He spat at her feet, and then waggled it at her in a way that was meant to be obscene. Which was not the most clever thing he might have done, and was almost certainly what she had expected, or even intended, that he would do next, because in a second she was up and had one of the wicked hatpins out and through his tongue into the flesh of his lip.

"I don't," she said, "appreciate insolence from them as I have hired with good red gold. And my Lord does not welcome insolence to those who are about his business."

She punctuated her speech with moments of pressure on the pin, then pulled it out, twisting it slightly as it came.

He looked at her in hatred and agony and spat blood at her feet. "I don't care who you serve. I have no time for Kings." His voice was twisted by fury and pain.

"You would have time should my Lord will it otherwise, for he could make it so that you never set foot on English soil again, that English soil would pull itself away from you in disgust like a lady her skirts from a beggar, and leave you sprawling in the gutter."

Nonetheless, he raised a hand as if to strike her, and she reached for the pockets in which she kept her pistols.

I had been interested to see Miss Wild at her exercise—I had feared that she might have become one of those who order excruciations but are too delicate to inflict it themselves—but enough was now enough. There is a time for instructive acts of violence, but not, perhaps, in the midst of a storm which does not care.

I looked at Stagg and then, in a spirit of fairness, looked at Polly, and after my look neither seemed minded to continue the matter further. She returned to her seat at my side, and I wrapped the tarpaulin back around her. He stood glowering at us with rain streaming down his face until the bleeding from his lip was almost gone, and then picked up a cudgel which lay handy and used it to belabour the nearest of his boys about the head and shoulders.

"You should not use us thus," the boy remarked in an oddly calm voice. He seemed to feel no pain from blows he made no move to avoid. "The lady said so and you knows it to be true."

"You are my sworn bonded men and less than men," Stagg spoke with the arrogance of all slaveowners. "And I will use you as I choose."

"Not as you choose, but for as long as you hold our bond."

The dead boy was calm as death and lawyer's language and I started to sense how this might play out in the end, this day or some other year, but sure as sand through a glass.

"I have it here." Stagg reached into his pocket.

"Then mind you keep it safe." I owed him that much of a warning, monster though he was, for I know a little of such matters and their consequences.

Stagg paid me no heed and laughed wolfishly in the face of his servant. "I can do what I choose." He pulled two small phials from his pocket. "For I have here shavings of the coin in which I paid the parish for you and ash of the hair of your heads and the froth I wiped from your dying mouths and the stench of your last poisoned breaths as I caught special, and the dirt of the graves from which I tore you to serve me."

I detest such magics at all times, but when allied to murder, as this clearly seemed to be, they come close enough to the Rituals to be something of which I need to take note. And I would have acted, no doubt, but a wave crashed over the boat and tore the phials from his grasp, to float in the bilges where he bent to seize them back.

The one of the boys who stood nearest to him kicked him in the

102

face with a seaboot that sent him flying with a crack of bone from nose and jaw.

He who stood further away reached for an oar and brought it down on Stagg's skull with a crunch of finality.

The first boy reached down and pulled the phials from the bilge water and tossed them over the side.

"Free." His voice was dull, and without joy.

He and his fellow knelt in the bilges over the body of their dead master, and were busy with their nails and teeth for a while, ignoring the storm and all else save the hunger that comes over the walking dead when freed of mastery. Then they fell to argument and shoving. One sent the other sprawling, holding him off with the blade of the oar while he tore away the delicate parts and spat on them to make them his.

"You promised me the privities," the other whined. "You said I could have the privities if I let you have the eyes, for they be the juiciest parts."

The first laughed and near choked on the fine things he was gourmandising. "Promises are things for those that live," he said. "We are the dead and have no honour."

He struck at his fellow with the oar and of a sudden the mere touch of it caved in the other boy's chest like the tap of a spoon on an egg.

"I am ruined," the smashed boy said. "He was the death of me, and now you is the ruination." He pulled one of the broken ribs from his chest and hurled it at the other, whose forehead it pierced as if it were a skull of sugar.

The boy with the pierced skull blinked as if remembering something. "We are the dead," he said again.

"Dead," said the other, "and torn from our graves, but not to resurrection or to life."

"We are dead ashes," said the first.

"And unto dust we shall return."

They reached out to each other, all fury spent, and clasped hands that started to crumble.

"Amen," they said, and then again, "Amen."

They fell to the deck, broken things, that had only lasted long enough to take their vengeance and luxuriate in the torn flesh of their killer, and then come to themselves again. Not the saddest fate for ones who had been human, and then were not, and were better dead than continue as ravening monsters.

Then a wave smashed over them, and another, and of a sudden they were fragments and orts that drained away from the deck when the water did, and in the next moment the wind dropped and the sea was calm, dead calm, and we were there alone, in a boat that still moved at speed, with the wreckage of the dead Stagg oozing blood and other fluids into the pools of water at our feet.

All this was in the nature of the sort of magics with which Stagg played, and this is why I have no relish for the company of such men. Their ends are condign, and messy, and often have inconvenient consequences for bystanders, as proved to be the case here.

I walked to the tiller. I have no great skill in such matters, for I have never needed to acquire it, but in any case it wriggled away as I tried to take charge of it.

"It will not serve you," said a suave voice, "for it is not yours."

"So who's this?" Polly asked, in the weary tone of one who has seen quite enough dark magic for one night.

I had, after talking to Jehovah about the musician he later killed, gone to see the opera that had doomed the Viennese. It was fine enough of its kind, and said the right things about not thinking yourself above the ordinary, and that all bills come due.

It also had a singing statue, and a chorus of demons, with goatee beards and little horns, and impractical pitch-forks.

One of the problems with human artists is that they give the mighty ideas; I suppose red tights and painted eyebrows were a better look for the fashionable imp around Hell than the black armour or satyr thighs that were standard in earlier centuries, but I still found it silly, myself, especially when it meant padded calves. Some looks only work with excellent physiques.

I turned to look at the demon who stood there by the mast, glowing red with his own internal fires, and a case in point for everything I just said. "Which duke do you serve?"

"I have the honour," he said, "of serving Duke Lucifuge-"

"Rocofocale," I cut him short. "And were sent to investigate when the man Stagg arrived in Hell suddenly and before his time."

"Just so. And to see if we could come to any useful arrangement with his killers. My master's mail must get through."

"That is your problem and your master's. Stagg's killers, his victims, are gone where they cannot serve you. And I and Miss Wild are already employed."

"Then perhaps"—the demon's voice had the petulance of all jobsworths,—"we can discuss your continued presence in a boat which is my master's property."

"I had a deal with Stagg." Polly was in a mood to haggle and stand by her rights. "I paid him guineas and he swore to get me to France. A deal's a deal."

"Stagg is dead," the demon said. "You have no deal."

I grew irritated. "In earlier times, when Lucifer was young, there was respect, in Hell, for contracts."

"Humans break them with us, all the time," the demon sneered. "Stagg is dead and cannot take you to France, and you cannot steer the boat we made for him."

"Ah." I had a thought. "And yet Stagg can still take us to France."

The apprentices' teeth had near disjointed his left wrist, but left the hand ungnawed—I needed but a knife-stroke to cut it loose.

It had started to stiffen into rigor; I struck it against the side of the boat a time or two, to soften it. Then I clenched its fingers tight around the tiller and grasped them with my own. As I had hoped, the tiller responded to the touch of the flesh it knew, even though that flesh was torn and dead.

"That's all very well," said the demon. "But the sea is calm, dead calm."

"As to that," Polly shrugged, and rummaged through Stagg's spilt guts to find his whistle. "As to that," she went on, as she reached over the side to rinse the blood from it before setting it to her lips and playing some patriotic English air or other.

"As to that," she said a third time, as the wind filled the sails almost as enthusiastically as it had for Stagg's piping, "I serve a Lord the which has jurisdiction of these seas, and the wind is obedient to him and so is to me."

"Thus," I told the demon, "your business with us is done, and you may reclaim your boat when we are done with it."

"That's all very well," said the demon, "but I must insist…"

"You are a very junior imp," I said, "and one who needs to learn his manners." At his indignant look, I added with a laugh, "You really do not know who I am, do you?"

"Every damned soul says that," the young demon said, but looked less sure of himself.

"Your Duke will not be pleased with you, if you force me to remonstrate with him. But, as you will…"

"I'll go and ask." He blinked away.

I sighed. "Jehovah and Lucifer claim to rule the universe, but they cannot even manage their own staff."

"What would you know about it?" Polly said. "You as is the 'Untress, who works alone. Like you always says. What you don't know is that there is a joy to training up young things to work for you, and to have ideas of their own, and become good at things, a joy you do not know, because you work alone, for fear of staff that might fail you. As staff do, bless them."

"You're here," I said. "And I let you and Voltaire help me."

"We were supposed to be flattered by that, were we?"

"You would be, if you knew how few people I have trusted that much, and who they were."

She shrugged as one who half-understands a compliment has been proffered, and continued to pipe. I continued to use the tiller, clasping it with Stagg's dead fingers.

After an hour or so of silence, we heard the first breakers on the

French shore, and saw the first glimmer of approaching dawn. Then, from out of the darkness, we saw a lantern, and a French sloop almost on top of us, and a voice hailed us.

"Good morning, English misses," a young man said from a few feet above us, "there are five pistols trained on you, and you are prisoners of the French Republic and of the People of France."

"You'd better skedaddle, 'Untress," Polly said. "No reason for us both to be taken."

"I fear, mademoiselle," the young man said, peering down at us, his moderately handsome face illuminated by the lantern he was holding, "that I have strict instructions. If one of you tries to escape, I am to hurt the other one, quite severely."

"Nothing I won't heal from," Polly said.

"You've not had a serious hurt since you drank it," I said.

"No," she conceded.

"Try and avoid them." I took my weapons from their sheath and laid them at my feet as two French hands swung down from their deck onto ours.

They gathered my weapons up, avoiding meeting my gaze, and then took Polly's pistols from her, as well as some small knives that she had in pockets up the sleeves of her riding habit. I noticed, with amusement, that they ignored her hatpins.

I looked at Polly. "We are both deathless," I told her. "But in very different ways. I cannot be touched in any way that I do not wish, not any more. Fire does not burn me, and blades cannot pierce me or slice me, nor poison corrode my entrails, nor plague corrupt my blood. You though—all those things can happen to you, if your assailants are persistent enough. You will get better, eventually—if you are let."

Young immortals so often learn these lessons in harder ways than being taken inconveniently captive. As I knew.

"And you were going to tell me this, when?"

"I had no plan for us to take ship with a lich-mongering wind-whistling ruffian," I said. "I had no plan to find ourselves bandying

107

words with some officious imp, or taken up by the French coastguard. I had hoped that questions of your vulnerability to acts of violence would not arise, but things have proved otherwise."

By now, a young officer, whose uniform was made of shabby stuff but was clean, and pressed, and had brass buttons that shone in the new day, had joined us.

"I am Etienne Chambord," he said. "At your service. You may be the enemies of France, but you are spectacularly beautiful women, and I could never be wholly the enemies of such."

He bowed, but not especially low or without taking his eyes off us, or his hand off the hilt of his sword.

I chose to ignore him for the moment, save for a nod of acknowledgement before turning back to Polly. "I had assumed that you were aware of the limitations of your condition."

"I knew early on as I could not travel through shadow as others can," she said, "but I never learned how before, so no great loss there. And the old man warned me that drinking it would like as not kill me stone dead."

The young captain cleared his throat. Polly glared at him. "Nous sommes—um—busy, occupées, si vous oh blast it, don't mind."

"The thing with shadow," I said, "did not apply with the other person I knew who drank the Elixir, but she had travelled through it often before she drank." I thought hard about some of my worst memories. "The thing with injuries is something she and I learned in the hardest of ways, and something that I mentioned to Newton when he was very far from being old. I fear that he may have omitted certain warnings out of malice; he is not a nice person, after all, and one with whom I shall remonstrate when next I see him. As it is, let's just say, that you should avoid serious hurt if possible."

Polly nodded. By this point, the young officer was tapping his foot impatiently.

"If you are both quite finished, mesdemoiselles," Chambord said, "I have orders to send you to Paris by the fastest coach I can procure."

"Our thanks." I turned back to Polly. "After all, we always intended to get to Paris, and long journeys by night sleeping in haystacks and avoiding roads are something to which I have never had to grow accustomed."

She smiled. "You do always look on the bleeding bright side."

"A certain habit of optimism crept in once I had survived two thousand years," I said.

"Why," the officer broke in, "are you talking to her in French, when she is answering you in English? I speak both languages, so you are hiding nothing from me."

"Whatever I say," I said, "people understand. It is a gift I possess."

"I did not say I understood," he said sharply. "You are talking superstitious nonsense as far as I can see."

I smiled at him and he took a step back—my gift of being understood extends, as a rule, beyond the words I speak.

"Tell me," I said. "Who informed you of our whereabouts? And how was he dressed?"

"Some spy, or other, obviously on his way home from a costume ball, for he was dressed as an imp in a costume borrowed from the Opera."

I love the unassailability of reason in those men for whom it is a religion, and so laughed aloud. "Come," I said. "Show us aboard your ship and thence to our carriage."

As I helped Polly to climb the rope ladder, I reflected that, when all this was done, I should, after all, have to make a trip to the Hell of Lucifer. From time to time, I find it necessary to remind beings why respect has to be paid to me, and inconvenience to me avoided.

We got to Paris two days later.

It sounded more like Hell itself than most cities manage even at such times—and I had Bartholomew's Eve to set by the side of this day, as well as London and both Romes in times of fire and sack, and other cities beside.

It was the sheer din of cries of "Traitor" that we heard as we stepped out onto a balcony overlooking a square where Dr. Guillotine's famous machine had been set up, and the endless cacophonous singing of that irritating march song from Marseilles. I had heard it whistled, hummed, sung and otherwise rendered tunelessly by our guards all the way from the coast, and had had time to grow as tired of it as I have ever been of any music.

Now you point it out, yes. Perhaps, "Forward go the standards of the King" annoys me more. But that took me centuries to arrive at quite that peculiar level of dislike.

Chambord bowed his head, with something that approached reverence, to the two men who were waiting for us there.

They drew my eye instantly, and held it. They were not alone—a variety of guards levelled pistols at us, and a large man held the blade of a pike to Polly's throat—and yet had I had to sketch the scene, they would have held the centre of my composition, no matter where they actually stood. It is often thus with those who have practiced magic; it gives them a certain extra solidity.

One of the two wore a finely tailored jacket, breeches and waistcoat, all of them striped in a variety of pastel shades of green until it quite hurt to look at him. Round his neck was an elegantly though fussily tied white cravat, and he had the face and broad smile of a toad; such men need no magic or beauty to enchant—there is something about their eyes that compels even me to pay attention. He did not yet speak, but I knew from how he held himself that he had every confidence that, once he did so, he would ravish everyone on the balcony with tones that would make a sentence of death sound like a lover's compliment or an announcement of the successful instauration of universal benevolence.

The other wore plainer clothes in simple black cloth, pressed and neat with almost geometric sharpness; he did so with the starving distinction of a poet or an eremite. I had seen such men as him rummaging in bookstalls, and others naked in desert caves, hard on themselves and regarding that as reason to take the lives of others lightly. He was a dandy where the other was merely a fop; what they had in common was the stink of dark magic, self-righteousness and self-regard.

These were the men of whom Talleyrand had spoken, of that I had no doubt whatever: men whom I should have to kill sooner or later. There have been ages in which I would have struck quick as a serpent, and trusted to my speed and skill to have them dead and Polly safe. Or them dead at least, and Polly cared for over the long months of her healing.

I was younger then, and harder. And less concerned with gathering knowledge of my real and eternal enemy, more busy ending the lives of temporary gods.

Chambord presented us to them. "Citizens, I bring you my prisoners, as I was ordered."

"My thanks," said the thinner man, Saint-Just, "and those of the people."

"We will deal with them in a moment," the other said. "After they have witnessed the justice of the French people."

All at once—it was like a blow to the face, the sudden absence of the din that had preceded it—the crowd became utterly silent and in all that great square you could hear nothing but the creaking wheels of a heavily laden wagon, that drew to a halt at the foot of the wooden steps that led up to the deadly machine.

The men who climbed down from the wagon were forced at pike point by their guards to stand in line on those steps. One of them, young and with a tragic look, tried to push past the pikes to embrace the largest of his companions, a great bull of a man who stared up at the balcony where we stood, and into the eyes of the two men Polly and I had just met, with a fixed gaze that combined hatred, respect and pity in almost equal proportions.

His friend never managed to get to him, but was beaten back with the flats of swords.

"Never mind, Camille," the large man said, without turning his gaze towards his friend, "never mind. Our heads may kiss in the basket—they can't stop us doing that."

111

One after another, and then Camille, and last the large man, they mounted the stairs, laid their heads into the machine, and the blade dropped, their heads fell, and the hooded man who stood at its side pulled the blade up, hand over hand on its rope and pulley, up again for another death.

I have seen men compete in murder, men who could flay a child in thirty seconds and an adult in a minute or so, or could strike off ten heads or hands in an hour and smile through it. What was different, and terrible, about this was its monotone quality—the Aztecs killed their thousands in great lines up the steps of their far greater killing places, but they did so with zest; this was a machine doing a machine's simple tasks and the killer and the victim were just parts of the turning of its wheels and cogs and gears.

I knew at that moment, with sickening certainty, that my great enemy understood the possibilities of clocks and pistons and armatures in a way I never would, that a future was coming that would be like the creaking of that rope and pulley and the swift swishing drop and thud of that blade.

And lastly the large man stood by his executioner and turned his gaze from his enemies who had once been his friends and out at the crowd that had once worshipped him and now stood there in sick expectation of his end, wanting to hate him and still yearning for him and waiting both for his destruction and for the last kiss of his words.

He paused and then smiled.

He clapped his executioner on the shoulder with a meaty palm and said, "Be sure to hold my head up high for all of them to see—it will be a sight worth seeing." Then he laid his head in its place in the machine as if it were the pillow of welcome rest. And there was a swoosh and thud no different in any way from those that had killed his friends.

I sensed the wrongness of those deaths, the bad faith and the betrayal of friendship, rush away from the machine like a miasma that the crowd briefly inhaled, and then breathed out again, and it rushed out and on to some other destination that doubtless I would find out in time.

The dandy in black and the fop in green turned to Chambord, whom the sight of the executions had turned quite pale.

"I think that concludes your business here, Captain," Saint-Just said.

He made as if to speak; and Robespierre stepped forward and laid a finger, admonitory, on his lips.

"Say nothing, Etienne," he said. "It would be best."

It was not wisdom that kept Chambord silent, but some force outside himself.

"What you have seen," said Saint-Just, as if he were demonstrating a theorem, "is the general will in action. You are its servant, as are we."

"As were Danton and his crew," Robespierre added in tones of withering contempt. "Until they thought themselves something more."

"And now do it one final service," Saint-Just said. "As examples."

They turned, as if they were parts of a machine or the finger and thumb of a single hand, and gazed at me intently.

"And you, Huntress," Saint-Just said. "What do you serve?"

Robespierre answered him before I could. "The weak against the strong. Or the English Crown. Like your companion."

"Oh yes, Miss Wild." Saint-Just turned to Polly. "We know who you are."

He appraised her, not as a lecher, but as someone who knew how she would look dead and longed for her corpse as a lecher would her naked body. Polly was a brave woman, but she shuddered under his gaze.

"And shortly," Robespierre said, "we will take you to see your kinswoman."

"Who has told us much," Saint-Just added, "as all men and women do in time."

Then they turned their cold dead eyes from her to me and I saw

Polly blink with wet eyes from relief that they had dismissed her.

They were not seriously interested in anything that I might say, I was sure of that. Yet Voltaire had spoken well of one of them, and I always try to offer people a way back to reason.

"I serve no King," I said, "and no god either. Nor do I stroke my pride with soft fingers and call it the general will, or bend men to my will with cheap tricks and call it statecraft."

Saint-Just turned to Robespierre and spoke as if no one else were present. "She jests with us, I think."

"And talks filth," Robespierre said, primly. "I had always heard that she was of low character."

"And a sapphist, like the companions of that slut the Queen."

"Women are weak and corrupt, and do not understand."

They spoke slowly to each other, their speech unslurred, but as if drunk on logic and death. I had no weapons, but were it not for the blade at Polly's throat, I could have knocked their heads together until their brains spilled. And yet I swallowed my rage, because it was not helpful.

"Listen, you two pettyfogging imbeciles," I said. "I know something of your plans and of your purposes. I am here to tell you to desist. As I have told kings and emperors in my time, even in this young city of yours."

I looked out at the square, which was emptying now that the day's business of murder had finished, and the holiday of blood was done. Children were skipping home alongside young parents who walked arm-in-arm, helping sober grandfathers leaning on walking-sticks or crutches. All of them left with grim empty smiles on their faces. And everyone, as if half-asleep and dreaming the music, sang or whistled those damned songs.

"As to the shedding of blood, you have your reasons for that, as the English did when they killed their king and good riddance to him. Yet even were you not meddling with the Rituals themselves, you have trapped yourselves and the people of France in blood-drunk madness."

The terrible thing was, they could not hear me; they could not let my words enter their understanding. I have seen few men possessed by demons, but many possessed by the tides of bloodshed that wash through history, as deadly as the giant of salt water I once saw destroy a fabled city.

Suddenly, Saint-Just looked at me with something like his full attention and the whole of his intelligence, as if he were seeing me again and for the first time. "Perhaps it would be useful to talk to you."

Robespierre smiled and for a few seconds I could almost have believed that he was not my enemy. "After all," he said, in a flatterer's soft tones, "you were killing gods and kings before Rome was built, or Athens."

"We are not too proud to learn," Saint-Just agreed.

They made to leave the balcony and I stood aside to let them.

"Huntress," they said as one. And, as one, they smiled at me.

"If you come with us," Saint-Just said, "we will show Miss Wild to her kinswoman and no harm will come to either of them. And then we can talk, alone."

"We are men of honour," Robespierre said. He turned to Chambord. "Captain, if you would see Miss Wild to her destination? Our guards here know the way." Then he turned back to me. "Whatever you think of us, you know that Chambord here is a man of honour, who would have braved us to our faces a few minutes ago had I not silenced him."

I did not trust him, but I was interested to see how this would play out. "Polly."

"Watch yourself, 'Untress. As for me, I'd best see Augusta and find out what's what with her. And there's this pretty lad to keep me company. Don't worry about me; I'll be all right." Then she laughed. "And if I am not—" she looked at the two masters of Paris and France with a sardonic eye, "—be sure that the 'Untress will see through your tricks and scupper your plans, and pay for me blood for fucking blood."

"More foul language," Saint-Just said confidentially to his friend.

115

Compulsions and the gift of tongues, I thought to myself; these two may not be making gods of themselves, but the mere backwash of the Rituals is making maguses of them. They may not be as easy to kill as I should like.

Another reason to bide my time, and learn more.

Polly and Chambord, and a party of guards that were more in charge of him than he in command of them, left the balcony through the door by which we had entered it. I followed Saint-Just and Robespierre across a broad room, whose walls were overcrowded with paintings of a heroic age that was never as grand as artists portray it, and through a small door, into a narrow corridor.

Saint-Just drew ahead of me and Robespierre held back, as if courteously showing me into the corridor and thence into some room of state.

In the room that lay beyond the corridor, Saint-Just suddenly reached out and pulled down a lever that had lain flush with the panelling; there was the clanking of gears and the sound of chains, and the floor of the corridor juddered slightly beneath my feet. A similar noise had come from behind me, and I turned to see Robespierre, his hand on the lever's twin.

"Stay very still, Huntress." Saint-Just spoke with the calmness of a logician, or a teacher of algebra, not a man whose long plan had come to fruition.

"Not for your own sake," Robespierre's voice was mellifluous, but equally calm, "but for that of others."

"Whom you would regard as innocents."

"And whose deaths we have dedicated to our project, so that, if they die, it will be at your hand and part of the Ritual."

The worst of such men is usually that they love the sound of their own voice; it does not help matters when they love as much the voice of their special friend.

I realized that I had best pay attention to what they were saying rather than rush to one end of the corridor, throttle one of them and then return to break the other's neck. Which was my first instinct, but I have learned self-control down the years.

"How, precisely," I asked, as calmly as I could, "can my moving from here be part of any ritual, or cause anyone's death? Saying that you will kill someone if I do or fail to do something does not make me a part of your actions—it does not work like that."

These are mistakes that aspiring monsters often make, as much as mis-drawing a pentagram. There can be no guilt without an act's being formally chosen, and without guilt, there is no Ritual.

"It's the floor you're standing on," Robespierre said. "That corridor is not exactly what it seems."

"It's the counterweight," Saint-Just added. "Once we pulled these levers, your weight is what holds it in place, and if you move, the corridor will swing up."

"And various things will happen," Robespierre said. "In various places. Deadly things. Floodgates will open in dungeons, harrows will descend from ceilings and blades will swing out of walls. We had competent men design it all. It's a very, very big machine, and you are the most important part of it."

Saint-Just gave his lever one light push, to ensure it was firmly in place, and smiled benignly at me. "To free yourself, you must pull both levers back down at once to free yourself. And we don't think you can do that. Pulling just one locks the whole system into operation. Fast as you are, allegedly, even if you knew where the other parts of the machine are, you would not get there in time. The gears and pulleys are kept well-oiled. We have given this a lot of thought."

"We knew you would come for us," Robespierre said. "So we laid our plans."

And so they had.

The horrible thing about these two was that there was no gloating in them—everything was said in a pleasant conversational tone as if they were asking me to take coffee with them, or expounding the patterning of a sestina.

Worse, I knew that they had done what almost no-one had ever

117

managed to do since the Bird, so many years before. They had trapped me. And the worst of it was that while the Bird had used its own vast power to steal me from myself, a little, these two had found a way to use my own nature against me.

There is no point, however, in refusing to acknowledge that an enemy has overcome you; it is graceless and charmless. I nodded to them both and clapped my hands in slow applause.

"My congratulations on your ingenuity. If all is as you say, and I have to believe that it is, you have successfully made me your prisoner. For the time being."

"Of course," Robespierre said, "you could give us your parole and agree to leave France to its own concerns."

"Or help us," Saint-Just suggested. "We are the enemies of tyranny, and everything we do, we do for justice. And freedom."

"I think not," I said, and sat down, and closed my eyes.

"You cannot just ignore us." Saint-Just was upset, just a little, but even now his voice had the calm rhythm of a clock. "You cannot just sit there and go to sleep."

Without opening my eyes, I answered him. "I think you will find that I can choose precisely to do that. It's called freedom."

I had praised their cleverness, after all, and acknowledged their victory; I would, of course, at some later point be free, and at that time, I would of course kill them both, or try to. That went without saying, and it would be crass to remark on it here and now, when, for the moment, it would be an entirely empty threat.

They said more but I was not listening, and after a while they went away.

I am used to sleeping in uncomfortable places, and at difficult times; here, on these floorboards, that pressed against me as if they yearned to move upwards yet were held back, with the sure and certain knowledge that, for as long as I stayed where I was, a number of people who might otherwise be standing in line for their deaths in the square outside, would be safe, by my choice, I slept easily and like a small child.

118

They had used my nature to trap me in my own choices. I could live with that, because I had made those choices an age ago.

After some time, I awoke, and the doors of the corridor were closed tight, so that I had no sense of whether it was day or night, nor cared.

I walked the few feet from one door to another a thousand times and then another thousand. I danced the moves of those combats from my past that so narrow a space could have contained—improving the angle of a bone-crushing kick here, or a heart-thrust there.

Even after so many years, my skills can be improved. And practice and memory are useful partners. Memory, come to that, was a useful companion in my solitary prison. A companion and a pastime.

I rarely have the time to sit and remember past joys—the scent of the grass as I ate an apple in Provence and listened to a clumsy lute player, two summers before the Death; the smile on the face of the boy emperor turned girl empress, Varius Bassianus, whom men called Heliogabalus, as she tickled the feet of one of her charioteers—she was a monster, of course, but few monsters have quite that degree of charm or so sweet a smile; the sheen of fat on a roast pig at dinner in the land of Chi'in; and the tipsy laughter of Krishna's milkmaids as they pulled clean laundry from a stream.

And with that laughter echoing in my mind, I slipped from reverie almost into drowsing, only to awaken to a tentative rap on the door at the far end of the corridor.

"Who's there?" I called.

"Friends, probably." The voice was that of a haughty-toned woman on the other side of the door. "Depending on who precisely it is that the Jacobins have imprisoned so informally."

I heard the noise of a lock-pick being applied to the mechanism of the door with no especial skill but some enthusiasm.

"You had best leave that," I said. "How many of you are there?"

"Just the two." Another woman's voice, softer but equally decisive.

"A perfect number, in the circumstances. You will notice—and will not touch—a lever in the wall at the side of the door. Do not touch it, on pain of many deaths."

"And who, m'dear," said the more aristocratic of the two, "are you to give me instructions?"

"Men call me the Huntress," I said. "Women, alas, are less likely in this age to…"

"I know who the Huntress is." The second woman spoke primly. "Not all of us have been deprived of the benefits of education."

"I need one of you to go round—it may mean going onto the balcony and coming back in—to the other end of this corridor," I said. "Where that lever has a twin. They need to be pulled down at exactly the same time. Or, as I say, bad things will happen. I suggest that when one of you is there, they rap on the door, and I will give you both a count."

They did as I asked, and again I heard that clank and felt that judder, only now the floor beneath my feet seemed safe and secure where earlier it had felt otherwise.

I heard the lockpicks applied again.

"By all means." I refrained from simply walking through the wall or the door. It seemed to me that I owed my rescuers some politeness for a moment or two, before I raced off to rescue the people I had kept alive by staying in my prison, who would now be at risk as soon as it was realized that I was free.

The door flew open and there stood two women dressed in shabby bourgeois clothes. The taller of the two wore her clothes as if they had been stitched on her body by the finest tailors money could buy, and the other as if she had found them at hazard and used them to cover herself merely.

At first sight, the smaller woman had nondescript pleasant features, until you looked into dark eyes that looked back at you with an intensity that burned. Her companion, though—in spite of a nose that jutted out of her face like a weapon, and a chin that would have looked determined on a man of destiny, she was one of the most beautiful creatures I had seen in an age. It was a beauty that came partly from the glow of her skin and partly from an intensity equal to her companion's, not in the eyes so much as in the lush promising mouth and the way she held herself, at once alluring, playful and decisive.

It was no longer the beauty of youth, of course, but that of maturity; loving Sof who so many times was born, grew older and sooner or later died, has given me a certain appreciation for the stages of woman.

I nodded to them in gratitude. "And you are?"

"Mary," said the smaller woman, and "Georgiana," said the other.

"Where can I find you?" I asked. "Because I must travel through shadow quicker than thought to free those whose chains and jeopardy have kept me here these many days. Since—how much time has passed since they killed the big man that had been their friend?"

Mary's face alit with recognition. "Danton? That was two months ago. And they have kept you here in darkness without bedding"— she cast her eye down the small space to which I had been confined—"and without food or water that I can see. Such cruelty. Even for them. How have you survived?"

"Clearly," Georgiana said, "she really is the Huntress and a being to whom no ordinary rules apply." She spoke in tones which indicated that she rather hoped the same was in some sense true of herself, and looked at me fiercely. "If there are innocents to be saved and freed, you should not dally here with us. Look for us in the Marais, at the sign of the Dark Angel."

I had questions to ask of them, but she was right—I had no time to waste, and slipped from their sight, and into shadow.

But only a little way, for I needed to travel in close contact with the lines of chains that connected the room where I had been trapped to those other rooms where people sat or lay or stood, in terror, waiting for their deaths. Fortunately, it was only in the higher floors of the building I had started in that the chains ran inside carefully constructed channels inside the walls—once I passed through those floors and down into the cellarage, they were strung roughly through great staples embedded in the walls of passages that led from cellar to tunnel to sewer to catacomb to dungeon and unknown oubliette. There was masonry down here as old as the city, or older; there were fresh footprints here, footprints clear and deep in centuries of dust and rubble. And there were dead men, lying rotted to stinking in a room off one of the passages, men with set squares and hammers, who had had their throats slit, and among them a man with a great roll of drafting paper that I took from his dead hand, because I guessed that he was the man who had served my captors so well by building the whole mechanism. And had died for it.

I had no particular wish to steal from, or dishonour, the corpse of one who had helped wrong me—but I hoped his designs would tell me where to look for his other victims, would save me crucial moments that would in turn save lives. Yet I found myself disappointed, for his designs had been smudged to uselessness by the flow of his blood and the decay of his flesh.

I rushed through tunnels and across bridges high above lost rivers that flowed stinking with slime, and past carved stones in languages that none spoke now save me, and under arches whose mortar was crumbling them into deadfalls and over the rubble where old vaults had fallen in to ruin.

Dust sifted downwards through the air, so thick in places that the real world was dimmer than the shadows through which I ran, and water dripped endlessly down walls in slime, or in places as a constant flowing cascade that I ran through without getting wet, pooling on the flagstones of the floor that I passed over with never a ripple.

Mostly I ran in darkness, and on stone, but in places I found myself running on planed wood, or even on the rags of carpet; in other places torches guttered, or lanterns burned, or light not natural shone from panels of green bottle glass in the walls that I did not care to stay and understand.

As I went, I heard the crying of children and the moaning of the old, and the prayers of the dying—at first in my imagination and anxiety and then in truth. These were the victims I had kept alive by my inaction and I hoped that there were enough of them to balance the others, elsewhere, that I could not save. I save those I can, always, and it is never enough, because the evil will of men never ceases from slaughter and I have only two hands.

I had expected to find guards, and guards there must have been, some of the time, for few of the people I found in locked cells were wholly starved. They had been fed through hatches in the barred doors of their cells—coarse bread and dry cheese and little enough to drink save the water that dripped endlessly down the walls.

Yet I met no guards. This caused me relief, for I would have wished to slay them without mercy, and would at the least have needed to put them out of my way, leaving them broken and bleeding, so that I could free the prisoners and care for the sick and dying—but I dared not kill any man in this city whose death might have been pre-dedicated to the Rituals, as I would have done, had I been a man of evil will who wished further to trap or corrupt my great opponent.

I was used to the villainy of kings and priests and should have learned from Newton, but did not, that the villainy of philosophers is worse yet. Sometimes I am a slow learner and it is indeed fortunate that I have had the time to learn better.

I used my rage, nonetheless, in the service of the weak, and if I could not tear the limbs of men, at least I could pull doors from cells and smash them to splinters of wood and metal shards beneath my feet. And though the parts of the mechanism—the harrows and scythes and pendulums and spikes—that had for all these weeks menaced the prisoners lay inert where once they had thrummed to the rhythm of my pacing in my corridor, nonetheless, I tore them from their fittings and smashed their sharpness into blunted trash, and in this I was partly the avenger of myself and the weak, and partly—I admit it—a petulant child in a mood of tantrum at so much time in which my will had been broken to other men's plans.

The men and women and children that crept from those cells

looked at me with reverent horror as they passed me and picked their way through passages and tunnels and the channels of streams back towards safety and light.

I had no words for those who could move easily, though. I took those who seemed fittest by the shoulder, and not kindly so, since to be best fed in this place was not to be of the finest morals. I indicated that they should let the weaker lean on them, and should carry the weakest, and close the eyes of the dead, whom I left where they lay, staring with dead eyes at the wet walls and broken ceilings.

It was in my mind that once the prisoners were all free I would make an end of this pit of ingenious barbarity, even if smashing the whole as I had smashed its parts would bring parts of the city above our heads down in ruin. There could be worse memorials to such dead than chaos and destruction.

In the last cell I found Polly, wiping with a dampened cloth torn from her chemise the forehead of Chambord, who lay tossing in fever.

"You took yer bleeding time, 'Untress," she said. "But no doubt you have a story to tell, for from time to time that bloody pair came and stared through the spyhole at me, and taunted me through the grill that my friend whom I had brought to be their ruin was their plaything and their caged bird."

"That I was, for a while," I said, "for the good and sufficient reason that they placed me where I could not move without killing you and all these others, and contributing to their damnable Ritual. I waited, humbled, knowing that nothing lasts forever—and in time and by chance, I was freed."

"You say that," she said, "in a tone of wonderment."

"Wonder and gratitude, now that I am done with freeing those in danger here. I have lived these many ages, and it has not come to me many times to be saved by the hands of others."

"So who was it?" Polly asked. "Some hero or archangel?"

"Two Englishwomen," I said. "Two of your countrywomen, who seem to be wandering around in the midst of terror, trying doors and picking locks, as if it were a pastime."

Polly looked thoughtful. "You didn't get names, by any chance?" she said, all business.

"Mary and Georgiana. One was a great beauty and the other not."

"You would notice that, even in chains and danger."

"As who would not?" Chambord, rousing himself, lifted himself on one elbow. "In times of peril, beauty is our consolation."

Polly looked at him and smiled. There was a mocking tender intimacy to her glance that told me all that I needed to know.

I felt no need to comment. "So, what ails the good captain?"

"I tried,"—he clearly meant to speak gallantly but it ended in a grimace of pain—"to appeal to the better natures of our captors."

I frowned. "A waste of effort. If they had them once, they have burned them away with hot irons."

"And then he told them that they had no honour and had abused his. And challenged them both." Polly's tone was all affection for his folly.

"I thought," he admitted, "that I had the measure of them. A skinny dandy and a pudgy fop…But I was mistaken." He pulled a sad face in clowning, and then winced in pain for truth.

Polly picked up the tale. "Saint-Just taunted him, and said that the day of honour and duels was done with, and then he reached through the door. Not through the hatch but through the wood, as you might through shadow, and his arm was longer than a natural arm. And he took my Captain here, and shook him like you might a kitten you were minded to wring the neck of, and then threw him down against the stones so that he lay bruised and winded."

"I think," Chambord said, "that my promising career in the French Navy is over, alas!" Polly and I helped him to his feet; he shivered a little and looked pale. "I am not well," he sighed. "Or I would be of more use to you."

"We all has our off days," Polly said. "There is no shame in that, my love." She turned to me, all business again. "Mary and Georgiana? Now there's an interesting pair, if I guess rightly. Any idea where they are to be found?"

125

"They said to seek them in the Marais, at the sign of the Dark Angel. Not a tavern that I recall." I looked at Chambord for assistance.

He shook his head. "Not a tavern. Not a tavern at all, but one of those stories you hear in taverns, when the night has been long and the conversation grows indiscreet."

"A bawdyhouse, then," Polly smiled as one who had owned many such in her time.

"No. I meant that sort of indiscretion which might see you flogged for heresy or broken on the wheel for mockery of the king, or these days, it seems, our democratic masters. This is Paris, where a mere bawdyhouse is nothing."

"So?" I asked more pointedly.

"It is said," Chambord went on, "that if you are in danger of the rack or the whip, for speaking your mind, or the like, and need to leave Paris without being stopped at the city gates, there is a house that will offer you safe refuge and safe passage, whether you are freethinker, Protestant, or even, it is said, a Jew."

I smiled in pleasure; it is always pleasing to me when my more random acts bear unexpected fruit. "I think I know where this would be. It is a house where once I lodged some two centuries ago."

"Oh bloody hell." Polly raised her eyes upwards in resigned irritation. "Don't tell me."

"I did the household some service on Bartholomew's Eve." I smiled in proud memory. "And they miscalled me an angel, and honour the memory of my service to them."

It took us many hours to find a safe route to the surface, by false starts up staircases that led nowhere, or corridors that ended in a blank wall or a pile of rubble it would have taken even me a day we perhaps did not have to remove with no certainty of its being of use. In the end, we waded down one of the least unsavoury streams towards a glimmer of light, and I tore out a rusted grill where its channel led into the gloom of another day's dusk.

I could have travelled faster and more directly by myself, of course, but I was not minded to; Chambord was badly lame and sick, and had been hurt trying to protect and free Polly, when I was not there and could not., She was my chosen companion in this fight, and thus so was he. I have the freedom of choosing which of my obligations to honour.

It took me mere moments, though, to find our way once I found the surface; it is a skill I have, and the path to the house was once my path to my chamber and to the solace of sleep. And though it had been patched and thatched and its masonry pointed and its doors replaced and its plaster laid on two centuries of repairs thick, still I knew it well.

We looked at its door from an alley opposite and saw no sign of danger. I walked to the closed door and hammered on it.

"Who's there?" a voice shouted from within.

"It is I," I said. "Mara, the Huntress, whom this house calls the Dark Angel. And I seek the hospitality of the house for myself, and two fugitives."

A man opened the door and looked at me in astonishment. He had something of the look of the landlord I had had in this place so long before, and the overlong moustaches of that landlord's nephew—sometimes a family face can last as long as a building.

"By god," he spoke over his shoulder, to those within, "it is as you said. Exactly as the story tells."

He ushered us in swiftly. The narrow hallway and siderooms that I remembered had been opened out into a single common room, and there at table sat other members of this family—again, I knew their faces as variations on those with whom I had once shared this place—and the two women who had freed me, cleaning pistols and sharpening knives as if about to engage in some new enterprise.

He nodded to his relatives, and they moved to a far corner of the room, to give us what privacy they could.

Two of them helped Chambord on to a table, and first inspected, and then began to dress, his injuries, smoothing sweet-smelling salve on his bruises and then wrapping some tight bandage around his chest, where the ribs seemed broken.

The woman Georgiana looked at my companions. "Ah," she said in lofty tones that skirted disdain. "Miss Wild. Welcome to Paris."

Polly looked at her with rancour in her eyes, but said only, "My thanks, your Grace."

"I did not think," remarked Georgiana, "that you ever left London, let alone that I would find you taking French leave." She turned to the woman Mary and explained, "Miss Wild here is the King's Intelligencer, and rules over all spies, foreign and domestic. She is also far older than she looks."

"I gets to leave London," Polly said. "I just have to ask permission, from those in authority over me. And I have business here in Paris, the which is more than I can say for you."

Georgiana waved a languid hand at her. "Don't fret, m'dear. The work we were doing in Lausanne goes ahead quite as requested now we are back in England. With my Bess and sister Harriet, there is far too little work to need me there too. Even now that funny little man Gibbon is dead and gone from us, in January last."

She took a sip of wine from the glass that sat on the table beside the pistol she was cleaning. "Harriet even has the child Carolyn helping file the letters," she went on, "once Bess has read them and chivvied intelligence from them, as Gibbon taught her. It was like watching someone eat snails with a fork, every last little shred out of the shell. He was peculiar, but he was very good at what he did." She laughed, a high laugh like glass bells that reminded me of an age long lost. I had been too long without sisters. "Harriet has no especial skill, but Carolyn has real talent. It runs in the family, of course; some of us are just born spies."

"And some of us is just born harlots." Polly was almost hissing at this woman.

"And some of us," Georgiana spoke with a calmness that must have been as infuriating as Polly's jibes, "have harlotry thrust upon

128

us. For the sake of England. I was a mere chit of a girl when you first used me in the work."

"For England," Polly echoed, in self-justification.

"Talking of born harlots," Georgiana said brightly, "what of you, Miss Wild?"

"Not born to harlotry, your Grace." Polly relaxed and then grinned. "Born crown princess of dollymops and abraham men, of coney-catchers and guttersnipes. I was born to a kingdom, I was, by God, with more subjects than any Spencer of Althorpe might dream of, or any Cavendish of Chatsworth for that matter."

Underlying the hostility, these two had a history that I did not even begin to understand, and levels of irritation and affection that I have had myself with the mighty down the years. We have lovers, and we have friends, and above all we have colleagues.

"In any case," Polly was now almost conciliatory, "I did not ask, what are you doing not in Lausanne? I asked, what are you doing here? There ain't no balls here any more, nor card parties."

Georgiana looked at her haughtily, down the length of that prodigious nose. "I work with you, Wild. Not for you. Not any more."

"You made that perfectly clear, back when you rallied half of Parliament to put the poor king from his throne."

"The king was mad." Georgiana spoke as if to a child who understands little. "He was talking to trees in Windsor Park."

"Like your fat Florizel would be better."

"At least he was sane," Georgiana said. "But then the king got better, and we left him where he was. No reason to go on arguing about it now."

"Just as long," Polly returned, "as you're not here just because you're bored, and fancy mischief, and hanker for the dead days, when you watched her late Majesty for me. From close up, closer than I had asked."

"Ah, 'Toinette." Georgiana had a catch in her voice. "Dead and gone, poor love."

She looked round at us with a small tear trickling down a perfectly enamelled cheek and a nostalgic smile on her face. "She was such an idiot, you know. No head for politics, none at all, which is why she lost it, but her quim tasted like marchpane."

She paused in happy sensual memory, and then the tear was wiped and gone. "I felt like an adventure. My husband won't let me go up to town, and the servants at home play for such low stakes."

"As it 'appens," Polly allowed, "your being here has been timely for all of us. But I'd still like to know what you and Wollstonecraft're doing wandering round public buildings in the middle of the night, picking locks and freeing state prisoners."

All this time Mary had been standing by, a smart intelligent woman consigned to silence while these two queens of the world bitched at each other like cats or opera singers. I watched her sigh, and then grow tired, and then grow angry.

"It's Thomas," Mary burst out in anger. "They've arrested Thomas and will kill him if they can. And the American ambassador hates him, and will do nothing to save him, for all that he has done for freedom."

"Thomas Bloody Paine," Polly said. "Wot's he done to piss off the Froggies, then? That made him a member of their assembly for his treasons, straight away that he got here?"

"He spoke for the King at his trial," Mary said. "He kept arguing against the killing."

That, at least, inclined me to his side.

Polly turned to face Mary as if she had finally properly noticed her. "What I don't get is what you and the Duchess here are doing together. You don't share her taste for unnatural vice, and you ain't a spy for anyone that I knows of. You just write seditious tracts and marry bigamous American rebels."

"She asked my help; she sent me a letter. And I was bored with running a letter drop and doing nothing else." Georgiana waved a hand as languidly as if it held a fan. "I am more capable than that. And I like the man Paine, even if he is a damned rascally freethinker. I beat him at cards once, at supper with Johnson the publisher. And there are plenty of others that flocked to Paris when the Bastille fell, that the Jacobins would kill for their trouble."

"More seditionists," Polly grumbled.

"Enemies of our enemies." Georgiana had clearly talked herself into this view. "A troublemaker locked up is no damn good to anyone, but a troublemaker running round free, makes trouble."

I saw the sense in this, but I had other more immediate concerns. "All of this is well and good. But Robespierre and Saint-Just have a plan that is far more than just killing random friends turned enemies, and I need to thwart them in that plan."

"What sort of plan?" The look in Mary's eye made it clear she had already guessed my answer. She obviously was both well-educated and astute. And someone who paid more attention than either her companion or my own.

"The sort of plan that brings me running," I said. "They plan to raise themselves a god, and, given the lakes of blood they have spilled in the matter, I doubt it will be any god of peace or kindness. What I need to know is when, and where."

Georgiana smiled the winning smile of someone who holds a high value card. "I should think that it will be tomorrow, at the Field of Mars, shortly after noon."

"That's bloody precise in its particulars." Polly eyed her suspiciously. "For a guess."

"Well," Georgiana said, "it's the big Festival of the Supreme Being, whom they declared back in October, when they changed all the names of the months. And if you were going to make yourself a God, you'd do it on a Sunday—which tomorrow is, even if you were pretending it was some numbered day instead. It will take years and years for all that to catch on, I'd think. I mean, I know this is supposed to be Prairial, but everyone knows it's June, really."

"All a matter of education," Mary said. "If you persuade the children to think of it by its new name, they will go on thinking it as adults. You will have seen this a hundred times, Huntress, will you not?"

"Yes." I said. "And nine times out of ten, their children in turn decide to make them angry by going back to old ways. These changes last a generation, usually—except when it's a Prophet, or a First Emperor, and they change things forever. You can only tell afterwards."

Georgiana smiled at my words, as if I had thrown more coin down at the gaming table. Every word that told of some danger or other was an excitement to her, a sharpening of the breath in her nostrils, a sense of the day's worth. I have seen other men and women like her down the years; some of them have raced to an early death and taken those around them with them, and some of them have built empires and placed those around them on thrones. And others, like her, grew more reckless once youth was over, as if they could win it back with a throw of the dice.

"They've built a big hill-thing," Mary said. "With a statue of Hercules on a pillar at the side, holding Freedom or some such. There's going to be choirs on it, and dancing children, as well as speeches."

Georgiana nodded. "It went up very quickly, without great wagons of earth moving through the streets. Does that mean it's gone up by magic?" She looked at me in the touching expectation that I would know for certain about such things.

"Perhaps," I said. "But more probably, it means that it's hollow inside."

"It's wet paper and wire," said Mary, "and bits of rockery and trees on top to make it look real." She looked at Georgiana. "Some of us go out and ask questions."

Georgiana shrugged.

"Shoddy work, then," said Polly, suddenly complacent. "Just a sham and a botch like this whole Revolution."

I grew a little impatient with her, because she had seen what the Jacobins were capable of, had been imprisoned by them and her lover hurt, and she still had the easy flip responses of a politician who thinks a war will be over by Christmas because she has her shopping to do. I raised my voice to get her attention back and spoke with asperity that she heed me seriously.

"Maybe, but not if it's supposed to be hollow because there's something inside it. Such as the place where you can complete your Rituals in peace and quiet, and then bring out your brand new god or goddess and have lots of people to start worshipping it. Polly and I should go to this false hill, and take a long look underneath it."

Georgiana turned to Mary. "I think you should stay here, m'dear. If things go badly, you'll need to find some other way of saving Thomas."

Then she turned to me with a gaze of deep exhilaration.

"I didn't ask either of you to come," and yet I suddenly knew that I had hoped she would.

"Miss Wild,"—Georgiana nodded to her old boss and then fixed me again with those sparkling excited witty eyes—"will tell you that I constantly go where I am not invited. I am famous for it."

I thought it best to at least try and discourage this woman I had only met a few hours before. She seemed competent, but Polly I knew.

"Miss Wild is an immortal and trained for this work."

"She's a mediocre swordswoman." The lightness of Georgiana's tone did not conceal the fact that she believed herself capable of appraising such things as one who knew. "And a terrible shot. Not bad with knives, of course."

I made a last effort. "This is a venture from which we may none of us return."

"The best kind," Georgiana laughed as if she were discussing a carriage ride around the park rather than desperate adventures.

"You'll not persuade her to stay out of it," Polly said. "I've watched Her Grace throw every jewel she was wearing onto the bezique table. And the livings and farms of two counties. And she's right, damnit; she's handy in a fight for a woman reared to be useless."

133

"Not just reared," Georgiana laughed again. "Bred to it for generations."

Mary looked at us, and smiled. She was a quiet woman whom I wish I had had the time to know better, because she spoke in the voice of one who saw to the heart of things, and knew her own limits.

"I learned to pick locks when I was a governess," she confided. "Because sometimes the servants try to starve you out of resentment and it is always handy to be able to get yourself bread and cheese in the night. But I have no other skill in these matters—if it is to come to swordplay and pistolshot, I would be mere baggage." She shrugged. "I will go to Ambassador Morris again. It cannot hurt, and I might find out from him where Thomas is being held."

I was relieved; she seemed a woman of character and sense, but not a companion in arms. Her friend was another matter: a risk perhaps, but better than nothing.

Chambord was clearly out of action—our hosts had given him a draught that had left him snoring. I walked over to the tables where most of them sat.

"I don't suppose," I began, "that any of you would…"

The oldest of them held up a hand. "We take no sides. We help people in danger leave Paris. If you come back here from your venture, with any such, we will help and harbour them and you. But they have to make their own way here, and we do not need to seek out the trouble they often bring with them."

I could see the sense in that, unwelcome as it was when we sought and needed allies.

On the other hand, desperate as our case might be, it might be easier for the three of us to pass unnoticed through the streets of Paris than for an armed band of twenty or more. We needed to enter the chamber underneath that mound in the Field of Mars and to get there we needed to cross the river. That ruled out the use of tunnels and passageways under the city, even if there were any useable charts.

I turned back to my companions. "We should set out soon. It will take us some two hours to get there and who knows how early in the day they will move to conclude their business."

"They start with choral singing and speeches in the Tuileries," Mary said. "And then they march in procession to the Field of Mars, across the Pont Royal."

"Plenty of time, then, to find out what's going on under that mound before the crowds get there," I said.

"And we get to skip the speeches," Georgiana added. "The thing I hate about politics is the speeches. Even when they're being made by my friends."

Polly looked at me with a sardonic smile. "I'll make my own way there. Don't know that I fancies a stroll across Paris in broad daylight with you two Bedlamites. It's important that you get there as soon as you can, and you can take her Grace with you into shadow, and travel fast, the which you cannot do with me."

What she said was undoubtedly true, and had crossed my mind, but I had not wished to suggest what she was now volunteering.

"What if I should find your kinswoman Augusta there?"

"Tell her that I shall be there shortly," Polly said. "She knows who you are, for that I told her stories of you when she was in small clothes and going everywhere with a rag poppet that she started to call Mara."

"How will I know her?"

"Wild blood runs true," Polly said. "Augusta and I could pass for twins."

I turned to Georgiana. "We must travel fast and unseen. Through shadow, of which you may have heard tales."

She looked at me with a hunger that was almost that of a lover. "I heard tales of such things from my nurse and yearned that they be true, that I might ride wild nights with creatures that walk in darkness."

She stood and carefully placed the pistol she had been cleaning in a pocket in the loose sleeve of her chemise. "And if we are to pass unseen," she added, "I can bear a blade." By the wall beyond the table at which she had been seated, was a long thin case, from which she drew a rapier and a sword belt, which she strapped around her waist.

There are people whom you have not seen—you think you have, but you have not—until they take on some aspect which completes them.

"I cannot help but notice, Huntress," she said, "a certain peculiar nakedness about you that does not tally with the stories that I heard. Allow me to remedy the situation." She reached into the case again and pulled out a long thin blade in the Japanese style, a blade almost as long as my outspread arms.

"I bought this as a curio from a Cathay merchant who swore that it was five centuries old and from the closed kingdom of Nippon— and never found a swordsmaster who could tell me the way of fighting with it."

"I know such blades well," I said, and she passed it to me. I ran my finger up the blade's flat and heard it sing to me from the endlessly beaten-out heart of the steel. "Not five centuries, a mere two and a half from an age in which the swordsmithying of Nippon was at its height."

It was not true that that land's nobles used their peasants' bodies to try the sharpness of their blades, but only a fable in part. I had known of smiths that tempered their steels cutting the necks of men doomed to die and of the fierce spirits that such deaths sometimes left possessing that steel, spirits whose anger was something I had once needed to pay attention to. The sword-spirits thought to make themselves a spirit king and raged in the hands of the samurai and ronin that bore the swords, dragging their supposed masters into battles that could have been avoided and affairs of honour whose punctilio was mere jealous madness. Above all, their masters despaired and died the noble death of suicide on what was little more than a whim, and not their own. Thousands died, at their own hand or the hand of others, but not through the will of men. The swords raged on, laying the land to waste, until a being of blood and iron was born of that rage, whom I destroyed in the hour of its birth before it became a veritable typhoon of bloodshed.

When I slew it, in its dark glorious beauty, I broke the hearts of many of those swords and they turned and shattered themselves in their masters' hands. Others lived to tell the story.

Even now, as the sword sang to its new possessor, it knew my touch and shuddered.

"Be still, little spirit," I told it. "You are far from home and have nothing to fear here from me. You are my newest weapon, come in need when I have no other, and yet I know you are worthy to hang on my back with a spear that saw gods and empires die. Rest easy and be loyal, little spirit, mighty sword."

And I stroked and sang it into loyalty that might have seen me as the destroyer of its kin and tried to betray me to my death, and broken its heart against my deathlessness. Which would have been a shameful end for a weapon of such beauty.

I stroked it to hear it sing loyalty back to me, one last time, and then I patted it at the hilt and swung it into the sling at my shoulder that had been empty so many weeks.

"I shall call you Needful," I said. Needful is the name of all swords, yet of some more than others.

It was only now that I was armed again, that I could feel the pull of my other weapons, the ones taken from me. Like calls to like, as they say. I turned to Mary.

"This mound they have erected"—I pointed in the direction towards which I felt called—"it lies there?"

"Yes. Beyond the river and the bridge they call new, on the Field of Mars."

I smiled, for if my weapons were there, it meant that aspiring sorcerers were falling into a trap that never goes well for such men, who have taken that which is mine from me before. For a time.

I rapped on the table with my knuckles. "We know our paths. It is time we were away and about our business."

137

"Indeed," Polly said. "Especially those of us who actually has to walk."

Mary nodded. "A moment more," Georgiana said, and hugged them both. "Two things," she went on. She reached into her case and passed a smaller box she found there to Polly. "I have been practising, but these belong with a more gifted mistress."

It was a plain wooden box, but the wood had the fragrance of the oils that had been worked into it to bring out its deep luster and grain. Inside it were two knives, as unornamented as the box and as fine. Both box and knives had a simple perfection of line, like the idea of a box or a knife made solid—I cannot say it clearer than that. They were precious things, and the knives were also deadly things.

Polly took one of the knives from the box, and balanced it, first by its hilt across the back of her hand, then when it tilted, moved her hand quicker than even I could see, flicked it up and caught it, delicate by its point on the palm of her hand with only a single bead of blood to show.

"They'll do quite nicely." She kissed Georgiana on the cheek. "Thank you, your Grace."

"La, Miss Wild," Georgiana said. "Much of that and you might turn a woman's head."

She passed each of us a glass and filled it with a token amount of wine—hardly even a taste, but enough for a toast—and then climbed onto her chair, kicking her skirts out of her way. She raised her glass. "To adventures," she said, and was not absurd.

I am immune to such things, as a rule, and yet I felt a thrill at her words, and saw a flush of pleasure colour the cheeks of the other two women, and even our stolid hosts. Some have the gift of leading, merely, and others' gift is to inspire. In some other age, what might that woman have become?

I raised the glass and sipped from it, as how could I not?, and then reached out my hand to her as she stepped down from the chair. Before her foot could touch the ground or the glass she dropped in surprise be heard to shatter, I swept her away into shadow.

It is always best to take those virgin in such matters by surprise, that they not resist and hurt themselves as they burst into a new world.

After the times I had had to measure my pace to the mundane world, and to Polly, trapped in its real like a fly in amber, it was so deep a relief to move at my own speed that I pulled the Duchess with me as forcibly as if she were a colt I were breaking to the rein.

She turned to me as we rushed across where the river lay and through the walls of the great cathedral and out again without pausing to see what remained of its past glory, what desecrations the Jacobins had wrought, and smiled—almost a lover's smile, or a seducer's rather, an invitation and a threat. I should have to talk seriously to her at some point when we were not busy.

"It's as I imagined," she said, breathless and flushed. "The sort of ride one gets in dreams." She held my hand the tighter. "I wondered why the tales spoke of you as one who was alone, and how you could bear it, but now I see it all. With magic and action and shadow, what need of further excitation?"

I could not work out, I found, whether this was us having that talk, her telling me we did not need ever to have it, or some more subtle stratagem, nor greatly caring, in the moment.

This was, after all, a woman who had agreed, in a second, to join me in what was not particularly her fight, and on whom I felt I could rely as utterly as I had very few people, and some few weapons, in all of my long life. Flirtation was a small price to pay for such security, and if she knew that I am alone by choice, then she knew the limits of such flirtation.

Yet her touch reminded me that it had been a long time since I had seen Sof in flesh rather than in memory, and caused me to shudder at the memory of that last time, and reflect that never, in all the ages of time, had I seen Lillit, and known her.

I felt a sudden melancholy and looked away from that avid face that raced alongside me, and she pulled at my hand until I looked back at her.

"This is no time to be sad," she said. "You are the hero of the ages, about to do yet again what you do best, and with an appreciative audience who will try to stay alive long enough to see you accomplish great deeds." Her earnest smile broke through the cloudiness of my mood, and melancholy was gone.

By now, we were pushing unseen through a great throng of people, in what remained their Sunday best for all that the day of the week was some number with a feast day drawn from the animal and vegetable kingdoms. All bore, somewhere, a flounce of red, blue and white ribbon, and all were singing that song.

"I thought they'd be going to the Tuileries," Georgiana said. "Perhaps there are so many attending there's not room for them there."

The crowd worried me—if another huge group was going to join them later, that would mean almost all of Paris would be here. A lot of people who might die if things went badly wrong.

"Still," Georgiana went on, "if there are speeches, that means at least one of that precious pair has to be there to give one. Unless they can be in two places at once."

"I'm glad to say," I said, "that bilocation is either a myth or a trick that no one I know has ever managed to learn. Not even Jehovah or Lucifer. If the Enemy can do it, he's managed to keep that fact very quiet."

"The Enemy?"

"Oh, there is one," I said. "An ultimate source of evil and all that. Just not Lucifer; he's no friend of mine, and not a very nice person, but hardly in that league."

Then we passed through one of the small hills at the edge of the Field of Mars and there it was.

I like to think that, even if I had not known it was a piece of fakery, I would have known it for such on sight—a lumpen structure some ten manheights high, with paths up its side and little shrines

140

dotted about it, and chalk cliffs that looked even more false than the rest of it.

"How terribly Gothic," Georgiana said. "Poor dear Horace would love one for the back garden at Strawberry Hill."

"Plenty of room inside that for mischief," I said.

"Horace might well like that too."

"When I say mischief," I said, "I do not mean the sort of harmless prank one plays at tea. I mean blood and damnation."

To this she had no ready reply.

And we passed through the side of the structure and into a gloomy hall with pillars around its edges and shallow arches between them. Torches flared from brackets in the pillars and an oil lamp, that looked as if it had once burned before a high altar, glowed from the ceiling.

Beyond the pillars there was a darkness that was not just shadow or the absence of torchlight and lamplight. The place smelled somewhat of new plaster and stale incense, but more of some terrible decay that wafted from the darkness between the pillars.

Saint-Just was there, laying out, on a large three-coloured flag, my stolen weapons in a row among many other swords and daggers, alongside what appeared to be the blade from the guillotine, and several smaller chunks of metal which looked as if they might be lodestones. Around him, clustered and whispering in his ear, were several young men dressed in dark plain suits, though none as neatly pressed as his.

Chained to the pillar nearest where the things lay was a small boy who looked to be about nine years of age, but was so starveling and filthy that it was hard to be sure.

And at that pillar's nearest companion, not even chained, but held there by her wretchedness and no actual tie, was a young woman who looked like Polly, and who screamed loudly and continually.

When he had finished laying out my weapons, Saint-Just strolled over to where Augusta lay, and kicked her in the stomach twice.

141

"Stop your howling," he said in his calm terrible voice. "I have holy rituals to prepare and I need to concentrate if we are not going to make some terrible error with young Louis here, the way we did with you."

But she did not cease from screaming, and it was hard to know how she could go on like this without tearing her throat to bloody tatters.

"Well," Georgiana said, "at least we know where she is, now."

"I would so like,"—my voice had in it all the regret I felt at having to wait—"to come out of shadow here and now, and take that young man's head from him with my new sword. But I need to know what ails her. I will not take back to Polly a kinswoman who is no longer the person she was, will kill her first to save Polly the agony of choice, but not yet, and not now."

I hated to wait, when something appalling had happened and something worse was imminent and intended, but gone are those days of my youth when I acted first and dealt with consequences later.

Mostly.

We waited and watched for two hours in near silence. Eventually, choristers, singing as they came, filed in from the left side of the hall, chanting wordlessly, followed by Robespierre, who was breathless as if from running. Behind him marched a small group of men whose imitation of his taste in clothing seemed to indicate that they were his jackals and his toadies.

"It all took so much time," he said. "Leading the crowd and riding in that jolting ox-cart, with that vacuous girl and her chatter about perfume. Can we not prohibit perfume? It is an unnatural thing that disgusts me."

"You're here now," Saint-Just said. "And it is time for us to proceed, so that we can lead our new god out when he is made, and show him to his people that they may worship him instead of that terrible old tyrant in the skies."

Robespierre cleared his throat. The choristers ceased their noise, and the small audience clustered away from the workspace, and their two leaders.

"We are here," Robespierre announced, "to bring a better god to earth. He impels the just man to hate the evil one, and the evil man to respect the just one. It is He who adorns with modesty the brow of beauty, to make it yet more beautiful. It is He who makes the mother's heart beat with tenderness and joy. It is He who bathes with delicious tears the eyes of the son pressed to the bosom of his mother. It is He who silences the most imperious and tender passions before the sublime love of the fatherland. It is He who has covered nature with charms, riches, and majesty. All that is good is His work, or is Himself."

He paused, "And there may never have been such a god before, but now there will be."

This was all going to end very badly, because these men were not only evil, but so deeply self-deceived.

From the banner, the two men picked up two lodestones each, and commenced to wave them around in complex spirals, chanting nonsense syllables that they doubtless took for some mystic language.

"Mesmeric passes?" Georgiana whispered in my ear. "I thought that the American Franklin had quite exploded such notions years ago. Surely that won't work."

"Magic does not have to work, like cookery or mathematics do," I said. "It has only to be believed in. It is a focus for will, in this case, evil will, whatever these two like to believe of themselves."

"Would it be so very terrible," she asked, "if they created themselves a god of justice and mercy and universal well-being? Even by terrible means?"

I looked at her and shook my head. "The crucial word in your question," I said, "is if."

The weapons and the blade of the guillotine levitated from the flag and commenced a dance around the two magicians, and then, to their evident alarm, drifted back to their original positions and slumped onto the flag with a thud and a clash.

"So it begins," I noted.

Robespierre looked petulant a second and then raised his lodestones higher above his head and chanted ever louder, while Saint-Just stepped back and let him take the lead.

For a second, the weapons raised up again and lines of blue force crackled around them. The lines of force and the lines of the lance and blades briefly formed an image of a four-sided four-legged pylon, and then crashed down to the flag again.

And yes, I know now what was to be built in that place and that some current of time and fate flowed past us at that moment, but I did not think of such things then. Because almost as an echo of that crash, there was a thud from the dark alcoves beyond the pillars, and a single severed head came rolling out, as if part of some game on a village green.

It came to the outstretched leg of the small boy and opened its withered jaws and clamped them into the flesh of his calf with an audible click.

He gasped in pain, but had no energy in him to scream. Nor was it needful for him to do so, because the maddened woman chained opposite him screamed all the louder for the sight.

The click of the one set of jaws was like a signal, because two more heads, both of them more withered and rotten than the first, came rolling out. One fixed itself to the boy's right hand, taking most of his fingers into its mouth, and the other hauled itself up by digging its teeth into the worsted he was wearing and then with a great effort fixed itself to his stomach, so deep that I was surprised not to see any blood. The eyes in the sunken sockets of those heads stared out upon us with mad rage.

Robespierre and Saint-Just rushed over and tried to kick the four heads that followed out of the way, and their acolytes and choristers did the same as eight more rolled out and then sixteen. Yet it was as if they were moving against a strong wind or through some thick syrup.

Those that were not already armed picked up swords from the row on the flag and hacked away with them, for all the good it did them. The heads were inexorable and swift and the smell of them grew ever more intense as more and more started to roll out without need of the noise of biting to summon them.

"Should we not be doing something at this point?" Georgiana asked, but I shook my head. My instinct had been that this was a woman to reckon with; she had that icy calm some achieve through years of meditation and some by being slightly mad. In her case, it was just who she was.

"You see how little effect those two and their servants are having. Such great grim magics have their own rhythm which even I would have trouble breaking into. Better to wait a little. Still, while they are preoccupied…"

I raised my hand and my weapons leaped into the air from the floor and out of the hands of those who had seized them. They vanished a moment and were then in shadow, rushing to my outstretched hand like falcons I had set to prey, and hovering there. The lance and the two short swords I placed in the sling across my shoulders, and I twined the three small sharp knives back into the knot of my hair.

By now, the boy was hardly visible under the mound of heads that had clustered around him; new heads and ever more were by now biting not into his flesh but into other heads, and yet somehow when Robespierre's men tried to pull them away, they could turn and snap ferociously at the prying fingers without falling from their place.

Suddenly the creature that the boy was becoming lurched up from the ground where it had lain and stood tall on feet that were heads squashed and malformed by the weight of a body made of so many heads upon them, and eyes stared, and teeth snapped, from those strange feet as much as from the other parts of the body. And its head was made of the heads of young children, younger than the boy who lay hidden somewhere inside the mass, and those heads moved in unison when it opened its vast maw, and mad eyes stared out from among great fangs that were like a shark's or the rot-infested teeth of the great lizards of the South Seas.

145

As one of the acolytes tried to kick at the heads that still rolled out from between the pillars, he stumbled and the beast was suddenly upon him, lifting him to that maw in those terrible strange hands and stuffing him inside itself as when a snake eats a frog or bird and you cannot believe that jaws could open so wide without disjointing. And of an instant, it reached out and took another of the young men that lay in its path, and then another, and each time it swallowed one of them in two or three great bites, the beast grew, visibly, adding their mass to its own as more and more heads rolled out and attached themselves to it.

And the worst of it was, that the heads of those it had taken and eaten appeared, the marks of their last agony among them, sprouting like new carbuncles among the cluster of heads around its mouth.

"My god," Georgiana said, "is every head that has been taken in Paris here?" and then answered her own question with a sudden catch of horror in her throat, a sob that told me that she had recognized two of the heads that rolled out next, heads with long hair, and the remnants of beauty blown and blasted by rot.

"I have kissed those lips," she said, then drew herself straight, her eyes blazing.

"A moment more," I told her. "When we come out of shadow, make it your mission to keep that creature from the girl. While I destroy it."

"Tell me," she said. "Is there any of the child left inside that brute? That might be reached or distracted? Or of the love that those last heads bore for him?"

"Perhaps. But if I were you, and fragile, I would not venture my life on it."

"Huntress," she said, "if you knew me better, you would know that long odds are the ones I play, and have not always served me ill." Then she laughed. "Except at the gaming tables, of course, where they have brought me much debt as the price of a moment's excitement."

The creature was grown now to a height where its head touched the ceiling, and most of the acolytes and choristers were either fled from that place or eaten and dead. Robespierre and Saint-Just were taking great care to stay out of its reach while inching around the edge of the room towards where Augusta lay still screaming.

"Now," I said and stepped out of shadow, pulling Georgiana with me.

Keeping her eyes fixed both on the ogre and the other two monsters, she dashed to the girl's side and took up her stance there, protective, sword drawn. I myself pulled my new long slashing sword from the sling and stalked towards the creature. It ignored me, turning its gaze on what it thought of no doubt as its more vulnerable opponent and its helpless screaming prey.

I had not brought her with me as bait, but in such fights it is a role that my companions nonetheless sometimes play. And usually survive it.

"Ah, you brute." She spoke in icy anger. With her free hand, she pulled down the flaming torch from the pillar beside her and waved it before the creature's eyes. It flinched a little.

"So you know fear, do you?" she said, but it continued to lumber towards her. And then she surprised me, because as it drew close and tried to reach out to her, she slashed at it with her sword, thrust the flame at its face, and started to sing, as one would to a child, slashing and thrusting to the rhythm of her song.

"Ah vous je dirai maman," she sang. Ah, shall I tell you mother of my torment, the sad little tune you English took and changed into a meditation on cosmology, which says something about both you and the French. The creature paused and was for a moment utterly tamed and gentled, as she sang, as if the music touched something deep within it, something more than the living child entombed in its fury and decay.

And in the moment that it stood so still, I took my blade and swung up at it, a blow that took one of those titan legs from under it, and then, as it tottered, its head and maw on the backswing.

I could have swung at its centre, but I feared to harm the child that was trapped within it. The souls of children distorted into gods by evil men I can only free into death, as a rule, but this was different because the child was living still, however damaged his mind and spirit might be.

Needful sang with pleasure in my grasp, a new friend anxious to prove itself to me, as I cut the other leg from under the creature and then took its arms as it lay at my feet. The heads of which it was made still snarled and snapped at me, but uselessly, for just as it could shield itself from its maker, so I was shielded from its malice.

As it was not from me. I replaced Needful in the sling at my back, and picked up the blade of the guillotine where it lay discarded on the bloodied flag. I raised it above my head and brought the flat of it down on head after head, smashing them to shards and rot and the stinking deliquescence that lay within them, and, as I smashed them, ran out at the ears and nose.

It is important to remind dead things that they are dead, by breaking them and unmaking them, and just as in the first flush of their raising they can grow and spread like wildfire or Japanese vines, so too, once you break them with your will, they will flush away like silt in a torrent.

The important thing is to strike at them at the end of that first rush of growth, after they have eaten almost all that is handily there to eat but before they get to move out to places where there is more warm flesh standing there for their taking. And yes, I have dealt with such things often enough to have general rules.

The time to destroy such creatures is before they get to eat the many thousands of people singing patriotic songs a mere few yards away from you.

Meanwhile, as I worked at a task that was onerous, repetitive and utterly necessary, Georgiana had moved her attention to the two men responsible for this horror, who had drawn their swords against her, but were clearly not especially accustomed to doing their own killing.

She had moved into a killing trance, glaring at them with eyes that were angry to a point that skirted, yet was kin to, the madness of the berserker. It was a joy to watch her toy with them, with blade and flame—she was by no means the best wielder of a sword that I had seen even among women, but yet she had grace, skill and power, and they were clodhoppers, already exhausted from the great work that they had attempted and which had drained them in their failure.

I wish I had seen her fight when she was young.

"Oh you bloody bastards," she said softly, "to kill my friends and then set their dead heads to do your work for you, and to set them to make a monster of their poor child."

Without taking her eyes off them, she spoke to me. "'Toinette, and her friend Therese. Friends of these men killed them both, and Therese, they cut off her head, and they cut off her breasts, and carved her, and put the pieces of her onto the heads of pikes and waved them under 'Toinette's window, and said, kiss your beloved now."

She thrust again at Saint-Just and then she stumbled slightly, her foot turning on some of the ooze the smashing of the heads was leaving behind it. He raised his sword for a killing stroke, but she parried and twisted and his sword was from his hand and she thrust the torch at Robespierre as he swung at her while she was concentrating on his friend. Saint-Just waved his hands, making the beginnings of passes and working some death-curse or other, but of a sudden he screamed in pain, for there was a thrown knife in his shoulder.

"Started without me, did you?" Polly had entered the room silently while we were distracted. "Sorry to have missed most of the fun, but the crowds were worse than Vauxhall on a Saturday evening."

She turned to Saint-Just. "Hurts, does it?" she asked, but not as if she was solicitous of him.

She looked over at where Augusta lay screaming. "That's my great-granddaughter over there, shrieking her lungs and lights out.

What the bloody hell did you do to her? Give me one good reason not to put the next knife into your heart."

With Saint-Just out of action, Georgiana closed in on Robespierre, who backed away from her with an expression of genuine terror on his face that I had not noticed even when the killings of the monster he had made were at their bloodiest.

I went to the child, whom the heads had left entirely now. What clothes he had had before were in rags and he was bleeding gently from a hundred superficial cuts and bites.

"Louis," I said to him, but there was no response.

I waved my hand in front of his open, almost unseeing eyes, and they blinked a second but did not change their blank stare at something a few yards beyond the furthest wall.

"What did you do to him?" I asked the two men in tones that brooked no silence. "And what did you do to Augusta Wild?"

"We did nothing to the boy Louis Capet," Robespierre said.

"It was not us," said Saint-Just. "It was Simon, the cobbler."

"We thought…" Robespierre hesitated, then plunged ahead, "we thought, well, he will never be king. So let's give him a trade, an honest trade."

"We did not know," Saint-Just said, "that Simon would be cruel to him and beat him about the head with his cobbler's stool and across his back with his razor strop."

"We did not know that Simon would be kind, as he thought, and debauch him with alcohol until he was nearly imbecile and with whores until he was poxed. And when we realized what Simon had done to him, he was a slate wiped clean, anyway, and we needed one such."

"Better be a god, than an idiot," said Robespierre. "Mistakes had been made and we were trying to put things right."

They had the gall to look at me pleadingly, as if there was some chance that I would approve of what they had done.

I looked at them with the sternness of a judge. "And Miss Wild, the younger Miss Wild?"

"Ah, well," Robespierre said, and gave a shrug of his shoulders.

"That went wrong," Saint-Just said.

"We needed a goddess of reason," Robespierre said, "and though she is an enemy, she gave us clever empty answers under the question, and I thought, perhaps if she became a goddess of reason, she would see sense."

"And tell us everything we need to know," added Saint-Just. "But instead, all we got from the ritual was this madwoman who screams perpetually."

I remember, from my childhood, the times when I fell and grazed my knee and how it felt for just that second before the pain and the bleeding began, and this moment was like that time of expectancy and dread. And then Augusta sat up and ceased her screaming, and stared at me with eyes that were not mad.

She looked at me and said, "I suddenly realized that I heard your voice. Mara, Sister."

She smiled at me once, for the first time in centuries, and then her eyes rolled back into her head and she began to scream again.

I had not seen her in so long, and then her eyes had looked up at me from nightmare, and it had been an age before that that she had passed me a honey cake as I walked out the door and pecked her on the cheek as one unmindful.

And nothing was mended and she was here again and in pain again, and my eyes were at once wet with sorrow and burning with rage.

I rounded on Robespierre. Seizing him by his fussily tied white stock, I picked him up off the floor and wanted to break his neck, but I am not that woman any more who does such things in mere temper. I put him down and looked at him in quiet rage.

"You fools." I was a quiet Fury, a raging Fate in that moment, for he had made me so angry that I near forgot the limits I have placed on myself. "You wanted a goddess of reason and you brought here this tortured spirit, a woman worth hundreds of you, who sought only to understand the workings of time and fate. Terrible things were done to her, and what you have done is terrible too. Tremble, little men, because you have done things to your friends and to your king and to innocent children. But this—this you did to the sister, the long-dead, much missed sister, of Mara the Huntress, whom few have seen in her wrath."

"Can we kill them now?" Georgiana said, and affected a yawn. "They are horrid little men who have done terrible things, and we need to be done with them."

Polly shook her head. "That's all well and good, your Grace, but there are reasons not to. About fifty thousand reasons, beyond that door, and I can't get out of here by any other means."

She walked over to Augusta and took her by her hand, and stroked the back of that hand comfortingly, and the woman stopped screaming. Polly turned to me. "She liked me to do that when she was a child. Your sister may be in there with her, but Augusta is still there."

That was at once a relief, and a complication; I wondered whether Augusta was screaming as well. I knew that Sof was, and I knew why; I had hoped that, when she was next born, things would have changed. Doubtless being dragged into someone else's body had not helped her situation.

Robespierre and Saint-Just looked at each other, and the thin man nodded to the pudgy man.

"You have us at your mercy," Robespierre said, "but the people of Paris and of France will judge you harshly if you fall into their hands."

"There is a tunnel," Saint-Just said. "Through which we brought the boy, and the woman, and the blades, and the heads."

"It's always bloody tunnels with you people," Polly said coldly, still looking into Augusta's eyes and stroking her hand. "I'll wager you see tunnels in your sleep, and count the bricks."

Robespierre ignored her. "I propose that you take one of us as your hostage, and leave the other stunned, or bound, to give yourselves a good start."

"And you dare not kill us, Huntress," said Saint-Just. "Or you, Miss Wild."

"We dedicated our deaths at your hands to the Rituals. Just in case this day would come when we were at your mercy."

"And," added Saint-Just, "we proofed ourselves against your weapons while we had them, though not that strange long sword you have brought with you."

"But that matters not," said Robespierre with a note in his voice that was almost smugness. "For you cannot kill us, Huntress."

"Nothing to stop me killing you though, is there?" Georgiana said. "And what you have done to the boy here is enough to make any mother tear your eyes from their sockets and the skin from your faces before you die. And I stroked his head in his cradle."

"Ah," Saint-Just said. "I had not realized until now who you are." He turned to Robespierre. "She is one of their Duchesses, but a meddler with real power. She is the mistress of their Mr. Fox."

"No," Georgiana said firmly, "really I'm not. Poor dear Elizabeth would be most put out if she thought anyone believed any such thing. Charles is a good and faithful lover, to her. I just run election campaigns for him—but tyrants like you wouldn't know anything about that."

"You will not kill us," Saint-Just repeated, "because, if we are found dead, it will be assumed that we were killed by enemies of the French people. And there will be reprisals, against all the foreigners that the justice of the people can find." This he said in an insinuating tone and staring at her hard for tells, hoping that she would let something slip.

I was surprised that Georgiana ever lost at cards, because her face remained utterly calm as if she had no friends in Paris to be put at risk.

Robespierre walked over to where Louis lay, pulled a small phial from his coat pocket and broke it under the boy's nose. After some seconds, Louis roused, rose to his feet and began to stagger around confusedly until Robespierre seized him by the ear and twisted it until he stood more or less still.

All this gave me a moment to think of a plan, or rather of two plans: the plan I would propose and the one I would execute. A pretty piece, not of treachery, but of ensuring that whatever treachery they planned in answer to my proposal could not be executed.

"I have a suggestion," I said. "We have a torn and bleeding boy and a woman in some distress and you, Monsieur Saint-Just, have a knife in your shoulder. Our other differences—and they shall be redressed, never fear—can wait; medical attention and the calming of what was Augusta and now appears to be Sof also cannot."

Robespierre eyed me warily. "What do you propose?"

"That we take Augusta and the boy and Saint-Just down the tunnel, and you follow us, just out of range of pistol-shot and the rather primitive death curses you seem to have learned. We will send him back to you, once we are out of the tunnel. No one dies, and we have a head start."

He thought a moment. "I keep the boy. We exchange him and Saint-Just at the end of the tunnel."

I had expected this—I looked at my companions. Polly nodded and, after a long second's thought, Georgiana pulled a face and nodded.

"If there is treachery," I said, "be assured that you will die."

Saint-Just shrugged. "You intend to kill us anyway."

"In due course. But I have lived seven thousand years, and I still know the value of one day more."

I do not make threats, but I am aware that some find my statements of simple fact unnerving.

And so it was. Polly took her knife from Saint-Just's shoulder; I did not give him the chance to stop and dress it, because it was not bleeding enough to threaten his life, and a man weakened by blood loss was less of a threat to us.

I prodded him forward at the point of Needful, which thrummed with pleasure in my hand, pleasure and a mild hunger for fresh blood to slake the disgust it felt from destroying so much that was dead and rotten.

There was always the chance that he might trigger some deadfall as we went, or fail to point one out that was waiting for the unwary, and I wanted to be sure to be able to kill him in the moment of such a betrayal. My new sword had an eagerness that might serve especially well in such a moment.

Polly kept her free hand stroking at Augusta's, and there were only occasional screams from behind me. Georgiana kept up the rear; she had taken the pistol from her sleeve and, as we walked, would periodically turn, stop and level it at Robespierre, as he walked behind us at the boy's slow, halting pace. I noticed with pleasure that she did not try to cover him the whole time, and risk an accidental discharge of her weapon. The best of schemes can fall apart through simple errors; precautions against such are one of the hallmarks of the professionally violent.

After some time, the tunnel sloped upwards and its sides ceased to be lined in brickwork, and started to be simple blocks of crude-cut stone. Then, quite suddenly, we came to a simple wooden door and Saint-Just threw it open, and there we were, in the daylight of the afternoon, near the Seine, with the bridge formerly known as Royal a mere few yards away.

"You may send us the boy, Robespierre," I said. "He walks slowly, so I will wait to send Saint-Just back to you."

He released the boy and gave him a shove, and the child Louis tottered towards us unsteadily. Once Louis was close enough to the light to have to shade his weak eyes, I gave Saint-Just a shove, taking care to hit him on his wounded shoulder. Pain stops people thinking too hard.

I put my sword back into its sling—I needed my hands free for what I planned to do next.

Saint-Just passed the boy and I worried for a moment that he would grab the child and run; but no, everything went according to plan: Saint-Just retreated down the tunnel, and the boy was almost with us, when Robespierre spoke up from where he stood.

"Come back to us Louis," he said. "These are evil women, who mean you harm."

The boy wavered, and started to totter back towards the darkness. Georgiana cried out, "Louis," and then started to sing that nursery tune again.

He paused and looked confused. "Louis," Saint-Just called out, "they are evil women, sluts like your mother the queen."

"They want to make you be bad again," Robespierre said. "And we have brandy for you."

"You like brandy, don't you?" Saint-Just coaxed. "They won't give you brandy, Louis."

Louis squealed and ran staggering from us back into the darkness.

Georgiana made to follow him, but I seized her by the arm and shoved her roughly out of the tunnel and out into the light, where Polly and Augusta already were. Then I reached out with my hands to the stonework of the tunnel and pulled out block after block and hurled them down into the darkness. After a very short while, because I am quick when I set my mind and my back to such work, the tunnel behind us collapsed—it would be a while before Robespierre and Saint-Just could make it back to the chamber where they had worked their ritual and thence to the open air to summon pursuit.

Sometimes it helps that I retain the appearance of the young girl I was at the start of things, because it means that men of evil will fail to consider that I am titan-strong.

I turned to Georgiana. "I am sorry," I said, "but the boy made his choice."

"They have warped his mind." There was all of desolation in her voice, for the world and the love she had lost and this last fragment of all that loss she had hoped to save.

"I know," I said, "but some things cannot be helped. I would have saved him if I could, but I fear that he was lost to us years ago. Had we time, perhaps—but we do not."

"And you want to save Polly's great-grandchild," she said bitterly, "who is somehow also your sister, and perhaps you can make sense of that choice for me. Because yes, she is your sister and your child, but he was the baby of my poor dead friend." She wept.

"Let's face it, your Grace," Polly said. "He's the poor crazed creature they have made of him, and that is another thing to their account. Also, he's the bloody King of France, when all's said and done, and I for one don't put myself out for such."

Georgiana continued to weep, and then, of a sudden, gave a great guffaw. "Don't ever change, Polly Wild," she said. "Don't ever change."

"Don't know as I plan to," Polly said. "Don't know as I can."

As she spoke, a wagon stacked high with newspapers and broadsheets stopped alongside us, and Mary hailed us from her seat alongside the driver. "About time," she said. "I wasn't sure how many more times we could drive this way without its looking suspicious. If everyone weren't busily singing patriotic choruses, we would have been noticed by now." She pointed to the back of the wagon. "There's space for you all among the bales of newsprint. And this wagon delivers to Dijon and Besancon, if it serves your convenience to head in that direction."

"Well," Georgina said briskly, hitching up her clothes as she scrambled aboard, "that does put us on the road to Lausanne. We have a sick woman to care for, who will get no kind treatment in Paris. Or anywhere in France."

"You're leaving, then, with Thomas still in prison." Mary's voice was heavy with mingled disappointment and resignation.

"I was seen." Georgiana looked almost abashed as if she remembered a promise unkept, a task undone, and could not apologize enough. "And those butchers knew who I was, by name. We stopped them doing something terrible, but they know who I am. So they will be looking for me in Paris, which makes me a liability to our enterprise."

"She's being modest." Polly had clambered up too and made herself comfortable on a pile of leaflets, while I passed Augusta up to her. "She beat the two most powerful men in Paris in a swordfight—with a little help—and they are pretty fucking vexed with her."

157

"Poor Thomas," Mary murmured, full of sorrow. "A great man left to die because gods and monsters had to be fought."

I liked her all the more for the fact that she said this without the slightest touch of irony, and I felt somewhat concerned that these two women who had done me an enormous favour had perhaps lost the chance to do the thing they had originally planned.

"I could probably free him for you," I said. "How urgently does he need to be rescued?"

"You have other things to do?" Mary's voice was calm and disappointed. She did not add, that are more important? but scepticism that anything could be was there as an undercurrent.

"I have the chance to talk to the re-embodied spirit of my dead sister for the first time in a thousand years." I tried to keep the steel from my voice, yet failed. "She is mad with the pain of what was done to her, so mad that she screams constantly, and has been forced into another innocent woman's body against both their wills, so actually, yes, for once, just once, I do have things I need to be doing myself, for myself, right now. If that's all right."

Mary stepped back, looking abashed. "Well," she said. Her next words were slower, and more deliberate as she considered and reckoned up the days. "The ambassador has sent home for instructions on whether to make a fuss or not—he doesn't want to and my guess is that Washington will not either. But messages will need to go back and forth. Morris sent a despatch yesterday, by a fast boat. I would say six weeks."

I was impressed yet again by her sense for practicalities. "You have my word," I told her, "that I will return to Paris in six weeks' time and free him before they have a chance to execute him. If the situation changes, I imagine you can find a way of getting a message to me."

I am not used to making schedules and sticking to them, but I can be flexible.

"We had best be away," I said. "My thanks to you, Mary, and I will see you on the 25th of July, or whatever they are calling it now."

"Oh," she said," thank my husband Imlay. He deals with the

Norway traders, who provide the lumber that makes the paper that the printers use. There is always someone useful, that someone you know knows."

"I've found this true," I agreed. "Among seraphim and demogorgons, as much as among tradesmen."

Mary got down from her perch, a bit stiffly, and smoothed out her skirts. "I will wait for you on the twenty-fifth of July, at the sign of the Dark Angel." She pointed to our driver. "He's called Julien. He is remarkably uncurious, and remembers nothing of what is said in his hearing." Then she smiled at us, turned and went about her business, which, from the stiffness of her back, was none of ours.

By now, Georgiana and Polly had helped Augusta up onto the wagon. She had ceased her screaming, but only because Polly continually stroked and petted and fussed over her, and I feared that she might start again at the most inconvenient of moments.

Polly produced a small phial from one of her pockets, and held it to Augusta's lips; after a strained moment, her head dropped and she started to snore gently.

I hate to do such things, but I cast a glamour over the entire wagon so that no one looking at it would see or hear anything untoward. They would see what was there—four women, one of them asleep— but would not notice anything particular. The rules that I have, about the use of magic, about the expenditure of power taken from those who ripped it from bleeding bones—well, they are my rules, so I can break them. On the rare occasions that I choose to.

The wagon rolled slowly out of Paris and across France and little of interest occurred, which was all to the good. Every so often, Augusta would drift back to semi-consciousness and occasionally I would see Sof looking at us in wonderment through her eyes, and then a tide of distress would creep over whichever of them was dominant at the time and Polly would stroke her forehead until she slept again, or would produce another of the small phials of sleeping draught she had for some reason bought with her in such quantities.

"I guessed," she said when Georgiana asked her, "that there would have been torture. And when you retrieve someone from that, sleep is often the thing that they need most."

I saw no reason to harrow them with the true story of the torture that Sof had endured, of which anything inflicted on Augusta, would, however vicious, be a tiny fraction.

In each town, Julien would hold up two fingers or three, and we would heave down that number of bales of newspaper into the hands of whoever was there waiting to receive them. They'd pass up loaves of bread and flasks of wine and some rough cheese, and occasionally joke with Julien about his luck in having so many beauties to help him in his labours, and he would smile self-deprecatingly and I would walk over and slap him on the back, or Polly would put her arm around him and rest her head on his shoulder, or Georgiana would blow him a kiss.

And he never spoke.

He had a tongue in his mouth, because that was my first dark thought, but he was whole, in body at least. And he was not one of those grim wounded men who never smile. I think he did not speak simply because he did not care to, and had spent time in a city where much talking—I do not say too much—had had consequences.

He listened to our talk—Georgiana spoke a passable if courtly French and Polly some coarser and more archaic cant she had picked up when young from criminals serving out apprenticeship or exile from the gangs of Paris and Toulon at the court of her father. I spoke as I always speak, and people understand me well enough.

Much of the time, I told stories, much as I have told stories to you, Crowley, because it passed the time and helped to calm Augusta, and Sof, when they were awake. Sof had heard many of the stories before when we had last been together, but some of course were new to her.

Georgiana asked me, in due time, how I thought the spirit of my dead sister had replaced the goddess those evil men had called for.

"They wanted a goddess of reason and wisdom," I said, "and there is no such thing."

160

She looked enquiringly.

"No woman who was wise or rational," I said, "would ever seek godhood or allow it to be forced upon her; it is contrary to the nature of the wise. And wisdom cannot be made immortal, because it is important that it grow old, die and be reborn. Ages ago, my sister chose to pursue wisdom above all else, as my other sister, whom I have never seen reborn, chose to follow her whims across time and for all I know, does so still. And I have seen Sof in different times and places, and known her, and have recognized the memory of her among men in places where she lived and died, and I did not meet her there but came later."

I bent and kissed the forehead of what was at least for a while the resting place of my sister's spirit.

"She has done much good in the world," I said. "And counselled great men that they might also be good men. For this she has been tortured and slain, and sometimes I have avenged her, as I will when I return to Paris, one way or another."

"Didn't they say," Polly asked, "as they have dedicated their deaths at your hands to the Rituals?"

"You saw in that cellar how little that precious pair understand the traps and torments that their chosen path brings in its train. I tell you now, that they will not die at my hands, and yet they will die, and I will be the cause of their deaths." I spoke calmly, as I do when I swear my vengeance on those who have spilled blood, and have spilled blood that was dear to me.

Occasionally, when her mind was at its clearest, and her memory of torment dimmest, Sof would speak to me. She did not reproach me for the choices I had had to make so many years before, but said that I had little to feel guilty about, though she knew guilt would nonetheless dog me always.

At other times, we spoke of private matters, in a tongue forgotten before Khufu built his pyramid, and I shall not speak to you either of what was, as I say, private.

After some many, but never weary, leagues, I became aware of a horse and rider that followed us at a distance that gradually, ever so gradually closed. After each town it would be a little nearer to us, but not so much nearer as would have been natural had he not been hanging back somewhat. He wished not to pass us at natural speed, or to follow us at a distance, but to approach us slowly.

I descended from the wagon and ran fast as thought back to him through shadow, and then stood athwart his road, so that a more wicked and more foolish man might have tried to run me down, or rear his horse's hooves at me. Instead he bent down over his horse's neck, and whispered to its right ear, a whisper that was wordless and almost like a kiss. The horse stopped its gentle trot, and he unwrapped the muffler with which he had hidden his face.

"Well met, Huntress," he said.

"Good evening, Captain Chambord," I replied. "Or should I say Citizen Chambord?"

"You might as well say Condemned Dead Man Chambord, for all that I care. Or know." He smiled. "By god, you kicked a hornet's nest in Paris."

"That we did," I said. "It was needful that we do so to save that city's people from the insane thing their masters had summoned in error."

"Need I say," he said, "that the stories that you hear in the cafes and the wine shops are different? That English spies have summoned an ancient hideous demon—which I take it would be you, Huntress—that attempted the destruction of the people's tribunes, who fought it boldly and destroyed it, taking a few serious wounds, from which they are recovered."

"Should I be concerned about pursuers?"

He shook his head. "Strangely enough, I have seen few on the roads, and I have travelled carefully, taking notice of anyone who might be my nemesis, or yours. I have no wish to fall into their hands, and shadowing you seems the best way to stay out of them."

"Perhaps," I said, "since we are so clearly leaving, they have decided to let well enough alone."

"That has been my thought. And, much as I love the divine Miss Wild, my principal reason for travelling in your wake, and gently accustoming you to my presence."

"Polly will be glad to see you." I lied, because she had said nothing, and yet I guessed that I did not lie, not really, because I had seen her smile when she looked at him.

I raced back to the wagon, and waved to Julien to stop. Chambord cantered after, coming level with us in a little while, and waving his hat wildly in what was part gallantry and part sheer exuberance as he drew level.

"Polly, m'dear," he said after dismounting and approaching us. And then, more softly, "How is your kinswoman?" for he guessed that the sleeping woman who resembled her so closely must be the prisoner of whom she had spoken when explaining matters to him in their dungeon. Then he bowed to Georgiana. "Your Excellency."

"That'd be her Grace," Polly said. "She's a good English Duchess, not some Austrian bawd."

"Your Grace," he corrected himself, and then, "I have something for you."

Strapped at the back of his saddle was a bundle of cloth which seemed unusually heavy, and which rang in a clash of steel on steel, when he dropped it at her feet. "I could not bring the case," he said apologetically. "The pearl and silver inlay would have drawn attention. The men at the sign of the Dark Angel said that they would keep it, for you or for your descendants, until it was needed. But I have those weapons that you left behind, and they are so fine that I tremble at the thought of the ones you took with you, into that place."

Georgiana smiled and offered him her hand, which he kissed with more fervour than might have been considered tactful with his light of love sitting next to her.

The kiss he planted on Polly's hand was, however, more fervent still, and was followed by an embrace almost too passionate for the open air. The embrace ended suddenly when Augusta, or Sof, moaned gently in her sleep and Polly and Georgiana turned from him at once and were all solicitude.

After a little stroking of Augusta's forehead, Polly said softly to him, "She is as she is—half-mad and sometimes screaming in her fit unless we drug her to sleep. Somehow they dragged the Huntress's sister into her out of death or heaven, and she screams somewhat too, while at other times conversing in ancient tongues."

For a man who mere months before had been an absolute sceptic, he nodded along to this with surprising equanimity. There is no teacher like experience, when it comes to matters arcane.

I had thought that passing the borders of France and into Switzerland might be a point of danger for us, and readied myself to fight our way through, but Polly, it seemed, had arranged matters; she worked after all for the Lord of Cliffs and Narrow Seas, and there is professional courtesy between such spirits for their servants when no harm is meant to the nations they guard.

When we crossed the border, Chambord got down from his horse, whispered in its ear again and slapped its rump gently. It snorted, and went off the other way. "It was a loan," he said. "It is a sensible horse and knows its own way; it is also a good French horse, whom I would not wish to lead into treason."

"You can ride with us, sweet man," Polly said, "but do not think to renew what passed between us in a prison cell. In jail, I could be your Polly, but in free Swiss air, I am Britain's Intelligencer General and you a French Captain."

"Love knows no borders," he said with a bow of the head that almost won her.

"No, my dear," she returned. "Borders are far more serious things than love."

By now, the bales of newsprint were all gone and we lay among boxes of vegetables and cases of wine—France was not at war with the Swiss and Julien, it appeared, had relatives in the grocery trade in Geneva, whose errands he was running at this end of his journey as he had those of printers elsewhere. Thus it was that he could deliver us to the trim little house in Lausanne where Gibbon had lived and where a couple of servants were keeping things in order for him. We got down from his cart, and he trotted off with never an adieu.

"Your Grace," they said when they opened the front door and saw Georgiana.

She nodded at them genteelly and with moderate affection. "Franz. Amelie. I have some sad news for you."

Franz said, in English that was only slightly accented, "We are aware that the master is dead."

"How efficient of his lawyers," she said.

"Ah, no, your Grace." Amelie's English was even better than his. "He told us himself when he took up residence again."

"Really? How splendid. I've got someone here he will really want to meet." Georgiana turned to me, radiant with a delight rarely associated with the discovery that one's old friend is now a ghost. "This is the most amazing good luck, Huntress. I've spent the last few weeks quietly bemoaning the fact that he never got to talk to you. And missing him, of course."

Polly joined us at the front steps of the house, holding the hands of a sleepy, and not currently distressed, Augusta.

"The late Mr Gibbon," in proud and proprietorial tone, "did much useful work for me, all gathering and collating and scribbling notes in the margins of reports better men and woman had died to send. I never took to the man, but he was thorough."

Her voice was full of reluctant respect and just a little spitefulness.

"And in the time he could ill spare from his work for me was a famous freethinker and historian who wrote a book about Ancient Rome, what takes as long to read as Rome took to decline and fall. I don't know what further good he can do for me and mine unless you are minded to 'ave him put my poor Augusta to sleep with his prosing."

"Oh pooh, Miss Wild," Georgiana said, "his book is a work of magnificent scholarship packed with information and occasional jests."

And by now the gentleman himself had joined us, standing just inside the hall in that diffident way spirits have when the necessities of their existence bind them to a single dwelling.

Gibbon proved to be a small fat man, with an unsightly protrusion in his groin. He must have suffered from it for a long time to be so afflicted even now. He looked at Georgiana, and at Polly, sighed with an air of resignation, and bowed awkwardly and with a slight wince. "Your Grace. Miss Wild." He looked at me, Augusta and Chambord, with little apparent interest, and then a thought struck him, and he smiled broadly. "Your Grace's niece is not with you," he observed.

"Caroline?" Georgiana said. "No, she is in England, with her mother Lady Ponsonby."

"Such a spirited girl," Polly said. "But not joining us."

Gibbon's smile grew ever broader. "Welcome," he said. "You find us all at sixes and sevens, of course. I keep little in the way of an establishment these days—the servants eat plain fare, and I nothing whatever, but you are welcome to share what little we have."

I have heard people say this down the ages, and it is usually more than I would want to eat.

Then he added, with a slight catch in his voice, "Spirited, yes, that's a good polite word for her."

I wondered what this child could be like, to be so dreaded; I would see her some years later, dressed unconvincingly as a young man, playing cards with the poet Byron. She had even less skill at the tables than her aunt. She surpassed expectation, not in the best of ways.

The servants had stood aside politely, and we joined the dead historian in the hallway of his house. He was not quite prepared to be unwelcoming, but was clearly not entirely happy that we were here. "I am quite busy," he said. "And leading a quiet life. Trying to get some work done, now that I am dead, and have no distractions."

"You'll hardly know we are here," Polly said.

Unfortunately, Augusta, or perhaps Sof, chose that moment to scream so loud that the windows rattled.

"Who is that troubled young woman?" he said.

"My great grand-daughter," Polly said.

"Inhabited by the spirit of my dead sister," I added, for clarity.

"Ah." He regarded me with marginally greater interest. "And you would be?"

"My new especial good friend," Georgiana said, in a proprietary fashion.

"What I knew, well, and fought alongside" said Polly, "before either of you were born."

Clearly neither of them were going to get to the point, so I made the sort of vague curtsy I regard as owed to elderly men of distinction, whether living or dead. "I am Mara," I said, "whom gods and men call the Huntress."

"You really should talk to her, Edward," Georgiana urged. "She knew all sorts of emperors and prophets; I'm sure she knows just why Rome declined and fell. She would be of such assistance in your work."

He looked even more horrified by this suggestion than I was. "I'm not trying to rewrite the book, your Grace," he said. "Just checking the footnotes for my peace of mind. While I'm sure your friend might have been of great assistance twenty years ago"—in a tone that implied that he was sure of nothing of the sort—"even then I would have had to verify any account she could give me of, say, the sodomitic perversities of Heliogabalus. It is not enough to know what happened—I have to be able to prove what happened."

"Quite so," I agreed. "Though everyone exaggerates what that sweet little girlboy got up to."

"His behaviour outraged Rome," he said, "so that they cast him into the public sewers in dishonour."

"Nonsense. She slept with the same charioteer as her aunt. No one cared, except for the aunt, but she decided to take offence, have Heliogabalus killed, and put her son on the throne in her place."

167

"That's as may be. But you didn't write it down, did you?"

"I have better things to do with my time," I told him. "Saving the world from gods and monsters."

Gibbon snorted his disagreement and frustration. "We have a sick woman to care for," I told him, "which is also one of the better things I can do with my time than argue about the making of histories."

Even the elderly ghost could see the point of that, and his servants fetched smelling salts, hot water, cushions, tea and a bar of soap in no particular order.

"There are probably some leeches, still," he offered. "We released them into the garden pond when I went back to England to die."

"Mostly she needs rest," Polly said. "In a comfortable bed, where she can catch up on her sleep. I've known people as were tortured before, and they find sleep a sovereign cure."

Which might be true for Augusta Wild, but I believed it would not answer for my sister Sof, whose hurts were far deeper than any sleep could salve, or leech suck away. And so it proved.

When Augusta was in control of the body they were sharing, she was calm and often lucid, and chatted with her kinswoman about the agents she had sent from Paris ahead of her own arrest, and their subsequent fates. Or with Georgiana about the latest fashions and a system for winning at faro. Or with Chambord about the plays of Racine, for which both of them had a taste.

But I could see my sister mad and frightened staring at me from behind those eyes, and when she burst free, it was still, mostly, as an embodied cry of pain.

It was almost worse when she was lucid.

"I am fading back into the place between deaths," she said to me. "I have no business in this woman's body for it is not one I was born into, nor do I wish to steal any more of her life from her."

I stroked her forehead in a way I knew she loved, yet not in a way that would show disrespect for the younger Miss Wild, whose tastes in such matters I could not consult.

She clutched at my arm. "I fear for the child I shall be when I am born next. That I shall scream in pain that I do not understand, and be taken for a mad thing, and locked away. I do not think, Mara, sister, lover, that I could stand to be locked away, and chained, and bled, and left in the dark. I think it would make me madder and madder each time I was born, and useless to the work, and unable to understand the workings of time and fate."

But then she would cease to talk and lie there in staring silence, her sides heaving like a horse that had been galloped too long, or would cry out.

Often she would call my name, or Lillit's, or that of young Josh—but no one in this time would ever think that strange. But at least once she cried out in fear the name of Cyril. And then screamed inarticulately as if her tongue were being ripped from its roots. She fell asleep then, and woke as Augusta, as if a storm had passed and left a calm behind.

Later that night, when the three English women were talking quietly, Chambord sat in an armchair reading a volume of Gibbon's history. The servants were abed or about their private business, and Gibbon came to me, indicating that he wished private speech. We drew aside, some little way into shadow, where he was more solid, and our conversation discreet.

"I know," he said, "that you have your secrets, Huntress, but I think I have deciphered one of them."

I looked at him, stern-faced.

"I know, I think, some little of what has left your sister mad. I have, after all, written of it in my history, but truly it is not something I wish to contemplate."

I made as if to end the conversation.

"Or indeed to discuss," he went on, raising his voice slightly. "But she makes no recovery."

"She dwindles," I said, "out of the body she was forced to possess. And I tremble for what will happen when she next alights in life."

He looked at me intently, and I wondered that I had ever been tempted to think of him as a fop or a pedant, for now he spoke as one with authority. "She needs to forget. I know that that must be a terrible thing, for those of you who hold a single nature from life to life. But my friend Jones tells me of India, where they know of such things. Memory is not spirit, they hold. And I, who never thought such things worth considering, find myself in a place beyond death, and yet myself." He looked suddenly weary and older than he had been when he died. "One day, when I tire of revisiting my studies, perhaps I would wish to be emptied, to be wiped like a child's slate when the lesson is done. That time is not now for me, but perhaps it is for her."

I could not bear the thought of what he was telling me—it might be true but I dreaded it as a child with toothache dreads the pincers that will end its pain. "What you say may be true, but I have no knowledge of such matters. I deal in the slaughter of dark gods and evil men, not in the clouding of minds."

"You need to listen to me, for I have a story to tell—of which I was too ashamed to speak in my Autobiography, but which may answer this case, and I will speak of it in your need."

I have noticed that on occasion, ghosts that speak of their own past will lose the semblance in which they most appear and adopt that of some other age of their life, and so it was with him, as he talked. For long moments, I found myself looking not at the elderly man with his swollen groin, but at the young dandy he had been on his Grand Tour, before he watched goat-herds lead their flocks through the ruined Forum of the eternal city and found his vocation.

He had been thin once, and, though small, almost dapper, with excessive lace around his neck and fine ankles for a man, and the sort of carved mahogany cane that was briefly an essential part of a young man's equipment. He had a sword in an impractical scabbard at his belt and pockets for watch and snuffbox; he was quite the thing, and looked entirely insufferable.

"I don't know, Huntress," he inquired, "whether you have ever been in Venice for the Carnival?"

170

"Once or twice," I said. "In the line of duty. Demons and sorcerers and necromancers always think that they can pass unnoticed in a crowd of people in masks throwing streamers and coloured powder at each other. They are, in general, mistaken in that belief; it's something stiff and preoccupied in their merrymaking."

"So you know how the streets are suddenly full of people singing ridiculous songs and swilling red wine from leather bottles that squirt in your face and ruin your linen if you do not know precisely how to hold them, and strangers playing lovesongs on mandolins underneath your balcony at the oddest hours, and eating spiced chicken legs someone threw you from a passing gondola or a sausage that fell on your head as men with swords chased each other across the rooftops." He smiled, and shook his head in a mixture of repentance and sensual joy. "I have no particular gift for that sort of pleasure, as it turned out. But I was young and it was nothing like Hampshire. And then there were the women…I did not know, before Venice, that lechery was a pleasure in itself, whether or not it led to actual fornication. That was the thing. You had no way of knowing. That nun in a purple habit split to her thigh—she might be a whore whose bravos would steal your purse or she might be the daughter of a noble who could have you drowned in a sack if you looked at her the wrong way. She might even be a boy—the Venetians are lax in such matters.

"I did not know which frightened me more—losing my gold, or losing my life, or catching the pox, or committing sodomy under misapprehension. So I danced with the revellers and drank their wine and helped throw their streamers and powders, and I thought I could observe and only enjoy the sight of such things and then, then I saw her."

"Her?" I asked, as one is meant to.

"I heard her first," he said. "It was a high laugh, but one that had a richness from notes deep in the throat. I thought at first that she was one of the castrates that sing there in the opera house, for their voices have that mixture of silk and steel, of pleasure and regret, but then I saw her and knew that any lust I had thought to feel for girls in the street, or whores in bordellos, was but a shadow.

"She was dressed in a way I thought illegal even at Carnival, one shoulder quite bare and one breast barely covered. No boy and no eunuch, then…And a half-mask loosely held in front of her and dark eyes gazing intently across the square at me behind it. Her free hand pointed at me, and then beckoned. I shuddered in a fear I did not understand and I obeyed as one who had no choice.

"'Young man,' she said, and I stared at her like the fox at the hounds that will tear it. 'Dumb, then,' she said. 'I had hoped for perfection in you.'

"'My lady,' I said, 'Dumb in truth, but only struck so by your beauty'—for I had studied books of compliments before making my Tour in the hope of the encounters boys talk of late at night in their last days at school.

"'A stranger here,' she said, 'as am I.'

"'I am English,' I said, 'a gentleman who hopes one day to be a scholar.'

"'Ah,' she replied, 'it is a long time since I had an English boy at my side, and longer since I visited your land. You would not believe how long. And a scholar, you say,' and she reached out her hand and ran it across my shaven chin and up the right cheek to tug gently at the underside of the long-nosed mask I wore, as one who revels with revellers must. 'I know many things, and I will take good care of your education.'

"I thought her some courtesan, but the sort of woman kept only by the richest and most well-bred of men, and my only concern was not that I lose my purse, but that it not contain enough to buy that for which I would have, at that moment, traded everything I owned.

"My gaze was still fixed on her eyes, and her mouth, and I did not look away or reach inside my coat to count the coins I had with me for incidental expenses, but she laughed at me in a way that contained both scorn and tolerance.

"'Emperors,' she said, 'have offered whole cities of loot for what you will receive gratis, this night, and been refused. I am not a whore, little boy, but Woman, and this night, you please my whim.' And she took me firmly by the shoulder—so firmly that I doubted her sex again for a second—and pulled me towards the canal, and a single black gondola whose steersman was dressed in deep dark scarlet with a black leather mask whose nose was a phallus as long and as hard as mine felt at that moment.

"Her mouth was upon mine as she drew me down into the cushions of the boat and her hand upon me. I had never understood before that moment that a woman can take a man as thoroughly as any rake a serving wench, and leave him without will or any say in the matter. I was raptured and ravished, and felt neither ashamed nor unmanned, whatever I have felt about that night since in the ashen and guilty watches of early dawn.

"Suddenly we were from the boat, so suddenly that I remember no climb to a pier and it was as if we had flown from the cushion into the entrance hall of some palazzo, a hall swathed in green brocade, or perhaps in marble carved and painted to resemble cloth, as is the Venetian taste in such matters. We walked hand in hand through that hall and up the steps of a large staircase and I was so full of joy and pleasure that I thought I would spend at every step and then die of mortification at disappointing her, and at each step that thought held me off a little and so it built in me like a megrim or a hunger that needed to be satisfied.

"And then we were at the door of some inner chamber and she said 'Wait here a moment, sweet boy,' and entered, and from behind the screen at the side of the vast bed therein I heard the rustle of her dress, and I placed my hand on the gold and glass handle of that chamber door to steady myself as I entered." And here, at last, he fell into silence.

"And then?" I prompted.

"I remember nothing more," he admitted. "Just the words we spoke in that moment, and awakening with all my goods, and more coin than I had had before, in a carriage two days from Padua and heading towards Florence. And a heartache that has stayed with me ever since, and a sense of fulfilment that I never knew again until the first volume of my book was taken from the press and placed in my hands. That is the woman you need to find, because she is the mistress of delusion, deceit and memory."

"And what were the words you spoke?" I asked him, fearing that I knew the answer.

"I said to her, 'You are my Fate,'" he said, "and she answered, and it is the last thing I remember of that night, 'Ah no, sweet boy, I am your Morgana.'"

I had guessed and dreaded where his story was leading, and his last word thudded into my ears like the last grain of sand that tells when an axe will fall.

The one person I most needed, then, was the one person I could never bring myself to ask for a favour, or leave myself owing a debt to.

I turned to Gibbon, and noticed that this memory of brief happiness had had at least one positive effect on the man. The unsightly swelling in his groin had subsided altogether as if memory had lanced it; the marks of illness persist in ghosts for a while after death, but are the first mortal thing to dissolve away.

"I know her," I said. "Or rather, I knew her when the world was new. Our paths diverged then and I see no likelihood of our meeting again. We will have to find some other way to remove Sof's memories of pain."

I had obviously raised my voice more than I intended to, because Georgiana and Polly looked up from the sofa where they sat with Augusta. I slipped from shadow; talking loudly while invisibly is generally considered bad manners.

"Now don't you go upsetting the Huntress, Mr Gibbon," Polly said. "She has a temper on her that you would not wish to see awoken."

"All I said," Gibbon said, "was that I once met an enchantress who had the art of removing memories, and that that would be a way forward for us."

174

"What memories could be so very bad that you would have to remove them? And leave but the shell of a soul behind?" Georgiana sounded shocked.

"Worse enough than you can imagine," Gibbon said, "that the very thought of them would keep you awake sobbing, your Grace. Believe me when I say that I am doing you a service in telling you no more than this. I could wish, for my peace of mind, that I had not uncovered this secret."

"So what's the problem?" Polly said. "We find Mr Gibbon's enchantress and she does our business for us, and we pay her whatever fee she charges."

I looked at her, stone-faced. "The woman in question is not someone with whom it is possible to do business, and paying her would be beyond our means."

Polly gave me an enquiring look, and then laughed.

"It's her," she said, "it's her, ain't it?"

I did not reply.

"You said as how there had been one woman once, apart from your Sof. In great heat and need, you said."

I drew in a deep resigned breath at the way these mayflies needed to know all my business. "Yes. And the fact you now know that, changes nothing."

"Can't you—" started Georgiana.

"Don't you—" started Polly.

"I think—" started Gibbon, all of them at the same time and all trying to shout the others down on their second syllable.

Even Chambord roused himself from his book and made as if to speak.

And yet the noise they made was not as loud as the thunder-clap of the knocker on the front door of the house.

Almost relieved at the interruption, I threw the door open to find nothing but the night, at first glance. Then there was a sudden flutter and a bird flew in from the darkness, a bird as black as that darkness with a red flame of sullen intelligence in the eyes with which it peered around the room at us from the bust of Hadrian on which it perched.

"My mistress greets you, Huntress," it said. "And you too, Mr Gibbon. As for you, the Miss Wilds, Captain Chambord, the lady Sof and your Grace the Duchess, she has not yet had the pleasure, but I am sure she will be glad to make your acquaintance in due course."

Gibbon looked at the creature intently, and his age varied a little as if he were trying again to remember being young and lusty. "Will your mistress will Morgan be joining us imminently? I can wake the servants and provide at least a cup of tea or a glass of brandy."

"No," said the bird. "She is indisposed, which is the purpose of my being here. A saucer of milk, and a small piece of beefsteak, or a rind of cheese, would be welcome."

Chambord rose, bowed and went to the kitchen, returning a few minutes later with the milk and with a rind of Parmesan, which he set on an armoire. The bird fluttered down from the bust and set about the cheese, tossing it into the air with its beak and taking small bites each time it caught it, and then slurped the milk noisily. It clearly enjoyed making us wait, and from the crafty glances it gave me, enjoyed making me wait most of all.

Eventually the cheese and milk were gone, and it had no further pretext. It returned to its perch on the bust, though, and I noticed that it was taking good care to stay out of my easy reach. "My apologies," it said, "but I have been flying for some days, with only the carrion of battlefields to sustain me."

There was a sleekness to its feathers and a sheen to its cruel beak that told me this had been no hardship and that it had fed well. Also, that it was an accomplished liar. For I had seen its sibs travel in shadow, and if it came the long way, pausing to peck an eyeball here, and a spleen there, it was only because it had wanted to.

This was the Morrigan of which warriors speak, that feeds on those dead in battle, and leads them to their deaths by inspiring forlorn hopes, and doomed charges. I had rarely seen it, and never met it, but I had seen the wake of its passage through wars, just as I had glimpsed its mistress through the smoke of battles and then walked rapidly away through shadow that we not meet casually.

It is no god of war that I would punish, though; it is a beast that acts according to its nature. It feeds on warriors' bodies and its mistress on the devotion of both those warriors who die in her name and those whom she inspires to live and conquer. She is a whore, for whom men die, but she does not kill them. Like others I could name, she keeps carefully within those bounds beyond which my duties lie.

It looked at the others confidentially. "How pleasant to see the Huntress, again," it said, "that nurtured me as a chick and helped destroy my Parent."

"Your Parent," I said sharply, "was the author of its own destruction and needed little help from me. And nurturing you and your sibs was the right thing to do, rather than something for which I would expect thanks."

"That's as may be," Hekkat's bird, or rather Morgan's, said. "You were harsh to my sibs that wanted only to serve you, and will come to you again before the end."

"So they reminded me. When I saw them among the Aesir and again when they rode on the shoulders of Barbarossa and when I saw them in the camp of Gustavus the Vasa. And each time I have said to them, that I wanted none of their help. I have seen what your sibs have done in the way of bad advice to Star and Nameless, whom men call Lucifer and Jehovah, and I want none of it."

"And yet the end has not yet come," the Morrigan said. "The end is not even near, and things change."

"Not my heart," I snapped. "And I have nothing to say to your mistress."

"She has a matter to say to you, nonetheless," said the Morrigan. "And that matter is, she needs a favour, and will do a favour. Quit for quit. She knows of your need, and will do this service, but you will have to rescue her in order to bring her here. And she will never be rescued without your help."

"Some things do not change," I told the creature sternly. "The blood on your mistress' hands and the darkness in her soul. And from what power could she need rescuing? She soiled herself gaining power enough to rival anyone save our great enemy, and your parent; the fact that in all these years even Jehovah and Lucifer have not sought to challenge her speaks for itself. You are not claiming, I trust, that she has finally managed to fall foul of the actual source of the Rituals? That would be ironic, considering her own past."

"Nooo," it admitted, "but she is in the hands of a new dark power in the East that you should be concerned about."

"Why do people always go on about dark powers in the East?" I said. "Does no one ever worry about things to the West of them? The darkest power I ever actually had to deal with was all the way across the Atlantic, but no, it's always to the East. Why not the South, come to that? Plenty that's unpleasant and dangerous goes on in the South. Dahomey, say, but nobody's ever bothered about that except me."

I became aware that I was sounding petulant, shrugged and reined myself in. "Fair enough. It's a dark power and it is in the East. And it has taken Morgan prisoner. Why should I help her, exactly? Given that she is as dark a power in her own way as anyone else."

"Because then she will help you to cure your sister."

"I am supposed to trust her to meddle with my sister's mind?" I said. "With blood and rottenness under those talons she calls nails?"

"Can this woman really be so dreadful?" Georgiana asked, from the sofa where she sat.

"She is a murderess and a seducer of men's hearts."

"And yet you loved her once," she pointed out.

"I never loved her."

"You were her lover then," Chambord said. "For your anger is that of a lover scorned."

"I broke with her," I said. "I stood on the shores of a new and bitter sea, and told her I would not see her ever again."

Georgiana looked at me amusedly. "Oh, my dear girl," she said.

"The ones you leave are always the ones who cut your heart out."

"All that's as may be," Polly broke in impatiently. "Me, I takes help where I can get it. No matter what dealings there's been between us in the past. Or what scores unsettled." She thought a second. "Not that I wouldn't hold a knife handy to the throat of someone I didn't trust. Anything else'd be foolishness, lover or not."

"Any dealing with Hekkat," I said, "or Morgan as she calls herself now, would be foolishness indeed. She has almost as many centuries of practiced treachery to her account as I have."

"Of obstinacy and bluster," said Augusta Wild, or rather Sof speaking calmly through her, in a tone so tense and strained that I knew it was all she could do to keep from screaming again. "Of saying you will not do something, ever more forcibly, right up to the moment you accept that it has to be done."

She looked at me as sternly as I had looked at everyone else. "I need you to do this thing," she said. "Treachery or not, it is my best, my only chance."

She spoke not as one pleading, though there was desperation in her voice, but as one arguing for her very life with one who would condemn her out of love.

Sof who had always been the calmest and most level-headed of us, was crying out like a child lost, feverish and confused, and to see her reduced to this was almost the worst pain of all.

The worst was the thought that if nothing was done, she might be like this forever.

I reached out my hand and stroked her forehead as if I were her mother, not her sister-lover.

And then she relaxed into troubled sleep behind Augusta's eyes.

"Speaking for myself," Augusta spoke, almost as soon as Sof was gone, "I'd welcome your doing this—I love your sister as if she were my own, but she is an unquiet bedmate to have in my skull. Sometimes I come close to screaming myself; if you find your enchantress, she can trim certain things from my memory while she's at it." She looked at me intently, then turned to her kinswoman.

"And I'm with Gibbon and the Huntress on this one. You really don't want to know what was done to poor Sof; that knowledge is a burden I would gladly have taken from me, no matter how wicked the person that does it."

And what I had thought my unalterable resolve and my considered judgement crumbled in a moment. I turned to the bird. "Will this take long? I have an appointment in Paris in a few weeks' time, to save a radical from their infernal machine. And I would prefer to keep my pledged word to one who did me a great favour."

"I'm sure," the Morrigan said, "that you'll resolve my mistress' difficulties in a few days. If we set out this night and do not dally."

"That is a thing easily said," I answered, "but the ease of its accomplishment is another matter. Something that could hinder your mistress is a matter of weight and danger. Tell me more."

"That I cannot." The bird preened as it spoke, picking some louse or graveworm from among its feathers, yet with all of its attention fixed on me with its knowing raptor eyes.

"A geas that prevents you?"

"No, mere ignorance," it replied. "What I have told you—her danger, her request, her offer—these are all I know because I have not been with her these last three years or more. Yet we have our understandings, and our ways and means of passing messages when in sorry case."

It hopped on to one leg and showed a talon on the other that was gouged and burned as if by acid.

"I had my troubles once," it said. "Pinioned to be eaten slowly by a plant in the Southern forests that staggered from place to place planting its roots and uprooting them again and stinging beasts to death as it went and crouching over their remains while they rotted and it digested them. And I called a passing bat to me with my harsh song, and it avoided the sting, and took a small feather from my side, and went to her, as bats will, through shadow. And she arrived with despatch, and blasted the creature, and all its kind, that it trouble none further."

"And her ways of calling you?"

"She has a mirror in one of the rings on her left hand," it said. "A shabby little ring of tarnished silver and agates, but it has a compartment with a small fragment of glass on which she can write words in her blood. And however far apart we are, I see those words pass before my left eye, where she scratched it once with the glass for just this purpose. She has talked to me across the years. And I know of you and what you mean to her. And she sent me these few words. Mara, she said, and sister, and forget and deal and save and then— she was weakening at this point and her writing was less clear—two names. One name you will know, and that name was 'Alamut.' The other I had never heard uttered before, and it was 'Agharta'."

"Alamut I know," I agreed, "and I was there at its end."

"Alamut?" Gibbon repeated. "The castle of the Assassins."

"The order of military mystics," I said, "whose enemies gave them that name to imply that their courage and their passion came from a pipe or a sweetmeat. They were pious men whose powers came from contemplation and devotion. Not that that made any difference to those they disembowelled with jewelled steel knives in the marketplaces of Acre or Damascus."

"Agharta means nothing to me," said the dead scholar.

"Nor to me. Clearly something has been happening that has escaped my attention."

"It's a rumour," Chambord interrupted. "Something that the sadhus of Hindustan whisper of, that a fortune-teller told me of in Pondicherry, saying that I would go there and perhaps meet my end. And I scoffed, because the next day I was to take ship back to France, with a letter of commission for my own small command in the narrow seas of La Manche, and with war with the English could be certain I would never return there."

"We all 'as our appointment in Samarra," Polly said. "So what did these rumours say, captain?"

"That an old man was gathering mystics to him. In a place which no maps show, and no legends speak except his call to join him.

Some said he plans conquest and some that he seeks transcendence, and some that he wishes the Franks to return to their homelands and trouble the world no more. Some said he was a Hindoo, and some a Mohammedan, and some that he worshipped none save himself."

I grimaced and sucked at my teeth as if there was something caught there that troubled me. "I thought he was dead, bone and ashes in the ruins of his home. I thought I saw his corpse, with the eyes and nose and lips self-cut from his face in the frenzy of his asceticisms and rituals. Clearly I was mistaken, and there is work half-done that I must do again. I shall try to return to Paris and rescue the man Paine, but if I do not return in time, someone else will have to ensure it."

"That I will," Polly said, "since you must travel fast and hard and I would be a burden to you, and my kinswoman here little more."

"I would love to see the East," said Gibbon sadly, "but my condition has its necessities. I am bound to my library and desk, with a leash that lets me come to this room, but no further."

"It is clearly my destiny," Chambord said, "to go to this place and face my death. I owe you a life, Huntress, both because you saved me, and because I put you to inconvenience. If I may, I will come with you."

"I will be glad of your company," I said, lying a little because I am the Huntress and I hunt alone, yet sometimes I break my own rules. And I do not argue with men's destinies when they become obvious.

"So, your Grace," Polly told Georgiana, "you'll accompany us back to London then."

The Duchess shook her head. "Alas, I am a dutiful wife and my husband the Duke has explicitly forbidden me to appear at court or in Almack's until the autumn. He assumed that I would stay in exile in the country and so did not order me to. I will not disobey his actual commands, but I detest the rural life."

"And so?" I asked.

"If you'll have me, I will accompany you into desperate danger

182

and the wilds of Asia. And stand at your side while you encounter this woman who bothers you still, and whom I die of yearning to meet."

"We may not return."

"And where would be the fun of an adventure of which that was not true?" She smiled. "I am a woman of a certain age, and my sinews grow slack from disuse but from time too. I have one last great game in me, and then it will be the tea-pot and the port decanter and a life of slow decline, with the card table and the chivvying of great men into common sense my only real diversions. I will come with you. If you will have me."

There was a sad eagerness in her which made me agree against my better judgement; I had seen her in desperate action, and there was truth in what she said. The company of mortals saddens me thus so often, because I see their sorrow at the losses of time, losses I do not share, save through sympathy.

"I can think of few I would rather have at my back," I said, and this was true as it had hardly been in eighteen hundred years. Since young Josh, and his accursed brother. Voltaire had been a good fellow to spend an evening of danger with, and a clever man to understand; and there was Polly of course, to whom I had not lied and whose courage I loved. Chambord was an unknown quantity, but Georgiana had won my heart as a sister of the sword.

I did not lust for her, I swear, and do not feel the words turn in my mouth. Sof had never been a fighter in any of her lives, and I had never seen Lillit once since her death. This noblewoman at the brink of middle age—she was one to whom I felt a pull that made me think, even in the company of Sof's maddened spirit, of how things were when we were young in the youth of the world. Beauty, wit and swordplay—there have been few such in all my ages.

I thought on this wistfully for a moment and then considered how we might go East a while and then South a while from this place to the first of the places where we needed to be. In this civilized age, I could not rely on some chance encounter with monsters and transgressors to blood Georgiana and Chambord to an extent that would give them the power to walk in shadow, nor did I want to teach them its ways lightly. I had done that before, when the world was young, and the world still lives with the consequences of my teaching.

Of course I could simply have pulled them with me into shadow, and borne their weight and resistance, but I am reluctant to do that for so many miles. Again it is something that has had consequences in the past.

The Morrigan caught my hesitation. It winked a dark eye at me and jumped up into the air, emitting not its usual caw but a loud whistle that echoed around the room and shattered two of the crystals on Gibbon's elegant little chandelier.

"I didn't know that you would wish to take company along," it said, "but I made arrangements with my poor scorned sibs, who are prepared to do you favours to show you kindness, even if you show them none. Without any favours expected in return, might I add?"

And whistled again.

In the distance I heard a whinnying and a thunder of hooves. At first the others did not react, but then I saw their faces catch alight with excitement. There are creatures that are not only themselves, but the Idea of the creature they are—that pompous oaf Plato got some things right even without having experienced them—and when you find yourselves in the presence of such, it is only human to bask in the pleasure of the moment.

All of us, save Gibbon, who could not pass his own front door, crowded out into the garden where a grey horse was grazing the lawn ferociously. Another, larger horse was scratching its soot-black neck against the small summer house with a vigour that threatened to demolish it.

The grey was all lithe elegance and supple power and you had to look at it a second time, cricking your neck slightly, before you saw its form blur slightly before your eyes and realized that it had eight legs. The black was a more normal looking sort of horse, except that after a little you realized that the smell of burned hair and charred wood came from it and not from some terrible accident nearby.

"I suggest, Captain," the Morrigan said, "that you take the All-Father's horse and that her Grace takes the steed of the Valkyrie."

I had seen both horses before, I realized—Sleipnir I knew at a glance from many battlefields, but when I had seen its foal before, it was a dapple roan.

The Morrigan caught my reaction. "She rode through the flames of the Volsung's pyre with her mistress," it said, "but where Brunnhilde chose to burn with her dead love, and become ash and legend, the horse chose to burn away its mortal part and ride with its dam."

Chambord walked over and bent to Sleipnir's ear; the horse bared its great yellow teeth and fixed him with a wild-eyed glare.

"One master of might; until world's burning.

Others endure and bear; none my lord.

No wily whisper-tricks; Loki's teaching," it whinnied.

"My apologies, Madame," Chambord bowed his head a little further, in genteel penitence. "I meant no harm."

"Harm is of evil heart,

None in mere kindness."

Georgiana, meanwhile, had pulled some dusty lumps of sugar from one of her pockets and was feeding them to the other horse, while stroking the single pale streak that ran down its forehead. She turned to me. "And you will run alongside, when this horse could carry us both?"

I smiled and said nothing.

"Hardy the huntress walking in shadow

lone and loveless shielded from friend."

"You won't get wherever you're going by lollygagging around." Polly came back out of the house with a small bundle, which she passed to Chambord. "A couple of spare shirts for you, m'dear."

The servants came out with a small basket. One of them had fashioned a crude sling from a leather belt and a piece of gaudy red brocade and passed it to Georgiana to secure those weapons that were not at her belt.

"Some cheeses," the housekeeper said, "and some pumpernickel bread that will keep well."

Chambord bowed to his horse. "Madame. I am unaccustomed to riding bareback, and we have food and weapons to carry. Yet you are the steed of a god, and unaccustomed –"

Sleipnir snorted derision at him.

"Broken the battleline smashed all Rome's legions
Goths rode with gear. Great was their victory.
Free foamed the horse's mouths blood on their hooves."

"She refers," Gibbon said from the threshold, "to the great victory of Adrianople, where Odin-worshipping Goths brought the stirrup to Southern Europe."

Chambord still looked blank.

"She means, dear," Polly told him kindly, "that she will allow you a saddle, but no reins."

"After all," I said, "she knows where we are going, and you do not."

"Seawards and southwards, river and saltspray
Mikklegarth the mighty fallen and risen
Fortress in Wilderness strong in its pride
Fallen the fortress; cast down its gardens."

"Yes," I said. "That's right. Alamut it is."

The Morrigan took to the air and darted to the South and East. "Last one to the Bosphorus is a salted herring," it cawed back at us.

But unlike the bird, we had farewells to make.

Chambord bowed deeply to Polly. "I go, perhaps to my death," he said. "I would not wish to leave without saying farewell."

"That's all right, dear. We are people of business, and sometimes we come to a parting of ways."

"I took you prisoner once, and then we shared a cell—but my heart will always be your captive."

"That's poetry, and like such, it belongs in a poem, and not on the

186

lips of serious people, but…" she flung her arms about him and gave him a hearty kiss on the lips, "…there's few as have pleased me since my Mackie, and he is dead some three score years. So take that as praise, my Froggie captain, and take yourself off to your fate. Who knows if we shall meet again, but if we do, and not across the battle lines between your country and mine, we shall talk, I make you that promise."

He bowed to her again, turned and busied himself with his horse. I meanwhile had made my farewells to Sof.

"Sister," I said. "We shall perhaps never meet again."

"I know that, beloved sister, but who can say what time and chance will bring? I understand them better than most, and I know not."

There was a catch in my throat. "And if I see you, I may not know you, and you will not know me. I thought I met you once, in Mexico, and it almost broke my heart to think you might have your reasons for denying me."

"That was not me," she said. She met my eyes and I looked deep into her and saw no deceit or uncertainty, then or ever. Yet I was still confused, for Malinche had been like her in so many ways.

"I am glad of it, for she was fiercer than I like you to be."

"Will you not return with the enchantress?" she said.

"Oh, my dear, I know what must be done. I see that it must be done. But I do not wish to see it done." For once in so many years, I knew what it was to feel fear. "I promise you," I added, "that it is not for fear of spending time in her company, but I would be distraught and my pain would make your pain worse."

Through her pain and distraction, Sof smiled at me. "I understand. I could not bear to watch you lose yourself, and my troubles have caused you so much pain already."

We took each other in a grasp that lingered and I felt her tears hot against my cheek, or maybe they were mine, or both mingled and I care not.

Then she sighed and shuddered, and screamed three times, and

187

then was gone away behind Augusta Wild's eyes. And I knew I would not see her again in this age, and I could not bear what had to be done and so must stay away lest I try to stop it.

I passed her kinswoman to Polly to care for. "Miss Wild, I would appreciate it were you to wait here until the 25th. I hope that we may transact our business in a few days, and it would be awkward to bring Hekkat to London to work her magic and find you and Augusta somewhere with a broken axle on a German road. I am sure that your realm can spare you a few more days, especially since I will do work in Paris that serves your turn."

"Freeing the traitor Paine?"

"That," I agreed, "but also bringing Saint-Just and Robespierre to utter destruction."

I walked over to where Gibbon stood dithering on a doorstep. "My thanks for your help, sir ghost. I wish that there were something I could do for you, or tell you."

"I have explained why not," he said, "but perhaps there is one thing. Something not relevant to my book but which I would wish to know." He looked at me. "The Camelopard. That the emperor Commodus had slain in the arena. What manner of beast is it?"

I have no special gift for description; I have known artists who could sketch a creature so that you can see it better than in the flesh, but I am not one of them. I have killed more creatures than you can imagine that I cannot put before your eyes with my words.

"It is a gangly harmless creature, long-necked and fragile-legged, and covered in spots. It is not like a camel or a leopard, yet one struggling to describe it might refer to them. They graze on the high leaves of trees that cluster in stands in the high dry grass and at night they whimper love to their mates and twine long necks around each other."

"Why would an emperor kill so harmless a creature? What sport in that?"

"He wanted to be loved, and the mob liked novelty. And he wanted to make love to everything that there is under the sun, and the creature frustrated his will by kicking the ladder away."

188

"He was one of the worst of them," Gibbon said.

"I have always thought so," I answered and bowed to him.

Polly called to him from the door of his house. "Since I am stuck here for days among your dusty manuscripts, Mr Gibbon, I may as well have you take me through the accounts from your time doing my work here in Lausanne. I do hate to be idle."

Georgiana had found one of the blankets from the wagon; she slung it across her horse's back and swung herself up to another battle-maiden's place as if she had been born to sit there. Chambord saddled Sleipnir and mounted about as elegantly as one would expect of a sea captain, which is to say with some efficiency and no grace whatever.

The horses set a fierce pace that I found bliss in outdoing. Through the mountains I ran and they rode, on and on, as if peaks and torrents were mere pebbles and spray beneath our feet; then on through the great forests of the Germanies and occasionally rattled on the cobbled streets of night-time towns. And on into the debatable lands ravaged by the wars of Magyar and Slav and Turk, where the sky was lit up not by a dawn that was yet far off, but by the red sullen light of burning haylofts and villages.

Chambord rode with gritted teeth and mild desperation in his eyes, Georgiana laughing and throwing her loose hair back. Whatever came of this, I was glad to see her joy.

In due course we came to the Great City as the dawn rose, the city that was Byzantium once, and is Istanbul now, but was always for me the city where one of the most evil of men, the tyrant Justinian, built the most beautiful of buildings, and dedicated it, all unknowing, to my poor sister.

I let the others go on ahead, for I wished this moment to myself. And I went and stood outside it and looked up at its great dome. Church it had been, and mosque was now—but it was a place of peace. I do not pray, for to whom would I pray? But I sent out entreating thoughts to the only man to whom I would have prayed.

"Josh," I said, "if you have any power, and are out there still in the world, think of Sof, whom you once loved, and her great need."

And then I was done and ran on my way past the old walls and out into the fields and on and on beside the shores of a sea that I had seen made, that lapped over lost lands that I had walked, and I thought of how things change and pass. We were going to a ruin that I had seen new-built, and betrayed, and at its height of power, and in its decadence and at its fall. And somewhere its Master, whom I had thought centuries dead, lived still and had to be dealt with.

Things fall and change and yet nothing is ever done with.

And with these thoughts in my mind I came up again to the two horses and their riders and the great battle-crow that flew alongside them, and my mood lifted again to see them.

We travelled up into the hills and beyond into the mountains and more debatable lands between Christian and Turk, and then the lands debatable between Turk and Persian, that hated each other as much as the Christian infidel over blood spilled a thousand years and more before and had become the difference between sects and cultures and nations.

We had left the sea that is called Black behind us as its shore swung North, and for a while we were landlocked. The mountains grew needlepointed and razor-sharp and yet the valleys between them were green with new growth and bright flowers.

It was a fierce late spring up here and there were scents in the cold air, scents of flowers whose names I had forgotten and never known. And the husky scent of wild poppy that I knew would be with us all the way East. If that was where our path lay.

We came to the scent of distant salt spray again—far below the feet of the mountains among whose highest ridges we rode was the sea that men call the Caspian in the west and Gilan of old and Mazandaran in Persia. A few centuries before, some had called it the Khazar sea, but few now remembered that hardy people who had vanished among the nations.

Quite suddenly, towering over a plateau full of fields run wild and ruins little more than heaps of stone, we came to the mountain called Alamut and the ruined fortress that had been the Eagle's Nest of the Assassins, a place of contemplation and training and scholarship that sent men out to kill.

The horses and the bird and I came out of shadow and stepped and flew respectfully up a causeway that would once have been viewed by a thousand watchful eyes, where to walk without permission would have been to be hedge-hog pierced by a hundred arrows and lances. Sometimes you walk in dead places with a caution that respects the places that they once were, just as you bow your heads in ruined temples to gods you never liked. Out of respect, not for the gods, but for change and loss and mutability.

Georgiana sat up straight on Gram. "How did a fortress like this fall? Could men starve it out?"

"In the end," I said, "all fortresses fall. But no-one could starve this one out. It had great granaries and cisterns—and the grain of all the valley below and many farms nearby. It had fighting men and scholars and wizards and women of fortitude and power. It had its founder to guard it secretly from shadow. And yet it fell as all fortresses fall in the end." I paused. "Its stones and its garrison and its guardian were all true, but its commander proved false. The last lord of the assassins was a coward, you see, who thought to buy his life from Hulagu Khan, even if the price was the lives of all who followed him. And his name is one I choose to forget, in token of his shame."

I remembered watching as he stepped out of Alamut's great gate and walked, head bowed, down the courtyard to the carpet spread before the Khan, the carpet which was to be the instrument of his death.

"Somehow, I know not how, he had tricked his ancestor, Hassan, the man for whom we seek, into that slumber which sometimes overwhelms the young and newly immortal. And he had Hulagu swear that his blood would not be shed. And he took with him all the keys of the fortress, and Hassan woke and called down to him

191

from the tower above the gate that he was a fool as well as a coward. And Hassan took a knife into his immortal hand and carved first the beard and then the skin and last the features from his face in rage, or as an attempt at some great working, and his heir ignored him and walked on, bearing with him the keys of the citadel. He handed them to the Khan and with them the lives of all who would die that day, and his own among them."

"Cursed be all cowards self curse among themselves
Traitors betrayed Justice of lords."

Sleipnir was obviously much taken with the story because she spoke almost clearly.

"Hulagu was careful of his words, like many tyrants who wish to feel good about themselves, and he did not shed the blood of the coward lord of Alamut, because he would not be foresworn and in the company of the traitor. And blood shed against his word would be a curse upon him and a curse upon the tribe. So he had two strong men throw the man down onto the carpet and hold him prone while they rolled the carpet over him and over him."

It had been a carpet of Samarkand, a city which had fought the Khans and died for it, but died bravely.

"I cannot bring myself to hope that he died of suffocation before they rode their horses over him until he was pulp of blood and bone that yet did not seep out onto the ground. The men and woman of Samarkand wove carpets that took much hard wear."

And the folk of Alamut died as all died who stood against the Mongol. I had thought that none walked away from that day but clearly I had been wrong.

"Hassan was a clever one," I said. "He had survived his own death once and must have done so a second time. Though he seemed like a man who had undergone the real death, the death that comes to gods and demigods, often at my hands."

"Was not the first of all captains of assassins," Georgiana said, "someone who should have come to your attention long before?"

"I take no sides in human wars—or almost none."

"War?" she said.

"Some send out armies to kill other armies. Hassan sent men to kill men. Some might call it murder, but for him it was just another way of waging war."

"He shed blood, and now he lives when he should be dead. Are not such men, Huntress, those whom you hunt?" said Chambord.

"Blood was shed in his name, and he died and rose as a god of sorts, and there was magic in the making of his new state, but no conscious use of the Rituals. So I let him live. For all the good it did him."

They looked puzzled.

"This was a godly man who had had men killed that he and his might worship god as they chose, and all in the belief that there was no god, but god. Imagine what it feels like to be so godly a man as that, and then awaken to your own godhood. And learn that the god you killed for was only just such a one as yourself."

I had first met Hassan I-Sabbah a few years after he rose from what should have been death, and the marks of despair and desperation were still on his face. I say met, but when I approached him, as to console one who had become my brother in deathlessness, and to ascertain that he was not likely to cause problems, he shuddered and tried to drive me away with curses.

Some might take exception to such insolence, but I ascertained his guiltlessness and let him live, not thinking that he would become a problem to me some centuries later.

My mercy always has its costs and the best of those are ones I pay in my own blood and time and not that of others. Yet, were I merciless, I would be unfit for my work. I have seen too many beings who confused harshness with justice, and I choose not to be one of them.

"He lived in seclusion for a score of years," I said, "talking only to those he sent out to kill, and to the scribes who took down his thoughts in theology, and to his wives when he wished meat to be placed on the spit for him."

His life after death was more of the same, except that he thought it wrong to compel women to lie with a dead man and told them that death had divorced them. And he had no further need of meat. They left his house, wailing but not in mourning as the bystanders considered. He was a man of blood, but he was loved by some.

He lived among the descendants of his people, and they knew him not, for all that many of them talked of him among themselves as one risen, hidden and teaching, although he walked among them, and taught them constantly. Alive, he had killed one of his sons for being tipsy and another for disobedience; ascended, he did no more than reason with his folk, and did so not from authority, but from logic, when for a while they thought his half-felt presence meant that they had no further of the Law.

"I liked the man," I said. "He was modest and ascetic. For a god." As I talked, I cast my eyes around the ruined fortress, hoping for some sign of where he had taken refuge. "He was someone I might have hoped would eventually join me in my work, but he was one of those men who take no account of anything a woman does and this seemed to me, after four decades or so, something he was unlikely to grow out of."

Sleipnir yawned—the trouble with magic horses is that they have the intelligence to become bored—and then tapped the ground with one of her mundane hooves, and then one of those that was mainly in shadow.

"Graven in granite under great fortresses
Room in the rock. Retreat from followers
Seek it in shadow, sealed from the world."

Gram had not spoken up to that point; I had considered her mute, though as intelligent as her dam, but she now proved that she was merely a horse of few words.

"She can see through things," Gram's neigh was huskier than Sleipnir's as if the smoke of Brunnhilde's pyre were still within her. "It is one of the things she does."

There is a trick which I have heard of, though had never had need to try myself, by which you take yourself through shadow into the heart of a rock, and you carve yourself a space there. It is a work of much labour because unless you chance upon a flaw or cavity on a first attempt, you have no room to work your tool in, and little time before you need to take breath; it is a work of great patience and therefore of great need to hide something. But it gives you certainty that no mortal and few immortals can come upon that which you hid.

I sank into the ground at the point Odin's horse had indicated, and some twelve feet into the rock I found a cavity just large enough for a roll of parchment and for a ring with a stone in it, a stone faceted with one edge that was sharp to the touch. I flicked at the stone with a fingernail, and it lifted to show a small cavity inside its setting, in which there was a single hair.

I brought both back with me.

"It is my mistress' ring," the bird said, needlessly. "My cut eye pains me just to look on it again."

I unrolled the scroll, and read it aloud. It was an admirable piece of calligraphy, almost too beautiful to convey anything as vulgar as information—I would have expected a poem, but instead it simply said "Alamut has fallen; Alamut is reborn. Take the road East to the Valley of the Idols, and then north-east into the high hills. I wait for those who wish to rest, in the land that was the Hellene's once, and the Scythian's once, but is now part of the kingdom of peace."

Chambord screwed up his eyes, as one trying to see if there were something obvious that he had missed. "A trap, surely."

"A trap, yes," agreed the Duchess with a grin, "but not for us in particular. Presumably it is a call to anyone capable of coming this way and delving down to it—the mighty of this world, which, my captain, does not include you or I, but would certainly include the Huntress here."

"I have been trapped few times in my years, one of those recently. I do not plan to be trapped again this millennium, but I will go visit my old acquaintances. If Hassan has found some way to hold Hekkat against her will, I will ask him to release her and then he too will be owed a favour."

195

"And if he does not wish to release her?"

"That is not likely." I spoke with a certainty I did not entirely feel. "Hassan was a wise man and then a wiser immortal; it is to be hoped that he has not grown into foolishness with the years. But if he has, that is a problem to be dealt with when it occurs."

"I do not know those lands," Chambord asked, "but how will we find the precise spot of his new home? Will we have to ask shepherds and goatherds for direction like gawkers? Letting him know of our coming days in advance as those we ask pass word?"

"For that," I gestured with the scroll, the ring and the lock of hair, "Hekkat has provided."

"My mistress is called Morgan, in this age, and for several ages past," her bird cawed as if offended.

"As you wish," I shrugged.

I caught myself wondering whether her nature had changed along with her name, and then mocked the moment of weakness that would change a decision I had made once and irrevocably.

And we had no time for me to think or discuss further because I started to run, with the Morrigan flapping above me, and the others took horse and soon caught up with me.

We left Alamut and its tragic emptiness behind us, and raced East for hours towards Bamiyan and its great statues. Which stood as I had last seen them, only weathered by time's slow chiselling. Statues part-Greek and part-Asian, and not at all resembling the Gautama I once knew, and fought against. I stopped at their feet and the others clustered around me.

I pulled Morgan's ring and the lock of her hair from the wallet at my belt.

"Ah, I see." Chambord spoke as one intrigued to see a trick done and thinking that he knew the technique. "You use the hair to dangle the ring and it serves as a pendulum which you use to dowse your friend's location. It is an application of animal magnetism and not really magic at all."

I smiled at him as one would a precocious child. "You might term this particular magic a use of animal magnetism, if you chose," I said, "but in all important other respects you are quite wrong."

With my right hand, I held the lock of hair downwards and stroked it with my left so that of a sudden it became rigid. I tossed the ring into the air and caught it in mid-flight with the hair—then let both of them go. Both floated a second and then pointed, almost due East and towards the distant high mountains, and began to move in the direction it pointed.

"That is our path," I said. "Bird, if you would be so kind?"

And the Morrigan seized the ring in one of its talons and did not try to resist the tugging of the hair.

We sped along old roads between straggly fields, through plains and across slow half-dry rivers. Everywhere we went, the air was heavy with the scent of poppies, some running wild and straggly and others cultivated, but as the grain of a field or the vines of a vineyard, not as the flowers of a garden.

"I had forgotten the smell of these lands," I said.

Up into the hills we went, and then the ring and the hair ceased to tug, and the hair went limp and floated free. The Morrigan dived for it, and took it in his beak.

Before the ring could hit the ground, I was there, to catch it. I placed it on the smallest finger of my right hand for want of a better place to bear it.

Below us lay a valley greener than most we had crossed or passed through, save where is was deep red, almost purple, with a mass of poppy. There were buildings here—no fortress though a couple of the larger villas or storerooms looked as if they could be defended in a pinch against a small force; they were white with a marble that was not quarried in these lands, and, though in repair so good that they might have been built yesterday, were in the style of the Greeks who had ruled here two thousand years earlier.

The place stank of magic, though not of the sort I concern myself with, and the air was full of the drone of bees, a drone that had been on the edge of our hearing for some miles, I realized, and which grew louder as a swarm of the things came together and rose up out of the valley in a cloud to confront us where we had paused on the road. Black and some six feet across with all the crowding lives it contained, it formed itself into the skull-like face I had seen on what I had taken to be Hassan's corpse, and its lips moved.

"Huntress," it spoke. "And Morgan's bird. And the horses of the impostor who calls himself the All-Father. Blaspheming in his folly. And two companions, whom I know not, but are clearly Franks of the West. I will not say you are welcome, but you may pass into this valley in safety and leave freely, when you choose."

I was disinclined to trust Hassan, but saw no reason why he would try to detain us, so took his word, for the moment.

"Greetings, Hassan-i-Sabbah," I said, "Master of Assassins and Lord of Alamut."

"These days," the cloud said in a harsh voice made of the noise of a thousand buzzing insects, and that terrible lipless, nose-less face formed itself into a parody of humility, "I rule none save my bees. And this land, my Agharta, is hardly an eagle's nest."

"All lairs are eagle's nests, if those who sit there have power. And you have power and to spare, more than you had before, if I am not mistaken."

"You flatter me, Huntress. Like you, I have a little power, and cultivate it well. And use it for a greater good and few purposes of my own. But come, take coffee with me, or wine if the heathen prefer it. And let your horses graze—I would not punish them for their master and you have come a long way, and that, if I am not mistaken, in a day and a night and a part of a day."

I had not thought that a face made of bees could incline itself in a bow, yet Hassan's changed its angle in what resembled a bow close enough to be taken for one. I noted the degree of control over his winged servants that this implied—noted and thought on. Aloud I said only, with a slight bow of my own head, "No journey is too long or too wearisome that brings me to the elegant home of a man of great virtue and wisdom."

"If such were here," he bowed even more profusely, "you would be welcome to it. As it is, you are welcome to my poor abode and my unsatisfactory person. Many of the mighty have deigned to rest here from the labour of their lives, and perhaps you will find interesting companions among them."

The man I remembered was not my idea of a friendly tavern keeper or a genial host, but people change when they become immortal.

Georgiana had dismounted while Hassan and I were speaking and had stood for all of a minute with her head bowed demurely and respectfully. But longer than that was not in her. "Goddamn," she said, "I thought it a convention and a fiction, but the pair of you duel with humility like characters in oriental tales."

"And the English," Hassan said, "even their women, are as punishably profane as rumour tells."

"Just so." Chambord dismounted from his horse in turn, and bowed to the face. "Yet I have found them the most delightful of enemies."

"You are a Frank," said Hassan. "Alas, your charm and flattery are lost on me. I knew your countrymen in centuries past, and found them smooth-tongued betrayers."

"For that I am truly sorry. Yet, I am a sea captain and a man of my word."

"That remains to be seen. And punished if it prove otherwise."

"You mentioned grazing for our horses," I said, wanting to move on from men bristling at each other. "I would be grateful, and so would they."

"Pleasure of pasture when journey is past
Green on the tongue great solace is
Happy the host who harbours the thankful –"

Gram stamped a hoof and whickered impatiently, "If you weren't following my mother, she means many thanks for the grass."

Hassan inclined his bee head to the horses. "I had forgot that the horses of the All-Father were rational beasts. I have known such in Arabia."

And of a sudden, the eyes of that lidless face closed, and the face wavered and dissolved. Many of the bees swarmed back down into the valley, though many stayed with us, as our companions, or our watchers, or perhaps something more menacing.

The horses tossed their heads in respect, then galloped down into the valley, where after some few minutes they made free with the grazing they had been offered.

And so it was that we descended into the vale of Agharta on foot with the noise of bees loud in our ears. Not captives, but not, I feared, entirely guests.

I thought of Hekkat, and the name she called herself now, and wondered what the ages had made of her. I also thought about the fact that Hassan had not asked why we were here.

After a half hour's stroll past the poppy-fields and some plots that grew other flowers and some that grew more mundane crops of squashes and pea-vines, we came among the villas and temples of what was now Agharta, but had once been, if I took its history right, the country estate of some Greekling lord in the centuries after Alexander had rushed through this land and so many others like a fever of the blood that rages, and then is gone.

Someone had preserved them down the years, and must have done so for a millennium before Hassan was even born, let alone come to this place from fallen Alamut. I wondered where that man or woman was now.

A small table with chairs in the European style had been set out at the foot of the steps up to one of the more elaborate buildings, and on it sat four cups and a small bowl of blood for the bird. Above the centre of the table a small flame burned of its own accord, and above that there hovered a large open pot from which the noise and aroma of fresh coffee emerged.

And at the head of the table there sat, wise-bearded and with his features intact, the Hassan that I remembered from before those last desperate moments at Alamut, in his own flesh and not that of bees.

"Take coffee with me," he said, "and be welcome to my house."

I was surprised and glad to see his features restored, though intrigued that, when he controlled the bees, his memories of pain and mutilation still imposed those ravaged features on his eidolon.

It is, of course, often thus, I thought to myself, and had a moment of smugness that I, at least, do not change.

"Our thanks," I said, and my companions made murmuring noises of agreement. "So, what do you do in this rural retreat?"

"I offer repose and withdrawal from the world to those who ask for it, and I take care of some small matters of family business."

"I had thought that there were no members of even your most distant kin," I said, "that survived the sack of Alamut."

His almost unblinking gaze twinkled a moment and then became stony. I realized at that moment that his lips did not move into a smile, and did not do so when he spoke. "Just so," he said, "as you say." There was an air of finality to this which at once demanded further questions, and brooked none.

Georgiana sipped her coffee. "It is devilish sweet," she remarked. "I prefer mine without sweetness."

"It is the custom of the Turks," Chambord said, "and doubtless their Arab subjects too, to brew their coffee with sugar in the pot."

"Merely a little honey from my hives," Hassan said, and his lips definitely did not move at all. I wondered whether the others had noticed this.

Georgiana took another sip—I had not tasted the brew yet, because it was still hotter than I like it. Suddenly she spat it back into her cup, and hurled the entire cup into Hassan's face.

"And that for trying to poison us," she snapped. "I tasted opium when I was young in France and I saw men sicken from it."

I put my cup down untasted, and Chambord did the same.

"I think you owe us an explanation," I said. "Or is this that same repose that you offer your guests?"

Where the boiling coffee had hit Hassan's cheek, it spread like a stain, a moment and then it became clear his face was melting and dripping away and taking with it the hairs of his beard and moustache. Beneath, with only those staring eyes looking alive, lay the red ruin he had carved his face into so many years before, with glints of bone and teeth white under the bloody pulp.

And from the doors at the top of the stairs a great cloud of his bees came forth, buzzing in anger as loud as grindstones on a battalion's swords. I looked into shadow, and the bees were there as well.

"Stay your hand, your Grace,"—for her hand was on the hilt of her already half-drawn sword—"you have made your point."

And then I turned to Hassan, around whom most of the bees were hovering, a cloud that was also a veil for his ravaged features, a veil that picked away the melted wax from the ruin of his face as we watched. An entire detachment of the creatures hovered a foot or so away, some darting in to retrieve the hairs of his beard, brows and lashes one at a time, others holding them, and others reattaching them.

"I thought you were our host and we your guests." I spoke in hurt tones. "What host is it that doses his guests unaware with the juice of the poppy?"

"One who knows that his guests have feigned friendship and come to take from him that which is his."

"We come for nothing that is yours," I said. "We come for her once known as Hekkat and now known as Morgan, who is her own, but of whom I have dire need."

"I too have need of her."

"I would not stand in my way, were I you," I said. "This is a personal matter. I have asked for little from the world in the years that I have guarded it, and this is something that the world, and those who live in it, owe me. Not for myself, but for another who has been much wronged."

"You are too proud for a woman," he said. "I have man's business to do."

"I am Mara, the Huntress. And no man, and no god, will stand in my way."

By now, the bees around his face had finished removing the features that Georgiana had wrecked. We watched in fascinated repulsion as, a filament of wax at a time, they wove him a new one. The worst of it was that he paid them no heed and went on talking all the while, as they reapplied each strand of his beard, each hair on his head.

They even replaced the small hairs of his brow and ravaged lashes. I admired the concentration with which he could control the finest detail of their work on his face while still glaring fixedly into my eyes in an attempt, if not to break my will or my gaze, at least to demonstrate his determination to me. I admired—but I was not about to yield to him, and it is a sad truth that a mere six centuries or so do not hone the will so much as six millennia. He put up a good show, but it was never in doubt which of us would lower their eyes first.

"What can you need the witch for, as important as my need?" he asked. "Have you come to take her back as your partner in unnatural lust? Or is there some actual serious purpose?"

"I will not take her back, and I have a serious purpose, which is my concern and not yours. It is a family matter." Then I added, for the form of the thing, "And though I would never take her back, there is nothing unnatural about any such lust."

"Family matters," he scoffed. "Women's concerns are always with such trivial matters. I too have family concerns to consider, but statecraft and the destruction of the mighty too. They killed my family—my descendants in the fourth generation and their sons— and they left my realm in ruins, and I will have my vengeance."

Chambord looked at him as if at a madman. "The armies that crushed your Assassins, and burned your Alamut, are centuries in the dust. Nothing is left of the Mongol realm but a few tents and herdsmen in a wilderness of grass."

Hassan returned his look scornfully. "And who do you think brought that about, Frank? I was not at the Bitter Springs and the Mongol realms of the West split and split again with only the occasional bit of help from me—but the prize was the Silk Realm, and the empire that Kublai built there. And that I brought to naught—his campaigns in the lands of the Viet and the Lao I chipped away at with

203

poison and plague, and his voyages to Nihon I brought down storms against. He died a disappointed man, and his realm crumbled round him. The Han speak not of him and his memory would be lost in the West were it not for that Venetian and his book. His empire lasted a mere century, and then the Ming came, and then the Manchu. And I was there at every turn, I and my bees."

He stared at us with eyes that were boastful and full of a fire that was beyond madness.

"Timur was a Turk, but he was the spiritual heir of the cursed Genghis, and I brought his conquests to nothing and his kin to ruin. And the khanates of Tartary, one after another—I caused them to war on each other, and then I raised up Ivan whom men called the Terrible, and he smashed Kazan with his great guns and those children of Genghis were brought to utter ruin."

He grew despondent a second. "Yet his cursed seed lives still, like some weed in a garden that you rip up and cast into the fire and yet grows back from a fragment of root, small pallid things that, if you leave a day or a week or a decade, will smother everything all over again."

He was almost ignoring us by now, rehearsing the story as he had told it a hundred times in self-recrimination.

"How was I to know? He was a boy king, Genghis' heir, yes and Timur's too. And all I had to do was bribe a few men, and kill a few more, and he and a few friends were driven from Samarkand and out into the wastes. It pleased me to think him there a lone starveling wanderer and I did not make certain—I thought he was one of the last, and I wanted to savour his slow lingering death. So I went North to Tartary, where there were always khanlings to kill and I forgot him save as a pleasant after-taste… His name was Babur, and I am still, centuries later, undoing the consequences of five years' inattention. For when I turned around, there he was, Babur the Tiger, the seed of Genghis grown again, seated on the Peacock Throne in the city of Delhi.

"It has taken me years, me and my bees and my wizards' powers, but the accursed Moguls reign to this day—though not, I think for long. They have lost their Peacock throne, stolen away by Nader Shah to Persia, and though the chair itself was but a bauble, emperors who fail to hang on to their baubles do not prosper. And one after another, the children of Babur met their fates, and their fate was often me.

"Humayun fell from a roof, stung by some insect perhaps, and broke his fool neck. Akbar—there was a man who had all he ate thrice tasted, and burned smokes that sent my bees to sleep in honour of his many gods and none. Jehangir was a fool who brought ruin on himself without my help—I had other concerns in those years. Shah Jehan though—I sent bees against him and then on a whim turned them from him to his Mumtaz. Why should he have her that men called the Perfection of the World, when my wives are centuries in their graves, and their gravesites trampled on by his ancestors' horses?

"And he frittered his reign away in grief and buildings until his sons walled him up in his dead wife's tomb where he could spend no more of the treasury. His sons were a quarrelsome lot—near parricides all of them and brother-killers too. I thought Dara the most able, so him I brought down—he rode his elephant into battle in the morning, and I had placed sleeping insects among the cushions of his howdah and in the heat of battle he met with misfortune and fell from his great beast into the hands of his brother. Who was not kind to him.

"That brother, Aurengzebe, I underestimated for a while—I thought him a common murderer, but he was a godly man, who would wade through blood to kneel at the foot of God. And after some thought, I let him be, because realms led by such men only prosper for a short time; he raised up enemies against him, and beat them over and over, but then he died as men do, and his children found the enemies he had made more than they could handle. Their throne totters—I give them fifty years, and then, perhaps, my war with the seed of Genghis will finally be done."

It is good for immortals to have a hobby, but I did not approve.

Some might see me as engaged in a similar quest for vengeance, but I only kill those who work evil and the Rituals. It is not at all the same sort of thing.

"You talk of rulers," Georgiana said, "and of thrones. But what of the people?"

Hassan looked at her as one who had never heard such a question asked before.

"You have brought ruin and war to the lands of India," she said. "What will replace the Great Moguls when they fall? I will tell you,"—she pointed at Chambord—"his people or mine. India will be the prize of wars fought elsewhere, and will know rulers far more alien to the land than the Moguls, far harsher and more corrupt. My friends are prosecuting one such, and I have read the bill of impeachment against the man Hastings, and I tremble for the land of India, and I tremble for what it will make of my countrymen, if they stay to rule it."

Chambord looked smug. "That, your Grace, is because your land is still ruled by oligarchs and aristocrats, even ones as charming as you. France will bring India the blessings of peace—not the excesses of Terror we saw in Paris, but the true revolution of freedom, of men living together as brothers, Yes, and women too, those that do not burn themselves for love."

"None of us are good enough to rule another people," she said. "Neither your people nor mine, but certainly not this man with his magic, and his bees."

Hassan laughed at her.

"Listen, you silly man,"—suddenly I found myself paying attention to the fact that she was more than an adventuress, that she was a woman who, in spite of being a woman, had statesmen at her beck and call—"you are out of your time and out of your depth. This is an age of reason and compromise and negotiation, and you had best get used to it."

"This is nonsense," he said. "Power is as it ever was, bloody and ruthless."

"No, it need not be. I tell you—the other year, our King went mad—not just slightly unwell, but wandering around talking to trees mad. And some of us who had detested him for years saw our chance. We would replace him with his worthless son who would owe his throne to us and do what we wished."

Hassan looked intrigued despite himself. "And you stand here, alive, without a bowstring or cushion cutting off your breath? Or are you an exile merely?"

"No," she said. "We failed, because he got better. And we backed down, and we made our peace. We are not an Oriental tyranny, or some Gothic state of lords and headsmen. We are civilized men and women, who backed down. No one died. We tried a gambit in the game, and it failed, and no one died. You could learn from this."

"Why am I forced to listen to the chatter of women? It is bad enough to have the Huntress appear in my realm and pry into my affairs, or to have the whore Morgan demand my help and refuge, but you and she are at least persons of power. I will not be lectured by some mayfly bitch from a barbarous land." He waved his hand. "I will have my bees sting your lips and tongue and throat so that you will never speak to your betters again."

"No, you will not, and that is for two reasons. One is that the Duchess is a brave fighter, my ally and my friend, and under my protection. And the second"—I held out a hand on which sat a large black insect—"is that while you have been explaining yourself to us, I have been in conversation with your queen."

His wax face could not move, and yet his eyes blazed behind it with effort and then failure.

"There are things at which I take offense," I told him. "One of them is magics that control the mind. I do not punish them, you understand, but I undo them where I can. You no longer have the bees in your thrall, for I have unpicked the tiny hooks you had in their minds."

The insect in my hand buzzed intensely and then rose and flew across and perched on Hassan's shoulder. And the swarm of bees which had hovered, buzzed peaceably around him, like a cloak or a shield.

"Oh," I said, "well, fair enough." And added, "Your Majesty."

Hassan laughed aloud in glee, and then looked less cheerful of a sudden.

"Some of us," Georgiana reminded me, "do not speak bee."

"Oh," I said, "I freed the bees, thinking perhaps that they would punish Hassan where I cannot. But it appears I was under a misapprehension." We watched as Hassan reached up and with a delicate finger stroked the queen between her antennae. "It appears that she minded being controlled, but is content to serve Hassan as his friend. He is good to his hives, tends their sicknesses, and cleans out their parasites. They will bring him wax and the honey that brings sleep and the venom that cures many ills, but they will no longer kill for him, save to defend the hive."

The Queen buzzed some more.

"I see," I said. "It appears that someone listened to your lecture on governance, even if Hassan here did not."

Hassan's waxen face had no expression, and yet I knew from his eyes that he had yielded to new necessity. "The Moguls will fall without my help," he said. "And it is clear that the chatter of women has more power over me than I had thought."

"Indeed so."

The voice came from the top of the steps, and there stood Hekkat who was now Morgan, hardly different from when I had last seen her as a friend, or less terrible than when I had glimpsed her on fields of battle. She had cast aside that aspect, and was still young, beautiful and strong and wrapped in a cloak as dark as starless, moonless, cloudless night. Around her there clustered men and women, some of whom I knew and some of whom I did not. The men were yawning into long beards and the women were brushing sleep from the corners of their eyes.

"Thank you Huntress," Morgan said, "and your friends, for entertaining Hassan here. I needed him distracted, and you have

208

managed that admirably. I hope he did not bore you too utterly." She looked at Hassan and smiled, showing her perfect teeth. "Honestly, Hassan, I don't know why you bother concocting sleeping draughts and drugged coffee; you would do just as well putting people to sleep by telling them all your grievances and all your schemes."

"You were asleep," he protested, petulant as a child caught out in some petty theft.

"Little man," she said, "I was brewing sudden death, deep sleep and the ecstasy of love before your Prophet was born. And I learned to convince my mother that I was asleep when I was a mortal child. Forewarned is forearmed, as they say. I was called here by your sleepers and knew of your treacherous hospitality. And now the sleepers wake."

She turned to me. "Mara, my dear, how nice to see you after all these years."

I stared at her in disbelief, at her impudence, her audacity, her control.

"I'm sorry to have brought you all this way, but I thought it best to settle this matter with overwhelming force. With you here, and needing my help with your sister, Hassan will have to accept that there is no point whatever in making me fight my way out of here. And I owe you a considerable favour now, which means that you can take my help and not speak to me for another five thousand years afterwards if that's what you want to do."

She turned round and gestured to the wakened sleepers. "Hassan, you will need to explain yourself to these people. Some of them aren't very nice, so you had better have a good answer."

Hassan stood up from the table and turned to face the men and women he had deceived and drugged. He was past petulance and too intelligent to bluster, and spoke as a merchant among merchants defending the quality of his wares.

"You came to me, all of you, seeking refuge. And refuge I gave you, safe from the enemies you had all managed to make for yourselves, men and kings and gods."

209

One of the men stepped forward. "Safety?" he said. "You poisoned me and leeched my power."

"When you came here," Hassan said, "there were men hunting you who would have burned the flesh from your bones by slow degrees, or wound out your guts on a spindle. They are in their graves, Herr Faust, and your sins are forgotten save in puppet-shows. Even gods and devils have forgotten you, while you slept—and if they were to notice you again, it would not go well for you. You would pay the host of an inn who fed and sheltered you for a night. Did you think my services came without a charge?"

"You might have asked." One of the women spoke up, her high cheekbones bright with rage.

"Perhaps," Hassan said. "But you, Melisande of Jerusalem, are in no position to lecture me on the duties of a host. And you will say that men you sent mad or turned to beasts were dangers to your son's rule and that all was done for the state and for the honour of your god. We all do what we must, and if need be, we pay for it."

Behind and around him, the humming of the bees, that were no longer his slaves but still his friends, rose to a snarl.

"You are free to go," Hassan said. "But, if you wish, you are also free to stay. Perhaps I should have asked, as the Queen of Jerusalem says. I have dabbled in your minds these many years, and I know you all, for I have watched you sleep, and cleaned you, and let you sleep away your hurts. And I know that the reason you came here is that you had nowhere else to go; and that has not changed."

What impressed me was that he had the sense not to use magic on magicians. He spoke to them as a leader of men talking, not to equals, but to subordinates that he respected.

"Come," he said. "Let us reason together. I am sure that we can come to an accommodation. And if not, perhaps you will succeed in killing me, but I assure you that my good friends the bees will avenge me."

He turned to me and my companions, and to Morgan who was once Hekkat. "I owe you my thanks, Huntress, Enchantress. You have obliged me to resolve situations in which I had perhaps not acted for the best. And your companions, Frank, Englishwoman, bird and horses—I thank you too. I am not a man to whom humility is congenial, but, as you say, it is a new age. And now, if you will, I and these good people have much to discuss."

He walked to the man Faust and clasped him by the hand, seizing his other arm with the hand that was free and looking him straight in the eye. And he bowed and set his wax lips to the hand of the lady Melisande, and of a sudden faces that had looked at him in stony rage were smiling, and Faust clapped him on the back as if his boon companion at some inn.

I caught the man's eye questioningly, and he turned to me, and bowed. "My name is Johannes Faust. If you have heard of me, you know that I have a history of making the best of a half-way decent bargain."

The snarling of the bees diminished to a comforting hum, Hassan's former victims clustered around him and went back into the temple with him, and we were alone.

"That did not go as I expected," Morgan remarked. "I had rather thought that there would be blood. But heigh-ho, I am a reformed character these days. I no longer seek conflict for its own sake."

I relished that she too had found herself irrelevant to a situation she had controlled for a moment.

She shrugged. "Faust summoned me in his dreams, and seemed quite vexed, but he was never the most reliable of men." Then, shaking it off, she turned to my companions. "But I am quite forgetting my manners—and the Huntress has never had any."

"I am but a French sailor," said Chambord. "I wish that I could be more and have more to offer so famous a lady, but all I have is my honour, my heart and"—he lingered a little over the kiss to the hand she reached out to him as part of the same dance of gesture as his bow—"my regard."

"Le Capitain Chambord," I introduced him. "A man who has come hither with me to seek his fate."

211

"And perhaps has found it." He stared at Morgan in worshipful lust. "And this is her Grace the Duchess of Devonshire."

"Your servant, ma'am," Georgiana said with a slight curtsey as one used to speak to queens.

Morgan nodded to her, as if to an equal, and perhaps rightly so. Lastly—perhaps not wisely so, as things turned out—she turned to her bird. "As always," she said, haughtily, "you are the best of servants."

"Mistress," it cawed, but there was something in its tone that did not sound as servile as one might have expected. "I had hoped that this would end in blood. I have flown so far, with only the odd morsel for my reward."

"You have fed so well in past ages," she said, "that you would prosper still if you never visited another massacre or ambush."

"I feed," it said, "because it is my nature. And I feed on the carrion of battle because that is what you trained me to, and it has become my nature."

"Natures change." Though Morgan spoke to her bird, she spoke also to me. "I have chosen change in these new ages of change. You would do well to imitate me in this."

She spoke to me directly. "For ages, I was battle-mad; I lived in rage and where war was, there was I. But I grew tired and thought better of such things, and then I heard of your sister's fate. I heard first what happened in Alexandria, and then what happened in Paris, and I wept for your pain and for hers."

I gazed at her, stone-faced.

"You will say, it was not my concern to grieve. But everything in your life concerns me, still. Besides, the pity of it—I would have wept at the tale even if it were not of someone I love."

She gazed at me a moment; I chose not to react in any way.

"You will remember the fate of my Amazons." I did, and shuddered at the thought. "Sometimes I have met those women again, in other lives, and seen that the pain of what was done to them lived on, in life after life, and drove them to harm and distraction. Such pain cannot be mended, save by wiping from them even those memories which pass from life to life."

"No hope of cure without that erasure?" I asked.

She shook her head. "None. None for them, and their case was not so bad as your sister's. I learned to take their pain away by long slow study, and when I heard of your sister, I studied all the harder. And study became my delight instead of battle, and I will do what I can for your sister."

"I will not reward you for it," I said. "You will have my thanks, but my thanks alone."

"That is all I hope for."

"So, Mistress," said the Morrigan. "When you have done what you need to for the Huntress and her mad girl, on what battle field shall we meet? War brews in High Germany, and Tartary, and in Africa where a youth called Shaka is teaching his troops new ways of making war."

She stared at him with scorn and waved dismissal. "Go where you choose, bird, and eat what prey you choose. I am done with battle, and if you cannot accept that then I am done with you."

Its eye glinted. "Take what prey I choose? Is that all you have to say to me after ages of service?"

Of a sudden, it flew at her and clawed its talons into her shoulder so that she reached with her hands to tear it from her flesh. And the cruel beak was at her face, and her eye was gone into its beak and gullet in a second.

Morgan screamed in pain, and for a second I thought of rushing to wipe the blood and juice from her face and console her. For a second only, because Georgiana was quicker and had a handkerchief to the bleeding socket before I could move.

The Morrigan gulped her eye down its gizzard and then spoke, with a sounding anger that was more that of its long-dead parent than of the creature I had thought I understood.

"I take my pay then. For ages of service and these last years of scorn. And I take your eye for the pain you caused mine. I bit deep and dark, so do not hope that it will return, or that you will gain wisdom from its loss, as Odin claimed to, when it was all the wisdom taught him by my sibs. I am the Morrigan, and I will be battle-crow alone, with no need of a goddess, a goddess to whom I taught much, and last of all taught to bleed."

Its fine speech ended in a caw of pain, for Chambord had drawn his sword and struck at it inexpertly, taking feathers from its tail, but doing it no mortal hurt.

"Do no war against women, Monsieur Crow," he said. And then screamed in his turn as the Morrigan struck at him with a talon that for a moment seemed long as a spear, and sank into his chest, and tore at him there.

The Frenchman collapsed in a heap. The bird flew up and clear of even my thrown lance, only to be brought squealing to earth again, its wing caught in the mouth of the steed Sleipnir, sprung into the air on those eight legs as if she had wings as well, and biting down hard with jaws grown terrible in her rage.

The crack of the wing was louder than Chambord's dying moans.

Sleipnir opened her mouth, dropped the crippled bird to scrabble on the ground, and trotted over to where Chambord lay. She spoke over him.

"Gallant and ready my rider. To avenge wrong.

Dying in honour, deed of grandeur."

And then she reached out her tongue, and licked his forehead tenderly as if he were her foal.

Georgiana had helped Morgan to the ground while she dressed the enchantress' wound, and now helped her rise. Morgan was pale and terrible as the moon in storm.

"And so it ends," she said.

"You ended it," the crippled bird rasped.

"I ended it as a parting of equals," she said. "But now, now, you will serve me forever. And not as an equal or even a trusted servant." She smiled at me. "You, Huntress, will remember. The Bird, this creature's parent, could split and divide itself."

She touched her bloody socket with a finger that she brought away wet and red, and touched it to her mouth, and licked her lips.

"This is the word of my shed blood, vengeful against this child of the Bird. I unmake you. I fragment you. I take away your mind, all save knowledge that something terrible has been done to you. You will flutter an eternity in pain."

She crossed her arms, hands flat the left in front of the right and splayed them like wings, fingers together and thumbs folded to the palms. Then, slowly she separated the fingers, unfolded the thumbs and slowly, so slowly, unfolded her arms and spread them wide.

There was a tearing and a screaming that had little of the caw or croak about it, for all that we knew whence it came. Of a sudden, the Morrigan was gone, and dark in the sky above us rose a hundred thousand smaller crows, whirring and whirling and making their din. In her hand, Morgan now held a hair-comb in the shape of a single bird, and she thrummed against it with the bloody finger, and then placed it in her hair, above an ear. And the sky was empty.

"Waste not want not," she said.

I had meanwhile knelt by the dying Frenchman, as had Georgiana, who took his hand and held it tight. I have never known what to do at such times save show concern. I have no gift of healing, save that one time, and all I can do is wait for men and women to pass, and then do what I can to give them choices after their death. Belief is a powerful trap for most souls, but I had hopes that Chambord was a man to whom I could give advice.

He spoke to Georgiana first, though. "Be sure to speak to Mademoiselle Wild for me," he said. "You may assure her that my heart was always hers, even if I died defending another."

I forbore to mention that he had come close to pledging himself to that other; after all, Morgan had that effect, and not on men alone.

He turned his face to me, all business despite his death agony. All men die, and dying is never a pretty business, but he ignored the catching of his breath and the rattle in his throat, and so, remembering his courage, shall I.

215

"Huntress, it has been a pleasure. I hope you do not mind that I and the Duchess here had already arranged that we would accompany the enchantress Morgan back to London. We overheard what passed between you and your sister and understand your desire to be elsewhere. Besides, you are pledged to duties in Paris."

I knew well what obligations I had and did not have, but it troubles me not to be lectured about such things by dying men; it is always worth being reminded of what is important.

By now, Morgan had torn a strip of dark velvet cloth from her cloak and tied it, fetchingly, around the side of her face that now contained an empty eye-socket. I caught myself noticing that it did not diminish her beauty in the slightest.

"I could ease your passing," she said, and placed a hand on his forehead.

For a moment or two his face grew calm as pain retreated, and then his expression grew intense as if concentrating on one real thing more utterly than ever before. Confusion passed through his open eyes, and he looked directly at Morgan.

"Venice?" he said. "Really? I was never there." He withdrew one hand from Georgiana's grasp, reached up and pushed Morgan's hand gently but firmly away. "Enchantress, it was kindly meant, but I would rather console my dying with my own memories than someone else's."

The effort to speak was the last he had in him, and his eyes glazed and he passed beyond consciousness into a mixture of agony and remembered happiness that flitted across his face and then was gone into stillness.

He was still there, of course, young and gallant, standing beside what he had left. Morgan and I had words of advice for his spirit, but those are a private matter. Suffice it to say that Sleipnir left us at that time, and she had both a rider and a burden, and her destination was not, as far as I know, the burned shell that remains of Valhalla.

Georgiana led the horse Gram away from earshot and busied

herself in grooming her steed, with a curry comb she produced from one of her endless supply of pockets. Tact was not the least of that woman's virtues.

"So, Huntress," Morgan said. "Are we at this long last quits for Atlantis and my Amazons?"

"When you have done what you can for my sister, and for Miss Wild."

"And are we friends?" The wistful tone in her voice suggested that she hoped for more but would not ask it.

"No, not yet. I have withdrawn 'never,' but not yet. You are still not worthy, less worthy by far than that mortal woman, or even that poor dead man."

"May I ask why?"

"You should not need to ask, but since you do...Friends come and make an offer, even when that offer would not, at first, be welcome. Friends tell one with a sick sister the depth of that sickness and of its cure. Friends do not make their offer part of some elaborate scheme of double-dealing and treachery. It is only chance that only two beings died here today, but one of those lives was under my protection."

I looked at her sternly.

"I have been rebuked, for improvisation and lack of forethought, but you have surpassed me here. I let Chambord accompany me here because he wished to confront the fate that awaited him and I had hoped that I could turn that fate aside. I could not, and the reason for this was your plans, your ventures, and the bird companion you chose to take on and then set aside. I am sorry for your eye—but this man lost far more."

Though she was, and is, a mistress of deceit, her contrition seemed genuine enough.

"May I hope," she said, "that you will forgive me one day?"

"Hope is every being's birthright and friend. And, in this case, not a delusion, perhaps." I looked down at my hand. "I have your ring," I said, and reached down to take it.

217

"Wear it as a token of my repentance," she said. "I took it from one who worked the Rituals and whom I slew in battle so that you did not have to. It has power within it that I have never taken." She smiled and I saw nothing in her smile that I could not trust. "Besides, if you ever have need of me, touch it and I will come, even to the bottommost Hell of Lucifer."

I turned to Georgiana.

"I entrust the enchantress Morgan to your care, and you to hers. Go by the fastest road you can, through shadow, to Miss Wild's private rooms; we have dallied long enough, and my sister and the younger Miss Wild need help."

I bowed my head to them both. "Your Grace, it has been a pleasure beyond my ability to express. I hope we shall meet again, but who can say? Enchantress, I commend Georgiana not merely to your care, but to your attention; she is one from whom you might learn." Then I laughed. "And do not break each other."

I kissed Georgiana's cheek and kissed the air near Morgan's, and was gone from their sight and, in a few short hours of untrammeled travel through shadow's heights and hollow places, to Paris, which smelled of hot weather, disease and unrest.

I came to the Inn of the Dark Angel, and knocked three times on its door. Mary herself opened it. "You've cut things fine," she said. "Tom dies tomorrow."

"I said I would return in time, and here I am."

She sighed. "I wish we did not have to rely on you in this— Gouverneur Morris might have helped, but chose not so, and the authorities in Washington declined to plead for clemency."

"What matter," I said, "if I am here to rescue him?"

"You are a goddess, or a demon. And Tom has spent his time in jail completing his book on the fact that no such beings exist."

"I don't see the problem."

"Tom Paine is a very stubborn man." There was a weariness in Mary's voice, clearly borne of many years of enduring men's high-minded perversity.

218

"Where is he? I may as well go straight there and honour my pledge to you."

"They at least did him the honour of housing him in the Luxembourg, a palace that it suited their fancy to turn to a prison."

I remembered my manners. "How have you been?"

"In hiding," Mary said. "Mostly here. I got them to smuggle me away from the city for a while and spread rumours that I was elsewhere, with Imlay, or in Sweden on his business. Paris has had a blood-drunk summer since you've been gone. The lists go up every day in the prisons and the guillotine is never idle."

"More slaying? I had hoped that, with the loss of their chance to build a god gone, Robespierre and Saint-Just might have slackened their efforts."

She wrinkled her face, as if there were a thought in her head that was like a bad smell she could not get out of her mind. "It's like some huge clock, ticking away. With blood on every cog. I don't think they control it any more—word is that they will fall tonight. But the clock will tick, even if their heads fall, and it will be a while before it runs down."

I remembered how, when Danton died, I had thought something similar. Then, at least, there was a purpose and I confused that with the idea that this age had to have wicked men to wind its clocks of death. Perhaps I was to be proved wrong. And so I have been.

"I fancy," I said to her with a smile that showed all my teeth, "that I shall endeavour to witness their fall. Those two may have ensured I cannot kill them myself, but I shall see if there is anything I might do to ensure their punishment."

They had, after all, managed to inconvenience me. Which is more than Augustulus Romulus managed, or Baibars the Mameluke, and they were better men than these.

Paris stank in the heat. There were no dead rats in the gutter or I would have thought it a plague season. And the beggars had stale crusts to chew and begged money for sour wine to soften it, so it was not a season of famine. It was the stink of blood, the stink of fear, the stink of something new, long awaited and long dreaded.

And that thing was not I, but I might be its friend and ally, if I chose.

The gardens of the Luxemburg, though, hang heavy with scent—the scent of fear but also the scent of flowers past their best bloom and shedding their petals, the scent of roses whose fleshiness has started to brown at the edges. It cloyed in my throat like cheap candy.

The smell of dead and dying flowers was everywhere in the palace too—some guard had thrown them in loose bunches along the corridors to hide the smell of blankets soaked in jail fever sweat and chamber pots too rarely emptied.

It was a prison, but its cells were basement rooms where cheese and potatoes were still stored, or where servants had shivered in winter, or a ballroom across which barriers had been thrown, where people sat on the floor and dared not look across the barriers for fear of the guards.

"I seek the American Paine," I said to a guard.

"That prosey traitor as tried to save the bastard king? What do you want to see him for?"

"I have been sent to ask him questions. There are always questions to be asked of traitors."

"Normally, I'd say good luck with that, because none of us like to talk to him for fear of being caught there with his tongue and his yap for hours while he talks treason and godlessness and makes it sound like good French sense. But as things are…"

I stared a question.

"He loses his head tomorrow, and is off it today. Gaol fever—no sense to be got out of him. Almost a waste to chop a man as will die tomorrow whatever happens."

"Take me to him," I said, as one who brooks no enquiry as to who she is, whom she serves or by what right she gives orders. Men who serve tyrants are bad at asking questions; it is a part of their sad trade.

Up two stair-cases from the ball-room were the rooms where the palace's upper servants, or lesser guests, had stayed; stinking still, but with some air blowing in from open or broken windows—I did not bother to discover which—still laden with the sickly stench of the gardens but at least chill enough to cut the endless swelter of a building stuffed with more people in distress and fear than it had seen in its days as a house of pleasure.

Some of the rooms had numbers chalked on their locked doors. And some had their doors wide open and were empty. I glanced at these in interest.

"They went today," the guard told me. "First thing this morning, the carts came for them and we counted them out, cell by cell. Same tomorrow. We put the number on the door—cell by cell, unless there's someone as is being kept, special. Like your man Paine was, until the Americans said they did not want him. And in the morning we count them out, and if one cell is short, we take from one that was not due. And if the sums don't add up, down where they load the carts, they take one of us, so we make sure to keep our accounts straight."

The cell he showed me to had 4 scrawled in chalk across it.

"Don't stay too long," he said. "They never punish us for bringing down too many for their carts. The guillotine has always room for one more."

"Leave the door open," I told him. "I want to breathe air, not the stench of fever-sick dead men."

"I can't do that," he protested. "They might escape."

"Do I look like a woman who would let enemies of the People go free?" I slapped him once on each cheek. "Do you think that the Tribunes of the People would send someone to ask questions who would let traitors and atheists carry their sickness out into the streets?"

"No." He cast down his eyes.

"Then leave the door as I say. And leave me to my work and get on with your own."

When the door was open, I pushed it against the wall, so that the number 4 could not be seen.

Three men sat round the tossing, turning body of a man in the depths of fever, themselves only well by the courtesy of comparison.

"Is this Paine?" I asked.

"And who are you?"

I looked to check that the guard was not lingering in earshot. "A friend."

"Thomas," the man said, and shook the dying man by the shoulder. Or rather, the man who was clearly not dying quite yet. Nonetheless, his voice had the faltering breathlessness of a man struggling to be awake when his body would rather be asleep or in delirium, and there was an unhealthy sheen on his forehead.

Paine raised his head from the stained pillow. "Who might you be?" He had the sharp features of a man born to ask awkward questions, and keen to get in his own answer while you pondered a response.

"My name is Mara," I said. "I am called the Huntress."

"Mary mentioned you," he said. "Though I am not clear why she thought a madwoman could help me."

"A madwoman?"

"There is God, a single divine spirit, and the world in which he is manifest. There are no miracles, no revelations, and no warrior women from before the dawn of history."

"Who am I then?"

"Mary mentioned that she had freed you from some private prison of the man Saint-Just. Clearly, you are some woman he tormented into insanity. I have no idea who you were before."

"I am here to free you."

"Which is very kind of you, but you could not free yourself. And why me, rather than all these other good men, who are less likely to die in the next few days? I will die, probably, even if my head stays on."

"I am here to save you," I said. "Because I promised Mary that I would."

He looked at me with infinite kind patience. "I am here because I chose to be, because I took actions that I knew would have consequences. As well tell Socrates that he could walk from the cell, and you know what he said when that was suggested to him."

"Better than you. You only know what Plato said he said, which leaves out most of the jests and all of the bawdy."

He laughed, and then coughed. "Sometimes I envy the mad. You at least enjoy your insanity, whereas to be sane in this world is to see injustice and know that the way to end it lies through death."

"Through death?"

"For the Revolution to kill the likes of me is to dishonour itself. At this point, there is no hope for the madness to cease save that."

"Mary tells me that the Jacobins may fall."

"And what of it? What follows them may be worse—men made rich on the wealth of the dead, or some adventurer who wishes to be crowned in the Bourbon's place. I would rather die with honour than see more." He laughed. "If you are as powerful as you claim, kill Robespierre and Saint-Just. Their deaths would ease my own. Otherwise, leave me in peace."

I could have dragged him from the place by the scruff of his neck, but he found enough comfort in his delusions that I thought it best to leave him for the moment.

"Done," I said. "I had planned to end them, as it is."

He looked at me with sudden concern. "You poor mad thing. Do not put yourself in jeopardy on account of my jests."

I turned to his companions. "Be sure that door stays open. The number that marks you for death is against the wall and I shall ensure that it stays there."

I walked into the corridor. Taking one of the knives from my hair, I drove it with the heel of my hand into the wood of the door and through it into the stonework that lay beyond the coarse plaster of the wall.

I went downstairs and found the guard again. He was not glad to see me.

"That door stays open," I said. "No one will leave that cell in the morning."

"But that will leave the count out for my floor."

I could have said that that was his concern, but did not. I merely left, through shadow, that he might have a sense of with whom he dealt.

I went to the Assembly, to the Convention, but had missed Robespierre by minutes. They were still arguing as to whether his speech should be printed as a decree—I took this as a good sign.

I wandered the streets, letting people see me as they chose, as a whore, or a merchant's wife, or a child. I despise such magics, but they are occasionally useful. And wherever I went, I spread rumour. Rumours that had enough of the truth that they would do damage: "Robespierre has a private temple where he conducts strange rites." "Saint-Just keeps women in secret dungeons." "Do you know what those two do with the severed heads of women?" "They debauched the child Louis Capet; that's just not right."

Such things are easy to say, and will find an audience when people are ready to hear them. Paris had changed so much since the time of de Molay, and yet some things remain the same, and what I had done once, I could do again.

I caught up with Robespierre for a moment at the Jacobin Club, but I watched him from shadow; his hour was almost upon him, but it was not ripe.

When, though, he shouted, that, if the people desired it, he would give his life for the fatherland, I let him see my face for a moment, just a moment, so that the cheers for which he lived would be poisoned for him. Then I moved on, and wandered the streets all night, talking to people as I went.

I was at the Luxemburg at dawn, when the carts came, and followed them to the scaffold. Paine and his companions were not aboard, and four guards, the badges of their uniforms torn off crudely so that the cloth was threadbare, were.

I watched them queue for the stairs to their death and then

pushed through the crowd. I seized the guard I had met and one of his companions by their torn collars and rushed them through shadow to a nearby cellar, then did the same for the other two. Two of them—one the guard I knew—soiled themselves in terror.

"Find some other trade," I snapped. "Mercy is rarely given to those who have shown none and your lives now belong to me. I shall be watching." Which was a lie, but in a good cause.

I went back to the club of the Jacobins. The mood of the people crowded into the room had changed. They smelled the possibility of fall and of blood; I only had to shout "Arrest them" once, and parts of the room took it up.

Saint-Just shouted above the din. "If we are traitors, cast us from the Tarpeian Rock."

"Wossat?" said the woman sitting next to me in the public gallery.

"It was a rock. They threw people off it."

"Throw 'em," she shouted, because she liked the sound of it. "Throw 'em."

The din grew louder, and, quite suddenly, Saint-Just sat down.

Someone shouted something incoherent about how Robespierre had threatened to arrest him and someone called back, "What, you too?" and someone else said, "You should be safe, you're not a pretty girl," and someone else said, "They're not all that fussy." And there was laughter, the enemy of all tyrants.

Robespierre stood up, and the crowd were quiet a moment. "I must defend myself. I am the true friend of my people and I will die for them if I have to."

A man with the cynical eye and clean throat linen of one who had done well from knowing when to change sides interrupted him. "Here he goes again," he said. "Listen to him. It's all about him, isn't it, lads? It's his revolution, his people, his country. But it's not his, it's ours. And you know what he'll say, old miseryguts, it'll be all 'Poor me, poor persecuted me' and he'll say 'They're silencing me' if someone moans when he goes on for two hours. The Republic is in danger, my dears, in danger of Maxie boring us all to death."

They were laughing out loud now, a room full of them, and it was a sound better than the shouts of "Arrest them" or "Throw 'em," because it was the sound of his magic breaking.

He stood up and so did I, up in the gallery. I caught his eye, and then drew a finger across my throat. He started to speak and his tongue stumbled.

"Danton's blood is choking him," I shouted. And others took up the cry.

He glanced across at Saint-Just and the two of them, and three of their friends around them, pushed their way from the room and out into the corridor.

They were arrested on the spot and hurried from the building with their arms twisted behind their backs. For a hundred paces at least, it looked as if they were in real discomfort, but the captain of the militiamen who had them never thought to tell his men to stop Robespierre talking. I watched, because it was as well to know how much of a problem I still had with bringing these two to their end, and because it is always as well not to count one's corpses before they are dismembered.

A hundred yards and the pressure of their arms against their backs relaxed, five more and their arms were released altogether to swing at their sides, a yard more and one of the militia men casually raised his musket and smashed its butt into his captain's head.

I heard Robespierre shout to them and to any idlers who might be listening, "The Revolution is in danger! To the Hotel de Ville!"

I wandered back into the Club of the Jacobins, where the clean-shaven man who had spoken before was lounging against a desk and talking complacently to his friends. Sometimes the sheer effort of will involved in breaking a magician's hold makes people mentally exhausted to the point of utter stupidity.

"Do you know where Saint-Just and Robespierre are?" I said.

"You need no longer trouble yourself with them, mademoiselle. They are under arrest and on their way to the scaffold."

His complacency extended to appraising my body with lust. I had no time for this and spoke to him as harshly as the occasion, and his impudence, merited.

"No," I said. "The troops you had waiting for them have already joined them, and they are marching on the Hotel de Ville."

"Shit!" He turned to one of his companions. "Barras, how many districts can you raise in half an hour?"

"It's hopeless," his friend said dejectedly. "I have prepared for this hour, but only to hold the square against any attempt to rescue them from the scaffold. I had told them to march in an hour or two, but not yet. It will take messengers ten minutes or more to reach even the nearest ones."

"Write me a despatch," I said, "and I will take it to them in seconds."

"And you are?" he said.

For one moment, I freed myself of all glamours and he saw the anger in my eyes. "I am Justice," I said. "I am the defender of the weak against the strong."

The clean-shaven man laughed. "It is some mad wench like Corday," he said. "Pretty, but I prefer my fucks both dumb and sane."

I picked him up by his throat-linen, threw him across the room and was there to catch him before he could injure himself. Sometimes I take exception to disrespect. Young Josh once rebuked me for it.

"It is as she says," said Barras. "I have the orders here."

"Add a requirement," I suggested, "that they bring their drummer boys and sound the tocsin. You must not let them hear him speak."

He scrawled some names. "And here are their locations."

I took the papers from his hand and as I did so, the clock began to strike noon. It was an elaborate mechanism, which played that damn tune, three verses of it, at the end of striking the hour. I was not back by the stroke of twelve—not Hermes himself, or the steed Sleipnir could have done that—but I returned by the end of the third chorus.

227

"It is done," I said. "Your men are on the march."

We stood some minutes in silence and then I heard it in the distance, coming from all the parts of Paris to the south and the west of us—the noise of drums and the shouts of marching men.

A boy rushed into the room, his face and hands smeared with ink. "I have it, patriots," he said. "Monsieur Barras. Monsieur Vadier." He handed them sheets of printed paper, the ink so wet still that it smeared, but only a little. "They are going up all over Paris," he said. "I gave your silver to the streetboys and had them wait for the decree and for pastepots."

Barras looked at his friend. "What have you done, Vadier?"

Vadier smiled. "I have printed a decree declaring them outlaws. All we need do is seize them, and we can kill them as soon as we choose."

"There has been no vote for that," Barras said. "The Convention…"

"The decree says otherwise, and do you think that if we kill those men tonight or tomorrow, the Convention will care? Or that if those two manage to arrest us, we will last five minutes?" Vadier turned to me. "Am I not right?"

I smiled at him and this time he bowed his head.

What I remember of that afternoon was watching the militias arrive, dripping with sweat from forced fast marches in the heat of the early afternoon, and the noise of drums, the perpetual noise of drums in our ears.

I thought of suggesting candle-wax as well, but dismissed it.

Men ran back and forth, shouting that one quarter had declared for Robespierre or that another had defected back to the Convention—Barras sent drummers wherever he could that might waver, and the growing smirk on his and Vadier's faces seemed to indicate success.

The heat broke, quite suddenly, and there was rain, bright rain in sheets out of a clear sky, and it felt as if a pressure had gone from behind the eyes and a stench from the nostrils, in spite of the constant pounding of the drums.

228

The drums, and more besides: young men with whistles, and pipes, and old women banging ladles against pots, and men with hammers striking sheets of tin. They marched behind the troops as we slowly moved towards the Place of the Revolution and the Hotel de Ville.

It was where I had started this visit to Paris, and it seemed fitting that it be where it ended.

Night was falling and I feared that some last dregs of the magic of the Rituals might still obstruct my justice. Such things are always strongest when no sunlight shines on them.

I raced ahead.

There were militiamen still there, but as the noise of the drums grew louder from every direction, many of them shook their heads as if awakening from drugged sleep. They threw down their guns and walked away, and even those who were still spellbound did nothing to stop them.

As the militias commanded by Barras arrived in the square even those last supporters of Robespierre began to melt away—or, rather join the angry mob, drumming and shouting and hooting.

Up on the balcony on which I had first met him, he appeared for a moment and tried to speak, but the drums were too loud and after a few seconds he gave up and went back inside.

The great wooden doors of the building, thick oak with great iron studs like the spikes of a fortification, were closed and locked against me, as if I could not simply have walked through them. I chose otherwise, pulling at their great handles until the chains that were holding them on the inside burst with a furious clatter that could be heard even above the drums.

I stood at the foot of the staircase and shouted up to the men who had come nervously from an upper room when they heard me enter. "Saint-Just! Robespierre! I have come to make an end of you."

I raced up the stairs.

One man struck at me with a crutch and I brushed him aside so that he fell sprawling and broken down the staircase. Another, who looked a little like Robespierre, took the time to aim and fire a pistol at me, but his ball struck me as gently as the rain outside. I took the pistol from him, none too gently, and cast it down. He pulled another from his belt and I took it from him. I threw him from my way and into the room.

There was a noise of broken glass and a scream.

"Augustin!" came a shout from Robespierre as I entered the room and walked towards him.

Though the drums were loud outside still, the room itself was a realm of silence. Another few weeks of power, or a serious effort, and they might have mastered shadow, and escaped to do more harm.

I weighed the pistol in my hand, and checked that it was fully loaded with powder and ball. Robespierre looked at me with hatred. "Huntress," he shouted. "You have killed my brother, who harmed none."

"And men like you killed my sisters, in ways a deal less merciful than a sudden fall," I said. "So I care not."

"What do you plan to do to us?" Saint-Just asked.

"End you."

He laughed. "And how do you propose to do that? We have charmed your weapons so that they cannot strike at us, and dedicated our deaths at your hands to the Rituals. You cannot kill us without breaking your own rules."

I laughed in his face. "Little man," I said, "I found ways around my own rules before Troy fell."

I hit him in the face, not hard, just enough to make it clear to him that I could do worse if I chose.

The Japanese sword at my back sang to me. "Mistress," it said, but that was not all it said. It could be a storm of steel for me, without my hand, if I freed it to fly.

"No, little sword, brave sword," I said. "We do not know what protections guard these scum still, and I would not have you stained with their worthless blood."

I smiled at Robespierre and Saint-Just. "I have not forgotten the weeks I spent in that room over there. But your death is not, in the end, a matter of my personal vengeance. I defend the weak against the strong, and it is always best that it be the weak who pull the strong down."

I raised his brother's pistol. "You have taken so many lives, and what you did not put into your gods, you put into that tongue and that voice. I take them from you." And I shot Robespierre in the face, smashing his mouth and jaw beyond any hope of repair.

He collapsed slowly, like a building whose inner walls have fallen, and there came a hopeless gurgle from his throat and red bubbles frothed at what was left of his upper lip.

I looked at Saint-Just and he looked back at me. There was not even hatred in his eyes—just a rational mind that knows it has come to the end and does not care. I had never seen that look before, but I have seen it since.

I walked from the room and passed Vadier and Barras on the stair. "They are at your disposal, gentlemen," I said and nodded. "I suggest that you take their heads as soon as ever you may. I do not think Robespierre can heal his wound, but I would not care to gamble on it."

"I never gamble," said Vadier with that dislikable smirk, "unless I am sure to win."

And indeed he was one of the few men I met in those years, apart from Talleyrand, who won the only victory on which no man can count. He died in bed, of old age.

Paris was cool that night, with the freshness that comes after rain. Paine was awake when I went to his cell to retrieve my knife from the door. His fever had abated somewhat.

"They have fallen," I said. "Shall I close the door and remind the guards of the warrant for your death? Or do you want to live another day?"

"It is a philosophic weakness in me, but I am not eager, any more. Perhaps there is a cause that needs me, or a book I can write. Leave

231

the door, mademoiselle." His voice grew more urgent. "And keep yourself safe. This is a dangerous world in which to be mad, though it is no safer to be sane."

Paine lived a decade and a half more, outliving both Mary and Georgiana, but the book he wrote in his death cell was the last thing of note he did. It is all to the good that he remained unshaken in his faith that I was mad, and magic a delusion. The world would have been the worse for his changing his mind.

I have seen Polly from time to time—I visited her and her great-granddaughter, but Augusta had little sense of whom I might be save a friend of Polly's, and we thought it best not to remind her. Once Morgan had wiped memory from Sof's troubled spirit, the ties that held her to Augusta had broken, and Morgan was thorough and kind in the way she took from the girl the months in which two tortured spirits had lain together and shared the worst of pain. She might have lived with the torments that had been inflicted on her own person, but not with what had been done to Sof.

I have not seen Morgan again, but it pleases me that she took pains with Augusta as well as with Sof; she did not just keep her word to me, but learned compassion. Or at least its image.

But that morning, I walked back to the Place of the Revolution, and watched my two enemies die, as so many had died before them.

I will not say that Saint-Just died well. He walked unaided up the steps of the scaffold and looked down at me, and the mob, with eyes no less dead in that moment than they were when the executioner Samson held up his severed head. He died quiet and uncaring and sober as a machine—I will not say he died well.

Robespierre screamed wordlessly every time the cart jolted over a cobble-stone. Someone had wrapped a rag around his shattered face, but it would have been hard to force laudanum past the wreck of his jaw into his throat and no one had tried. His eyes kept darting round the square, fixing on something and then looking away in horror. I do not know what he thought he saw—I saw no ghosts there myself.

232

He stumbled up the stairs of the scaffold, and the mob laughed as at the falls of a drunk or a clown.

Samson knew his audience, and with a deep bow and a flourish, he ripped off the bandage and showed the extent of the injuries to the crowd. If Robespierre had screamed before, what we heard as the bandage ripped away was something fiercer and wilder; I have heard gods and great beasts make less fuss about their dying.

Samson forced Robespierre's head down into the machine, into a groove that his broken jaw hardly fitted any more. The executioner's hands were covered in the blood from wounds that had torn ever wider open.

And that scream went on and on. The blade came down and the head fell, and somehow the severed head Samson showed to the crowd went on screaming without throat or lungs until those angry eyes finally clouded over.

I think that scream was his spirit dying along with his magic. And that the spirit of Saint-Just died silently some hours before his body.

I do not know.

Hell does not hold them. I went there to look.

# Extraordinary Renditions

## London and Basra Province 2003

There was a burning ache in the back of Emma's throat.

It was a bit like a bad cough about to start tearing her lungs apart. It was like an urge to vomit herself empty, or as if she had vomited already and the burn was acid and bile, but it was none of these things.

It was fear.

She recognized it; of course she had been afraid before. She had been afraid and she had coped and she hadn't died. She could have died, all those times, but she was not as afraid then as she was now.

It wasn't the two large men in dark glasses and telephone headsets who were following her down the street. They seemed to get closer every time she looked back at them, without ever looking at her, or seeming to get faster when she looked. She'd seen how fast they could move when they wanted, and the fact they hadn't overtaken her meant that they were waiting- for her to be alone, or for something else and worse to join them.

Nor was it the sense that that something else, something grim and inexorable, was trying to burst its way to her from some bad place.

It was partly that, somehow, for twenty years, she had had Caroline there and now did not. She was used to having her—not holding her hand perhaps, because a ghost cannot do that—but just there, to help her talk, think or charm her way out of danger.

Not having her there was the worst of sadness, except for worrying about where she was and what was being done to her. It was the fear that each of them might spend eternity worrying what had become of the other. Not knowing would be a torture as bad as anything else that their enemies might do.

Fear and sadness mixed—that was what made this the worst of fear.

The two men might close with her in the twenty yards to her front door. Or when she got it locked behind her, there would be something bad waiting for her in her favourite armchair.

Of course it was those things as well.

She had faced ultimate evil, and devouring appetite, and things that could erase her world with a pure thought. But now she was panicking and struggling to make herself breathe like a proper sensible person, and not start running and probably turn her ankle and look like a fool. Shortly to be a dead fool.

Another ten yards and at least she would be inside her front door.

What if they shoot just as I'm turning the key? Or what if the lock is wired to electrocute me? Or what if there is a bomb?

It's arrogance, she said to herself, it's sheer bloody conceit, Emma Jones. You're afraid because the sort of gunman, the sort of third-rate demon, that are on your trail, are not up to the standard of the menaces you have survived. Death is supposed to be special; the universe is supposed to lay on something as big as your own sense of importance, some distinguished thing. Maybe you just get killed, and it isn't that big a deal for the universe.

But not right now, she thought as she got to her front door and locked it behind her.

She ran up the stairs to her flat, and opened that door, and locked that, and engaged the expensive system of locks and bolts she had put in a year or two earlier, and activated the charms she had bought from a kobold in southern Bavaria and a rakasha in Cawnpore. At least now she had a moment or two to think. They might get through to her eventually, but perhaps she would have an idea. Though they seemed ever further from her mind as her brain itched with stress.

Downstairs, the outer door was being hit with something heavy.

They'll bring a ram, she thought, and that will get them in down there. This door will be harder, though. Perhaps she should call the police, and perhaps that would just get some policemen killed along with her. Or perhaps they were the police, or people to whom the police deferred.

She caught sight of a bright light off to her left. It was a silver statuette she had bought on Portobello—some representation of abstract good that she had bought because it had looked so forlorn on a stall with no one worshipping it.

Caroline had sneered that it was a hideous bit of deco crap, and had then looked at it again, and said that maybe it would grow on them, maybe it was better than she had thought. She had had that look which sometimes meant that she was being told things by their employer and sometimes just meant that Caroline was being unusually nice.

That made Emma think of Caroline again, with pleasure and regret and terror.

Now it was glowing, glowing harshly, as if something were trying to push past it and it was pushing back so hard that it was burning from the inside with the effort.

Stand there for me, little statue, she said to herself, and reached out, thinking that perhaps this was imagining things and perhaps it would burn her hand.

It was cold to the touch, but seemed to throb with relief that she had touched it; hanging on to it seemed like the most important thing she could be doing right now. It wouldn't stop the men beating at her door, but it might help buy her time.

So she clutched at a statue, a statue that probably wasn't even that of any goddess anyone had actually worshipped, that had no power at all. She hung on to it because she had no idea what else to do and it felt as if she should.

"Help me." She was shocked to hear the desperation in her own voice. "Help me, whoever you are." Her friend was gone, and she felt as if she had no other friends and no other allies left to her in the world.

There was a noise of something giving downstairs, of splintering and bursting and of angry feet on the stairs.

And Emma struggled to be calm, and to think of what to do next and of how she had got here.

One of the disadvantages of a ghostly girlfriend was the constant heckling.

"Walk out, now." Caroline's voice was nonetheless urgent for the note of teasing in it. "It's not too late, and you'll look less of a twit than you will on their hideous show answering any of their damn fool questions or arguing with that horrible man."

Emma hadn't wanted to be on this awful chat show to begin with, but her agent had pleaded with her.

"You need more exposure." Natasha had made a little pleading face. Almost like a hungry child.

"Exposure?" Caroline scoffed. "That's like being naked in public, for money and not for fun."

Emma affected to ignore her and gave Natasha an equally earnest glance in return. "I've had about as much exposure as I can handle, recently." Her voice was full of reproach. "Last time you put me on television, my flat got picketed."

"Well, it got you in the papers. Being hated by religious fanatics always makes you look good by comparison."

"They threw fruit; it got everywhere."

"You always look fabulous, dear. Even with mashed banana in

237

your hair." Compliments from Caroline were always welcome, but not much use given that Natasha couldn't hear them.

"Please, pretty please." The note of pleading in Natasha's voice got so embarrassing that Emma said yes to stop her. Because, after all, she paid Natasha to know about these things, so she was probably giving Emma good advice.

Now she had got to the studio, only to find the man who had led the picket sitting in the green room sipping peppermint tea and ignoring her. Clearly bigotry was doing well for him because he had an expensively cut grey suit and the sort of horrible glossy sheen on his forehead that seems to go with ill-gotten prosperity.

"Don't look at him," Caroline did a completely unnecessary stage whisper. "The moment you turn your back on him, he looks at you as if he wants to kill you by slow torture, which he probably does. But he's very quick, so you won't catch him doing it."

Emma reached into her large shoulder bag and a small pink hand passed her a mirror. She used it to glance behind her and Caroline was right—somehow, no matter what the angle, the man was managing to avoid her gaze.

"What's Rodney Black doing here?" Emma whispered to one of the sharp young men in skinny jeans and t-shirt who zipped around the room like elegant mice, dispensing coffee and making themselves look useful.

Then she added, "You're Justin, right?" Because at least trying to get people's names right gives the impression that you are paying attention to them, even if that is not really true.

"No, I'm Jason. Justin's over there."

He seemed quite OK with her having made the mistake, so she did her best to fix who was who in her mind. It's always best to make the attempt, she thought.

"He was in for a news programme earlier," Jason explained. "Margaretha asked him to stick around when one of our other guests dropped out—because let's face it, dear, having the two of you on at the same time is liable to be amusing."

238

"What was he on the news about?" Emma sucked her lower lip under her teeth in malicious glee. "Surely he never has anything new to say except that people are bad and ought to be punished."

"Oh, something about some earthquake and how it was our fault for being gay."

Emma found this moment of solidarity rather charming, and flashed her best and broadest smile at the boy.

"You are, aren't you?" he said, nervously. "Only I've got in trouble before now for assuming about guests."

"Oh, charter member, darling."

"Only no one ever gets mentioned as in your life?"

"There was a friend at Oxford," Emma put on the most solemn voice she could manage. "But she died."

Caroline stood next to her and made loud gagging noises. Then she was suddenly sad—"I was killed"—but only Emma could hear.

Jason looked appropriately mournful a second, then leant in enquiringly. "Justin said that you and Elodie…Back before she was a star."

"Ah." Emma's smugness gave the lie to her words. "That really does fall into the category of, I can neither confirm or deny."

"That's what I hate about homosexualists," Black boomed from the other side of the room. "They pretend to be this vast family in which they all know each other, but actually they constantly tear each other down, as well as everyone decent."

Emma turned and fixed him with her coldest superior glare. "My experience is that that's a fairly good description of families, actually. Even the nice ones."

Black tried to brush her off. "Not good Christian families."

Emma laughed at him. "The number of good Christian families I've had to help. Along with good agnostic families, and good Muslim families and the rest of it. Bad feng shui and dodgy bits of karma are no respecters of faith."

Black became louder and more hostile. "All these things are like you, trips and traps and servants of the Adversary."

"Satan? I wouldn't know. I've never met the man."

"Yet you serve him."

"No, really I don't. I have an employer and they are not he."

"I am a servant of the Almighty God—and everything I do, I do because God Wills It."

"I really doubt that. You don't at all seem the sort of person that nice old gentleman would hang out with voluntarily."

"Blasphemer."

"You know, just because someone's circle of acquaintance is bigger than yours is no reason to throw insults around."

By this point, Caroline, in an unbecoming cheerleader's outfit, was dancing around with pompoms and blowing raspberries on a whistle out of a Christmas cracker.

Black turned round in a rage. "Will you stop that?" he shouted and then had the slightly embarrassed face of a man who has given something important away. As in, he could see Caroline and was thus obviously more involved in the world of magic and shadows than a man of his profession and pretensions might be expected to be.

"If you're going to shout at each other, dearies, keep it for on camera. Mummy has a headache."

From the look of her, Margaretha, link woman of Mid-Morning, had not slept much the night before and had not so much got up on the wrong side of the bed as rolled into bed that way and then fallen off again almost immediately.

"Well…" Caroline ostentatiously dropped her pompoms to put on a pair of dark glasses. "She's a friend of Dr Stoli and Miss Spliff, clearly. Red eyes at morning, journalist's warning." And she turned to Black. "Mind your manners when you talk to my beloved," she snarled. "Our employer says that you were already in his bad books, and believe me, that is not a place you want to be."

"I don't talk to familiars," he said stiffly. "Especially familiars who are the possessing demon of unnatural lust."

"Well la-di-fucking-da," said Caroline, blowing another raspberry.

"Listen to little Miss Etiquette."

Black went red in the face and started batting at her—immaterial as she was, Caroline found it fairly easy to avoid his blows. And do a sort of ballet dancer cum ninja pirouette thing at the same time. Of course, from Margaretha's point of view, Black had just started spouting nonsense at someone who was not there and hitting the unwounded air.

"Are you quite all right, Reverend Black?" she asked. "You can go and lie down if you need to."

He turned to face her, took three deep breaths, and it was as if he had never lost his temper. He went back to radiating utter calm. Emma was impressed in spite of herself, and even more sceptical about this man's pretensions to be merely a man of God and in no way involved with the wonderful world of magic.

"I wish I could control my moods like that," she muttered under her breath.

"You'd be a lot less fun," said Caroline, "and you probably would not think nearly so fast on your feet."

Justin put his head to one side, listening to an earpiece, then waved his hands about in a way that was meant to look efficient.

"We'll be ready in five." Margaretha came over to Emma with a confiding look in her eye. "I've been meaning to ask you...Who does your work? Because you look amazing. You could be twenty. You couldn't slip me his address?"

"Oh," Emma said, stalling. She really couldn't explain that her youthful looks and scarlet hair were the result of an encounter with solid geometry. "It's just good genes and washing my face in cold water every night, and letting it dry. That's the important bit, my grandmother used to say, but it was her I got the good genes from, so what did she know."

"It's a pact with the devil," Black said. "Thou shalt not suffer a witch to live. She should die by fire. God Wills It."

"Oh, please say that on camera, sweetie," Margaretha wheedled. "It would do wonders for our ratings."

"Don't think so," said Emma. "Incitement to murder a bit of a problem."

Black spat at her. "It's the unchanging word of God, that people like you should be killed." He raised a hand as if to strike at her.

Suddenly there was the most terrible pain in Emma's hand, as if something were trying to bite her fingers off. She heard a screaming in her ears so loud and full of terror that it took seconds to realize that some of it was coming from inside her head and some from her own tearing throat. It went on and on, the pain and the screaming, so that she lost track of herself for what seemed a moment, but was actually several minutes. She found herself coming to, confused, on one of the greenroom couches with a damp towel around her head and Jason fussing over her.

Caroline was standing over her too, looking concerned and not wearing anything out of the ordinary. Just the spectre of t-shirt and jeans, though rather nicely cut ones.

"Did he hit you?" Jason said. "It looked to me as if he hit you."

"No," Emma said. "He didn't hit me. I just had a migraine or something. It was nothing to do with him."

"Only it looked as if he cursed you. Or whatever Christians do instead."

Emma just wanted to get herself home. She was still holding her mirror, she realized, and when she looked in it before putting it back in the bag, she was worryingly pale. "Can you get me a car?" she asked.

"It will be waiting for us downstairs," said Jason.

He helped her to her feet, and Caroline dithered in that on-one-foot-and-then-on-the- other way she had when she was worried.

"I really don't know what just happened," Emma said, not actually to him. "It's not something that's happened before." She was used to attacks, but only those that came from outside her and that did not stop her thinking while they were going on.

"The Boss has some ideas," Caroline said. "But nothing definite. Just take it easy, if you can."

Emma found the lift small and panic-inducing in a way it had not been earlier.

"You'll get your fee," Jason said, bracing the door open for her. "Because Margaretha thinks that he did it somehow. And because it will annoy him even if he didn't."

"That's nice," Emma said, though mostly she was trying to remember what it had been that was trying to eat her fingers.

And then, quite suddenly, she couldn't breathe; there was a great hand on her head, pushing it forward and she was straining for breath and falling to the floor and then she could get air back into her lungs in great straining hoarseness, and she was vomiting dirty water.

Then again, she could not breathe, only this time she knew what was coming and kept her eyes open and saw the face of a man mirrored in the water into which her head or what seemed to be her head plunged. She could see the nails of the hand that was pushing her head.

She struggled for breath, while Jason fussed and Caroline hovered. The lift door closed and off it went without them. As soon as Emma could speak, she looked up at Caroline. "Can we block out thoughts?" she asked urgently, not caring that Jason could hear her talking to someone who was not there. "Is there some way the Boss can do that for us from wherever they are? Because this is going to go on if we can't and I don't think I can cope with it."

It wasn't just the torture, it was the sense of someone else's screaming panic pouring into hers and calling out to her for help that she was in no position to give. She knew now who it was, and had some sense of what was being done to him, and if she was going to be able to help him, she needed to shut him out for the moment.

She sat down on the padded bench by the lift and tried to put her thoughts in order.

"Tell the cab to wait a bit, Jason. And could I please have another coffee?"

She wanted to get the taste of the water out of her mouth, and she also didn't want Jason listening in. He seemed a nice enough young chap and she had a sudden awareness that her friendship could be dangerous right now.

As soon as he was off down the hallway she turned to Caroline. "It's Shallock. Someone is water-boarding John Shallock. I saw his face reflected in the bath as they plunged us under. And something is trying to eat his fingers, though not at the same time."

"I knew bridge was competitive and mean," Caroline said. "But I didn't think they went that far if you missed a bid."

"I don't think this is anything to do with bridge."

Emma thought for a second—reasoning things through was always her best way of not being scared or in pain. "Who water-boards people?" she mused aloud. "Lots of people apparently, or so the papers say."

"They're all part of the -cough splutter sarcasm—intelligence community." Caroline said. "The boss knows no more about any of that than we do. Though what would the twit Shallock be doing that any spy would care about?"

"Well, he does have a day job, remember. Moving money around."

"So maybe he's been moving money for some bad guys?"

"I don't think so, or at least…Look, there's another thing. I felt and saw the hand that was pushing his head underwater and it wasn't human. Not a bit—some sort of demon, huge clawlike nails."

"Poor John," Caroline said. "Such a civilian to get caught up in our world. Why are you picking up on him?"

"Back during all that stuff with the vampires and the elves. I gave him my card. I was showing off, was all. I didn't think it worked like that; I thought it was more like a phone call."

"People in trouble scream down the phone," Caroline said. "The odd thing is that he had the card to use—not something you would expect demon torturers to let a chap keep. I mean, they tell me it's hard enough to get the police to let you make a phone call. You have to consider the possibility that they are letting him get through to you and that it is some kind of a trap."

"Is that what the Boss is telling you?"

"No, sweetie. It's how things are. I'm not saying that we shouldn't look into whatever has happened to that nice Mr Shallock, idiot that he is—just that we will need to watch your back."

Emma felt a large clawed hand twisting Shallock's arm behind his back and caught sight of a long white corridor that seemed to stretch forever before a blindfold was pulled back down over his eyes.

But this time the pain was at a remove and was bearable, more like a piece of unwelcome information than an imminence of dying. "What did you do?" she asked Caroline.

Caroline looked slightly drawn, slightly grim. "The Boss and I are sharing it with you," she said. "I'd forgotten how much being in pain sucked. Typical of my luck that the first time in years I feel anything whatever it's pain, and it's John Bloody Shallock's pudgy body I'm feeling it through."

By this point, Jason was hovering with a rather good Americano. Emma followed him into the lift, sipping it all the way down and letting him walk her out to her cab. She hitched her bag firmly onto her shoulder; its comfortable weight let her feel business-like again.

"My advice," she said to him, "don't ask the likes of Black onto the show again."

She didn't think for a second that Black had anything to do with what had happened to her, but there was nothing to be lost by doing him a bad turn.

"Where to?" the driver said.

"New Scotland Yard," Emma said, because she had always wanted to have an excuse to say it. "And step on it."


There can never be too many policemen that owe you favours. Emma thought it best not to cash in any, but to go to the two people at the Yard that she thought of as actually her friends. These days, Sharpe was a Deputy Commissioner but his major interest was still the Spook Squad, even if he kept a watching brief on a bunch of other specialist units that no one wanted to talk about—non-human liaison, alchemy, that sort of thing.

Tom was officially a civilian consultant, though he had a permanent desk in the building and regularly practiced at the shooting range. Apparently he was one of their best pistol shots, and a gifted sniper, but those were things he didn't care to talk about.

The cheap thing to say would be that he was making up for all the things he could not do, by being the best at everything that he could. And just because it was the cheap thing did not mean that it was not, in some important ways, true.

Emma imagined that he had probably killed people, and did not want to know this for certain. There were people who had met their deaths through her and that was something with which she had made her peace; and there were people whom she could wish were dead. As yet, she had never been in a position where she had had actually to kill anyone herself, and she did not want to know or think about it. There were innocences she might lose sooner or later, but that time had not yet come and hopefully never would.

Tom looked older than when she had first met him, to a degree not entirely explained by the passage of the years. It was not the lines round his eyes, just a sense that he had seen more with those eyes than he would have wished. Had things been otherwise.

Whenever she thought of Tom, she thought of how much she liked him, and then of how terrifying he must be to the men and women he took down—a man in a wheelchair who could appear anywhere, shoot them, and leave in an instant.

Perhaps—and she was not sure this consoled her—he didn't need to kill often, because the rumour of him must be as terrible as the actual man, and dead people spread no rumours. Or perhaps he just refrained from killing witnesses.

She really did not want to know, because she liked him.

She had rung ahead—a trim young woman in uniform was waiting for her in reception and already had a name tag for her.

246

"No one ever has a name tag for me," sulked Caroline, and made up for it by instantly causing a very large badge, covered in shiny sprinkles and dayglo happy faces, to appear on the lapel of the excessively tailored pin-stripe suit she was suddenly wearing.

The conference room looked big and empty with just them and Sharpe in it, and only a little bit less so when Tom, after a minute or so of awkward silence, joined them, not through the door.

"So," Sharpe gestured Emma to a chair, "nice as it always is to see you, Emma, what is it that you could not tell us over the phone? I am quite busy these days, you know."

Tom was more cordial. "Morning, Emma. Morning, Caroline. Glad to see you're better—I was looking forward to seeing you on television and they said you had been taken ill."

The chair was a lot more comfortable than Emma had expected—firm against her back but yielding where she needed it to. Gosh, she thought, I am sitting in an ergonomically designed metaphor for contemporary policing.

"Not exactly ill." Emma settled all the way into the chair. "More, suddenly in involuntary telepathic communication with a friend who was being tortured by demons in what looked like some kind of American military prison."

Sharpe tapped a pen against his teeth. "Didn't know you knew terrorists, Emma."

"I don't. This was a middle-aged merchant banker who spends most of his time playing bridge. A man called John Shallock."

Sharpe nodded and looked more sympathetic. "I met him once. Didn't know you knew him. Deeply boring, quite likable, looks like a frog. His tailor works miracles, but still a well-dressed frog."

"He's wearing an orange jump suit now," Emma said. "And he is inside my head whimpering."

Sharpe shrugged. "Not really our thing."

"I could ask the Americans," Tom offered. "I've helped them out once or twice in the line of work." He said this in a self-deprecating tone of voice that implied its own two-figure body count. "But if I

247

ask the Yanks, it means they know we know that they are up to something, and they would probably lie about it anyway."

"She should probably ask Miss Wild," Sharpe said. "She might know." He seemed amused at the idea of asking this Miss Wild for anything. He looked across at Tom as if the pair of them were in on a joke and Emma was outside it.

Boys, she thought, bloody boys the pair of them.

"You really should meet her anyway, you two," said Tom. "You cropped up in conversation once, and she was rather impressed that I knew you."

"Who's Miss Wild?" Emma said. "Caroline?"

"Ah," said Caroline. "You know that sometimes the Boss doesn't tell me things and I realize ages later that we were supposed to find them out for ourselves in the fullness of time. Like we never seem to hear in advance from the Boss about any major player so we get to have our own ideas about them. That would be one of those times—which means she's some sort of player."

"So," Emma said. "Miss Wild...Some sort of spook—a ghost perhaps, a spook spook, or is that a spook squared?" She noticed herself drifting into the excessive verbal inventiveness that afflicted her when she was exceptionally nervous and stressed. Oh god, she thought, puns next.

"Tom knows her better." Sharpe was clearly in a mood to tease everyone. "The old woman has a bit of a thing for our Tom."

"Not old." Tom looked smug at the thought of whatever thing it was she had. "Except technically."

"So another immortal," Emma said.

"Oh goody." Caro yawned for both of them. "Someone else with thousands of years of back story that I have to relay to Emma late at night when we'd rather not be talking about other people's complicated problems."

"As immortals go," Tom said, "Miss Wild has only got three centuries on the clock."

Off Emma's look, Caroline said, "Oh sweetie, with your upgrades, you'll make that easy. But it's not like Morgan, is it? Or Sobekh, or even the dryads and the faun. Let alone the real players."

"Like Jehovah?" Tom said, knowledgeably.

"Don't think so," Emma shrugged. "Nicer old chap than you'd expect, but not that old, as these things go."

"Emma met Ultimate Evil Person once," Caroline explained to Tom. "She feels very smart because she kicked him in the goolies and got away with it. It's one of her things."

Sharpe broke in, clearly irritated. "When you are quite done, some of us mayflies, who expect not to last very long after retirement, are getting bored with conversations with invisible and inaudible beings about a whole bunch of immortals I hope never to meet, as opposed to the one—apart from possibly Emma here - with whom I have to deal regularly."

He cleared his throat and everyone looked at him abashed.

"Polly Wild is apparently several centuries old, and has been running bits of intelligence most of that time, but has not been getting on with her lords and masters all that well for the last two decades. So she is a little out of the loop, but probably someone you should talk to anyway."

Emma looked at him questioningly.

"Thatcher didn't like her; she laughed at Major; Blair and she never got on. He refuses to believe that she is real and she told him that going into Afghanistan with an army never works and that goes for Iraq too. Then she told him some complicated story about the Peninsular War which didn't work very well because the Prime Minister was pretty vague which Peninsula and which war. And she told Alastair Campbell that she'd been sworn at by the Duke, the Prince Consort and more than one Churchill and he couldn't say anything that she had not heard from his betters."

"She sounds like fun," Caroline said.

"All I want is someone who can help me find out what is going on with Shallock," Emma pleaded.

"Well," said Tom, "that pretty much means someone who is part

249

of intelligence but is not hopelessly in bed with the Americans. Whom Miss Wild does not like because she thinks that they are canting rebels who have got above themselves. Apparently she said that to Harry Truman once, and he threatened to cut off the Marshall Plan."

"Anyway," Sharp broke in, "now she doesn't have the ear of Government so much any more—which is pretty stupid given that she pretty much ran the British Empire for a century or so and then started telling everyone when it was time to wind it down rather ahead of the curve—she has got terribly into surveillance. She has resources the rest of us simply don't have."

"I used to date one of her IT girls—she picks her systems people for their looks on the grounds that if she can't understand a word they are saying at least she can watch pretty mouths making sounds—and she showed me Miss Wild's Map Room, which is a table top the size of a football pitch with screens on it that give you real time coverage of most of the world and large parts of shadow. She's very keen on watching shadow because she can't go there herself."

"Well, neither can we," Emma pointed out, "or not much and only really when we are invited. Obviously enough to do the fast time thing and the quick escape thing, but not for any distance. Never bothered us."

"Well," Tom said. "She's mates with the Huntress and it really bugs her that Mara can bomb around the universe in the blink of an eye and she is stuck in the mundane world. So she has orbital satellites in shadow, and that costs a pretty penny, I can tell you."

"She resolved the Cuban Missile Crisis," Sharpe said, "by telling Kennedy and Krushchev that she could neither confirm nor deny that she had her own nuclear strike force hidden in shadow. Macmillan sat in the Cabinet War Room getting more and more upset with her, but she told him politely to shut up and let the professionals deal with the problem. She told Krushchev she'd set Baba Yaga on him, and she told Kennedy that she'd shag him, which is more than she'd let his father do. Bit of a last hurrah for her that turned out to be, because LBJ wouldn't talk to her. He said that, when you're the President of the USA, the world is your bitch, and you don't need to be some bitch's bitch."

"So," Emma asked, "when do we see her?"

Tom looked at his watch. "She receives for coffee at 11.30 sharp, which is,"—he seized Emma by the hand and Caroline reflexively grabbed the other—"just about now."

And suddenly they were in an entirely different room, a rather elegant drawing room with soft lighting, a refreshments trolley and a number of mildly worn and baggy leather armchairs that belonged in a gentleman's club and seemed to promise endless sleepy hours of comfort.

There was also a chaise longue on which sat an alarmingly young woman in a Never Mind the Bollocks t-shirt and some very tight-fitting leather trousers. Her hair was bottle blonde with just a touch of something darker at the roots.

"'Allo, Tom," she said. "Who's your friend, and who's the ghost?" She looked a little closer. "Scarlet 'air and a ghost doxy—well I do believe it must be Miss Emma Jones. 'Onoured, I'm sure—we've bin 'earin' things about you for lo! the last score of years and I do believe you surpass bloody expectation. Welcome to an old unfashionable woman's chambers and what is it I might do for you?"

Emma looked her in the eye.

"There's a man named Shallock, John Shallock, and he is in the back of our heads, screaming. It's something to do with the Americans and something to do with Hell. Any ideas?"

Miss Wild was silent for a second, flipping through the circular files in her brain. "This would be Shallock the bridge-playing banker, I take it, rather than his cousin the Assyriologist?"

"Yes," Emma said. "I didn't know about the Assyriologist."

"Well, there you are," Polly said. "One possible lead already, 'coz Assyriologists know the summoning names of all sorts of demons and gods which pretty much amount to the same beings. If as you're an Assyrian."

"Oh," Emma remarked, "we met some once, come to think of it."

"Friends of Sobekh." Caroline was doing her best to emulate Miss Wild's look in every particular and not bringing it off nearly as well. Clearly, Emma disloyally thought, when it comes to chic, three centuries trumps being dead.

"So if you knows them socially, you could probably sod off to the Hashmolean," Miss Wild said, "and ask them if they've seen him. No, not really—they're terrible conversationalists, silly old sods."

"Good in a fight though," Caroline said.

"Forgotten that was you, when you turned up," Miss Wild said. "Owes you a favour for that, I do. Those bloody angels needed a seeing to and you saved me a load of grief and paperwork." Her grin grew ever wider. "Come to that," she added, "seeing off the elves and the vampires saved me a lot of work too. Rich gits who live a long time always bear watching, in the national interest, because they get to think they own the place. Your ordinary Lords and Ladies are bad enough, but they usually die before they get to be a problem. My boss—not the Government, you understand, though I work for them too—my real boss—he says his brother the Border Agent speaks highly of you. Then there's saving the universe—that counts as a favour too."

Her smile grew broader. "You are definitely one of the people as can call me Polly. Make yourself at home and take the weight off. Friendship has its privileges."

"I don't quite follow you," Emma said.

"I think she means," Caroline said, "that you don't have to be shy of asking her for help."

"Practically works for me already, she does," Polly said. "As well as for this mysterious employer of yours. Which means I don't have to put anything on paper, because of all these damn fool attempts to make us operate an internal market. Used to be, I could just ring Five and Six and ask for things; now it all has to be budgeted for. To which I say, bollocks, whenever I can. So anyway, your man Shallock."

She got up and waved them to a door at the far end of the room.

Tom's wheelchair negotiated the furniture remarkably efficiently, given the extent to which he was staring at Caroline's spectral arse; presumably he could afford the best robotic guidance systems. Or maybe it was magic, or one of the mutant powers he seemed to have instead.

"This is my map room," Polly said, though what was in the new room, a room which seemed to stretch on for half a mile and more, was a mixture of monitors and tables that had screens set into them. "Move with the times, gal, my da said afore they hanged him. I remember when I were a chit of a thing and someone taught him double-entry, and in six months he had four separate sets of books, all of 'em works of art. He started the map room, he did, back in the year of the old pretender. And it's grown ever since."

She picked up a heavy piece of plastic with about a hundred buttons on it. "Of course, back then it were mostly keeping track of houses we owned, and where beggars pitches were. He was working for the Master of the Mint keeping an eye on the realm for him, but he hardly used the map for that. Then French Franky taught me the way, god rest 'im, the way to really use maps, and then I brought myself into the work of the realm when the Master proved false."

She pressed a row of buttons and suddenly the screens were full—satellite views of Western Europe and street maps of London suburbs and random shots from the inside of tube trains that were not all of them the London Underground, and an endless flat scrub plain on which a group of centaurs were barbecuing something on a spit that had more legs than four.

"Hardly maps any more, as we used to use them. Put all of them in the archive a few years back—they weren't good for much except gathering dust after the walls went down."

She walked over to a keyboard, put the control down beside it and typed for a second. On an adjacent screen faces flicked past like the dealing of cards and then the screen settled on a not terribly flattering but very clear picture of John Shallock.

"This 'im", Polly Wild said, not really asking. "Let's look. Last day on the grid?..." The screen flickered and there was a shot of the top of Shallock's head, and a time stamp from a week earlier.

"That's handy," she said. "London Bus C10, from Victoria to Canada Water, and there he is, getting on at Pimlico."

She looked round at them with a grin.

"Not that I couldn't have told you where he was if it had been a bus in Shanghai, but I'd have to ask the machine."

They watched the closed-circuit feed as Shallock sat down and pulled a sandwich box out of his briefcase. He opened it, pulled out a Kit Kat, unwrapped it very carefully without tearing either the outer package or the silver foil, snapped off one chocolate finger, ate it fastidiously a single small bite at a time, and then folded the silver paper back round the rest of it, slipped it back inside the outer packaging, put it back into the sandwich box and put it back into the briefcase.

All this had taken a while. "Slow eater, your Mr. Shallock," Polly commented.

At Elephant and Castle, a man in a pink baseball cap and a grey hoodie got on. By this point the bus was quite crowded and he plonked himself down next to Shallock, who wrinkled his nose enough that the CCTV showed it quite clearly.

The man had a very grubby white plastic bag clutched in both hands as if it were heavier than it looked. It had something cylindrical inside—a large jar. Pickles perhaps.

The man reacted to Shallock's flinching by moving even closer to his personal space and mouthing at him. Then he turned and stared at the camera and mouthed exaggeratedly at that too.

There was only a stub of tongue in his mouth.

Emma tried to read his lips, but he did not seem to be making much sense. Or not in any language she knew.

"Times like this," Polly said, "we need the Huntress. She speaks everything."

Suddenly the man with no tongue lurched to his feet and pulled

254

the alarm. Then he shoved the dirty plastic bag at Shallock and staggered to the front of the bus where he vomited darkly onto the driver, who pulled to a halt as the man collapsed. The driver started shouting into his radio and tried to open his gate, but the man had fallen against it.

A woman who looked as if she knew what she was doing came over and felt the man's wrist, and then his throat and then the wrist again; she shook her head at the driver. When she let go of the wrist the second time, the man slumped over sideways and she stepped back in horror as his hand fell off as if it had suddenly been dried to salt. Not only his hand, but his hooded jacket and his jeans and the face that had been visible and the body that one assumed.

He turned to powder, and did not so much blow away as just not be there anymore.

Everyone on the bus looked at Shallock, except for a couple who were too busy screaming. He looked embarrassed and then innocent. You did not have to be able to read lips to know that he was saying "Nothing to do with me" and "I never met him before" and "Oh my god, what was that?"

Then he looked inside the plastic bag.

What he saw there made his face go grey with shock and made him pull the edges of the bag tightly together again. And hang onto the bag as if it were the most important thing he could think of.

The bus had stopped somewhere nondescript up towards Borough Tube station and a couple of police vans drove up and a constable knocked on the door of the bus which the driver opened. The passengers rose and started to leave the bus, Shallock among them.

Polly rapped on another of her screens. The next moment there were two views, one from inside the bus and another from a camera somewhere on a wall just to the side of what happened next.

The driver pointed to Shallock, and said something, and two policemen grabbed him the moment he stepped off the bus. One of them snatched the bag from him while the other slammed him against a wall.

The policeman looked inside the bag and reacted with even more shock and horror than Shallock had. He put it down on the ground, stepped away from it and then aimed a sharp sudden punch into Shallock's kidneys.

By now Shallock was crying out in pain—the officer who had him against the wall had twisted his arms over to one side to give his colleague access. John seemed to be mouthing over and over "I didn't know him" and "My god, what is that thing?"

The policeman who had hit him once, hit him again, and the other passengers clustered around, and seemed to be cheering this on. More police arrived and shoved the passengers away, forming a cordon some ten feet round about Shallock.

A door opened in the wall where there had been none before, just where he was being shoved and punched, and the policeman who had his arms shoved him staggering through it.

The watchers, pressed in around the screen, caught a glimpse of Shallock falling to his feet on the white plastic flooring of an endless white corridor. Then the door shut again and the wall was unbroken where it had been open.

The policeman who had put the plastic bag down picked it up gingerly, while a colleague brought him a large container that looked heavy enough to be made of lead. He put the bag inside it and closed the container. The door in the wall, suddenly visible, again, opened once more, and they carried it through as the door closed behind them.

Each time they saw a flash of an endless white corridor, and each time when the door shut it was as if it had never been there.

One of the policemen clapped his hands, and the people from the bus who had been milling around in a vaguely mob-like manner suddenly blinked, all of them at once, looked at each other in confusion and dispersed in various directions as if they had no idea where they were. The remaining police got into their vans, vans which displayed no numbers, nor even plates, and drove away.

Along the road for a while, into the blank patch of anonymous office buildings between Borough and the Elephant and Castle roundabout, and then suddenly down through a hatch that opened in it, and into a rather larger stretch of white corridor. Again, once the hatch closed, it was as if it had never been there.

The worst thing about it was, none of the pedestrians seemed to notice it happening, and a motorcycle courier swerved to avoid it, as if he saw things like that every day.

"Well," Polly said, "that's a pretty piece of villainy."

Emma looked sternly at Tom, who was very slightly open-mouthed. "Those weren't any part of the police you know about, were they?"

He shook his head. "No numbers. Wrong buttons. We don't own a corridor. We don't need one because we have me."

"That's what I thought." Emma looked round at Caroline, who was uncharacteristically silent.

"I've always loathed the man," she finally said. "But poor bloody John."

"Poor all of us," Polly said. "I've no idea what's in that bag, but something nasty."

She tapped a screen that now showed a blown-up still of one of the policemen hitting John. His sleeve had ridden up, revealing a tattoo there, a spiral and a cross.

"Now that I recognize—your man Green owns a security firm, as does all the Yanks' work what is too dirty for all the agencies with initials. Burnedover Inc., they call themselves and they hire every bad bastard the armies of the world discharge for being too bastardly. That's who's got your friend."

"Evildoers who should never have entered my realm without our knowing of it," said the loud voice of a presence that was suddenly in the room, towering over everyone with more than height.

Emma had never seen the constantly changing flickering being before, but she knew who he was, or perhaps they were, from a sudden lowering of Polly's head more subservient than a curtsey would have been, and from a family resemblance to the Border Agent she had met in California.

257

"My Lord," she said politely, bowing her head in turn, and Caroline and Tom imitated her.

"Miss Jones," the Lord of Coasts and Cliffs said, "fair spirit, prince without a throne. I have much to thank all of you for. And will do so on some other day."

He was more courtly than his younger brother, with more grey in the hair at his temples. And sometimes he flickered, as if this was only one of his faces, the one he chose to show to Emma and Caroline.

He looked at Emma's bag with sudden attention. "And Miss Jones' other companions," he added. "You have all served, and are all welcome."

He turned back to Polly.

Emma realized that he was at once the biggest personage she had met in some time and one who could move through this room full of desks and screens and files with the elegance of a dancer.

"Someone has found a way in, of which we knew nothing. We should not be surprised—of late, too many of the men and women who have power in the land have no care for the land. They care for rule and for wealth, but not for the land or its people. I guard the borders as I always have, but there are holes at the heart."

A terrible sadness resonated in his voice and Emma found herself moved; he had the gift of compelling loyalty and she had no wish to resist.

"Always have been, some," Polly said. "There's a place in the City, as we call the Dutch Liberties because it doesn't belong to London any more. Charles—that dour sod people call Merry—signed himself away to the Frogs there, and we lost it."

"I had no jurisdiction there," the Lord said, "and no power to keep things from coming into it from shadow."

"Bad things. Worms and such." Polly shook her head. "Like of which we've never heard the like of. Even in shadow. Dutch Willem fixed it, but he was never the same afterwards. And he couldn't make it England again."

"In his bones," the Lord said, "he was a Dutchman. Though a good King of England."

"Better a bit of Holland," Polly agreed, "than a great tear into shadow. Good place to go if you know it's there—decent drop of pea soup, or a spliff if you're so inclined."

Her Lord looked unamused.

"It ain't about their being foreign, them as is," Polly said, "because you can have someone foreign, like the first Georges, and it doesn't make a problem, first as they have someone like Walpole to run things for them, and second because they care about where they're from and that makes them come to care for here." She looked for a second as if she wanted to spit. "Queens and bloody kings ain't the problem any more."

She turned to her master, who seemed about to disagree, and then back to Emma. "He's set in his ways, old dear. And he got used to them down the years. But really, most of them might as well be so many codfish for all the difference they make—young David bad combination, stupid and selfish. But we got Baldwin to settle his hash, no problem."

She smiled one of those smiles of utter vindicated hatred you never want to see pointing at you. "Thatcher, though."

"Why did that woman get to rule my realm?" The Lord spat the words through his teeth as if he had rather use them to tear something apart.

"Comes in here, bold as you like, and says, 'What's the point of all this then?' So he says he is the guardian of the nation. 'Ah,' says she. 'So I come to you about immigration?' And 'e says, 'We have always been a refuge and been enriched thereby.' And she turns to 'er minions and she says, 'I thought this was someone of importance and it's just some Guardian reader.' So I say to 'er, 'He's a tutelary spirit,' and she looks as if the only spirit she is interested in is Dewars. Then she asks what we are going to do about the miners for her, and then I realized we had a real problem. Because she saw that as a war, a war she was going to win. Agin her own."

"There are holes in the nation," the Lord said, "it will take a century to knit, and another like William, prepared to sacrifice his peace of mind for the realm."

"So I asked wossisname, Major, when he took over, was he up for sacrificing himself for the Land, and he said he would rather not. And went off to the cricket. Which was at least a very English thing to do, and did no more harm. And now there's Blair."

"I cannot see the man," the Lord said. "Others have torn holes in the realm, and he is just such a hole."

"'E's the sort that would sell the realm to the devil and think it a smart bit of revenue raising," Polly agreed.

"So, anyway." Emma was enjoying the diatribe but wanted to get back to actual business. "What you're saying is, that as a result of government policies of which you disapprove, John has been abducted by Americans over whom you have no control."

"Pretty much," Polly said. "Galls me to admit but I didn't even know about this white corridor until just now." She thought for a second. "Dunno how I'll get my eyes into it, but we'll manage. Eventually."

The Lord looked pensive for a moment, and then vanished. And flickered back two minutes later.

"My brother the Border Agent has no knowledge of it either," he said, and vanished again.

Polly gestured them back into the drawing room. "I wish I could help," she said, "but it seems as I cannot."

"Poor John," Caroline said and then winced. Both she and Emma had felt something unpleasant with sharp teeth gnawing on the little fingers of their left hands.

"Oh bother this," Emma said. Because this time she was expecting it, and felt back along the pain.

Somewhere underlying the agony, there was a skein of connection. Emma kept her mind close to that connection and summoned flame, just as if she were setting fire to some small thing close at hand. Because it was close at hand, at the end of the connection, which might be with something in the white corridor, but was also something as close as her own mind.

"Sorry John," she said. And set fire to the small business card that he still had somewhere in his possession.

Momentarily, she felt the burning of her own fire, and then it flared up, and stopped, and the pain in her finger as well.

Caroline looked relieved. Though then she started sucking her finger exaggeratedly and was suddenly sporting an enormous white bandage on it.

Emma groped around in her mind, and found a wisp of the skein of connection still there.

And a bell started ringing, until Polly snapped her fingers and it stopped.

"Now that's one thing we don't allow in here," Polly said. "Prying eyes as we have not invited."

Suddenly the Lord was back, and placed his hands on Emma and Caroline's foreheads.

When he spoke though, it was not to, but rather through, Caroline. "I shall, of course, respect your confidence," he said, presumably to their unknown employer. "I really had no idea."

He turned to Emma. "I take it that you are now rid of your friend's pain. I have rid you of a spy as well."

"Of course," Emma said. "My Lord, Miss Wild, I had no idea that it was a conduit through which John's torturers could track my whereabouts, or spy on us."

"No reason you should," Polly said. "And I don't think they can even have tried it, until just now. Which means that when we looked at the tapes, something felt us look."

"It is," said the Lord, "as if the White Corridor is a realm all of its own, but one new enough that its Lord knows not how to talk even to their own kind. My cousins in the Arab lands and beyond have felt their presence but cannot make them listen. It is as if they are some Lord of a realm not of this world, or anything but the Farthest of shadow."

Caroline frowned in concentration, listening to the latest from their Employer. "Boss says that it felt like something was trying to get a fix on them. And no one has managed that in centuries."

"Perhaps," Emma said, "the Boss needs to consider what sort of being might be able to do that. Given that some very important players must have been trying to find the Boss forever. Perhaps the Lord of some other realm entirely, since not even the Enemy has ever come close to getting a fix on the Boss." She thought for a little, and pulled a face. "Last time we dealt with anything from Outside, the world nearly ended."

"Trouble with Outside," Polly said, "is there's no real way to spy on it. Makes shadow look easy. Your friends the Solids—we never got a fix on where they are since their little incursion. Believe me, the Lord and his sibs have tried. As scary for them as for everyone, that was."

Emma shook her head. "This is something new. The Solids won't be back."

"Wherever this realm is," the Lord said, "it will have borders and its Lord will wish to protect them."

"Well," Emma wrinkled her face in thought as she spoke, "that's the thing. You're assuming that all realms are the same as the lands you and the Border Agent guard, and that guarding means the same thing. But the Solids not only had a realm, but were it. And yes, you could say they were keen to protect it from contamination, because that is why they went away. But this White Corridor Being is quite prepared to fill his realm up with Americans and demons and unfortunates like Shallock—we have to ask ourselves why."

"Money?" Polly suggested. "Always a sensible wager."

"Wouldn't work with the Solids, and this might be at least as strange as them."

"I've known few gods or demons," Polly said, "that you could not buy. The Huntress, of course, but she knows what money is. Just chooses not to need it."

"Of course," Caroline said, "apart from money, there are two other things beings want."

Tom had the face of someone who is not going to be the person who asks. She gave up waiting for questions and launched into "Beings want to eat and they want a fight for its own sake."

"Two things I would rather not contemplate." Emma had the morose face of someone who already contemplated such things far too much. "Let's hope that the White Corridor is just here so that the Americans can pay its lords and masters a lot of money in rent for using it as their mobile torture chamber."

"Cheery soul, ain't you," Polly said. "I've people who might be able to find out about that."

Caroline looked interested. "Clairvoyants?"

Polly smiled and showed her teeth again—god, those are good teeth for someone three hundred years old, Emma thought. "I have my ways, and my means, and I don't talk about them even to myself."

Polly and Caroline were engaging in the sort of mutual staring that for the aggressive counts as bonding, and Emma thought some more. So much to learn in the world, and if you're me, half the time people assume you know it already. "Before the Solids," she said aloud. "did anyone even know that there was anything beyond the world and shadow?"

Polly shrugged. "Not the sort of thing I even bother thinking about, makes my head hurt. But back when I took this job, the Master of Coin, 'im as held my place before me, came to me once. Ten years after he died, and we talked. Mostly about the Elixir and such."

"Once we dead people start talking," Caroline said, "the problem is usually shutting us up."

"More's the pity," said Tom, and then flashed a boyish smile. Caroline stuck her tongue out at him, and then sat in his lap.

"The Master said that he had been out at the moons of Jupiter and their shadows—and there were things there that troubled him."

"What on earth was he doing there?" Emma asked, startled. "Never occurred to me that spirits could do space travel, which is silly of me really."

"The Huntress sent him there," Polly said. "He was a new-minted demi-god and there are those as don't care for such, like His Nibs and Him Below. And I was angry with him for good and sufficient reason, and Mara had scores of her own to settle with him. So sending him off to look at something he was liable to be interested in seemed good to her."

"So what did he find?" Tom had the avidity of someone afflicted with far too much sense of the miraculous and wonderful for a man who had made his business the dispensing of murderous violence.

"He said as there were no words to tell it, and no mathematics either, until he had finished a new calculus. He'd been and made his peace with Heaven and Hell, but said no one there had the intellect to help him describe what he had seen. Something stretched, he said, something that pulled. Made my head hurt when he tried to explain."

Caroline jumped up from Tom's lap, sticking her hand up. "That's easy. Magic Black Hole. Obviously."

Emma did not feel nearly as confident in her understanding as she managed to make herself sound. "Not sure how that would work. Because we already know that in at least one of the places Outside, mathematics are different. But yes, kind of. Maybe."

"Clever clogs, the pair of you," Polly said. "So off he goes and takes a spare chair in Jehovah's study when it's offered him, and he just scribbles away for a century or so, and then he comes round to me and he says is there anyone I can think of that could help him. So off I sends him to that nice Mr. Einstein and they come back a few years later, when Mr. Einstein 'as joined him in demi-godhood, to his major bloody embarrassment, godless as he was. And they're still foxed."

"What about Hawking?" asked Tom

"Tried that," Polly said. "Nice chap, really clever. Just spent all his time being in awe."

"Well," Emma said. "Newton and Einstein, you can see."

"Hmph" Tom grumbled. "Just as important as them."

264

"Oh," Polly said. "I didn't know as you knew that it was Isaac I followed in this job, pox on the little creep."

"Pretty obvious," Caroline said.

"Really," Tom said.

"We all grew up watching University Challenge," Emma added. "Tom was on a team one year. We know stuff."

Polly looked miffed, but continued. "So last time I saw him, I asked him if there was any news and he said there were many interesting realms that we know not of. In the mind and in the past. Where the sleepers are. But then he looked scared and said I need not trouble myself and to forget until it was time."

"The sleepers awake, and the ring of flesh bursts and all is undone," Emma and Caroline said, in chorus.

The Lord of Cliffs and Shores looked at them aghast. "How do you know of such things?"

"Goes with our job," Emma said. "We are, after all, about the Boss's business." She turned to Polly. "It's some sort of prophesy, supposed to be a huge secret and no one knows what it means but it crops up all over the place. Egyptian fauns, Sumerian tablets, those sorts of thing. Lord of Ultimate Evil person tries to suppress people knowing it. And now, it seems, Isaac Newton."

"Black-hearted alchemical bastard as did for my dear old dad," Polly said. "But yes, he said that stuff along with all the stuff about mathematics he hadn't invented yet and it just sounded like some of the nonsense he went in for some of the time. When he were alive. Mad from mercury and not even from 'aving the pox or the fun as goes with the pox. I think he is mad still; last time he and Einstein came, he took back his books of alchemy, what I seized from him in Anno Domini 1727."

Alchemy, Emma thought, now that's interesting—but she never got the chance to complete the thought. There was a blast of hot air at the back of her neck, followed by two heavy hands on her shoulders. She felt herself pulled backwards and lifted and saw the faces of her companions, even that of the Lord, display sudden alarm.

She heard, and saw, Caroline scream in terror.

And as a white door slammed suddenly shut before her eyes, she realized that, for the first time in years, she was utterly without any sense of Caroline and their employer watching her. When the elves had pulled her behind their barrier, it had been bad enough, but this felt like a far more radical disconnection.

The hand on her right shoulder let go of her; that on her left spun her around.

There stood someone who might have been the Reverend Black, save for the fact that he was a decade younger and had a tight buzz cut. His look of passionate hatred was the same.

She looked at the insignia on the grey, white and brown camouflage uniform he was wearing "Captain Black?"

"No"—his glower grew more intense—"Major Green." And then he slapped her, so hard that it felt like a punch. "You needn't think your fine magic friends can help you here, witch."

"I don't suppose," Emma said, "that there is any point in my pointing out what you have just done. Kidnapping a foreign national, invading a government installation of a friendly power, then committing assault."

"I don't answer to anyone who cares about such things, I am a patriot and a Christian and an executive manager at Burnedover Security Solutions, Iraq branch office. Whatever I do, God wills it."

Emma looked at him, considering how his face would fall away from all that tension and animal aggression once he was dead. It really would be an improvement. "I was kidnapped once before, you know."

Green looked sublimely uninterested.

"I had no weapons, and no powers, and no magic friends. And before the end of that day, my kidnapper had lost everything he cared about and was a broken shell of what he had been before."

"Are you threatening me?" Green spat in her face, and slapped her again. It hurt even more the second time.

Emma blinked back the water that filled her eyes along with the pain. "No, just pointing out that actions have consequences."

She knew, in theory, how this all worked. They do their best to break you, and in the end usually succeed; you resist by not making any concessions whatsoever and hope that you can hang on to yourself long enough that someone organizes a rescue or negotiates a release.

People knew she had been taken—but the same people had, she knew, no idea at all of where the White Corridor could be found except that it involved Americans and demons, all of them probably deniable.

Still, at least she might manage to find out where John Shallock was, and why they had taken him, and to bring the poor man some sort of comfort. She might not be the reason why he was in this mess, but she still felt responsible for him.

And then she realised that Green had slammed his elbow into her stomach and she felt like puking, but somehow it was all miles away.

"She's one of the clever ones," a slightly accented voice said.

"You'll never break her like that," said an older man, with a different accent. "She's gone inside her head and is thinking. You would think the intelligent ones would be easiest to break, but I assure you it is not so."

"That, dear colleague, is because you never had access to electrical current. I found it good at breaking eggheads, usually."

"She's just some stuck-up English witch bitch," said Green. "Nothing special."

"You clearly didn't read her files," said the first voice. "She has protection. You got lucky."

"The All-Highest likes her, apparently," the second voice said incredulously. "Even though she is a godless pagan who practices necromantic and unnatural lust."

"He moves in mysterious ways," Green said. "We should not question. Whatever I do, God wills it."

A hand prodded Emma in the ribs, where she was sore from Green's punches, but so gently that it was hardly painful.

"Pretty lady," said the first voice, and she looked up and saw a handsome blond face, marred by a strange rictus, as if his face were largely paralysed, and a tongue that lolled wetly. There were several neat holes punched in the jacket of his tailored black uniform. Somehow the lolling tongue and ventilated lungs did not give him any sort of speech impediment, but then why should she expect logic when dealing with the walking dead?

And she hated him, not merely for what he was, or what he was going to do to her, but because he and his colleague had pulled her out of the safe space in her head to which she had run from Green.

"Would you like to see your friend?" he asked. "We will take you to him."

"This is what we do, Green," said the older man in lecturing tones, and then turned to smile benevolently at Emma like a jolly uncle. If a jolly uncle had skin that was weathered and brown like an old apple that had sat in a drawer too long and gone to dust inside its skin. He wore voluminous brown robes tied at the waist with a simple piece of rope that wrapped around twice, and looked to be skin and bones inside it all. "We get her attention, Green," the jolly uncle went on, still smiling, "by feeding her a little bit of hope, and then we tell her, as I do now, that there is nothing to hope for. That she cannot help her friend, because we have broken him already as we will break her. There is no need for any more brutality, because we will hurt her through her feelings of friendship and compassion. And tell her what we are doing, so that it hurts more."

Given that she had been threatened by the lord of ultimate evil, or something like that, she felt that there was something a little perfunctory about the old man's performance. She also noticed that he was looking sidewise at Green as if he was hoping for a good report. Green looked mildly impressed and more than a little bored.

"I'll leave her with you two then, Reinhold." Green looked at his watch.

"Reinhard," the other said, a touch of anger in his voice.

"Whatever," said Green impatiently. He reached out and slapped the wall of the corridor three times on a tile that was slightly discoloured if you looked at it against the ones surrounding it.

A door opened in the wall, and Emma watched as Green stepped out into what looked like a large car park, except that there were tanks in it as well as cars, and everything was covered in a fine white dust on which the sun glinted so hard it made your eyes water.

The door slapped to behind him with something more like a squelch than a slam.

"Come, Miss Jones," said the older man, tugging at her with a clawlike hand. "Come and be broken. You will be grateful by the end, I do assure you."

"Or not," said Reinhard. "You may care about her soul, but I don't. She is as damned as we are, but she is still warm. I would take pleasure in breaking her for that. And then killing her. But I do not care about her soul, or whether she wants to have my children afterwards."

"Damned?" The older man spoke with a passionate certainty that made him sound quite mad—or perhaps, Emma thought as he went on, not certainty at all. "You may be, for all I care, godless pagan that you are. I am in Purgatory, and part of my curative torment is to be told that I am damned, but I do not believe it, for all I did and do was to the glory of God. I am visited and tormented by visions, but I do not believe what they tell me. And my faith is being tested, as Job's was, though his comforters were less irritating than that man Green."

Yes, she thought to herself, I know that tone; that is the voice of a very intelligent person trying to convince themselves of what they know to be untrue. She knew it because it was a voice she had heard inside her own head, but this did not make her like Tomas more.

The blond snickered. "Tell yourself that, Tomas, and perhaps you will never be in Hell at all, because you have the delusion of hope. Which I am too sane to need."

He doesn't sound sane, Emma thought, but while they are bitching at each other, neither of them is doing anything to me. Also, the way that they glower means they must dislike Green only a little bit more than they dislike each other.

She hitched her bag firmly on to her shoulder.

"So, gentlemen,"—she might as well take the initiative—"if we are done for the moment with the physical indignity part of the proceedings, perhaps you would show me to my cell—or perhaps to Mr. Shallock, if you would. I would say, if you would be so kind, but in your profession that is probably an insult."

She started down the endless corridor and they fell in beside her, though not in such a way as to feel obtrusively like her jailers.

The older man looked at the younger man and laughed aloud. "They told me she was fearless and insolent, but I had not quite believed it. Clearly the world moves towards its end that has such unnatural creatures in it."

She noted a surprising avoidance of actual violence towards her from them—but then, whoever they were (though she had a pretty good idea), they were clearly only the hired help, and with Green gone, they considered themselves off the clock. And Green could not even be bothered to keep their names straight. What kind of villain misses that particular trick? You don't hire the best and then disrespect them—bound to cause trouble.

These were two of the worst people she would ever meet, but somehow, for them, she was an interesting break in routine.

Reinhard looked at her slyly. "We hear things, even in Hell."

Emma found it amusing that there was gossip in Hell—but then, hardly surprising. "What precisely have you heard?" Her tone was frosty, but not enough to cause offense.

"Well…" Reinhard's voice dropped, almost shy. "Little Boots told us, that he'd heard from Belial, that you are…"

Tomas looked scandalized, impatient and very slightly prurient all the time. "It's a thoroughly blasphemous rumour that you and the Lord God, who does not do such things –"

Emma caught on, and was mildly offended. "Oh, how ridiculous. I only met him the once and there were all sorts of other things going on around us. We ate cake and I poured him a cup of tea and my girlfriend was a little jealous."

270

They were nonetheless impressed.

"So you have actually met him?" Tomas sounded shocked. "Your file said so, but…"

"I saved the universe, and he thanked me." Emma felt smug saying this, because it was not only devastatingly impressive, but also true.

They'd all been walking down the endless corridor as they talked, and they came to a door beyond which Emma could hear moaning.

"We have to chain you up in here, if that's all right," Reinhard said.

"That's all right"—Emma felt that being gracious was better than showing even the slightest sign of fear—"and after all, you're only doing your job." Then, on a sudden inspiration, "That you're being paid for."

They glanced at each other like men with a grievance.

"Ah, I misspoke. You don't see a penny, do you? It all goes upstairs—no, silly me, that would be downstairs."

Reinhard grumbled like a soldier having a good moan where none of his superiors were there to hear him. "We get out of Hell for a bit and we get to eat American army rations, which are full of preservatives and fat, but better than flaming dung."

The older man looked slightly wistful. "I rather like the little fried sticks."

Emma was getting impatient. "If anyone important—like God—ever asks me, I will say you were perfect gentlemen and only obeying orders. Now take me in the cell, chain me up and let me talk to poor old John,"

Reinhard reached into the pocket of his well-tailored black uniform jacket and produced a keyring—impressive, Emma thought, that there was no bulge. Is that magic, or just Hugo Boss? He put something high-tech looking against the door and it beeped and swung open. Shit, that's not going to be pickable.

The room was brightly lit, and yet somehow John had managed to cower in a corner, so pathetic looking that it was as if he had had to create his own shadow to give himself a place to hide.

"Hi John, how are you?" Because what else do you say and how do you tackle the situation except by being perky?

He didn't seem to be restrained, except by a single long chain and cuff around his ankle.

"I'm afraid, Miss Jones," the older man said, "that we will have to restrain you rather more thoroughly than your friend. We have, after all, read your file." He reached into his robes and produced a small electronic device that he ran over Emma's jacket and hair.

She handed him her bag. "There's not much in there," she said. "Some pills and some tampons and a notebook."

He took it with distaste, and passed it to Reinhard as if it was going to make his hand sticky. Reinhard put it down hurriedly in the corner of the room furthest from John, and from the elaborate set of manacles towards which Tomas shooed her.

"Whatever is in there," the German said, "neither of you will be able to reach it."

Ah, Emma thought to herself, either they have not read my files as thoroughly as they like to think or their files are not especially detailed. She sat down and looked over Reinhard's shoulders as they busied themselves attaching chains to her. Good old-fashioned locks with keys, though I don't know how we are going to get out of the cell if it's got some kind of fancy fob thingy.

Sufficient to the day, she thought. As her eyes adjusted to the brightness she noticed a shelf halfway up the wall, and upon it a transparent jar like the one she had seen John be given on the bus, only rather larger. Something was writhing gently inside it, and she saw Tomas glance at it uneasily.

"Are we done?" he said to Reinhard, who nodded. As they retreated towards the door, averting their gaze from the jar, Tomas kicked something that clinked; he bent down and picked up his own set of keys.

"Why can't you wear something sensible? With pockets?" Reinhard tutted with annoyance. "For some reason, Joseph has been allowed an entire closet full of his best suits and you'd probably fit them. More or less."

Tomas waved the keyring at the door, which obstinately failed to blip even when he touched it with his fob. "I hate magic," he snapped. "But at least you could rely on it, once you burned the people who made things for you. Not like all this alchemy or whatever it is."

Reinhard looked at him pityingly. "Tomas, Tomas, perhaps now we are in a new millennium, you should consider asking the Old One if you can stay in a nice quiet part of Hell simmering gently. Or you could try"—he emphasized his words as he waved his own fob and got the door open instantly—"getting a grip." He walked through the door and made as if to slam it leaving Tomas inside, before catching it before it snapped locked, and elegantly bowing him through.

He waved an elegant hand at Emma. "Auf wiedersehen, Miss Jones, though I fear it may well be Goodbye."

"Behave yourself," Tomas said, "and they will probably not pursue things to any unpleasant conclusions. And, remember, we treated you as well as we were allowed."

Emma got the impression he wanted to say more, but she had more important things to think about and waved the pair of them off.

When the door slammed shut, John gave a last terrible whimpering moan, and then, once their footsteps retreated down the corridor, sat up and tried to smile. "Long time no see."

His attempt at perkiness nearly broke Emma's heart. "You needn't pretend, John. I know just how much they hurt you. I was there for some of it. And presumably my setting fire to the card didn't help."

John gave a sad little laugh.

"Oh, I didn't have it anywhere near me by then. Once they'd set up the link, they tried to keep it well away from me, especially after I grabbed it and tried to eat it. You started a very spectacular little fire on my interrogator's desk—took out his keyboard, his coffeemug and a picture of his hideous wife. And once you'd done that, there was no point in keeping me out of this room, where they want me to be close to that."

He pointed to the jar, and the thing Emma couldn't quite see writhed as if reacting to his attention.

"What is it?"

"Dunno, but it tries to talk inside my head. And asks me to love it."

"That's creepy."

"You've no idea. When I say love, what it seems to mean is, bite off my fingers one at a time and feed them to it. The man who gave me it didn't seem to have many left—and he didn't have a tongue either."

He held up his right hand, and waggled his fingers proudly, all ten.

Emma smiled at John, impressed. "They've had you for days, and you're a civilian. How on earth have you kept all your body parts?"

"Mostly I rehearse bidding strategies, in my head. Also, no way I could play serious bridge without my fingers, is there?"

She glanced over at the jar again and then looked away. Somehow, the more you looked at it, the more it moved. "What does it look like? All I've seen so far is a lot of writhing."

"Pretty much all there is, from what I saw when I had it close. I was hoping, Emma, that you'd have some sort of idea. It's like odd bits of flesh that are sort of vapour and occasionally liquid and every so often you'll see an eye or a finger-tip. Either bits of people it's eaten, or just odd bits of junk."

Emma thought for a bit. "Not quite all there, and wants to be loved, and wants to eat you a bit at a time. Sounds a bit like worship to me."

"What?"

Emma remembered that John was a churchwarden.

"I'm afraid, John, that I have to tell you a couple of things you won't like. There are several gods, of which yours is only one of the more powerful and comparatively nice. They seem to thrive on abject devotion—even this woman I did some work for, who seemed to be coasting a bit, had this whole army of men who were prepared to die horribly for her, screaming her name in passion."

He looked vaguely grumpy.

"And that?"

"Well, I think maybe when no one worships them any more, they get sick and die. Like goldfish if you forget the ants' eggs. They live off their fat until they fall apart. Only this one seems not quite to have died off entirely. Someone found it and put it in a jar and fed it, and now it seems to have perked up a bit."

John sighed. Deeply.

"Whatever it is, it's weird being near it. It's as if I am tired all the time and never seem to need to sleep. That's apart from the wanting me to feed it bits of myself thing. It's like the third day of a tournament when the rush went long ago and you have to keep going and thinking clearly but there is somehow less of you to do it with but you still want to win."

The poor thing sounded so depressed that Emma thought she had better do something to cheer him up, like start organizing an escape. She pursed her lips, and whistled gently.

Her bag got up on little brown cat feet and wandered skittishly over to her, and a small pink hand poked out of the top of it. It made a small row of things beside Emma's nearest manacle—a hatpin, a hair grip and then a couple of actual lock-picks.

"Well-done, both of you," Emma said.

Then the pink hand went back into the bag and came out with Emma's keyring. She didn't understand at first, but then it waved the keys around a bit until she realized that there was an extra fob on it.

"Clever, clever larcenous dears," she said, extremely pleased. "Now you're exactly what the Spanish Inquisition does not expect."

John looked over with interest.

Emma smiled. "I don't know how they do it, either. The hand just took up residence one day and started doing things for me. Whatever it is, it's the sort of thing that brownies are supposed to be, except I don't have to put milk out for it, just occasionally spill a drink into my bag. Which, since it came alive, has developed a bit of a booze habit too. I've no idea where it got the dud extra fob from— I think it sometimes steals things for the sake of it."

John smiled wistfully at her. "I'm glad you've got friends, even odd little silent ones. I always worried that you were very lonely."

"Of course I'm not lonely, John. I mean, apart from these two, there's Caroline."

He looked genuinely puzzled and for a second Emma couldn't remember why.

"She shared a set with me in our second year," she explained, "and she got eaten, and they stole everyone's memories of her. She's shared my life ever since she became a ghost."

John furrowed his brow a second and then light seemed to dawn. "Oh, hang on," he said. "I do remember. Why would I remember? Blonde woman, sarcastic, very grand."

The fact that someone's very powerful, very dark magic was no longer working on John was not even a bit reassuring.

Emma looked urgently at the hand, which worked faster on the third manacle, snapped it open with a click of its long delicate fingers and then closed it gently but without letting it relock.

She realized that, as they had been talking, the jar had been making a noise, a bit like rustling and a bit like humming. And John was looking paler and more drawn by the minute. He seemed almost to drift asleep for a second, and then came suddenly awake with a look of terror on his face. He held up his left hand, now little more than a stub.

"I don't remember," he said, his voice at once dreamy and staccato, "I don't remember that happening. I remember saying no, and no, all over again. I know I did, and oh it must have been out of its jar and nibbling at me and whispering in my ear."

And then he said nothing else coherent, just kept saying, "whispering."

Emma was free now, and the hand passed her her keys and she stood up and took one of the lock-picks and started to fiddle with the single manacle around John's ankle. He was mumbling and trembling with the most terrible of agues.

She felt the manacle lock click open and almost at once, all that was inside it was John's trouser leg, empty, and he was gone to dust, gone to dust even faster than the man on the bus.

The worst thing was, that the dust was on her hands, and she wiped them against each other to be rid of it, and on the empty trouser leg, that it not be on her own clothes, and he was gone and she wanted rid of his last remains.

He had never been one of her closest friends, but he was possibly one of the last people who remembered her before she had responsibilities. However young she now looked, she felt his death in her heart like years' worth of ageing.

From outside the door came laughter, and clapping.

It was Green, she saw through the small glass window in the door. Green and a couple of other soldiers who looked just like him. Smug, crewcut, square-jawed bullies who thought they owned the world, and owned her.

"Sit down, Jones," he said, "and I'll send someone in to sweep up your friend and prepare you to be the next meal. There was only ever one way this was going to end. As God wills it."

"As God wills it," the two other soldiers echoed, in voices exactly like his.

"Really?" Emma was caught in a precise moment of cold steel. She was watching herself and the moment went on and on. "Really?"

She leapt to her feet. Dashing to the shelf, she hefted the jar with one straining hand and waved the fob with the other. There was a beep and the door sprang open. She reached up with the hand with the fob and with both hands hurled the jar, and the thing inside, out into the corridor. As she slammed the door shut and used the fob to lock it again, she heard the breaking of glass and the humming and whispering of which John had spoken.

"See how you fucking like it!" she shouted and was appalled, a little, that she felt no guilt when, through the door, she heard one shot, and then heard Green scream. And then his men scream. And then a silence that was worse than the screams.

At last she stood and looked through the window, because we should always see the awful things we have done, but all she could see was a swirl of body parts not connected to anything, a whirlwind that grew redder the longer she looked.

Then there was a sudden thicker splatter that blocked the window altogether for a few moments, and left distorting streaks where it cleared at all. There were screams again now, and the sound of automatic weapons fire, but all moving further and further away.

There was nothing to stay in the room for. John was dust and less, and a torn shirt and some elegantly tailored trousers stained to ruin. Emma picked her bag up; it snuggled in against her comfortingly, while the hand reached out and stroked the back of her wrist. She waved the fob again and opened the door.

There was no sign that anything bad had happened here except that the corridor was almost sparkling clear, as if it has been scoured and polished. Picked clean. I guess, Emma thought, that newly risen zombie gods cannot afford to waste a single mouthful. All that was left were a few brass uniform buttons, as shiny and clean as everything else, and the parts of a gun, disassembled and left in a neat stack.

Emma started down the corridor and, as she passed, looked through the window in each cell door. Most were apparently empty, but three down and over to the left side, she heard shouting and stamping from a cell.

She could hardly leave anyone to die, die as horribly as John, but she was a little disturbed to notice that the prisoner was a young man with stubble who shouted "Allahu Akhbar" repeatedly as he stamped with seven hole black Doc Martens on what was left of another small dead, very dead, god. It only reassured her a little that his Arabic had a pronounced Yorkshire accent.

She opened the door, and coughed significantly. She needed an ally and could not afford to be fussy, though she almost reconsidered when she saw him avert his gaze from her face.

In the circumstances, "Come with me if you want to live" really did not seem appropriate.

"We need to get out of here." She scanned his face for some sign of understanding. "That thing is going to go on killing, and we need to stop it."

"It's killing fooking American kaffirs." Definitely Yorkshire. "Why should I care?"

"Because sooner or later it is going to get beyond these walls and start killing whatever lies outside them at the time. Which last time I looked was no longer London, but somewhere with bright sun, tanks, and fine white dust all over everything. Sounds like somewhere you might care about? Because it really did not look like New Mexico."

He thought for a second, keeping his face as impassive as possible, and still avoiding eye contact, and then he looked up and smiled.

"You used the creature to kill Americans, knowing it would grow, and kill more, and now you want to kill it, when it is harder to kill. Why?"

Emma realized she was going to have to face up to something which might forever change how she thought about herself.

"They'd killed my friend and threatened me. And I was angry and didn't think it through."

The worst of it was that, though she had her dead that watched her reproachfully at night for failing to save them—and John would be there too next time she got to sleep—she knew Green and his men would not be among them. Any more than Elodie's father had been, or all the other vampires and elves.

I'm a vengeful bitch, she thought, and I don't care about perpetrators who put themselves in harm's way. And then realized she had said that aloud.

"Pretty hardcore, Emma Jones. Let's see if you live up to your reputation. I'm Syeed, and I hope you won't have heard of me."

Emma sighed resignedly. "My reputation?"

"Are you kidding?" He got more Yorkshire and less austere-sounding as he went on. "When I was young and before I got serious I was a huge Elodie fan. And the tabloids were all over whether you were her gal pal or just her psychic. And these days the brothers have an interest in you—because you've been seen out with Ruthven the Killer. Wheels of Death, they call him."

"I'll be sure to tell him. But if you are coming with me, we'd better get a move on. Before the Americans and their subcontractors get over the creature and come looking for us."

As she spoke, the floor bucked and it sounded like the entire corridor was screaming for a second.

"What the fuck?" Not Bradford, possibly Huddersfield.

"I think the creature has grown. It is tearing down walls. I wondered whether the corridor was a living thing, and now we know."

"The creature?"

"Technically, it's some sort of zombie god—not a god of zombies, a god that is a zombie." Shut up Emma, he's not interested, not really. And he's a believer so he really doesn't want to know. "But let's just say creature rather than get bogged down in theology."

He looked the whole time as if he was simmering with vague fury. "How fooking considerate of you, but let's not pretend you're not an unbeliever and anything you want from me isn't going to end in betrayal."

"Whatever."

At least he had the grace not to say that she would betray him, when she knew perfectly well that it was likely to be the other way around.

Emma looked out into the corridor and walked in the direction away from the few remaining screams, not looking to see whether Syeed followed her. After a moment, she heard his footsteps behind her because, really, what else was he going to do?

And letting him come up behind her was a demonstration of trust and his doing so without attacking her was a demonstration of trustworthiness, or at least of common sense.

After a while he caught up with her. He was diligently not looking at her face, but he kept sneaking peeks at her hair.

"That's not dye, is it?"

"No."

The floor bucked again, this time so violently that they were thrown down in an untidy pile. When Emma looked around, they were in an entirely different stretch of the corridor, broadening into what was almost an open-plan office with desks and chairs.

Suddenly their ears exploded with gunshots and running feet and a group of the American guards who all looked alike were surrounding Emma and Syeed. One of them held a gun to her head but most looked back down the corridor.

Reinhard was there, his side-arm drawn and held ready. He paid no attention to the captives but stared fixedly in the direction from which they had come.

There was a heavy tread; it was as if something were walking at a funereal pace, but it rushed towards them far faster than the sound of its terrible stride. The small muddle of parts had become a creature that filled the corridor floor to ceiling, and out to the sides as well—a titan, a noble human face with lips that drooled and dead, dead eyes, almost no neck or legs, one arm that ended in a trailing hairy-knuckled hand and another in something like a lobster's claw. In spite of the noise of feet, its lower extremities were still slime and chaos; perhaps what made the noise of pacing was its memory of feet. Or the feet it would have when it ate more men.

And fleeing ahead of it, somehow keeping pace and reeling away from that claw as it snipped at him, was Tomas, unarmed and running as if he could escape Hell.

With no care for his colleague, Reinhard shot wildly—at least one of his shots tore into the friar's robe. The Americans fired too, but somehow Tomas avoided the hail of their bullets and the creature ignored them altogether. The bullets passed harmlessly into it and through it.

Reinhard threw his weapon down, drew himself up straight, stuck

281

his right arm up in a swift salute and shouted "Heil Hitler."

Then it was upon them—for a moment Emma found herself surrounded by a cloud, a soup, a jelly—and then it was gone, leaving her and Syeed untouched but still sprawling.

This time it had been less efficient in its eating. Still not much blood, but the floor was littered with skulls and large bones and drifts of the white dust, and a lot of metal and empty cloth.

Syeed reached out and grabbed at an automatic weapon and then pulled his fingers back, swearing violently.

There was a sudden ripping of cloth. Tomas emerged from behind one of the over-turned desks, walked over and passed Syeed a strip of his robe. "You had better wipe that," he said. "Quickly. It is some kind of acid and will char you to the bone if you leave it. Back down there I saw the creature spit it at soldiers as it rolled forward, and they died. Unpleasantly."

Digestive juices then, but there were things Emma needed to think about far more urgently.

"Reinhard?" she asked.

"Burned, eaten and gone." Tomas' voice was at once exultant and gleeful. "It ate him as readily as it did the Americans. Which surprised me. Clearly his feelings for his dead leader amounted to worship and to faith."

"I got the impression you did not like him very much."

"Bloody murderers, the pair of them," Syeed said.

"Ah yes," Tomas agreed. "But of which of us here is that not true? You by intent, at least, me by long practice. Perhaps Miss Jones here, since she seems to do it with reluctance."

Emma had been wondering where the exhilaration came from, and the salty taste in the back of her throat.

"Not so much." She heard the ruefulness in her voice. "Slinging that thing at Green pretty much took that particular virginity."

"He needed killing," Tomas said. "In any universe."

"You talk of more than one?"

Tomas was a small man, but he made himself as tall as he could, and Emma reflected that, in his day, he must have been a powerful preacher.

"The universe in which I thought I did God's will. I killed people by the score—I stood by the fire as the executioner lit it, and blessed the flames in which men and women burned. I watched as children's feet were crushed to make their parents repent, and I thought it a good act that might save them from Hell. And that universe was a lie, was it not? The universe in which we live is one in which I was damned to Hell, and let out to torture some more. There is no justice, and I am still here and it was Reinhard, who did not want it, who gets the peace of annihilation."

There were still shouts and screams coming from somewhere behind them and to the left.

Emma was confused. "I thought the creature had gone. Or were there other prisoners who have escaped?"

"It has escaped," Tomas said, "but in other parts of the corridor, it has yet to finish eating Green, and you are still in your cell. Doubtless in other parts of the corridor, it is tomorrow, or yesterday, and the more it bucks and jumps, the messier that will become."

"I saw an episode of *Star Trek: Voyager* like that once," Syeed offered.

"They are shadows, merely," Tomas shrugged. "They may sound terrifying but they are in a different time, and cannot harm us."

As if to contradict him, a door opened and six shambling beasts strutted out. Emma had seen their like in Los Angeles, and seen them eaten, but it seemed unlikely that any god would intervene to save her here. Their eyes lit up with greed.

"Snacks," one said.

Tomas narrowed his eyes and stepped in front of them.

"*Exorcizamus te, omnis immundus spiritus, omnis satanica potestas, omnis incursio infernalis adversarii, omnis legio, omnis congregatio et secta diabolica, in nomine et virtute Domini Nostri Jesu Christi, eradicare et effugare a Dei Ecclesia…*" he intoned.

One of the brutes held up its hands in the universal sign of giving up.

"There's no need to take that attitude," it growled petulantly and turned huffily on its heel. With its cohorts, it marched back through the door and slammed it behind them.

"Well." Emma's interest was piqued. "I wasn't expecting that to work."

"Nor I," Tomas admitted, as they trudged down the endless passage again. "Centuries in Hell being shoved around by creatures like that and it never occurred to me before that I still could compel them. Apparently, though damned, I am still a priest forever, according to the order of Melchizedech. And the followers of Wycliffe are not only heretics, but proven wrong."

"But you're not a believer anymore." There was an unbecoming note of gloating in Syeed's voice.

"None of us are," Tomas said "Or we would have been eaten already."

"You mean it eats faith?" Emma could have kicked herself. "Or rather the faithful."

"So it seems."

"I am a warrior of God," Syeed shouted proudly.

"You are a silly boy trying on faith as if it were a new style of beard." The contempt in Tomas's voice clearly stung Syeed as badly as the acid had his fingers. "In my time, I would have broken you in hours."

"Where does that leave you?" Emma said. "Because you just used ritual, and it worked."

"Doubting my own doubts," Tomas said. "And among them doubting that I will be quite so unscathed next time we encounter a dead god."

Ahead of them, Emma saw a hole in the wall that oozed a sort of white liquid and seemed to be rebuilding itself as the liquid set and hardened, like a scab on a graze or cut but faster than one would see on one's finger.

Through the hole, she could see stars sometimes and the night sky, and then a fibre at the heart of the wound would blink up and shut a second, and then it would be the car park, or for a second

284

Polly's office, or some street in a city she did not know. Near the hole, but in a part of the wall that seemed not to have been torn, she saw one of the tiles of a slightly different colour. She walked over and slapped it three times, and a door opened, alongside the wound, but a different sort of thing altogether.

The door opened on the car park she had seen before. It echoed with an endless warning siren, which no one seemed to be answering.

"How do we know that's where it's gone?" Syeed was clearly not one for the optimistic side of things.

"Well," Emma pointed out, "they do have to supply this place from somewhere, and Green did talk about the Iraq office…"

"Pretty fancy reasoning, but if you're going to wander out looking for something that might be elsewhere entirely –"

"The Moor is right, how can we be certain?"

She had no reason to trust Tomas, but he seemed to be throwing himself into this enterprise as enthusiastically as she could wish.

"Because of the tank lying on its side with great claw marks that carved their way into the side. Or is there some other monster apocalypse booked for today that I am unaware of?" Emma said.

She looked more closely—there were piles of clothing and bones scattered among the vehicles. Clearly guards and more guards had answered the alarm, and suffered death.

Stepping out into the car park was to step out into blistering heat and to find her eyes stinging from dust. She had never been more glad she kept sunglasses in her bag, though she wished she had also packed a bottle of water and some sun-screen when she set out.

"We need to get cover, quickly, those of us who are not dead and used to the flames of Hell."

Cover was easily come by, she found, because all of the vehicles had their motors and air-conditioning running. She tried the door of the first vehicle she came to that was not actually a tank and found with relief that it was unlocked. It even had keys in the ignition. Which reminded her.

"I can't drive."

Syeed was peering under the tarpaulin on top of the vehicle with an excited expression.

"It's all still here," he said, "Arrogant fooking kaffirs arrested me the other side of their car park and didn't bother to look see what I might have already put together."

He flipped off the tarpaulin, and there, mounted in the middle of the roof of the vehicle, was something that looked even to Emma's untrained eye like a rocket launcher. And several rockets dumped alongside it.

"Get me near to that thing and we'll see what it looks like with a couple of these up its arse," he said. "Only I can't fire and drive."

"I could try," Emma said. "How hard can it be?"

"Hard enough," Tomas said. "It took me weeks to master it when I was sent back to Spain some years ago. Lucifer was paid handsomely for my services. And I acquired one or two useful skills by way of compensation for my time."

He was a terrible driver. Emma found herself jounced about in the seat next to him and just hoped he could keep the Humvee from tipping over. At least it was pretty clear where the dead god had gone—the perimeter fence had been ripped apart and was lying on the ground, parts of it still spitting electricity and some kind of magical energy.

By now, the god seemed to have grown feet, and perhaps legs, because it was leaving great footprints with a running stride in the dusty ground. By the time its tracks reached a tarmaced road, it was clear where it was going. They had gained on it enough to see it heading towards the smoke and clamour of a small town.

"We don't let it get there." Emma made sure to sound very serious indeed. "Whatever the cost to us. If it eats that many people, it would take the Huntress to stop it."

"We could..." Tomas seemed to be thinking through an argument aloud, probably to dismiss it, "we could let it feed and hope that, in due course, one of the powers would come for it."

286

"Those are my brothers it's going to eat," Syeed said. "And my sisters."

This was clearly a little bit of an afterthought, and aimed at Emma's sensibilities, but still, it was a concession.

Emma found herself wanting to shout and swear, but contented herself with tones of cold annoyance. "I don't fancy explaining to the Huntress that we let it become a real menace because we were concerned about our own skins. It's my responsibility; I let it out; I didn't know how quickly it would feed and grow."

"That is a good reason too." Tomas had moved through considering into a final certainty. "I will tell you mine. Perhaps I believe enough that it will chase me, if the rockets do not destroy it. I am weary of guilt, and one of my visions promised me peace. Perhaps this hunt will lead me there."

Emma reached into the icebox she had found under the seat and pulled out the two bottles of water it had in it. She passed one up to Syeed and offered the other to Tomas, who waved it away. She took a sip before speaking.

"You mentioned visions earlier. I didn't know that damned souls got them…"

Tomas shrugged. "Nor I, which is why I sometimes managed to fool myself of late that perhaps I was not damned. She came to me in the night, the Blessed Virgin, not as I have always imagined Her, as young as when the angel came, but a woman still young but of mature years. She looked at me sorrowfully and said, 'Tomas, Tomas, there is no hope for you in Heaven or in Hell.' I said, 'Where then can I find peace?' She said, 'Perhaps in annihilation, or what lies beyond it, but nowhere in heaven or hell.' I wanted to believe it a dream and no true vision, but She caught my look and would not be gainsaid. Of a sudden, She had all of Her son's wounds and said, 'If you doubt me, Tomas, you know what to do.' And I knew that to touch those wounds would be a profanation. I believe nothing else, but I believe that was a true vision. And I see my course."

"Virgins. Wounds." Syeed sounded unimpressed. "You're supposed to be People of the Book, but it all sounds like bloody idolatry to me."

"Oh hush," Emma said. "Let's keep our mind on blowing the crap out of that thing we're chasing. And you're neither of you right. I happen to have met God, and he is a charming old gent, but nothing special."

Syeed grumbled under his breath.

"She has, you know," Tomas said. "It's in Lucifer's private file on her."

"Shut up the pair of you. Syeed, surely we're close enough to…"

"Helmet," he said, and then, as she grabbed the one she found under her seat and jammed it on her head, "Now, duck!"

There were a series of explosions that were deafening even with the earmuffs built into her helmet, and a sense of something whizzing not nearly far enough overhead.

Half a mile down the road, there was a crater where Syeed's first rocket had not quite got the range right. A few yards further on, there was a cloud of red smoke, or rather of smoke from the explosions and particles of whatever the god had for blood.

When Emma's ears stopped ringing, and she took the helmet off, she could hear a noise a bit like a lion's roar and a bit like a dentist's drill in the way it penetrated into your bones. It was a dead god moaning its hurt, but no deader than it had been before.

"You've managed to blow its leg and its claw off." Tomas swung himself out of the driving seat. "That will come in handy when it chases me." He slapped the door of the vehicle from his place on the ground. "Now, young Syeed, get down here and drive back to the base. I'm sure you and Emma can come up with some sort of nasty surprise for the creature."

"But how will you get it to chase you?"

Tomas smiled. He looked almost like a saint in a painting. "I have lots of practice at talking myself into what is convenient. I may not have faith, not the sort that moves mountains, but I can summon enough of its appearance to fool something large, hungry and in pain. And I believe in my vision and I hope to believe in Her promise. I do not choose to exist and I was brought up to pay my debts, all of them."

As he walked down the road towards the crippled god, he shouted back, "I believe that we can kill it with fire. Fire purifies, or so I have always believed."

Emma thought of all he had sent to the flames, and shuddered. And guessed a part of his meaning.

Syeed swung himself down into the driving seat.

"We'd better work fast." Emma noticed his smug, toothy smile and looked at him enquiringly. "Or is this going to be a case of something you prepared earlier?"

"Let's go have a look, shall we?" Syeed said. "The brothers always told me that security firms were sloppy, but this lot are pretty much beyond belief. They missed one of the stashes I put together. Maybe they really did think I'd just got to the base when they caught me." His smile grew broader. "Inshallah."

Clearly the day-to-day stupidity of the Burnedover people was on the same scale as what Emma assumed had been some kind of scheme to weaponise bits of dead gods as instruments of mass destruction against populations of believers. Was that really what she thought they had been up to—horrid when she suddenly put it together.

And they put their base camp near a town so it would have plenty to eat.

In any case, short of Syeed's having painted a sign that said "Ignore this large stack of fuel accelerants, oxygen cylinders and white phosphorus grenades" and stuck it on the tarpaulin over the stack, a tarpaulin carefully weighted down with full petrol cans, they could hardly have done a worse job of finding his preparations for some sort of mayhem.

She looked at him quizzically.

"In the jihadi camp,"—his smugness got more unbearable the more he knew how indispensable he was being—"th'instructor said,

'Always be neat. People never notice stuff that's neat.' And he was right."

Laying their trap required little more effort, in the end, than moving the neat pile into a central empty area of the car park as quickly as possible, and then emptying the petrol cans over it.

"I hope you've got matches," Syeed said, "They took mine off me."

Emma, aware that so far her contribution had been minimal, amused herself with the possibility of letting him suffer for a couple of minutes, and then just said, "Setting fire to this lot—really not a problem."

"Long as you're sure," Syeed said. "We'd better lay some sort of fuse, or maybe make a couple of cocktails. Not the kind you're used to."

"That won't be necessary." She took great pleasure in making her smile as lofty and mysterious as possible.

"No, really." He looked genuinely anxious. "I know all about making a big bang, but in jihadi school they weren't big on safe distances. Which I didn't care about then."

"And now?"

"Let's just say I'm taking this whole fooking martyr's death under advisement a bit."

They laid a long petrol trail and retreated to the far corner of the car park where one of the gates was, and ducked under the no longer manned barrier. Emma retrieved the helmet and put it back on.

They had a worrying few minutes, hoping that no surviving Burnedover people would suddenly turn up from out of the corridor, which still seemed to be in place where they had exited it. Emma had not known how to shut the door. It was still there, and some of the time the wound was there beside it, though largely closed and scabbed. They were also worried that the god would have caught Tomas—he was after all centuries old and had spent much of that time in Hell. Just how good was he at taunting, and believing, and running, and doubting, all at the same time? On the other hand, he had shown a nifty turn of speed in the corridor…

In the event, their worries were irrelevant. A bell rang, and something crunched on the stones and sand behind them.

"I found a bicycle," Tomas said unnecessarily. "Another of those skills I picked up in Spain."

Syeed clearly wasn't getting the emphasis, and Emma really did not want to know which side had been hiring famous inquisitors. Either answer would depress her.

The roaring they had heard on the road was close now, closer than they had been to it before.

"It's coming." Tomas said. "That your trap? Nice neat work."

He got off his bike, then walked, his head held high, to the middle of the pool and clambered to the top of the stack of combustibles and explosives, pausing along the way to tuck a petrol can under one arm, and lay down upon the jagged, evil-smelling heap as if on a soft bed. He upended the petrol can and poured its contents over himself as he lay there.

Syeed was aghast. Tomas raised his head and looked at then sternly. "What you would do for the hope of Paradise, I do for the hope of nothingness. Be warned, both of you, where certainty leads you."

The roaring of the god was nearly on top of them now but Tomas, without shouting, managed to speak so loudly that they could hear him clearly from yards away.

"I was not only inquisitor," Tomas Torquemada said, "but judge. And I judge myself not fit to exist any longer, nor do I wish to."

Emma grabbed Syeed by the arm and they ducked behind the guard post by the barrier.

"No, seriously. How are you going to set fire to it from here?" Syeed was really very anxious indeed, sweating in fact. Emma favoured him with a grin as toothy and smug as the one he had been laying on her for the last twenty minutes.

"Inshallah," she said, rather hoping her pronunciation passed muster.

The god hurled itself on Tomas as if he were the meal it had longed for for days.

"Into the hands of nothing," he screamed and started to crumble.

Emma stood up, and flicked one of her sparks on to the thin line of petrol they had trailed behind them.

Syeed gawped and she grabbed his arm. Suddenly what had seemed a safe distance five minutes ago seemed horribly close now.

"Run," she screamed, hoping they could make it to absolute safety before the heavier things went bang.

Not even looking behind her to see if he were catching up, she covered as much ground as she could and then hurled herself down flat with her hands over her ears. She caught sight of Syeed doing the same a few feet away.

The series of explosions that followed, and the shower of metal debris, fragments of divine flesh, and the white dust that had been a man and a priest and a repentant monster, seemed to go on forever, and for a short time, and for no time at all. It was a caesura in reality.

At the end of it, she and Syeed, slightly deafened—she had to shout to be sure he was hearing her—stood up and watched the pillar of flame and knew that their work here was done. Flames had even shot through the open door of the corridor and Emma could see things burning in there.

A cough behind her, and the noise of wheels on the dusty tarmac.

"If you're quite done here, Emma," Tom's voice feigned something quite like boredom as if blowing up dead gods was something he did every day, which for all Emma knew, he did, "I can offer you a lift back to Miss Wild's."

"That would be handy." Emma tried for a similar note, in an attempt to seem professional. "Caroline must be quite frantic."

"She was, while you were in the corridor, but Polly picked you up on a scan the moment you and your two friends came out of that door."

He pointed at the hatch, out of which smoke was pouring. Suddenly the whole area of space around it convulsed and a quantity of burning furniture, bits of the dead, and random weaponry ejected, along with what looked rather like vomit. Then the door spat out a quantity of dirty water, shook itself again, and shut. For a second, there was an afterimage of something oddly nodular, like a ginger root, or a mandrake, and then the air popped and it was gone.

Tom looked round at Syeed, who was hanging back as if thinking of making a futile run for it.

"Nice work, Mr. Rahman, isn't it?"

"Don't patronize me." Syeed stood melodramatically tall. "Just get it over with."

Tom tutted. "My dear chap,"—he was being quite caricature posh, Emma thought—"no need for there to be any unpleasantness at all today. You did us all a favour, and it will go in your file."

"I don't do favours for British Intelligence."

"You misunderstand me, dear chap. I don't mean anything that parochial. I mean, the human race."

Syeed looked at once embarrassed and truculent.

"Now of course," Tom reached up and patted him on the arm, "it may well be that, over the next few years, because of these bloody stupid wars my political masters have got us into, we shall meet again in less happy circumstances. I do want to assure you, it won't be personal, and I won't take any pleasure in it at all."

"Oh, stop it the pair of you." Emma always found it particularly irritating when boys high on testosterone tried to play politeness games. "Can't we just cut to the chase?" She really did want to get back and be with her girlfriend. And have another cup of Miss Wild's excellent tea.

"I'm sure I don't know what you mean, Emma."

"I don't get what you think this kaffir ponce and I can possibly have to talk about."

"Enemy of my enemy."

Emma felt she had better clarify, just in case it wasn't what they were quite ready to admit to proposing to each other.

293

"These Burnedover Inc. people aren't anything official, they've been doing covert abductions and god knows what else in the UK, and they were prepared to test mystical WMDs on civilian populations here. Syeed, can't you fight your war with them? I'm sure Tom's people would be most awfully grateful."

Both men now had slightly piqued expressions, as if she had trumped them on what each of them was about to propose to the other as if the other couldn't possibly have thought of it himself.

"That's not quite what I was going to say." Tom clearly did not want to let Emma set the agenda. "But, well, just because we are fighting a war right now, doesn't mean there shouldn't be channels of communication."

He paused for effect and for a prompt; when Syeed refused to oblige with anything but an irritatingly impassive stare, Tom gave up and went on. "I joined the game back when we were not talking to the IRA. We were so totally not talking to the IRA that actors had to play them on the news. But of course we were talking to the IRA. And one of the things we were talking to the IRA about, was, they really didn't much care for the Libyans who were giving them gold and arms. And nor did we, and not just for that reason. Like I say, channels."

"So how would that work?" Syeed sounded interested but unconvinced.

"I talk to my masters; you talk to yours. We agree not to try and kill each other personally while they're making up their minds, unless we really need to. You know the sort of thing. And every so often we meet in St James Park and walk around with our hands behind our backs and cough meaningfully." Emma was not entirely convinced either. "It's better than killing each other."

"Have to admit," Syeed conceded, "I've taken a particular dislike to Americans."

"These were very obnoxious Americans, indeed, Tom. Arrogant and stupid and they all looked bizarrely like each other. Almost as if…"

Emma really did not feel comfortable speculating about something that wasn't magic. Magic she could do. She needed to think; the boys needed to talk.

She wandered a little way and then a hatch opened, and a weeping white wound beside it. When she peered in, it hardly looked like a corridor any more—most of the tiles were gone and what had replaced them was reddish brown and covered with slime, or maybe mucus. It was like the inside of a throat, now, or some more unlovely biological duct.

And squelching through the sogginess that had replaced the floor came Reverend Black, missing a shoe, his elegant suit torn at the lapels.

Emma was sufficiently startled to see him that she didn't turn to run away from him and did not realize that the redness of his face was sheer blind rage until he had his hands around her throat.

He was screaming something about the Scarlet Woman, and she didn't think he just meant the colour of her hair. He also screamed, "God wills it," but it sounded more like a reflex than something he was thinking about.

Oh, this is really too fucking much, she thought. An entire miserable day and it is all this bloody man's fault somehow and the last thing I need is for him to kill me at the end of it. She ignored his hands for the moment, and reached up with both of hers, and pulled him sharply down by the ears, digging her nails into his cheek so vigorously that something tore underneath her clutching fingers. She butted him, hard, in the face, and kneed him, harder, in the balls in the same moment.

There's a secret to violence when you're small. You have just not to care that it's going to hurt, so long as you make sure it hurts them more. The helmet meant that she hardly felt his nose crunch at all.

Black's hands were off her throat and he was pretty much writhing on the floor almost before Emma had a chance to think of it. As she collected her thoughts a little, she felt her bag disengage itself from her shoulder—I never thought of its strap as a sort of limb or prehensile tail, she thought, but live and learn.

295

As Black lay on the floor, the bag stalked up to him, opened wide and teeth-filled jaws, and tore his ear off. Emma reached down before the bag could eat it, partly because you don't want your luggage developing a taste for human flesh and partly because if her idea was right, it might be evidence.

She put the ear in her pocket. The blood would probably dry-clean out and if it didn't, this outfit was pretty much a write-off by now anyway.

Black clapped to the place where his ear had been the hand that was not cradling his balls. Emma took a step towards him and he retreated back towards the door of what really was not something you could call a corridor any more. He stepped inside, his face still flushed with anger, then leaned forward and started shouting again.

"You haven't heard the end of this, Emma Jones. I have friends, friends so powerful you've no idea..."

But clearly no friends here, because the door suddenly snipped to—not like a hatch closing at all, more like a hungry mouth making a decision.

Most of his head, and the hand with which he had been gesticulating, fell plop into the dust at Emma's feet, and there was a small, silent and horribly final-sounding plop as all vestige of the creature the corridor had always been, really, disappeared.

Not just from here, Emma found herself thinking, probably from the world and from shadow too. Hope it never comes back.

Annoying to have a head and a hand as well when she'd already bothered to pocket the ear, but you can never have too much evidence.

She picked the head up by its remaining ear and picked the hand up with her other hand and wandered back to where Syeed and Tom were still hammering out some kind of agreement.

They looked at what she was carrying in mild shock and awe.

"Don't mind me, I just nearly got murdered. Again."

Syeed stood there with his mouth open; Tom opted for an *oh, this again* lazy smile.

"Who is that? And what did you do to him?"

"I hit him, he stepped back into the corridor, and it ate most of him and went away. His name is Black and he is—was—a television evangelist, who didn't like me much."

Tom produced a heavy-duty plastic evidence bag from somewhere inside his wheelchair. "Put what's left of him in here, and we'll take it back with us."

Emma was only too glad to get rid of it and wipe the worst of the blood off her hands with the wipes that Tom produced from another compartment.

"Let's get you back to Ms Wild's and get you cleaned up. Syeed, you can make your own way wherever you're going?"

It wasn't a question, more of a goodbye. Tom took Emma by the hand and she managed a quick wave to Syeed before she found herself back in Polly Wild's office.

The first thing she did, was throw up. There wasn't much in her stomach except the water she had drunk in the Humvee missile platform, but she brought it all up anyway. She had just enough presence of mind to drag the helmet off her head and over her face, and most of the vomit went into that.

Polly snapped a finger and a fetching young thing in a maid's uniform was there and had the floor clean almost before Emma had finished retching. She also took the helmet away—Emma wondered whether they'd bring it back, cleaned.

Caroline was there, cooing and caring, and Emma was conscious, amid the nausea, of how pissing off at such moments it was to have a girlfriend who could not actually hold your head in her hands and stroke the back of your neck.

"John?" Caroline said.

"I found him, but he didn't make it." Emma had never longed to see John when he was alive, but the taste of ashes in her mouth told her that she would miss him for the rest of her life.

"Didn't like him much, but that shouldn't have happened." Caroline clearly knew that insincerity would be more annoying than otherwise.

297

Emma turned to Polly Wild. Polly had been joined by the Lord, and by Sharpe, and by several other senior looking figures, most of them human, whom Emma did not know.

She thought she had better make this sound official.

"An American security firm, Burnedover Inc., with links to Evangelical preacher Reverend Black, has been kidnapping British citizens and probably other nationals and using them as experimental subjects to reanimate dead and forgotten gods as weapons of mass destruction aimed at civilian populations. I and a colleague destroyed two of the dead gods, one of which had earlier got loose and wiped out the security staff, but no civilians. Reverend Black attempted to kill me, but was eaten by his base—we acquired some remains for respectful disposal, perhaps after evaluation, scientific or magical. His staff all resembled him closely. The base has reverted to being some sort of alien incursion of an organic nature, and seems to have returned whence it came. Ma'am."

"That's the most succinct bleeding report I've had in seventy years," Miss Wild was clearly impressed. "This ain't a job interview, you know."

"I have a job," Emma shrugged. "I wasn't reporting to you, any of you—regard it as a cc. You need to know this stuff, I guess. All of you, especially the ones I don't know."

"Boss says, well done." Caroline looked round and so did Emma. Most of the people they didn't know had no idea that Caroline had spoken.

One of the men in suits looked round at his colleagues. "Are we supposed to take any of this seriously?"

They looked at him stony-faced. The man standing next to him said to him, "You really had better learn to shut up and listen. This is how things work, a lot of the time."

Emma hadn't really thought about how much the average mandarin knew about her work, and her world. Clearly, more than she might have thought. It was also, though, that the grownups wanted to talk and no one was going actually to come out and ask her to leave. She turned to Tom and Sharpe.

"I don't think there's actually anything very much for me to do here, now. Perhaps a car…"

Tom was suddenly acting as if he were some very junior cop at Scotland Yard, just at the meeting to show people in and out and not say anything. Emma supposed that if you were the Wheels of Death, Ruthven the Killer, it would rather spoil the point if everyone knew about it. He hadn't reported, not even to corroborate what she'd said—so he was kept more secret than, say, murderous American evangelists kidnapping British citizens.

Whatever. It was something she would ask him about someday soon. When she met to discuss with him the very dim security guards who all looked alike and the not especially bright officer who looked quite like them…

Caroline prodded her awake when they got home. Emma was still feeling a little sick, but she hadn't eaten all day, so she stepped into the bagel shop to get a smoked salmon and cream cheese onion platzel, and a tea, because then she wouldn't have to boil a kettle.

"I'll see you up there," Caroline said.

Honestly, Emma thought to herself, hours apart and her worried and me in danger, but she still can't be arsed waiting around for five minutes while I queue for food.

When she got up to the flat, she put the bag with her bagel and cup of tea, down on the floor a second while she unlocked the door, and disengaged the alarm. She held the door open with her foot and bent down to pick them up and so was not paying entire attention when she walked into the living room to find an elegant man sitting on her sofa. And no Caroline.

He was brown-skinned, and was wearing the sort of sunglasses you see on dictators on newsreels. Emma knew nothing about the higher levels of tailoring, but that suit was clearly just the sort of thing she knew nothing about; it had lines that seemed to cut the air about them when he moved.

"Perhaps you can help me." His voice had a clipped authority that both bullied and wheedled. He was clearly used to people finding him charming and not noticing how rude he was. "A part of one of my collections has gone missing."

There was absolutely no question in Emma's mind about who this was, and what he was looking for. "Tomas sought and found annihilation. His idea, his plan and his choice."

"I see." There was a lazy malice in his voice, as you would expect.

There was an awkward pause. She wasn't going to ask him for anything, even to speak. She *wasn't*. The effort of not saying anything made her neck muscles ache as if she were using them to lift something heavy.

"You were involved in me losing something I valued. I've taken something of yours away. Actions have consequences."

There was no smell of sulphur or clap of thunder. He just was not there any more. And neither was Caroline.

"Actions have consequences," Emma smiled, and knew that there was no humour anywhere in her eyes. "Oh, yes, they do."

She sat down and ate her bagel, which tasted stale even though it had just come out of the steamer. Her tea was salt with the tears that streamed down her face. None of this mattered, only that she was more desolately alone than she had been in twenty years.


The Tsar was dying. His courtiers looked at his young son like wolves.

Emma knew that the sadness she was feeling was at not having Caroline with her to moan about having to sit through the music, but the music was so perfect for her mood. It was high tragedy and something that had been earned by arrogance, and it was a sense of universal doom.

So much better in the original version, harsh and uncompromising, she thought, and then felt ashamed at thinking about such things when her girlfriend was in Hell.

It was the closest thing to a first night she could think of—a revival, but with a major singer doing the role in Russian for the first time—and it was the full text. Somehow Emma rather thought the Lord God was a man to get his money's worth. And that really did look like him, beard and eyebrows and muscles and brocade waistcoat, yes definitely.

Down there in the stalls. You'd think he would spring for a box but maybe he likes the sense of being incognito among his people, only not very incognito given how much those seats cost.

Not that she could talk. In a box all to herself. How convenient to have saved the place from a salamander summoned by someone who took Boulez too literally.

She'd have to go down and pay court, but he'd almost certainly seen her. Or one of his minions had. He hadn't had so many obvious minders in Brazil, but then, that was a night the world nearly ended, and he hadn't made his entrance until after the battle and the assassination attempt.

Boris died and it was the long scene in the forest with choruses acting badly and a symbolic Shakespearean fool singing woe to Russia. Personally she preferred the shorter highlights version. Anyway, she needed to slip out and be downstairs to join the queue.

Once you knew they were there, the demi-gods and saints and other beings were as obvious a part of the crowd as the corporate sponsors and the opera queens. It was the way they wore evening dress, she thought, as if it were civvies and a proper person wore armour or robes.

Still, these days, Emma was one of them. She still didn't think of herself that way, but she so was. When she slipped in past the curtains, the ushers didn't stop her even though the chorus was still moaning about Jesuits. And the two elderly incarnations of the living Buddha she found herself standing next to bowed to her, and she gave them the little smile she'd seen the Queen do on TV.

Back when she was a civilian, she'd never noticed all this

301

protocol going on, but now…Without Caroline to take the piss, she thought, you could get to enjoy it too much.

The chorus ran off stage and the idiot went "Woe to Russia" a few times and that was that. Very nicely done, on the whole, though the chorus really was a bit ragged. Still, Tomlinson was an amazing Boris.

She got into the spirit of things and shouted and clapped, then noticed that Jehovah was positively Italian in the way he screamed, whistled and threw flowers. Then he turned around, obviously feeling her eyes on his neck. And was all smiles and charm.

If there had been a queue of suppliants, she had obviously jumped it by being there. Saving the universe will do that for a girl.

"Oh look, it's young Emma Jones," he boomed in a voice that penetrated past the ongoing applause. "The rest of you can wait outside. I want to talk to my favourite young Magus."

Emma looked apologetically at the Living Buddhas, who bowed again. I suppose if you extinguish desire, you don't mind waiting, she thought.

Jehovah moved through the crowd. You couldn't compare him to anything—a thunderstorm or an elephant—he was just this person out of whose way everyone got without even thinking about it or knowing they were doing it. What you did know about, she found when it happened, was his arm on your shoulders and a sort of fatherly hug that was a bit too much like a grope.

"Where's the girlfriend, Emma Jones? Doesn't like the opera? I've got a couple of those miseryguts, so I leave them in Heaven." Then he caught her mood, and looked serious and chastened and, yes, apologetic, how sweet of him. "There's a problem?" His voice combined concern and vague pique. "I put out the word that you were under my protection. Won't save you from His Darkness, or Berin, or whatever he really goes by. But anyone else."

Emma looked up at him. He clearly wasn't lying and didn't know. "She was kidnapped from my flat a couple of days ago." She kept her voice flat and affectless so that she wouldn't let him see her cry. "Lucifer took her."

He looked shocked. "I told him quite specifically." Clearly, he was more concerned about the disobedience than about her loss.

Emma was not quite sure how to put this next bit. "I know one or two things that I would have assumed you knew. We need to talk." She felt a beautiful quiet confidence. *Actions have consequences, you smart-suited bastard.*

Jehovah harrumphed and was vaguely embarrassed. "I never said I was omniscient. It's one of those things people say about me and it's tempting to believe it's true when it mostly is. You know how it goes, Emma Jones." Then he made a decision. "If this is something serious, let me just shake hands with these chaps, and those other chaps, and then we'll go somewhere quiet and have a pint."

Oh god, Emma thought, Jehovah's a bloke.

What was worse, once they got into the large black limo with a driver behind smoked glass, and a couple of minders in the seats opposite, who looked just like the angels she had met on her first day on the job, he shouted through to the driver, "Take us out East."

He turned to Emma. "Bethnal Green, isn't it? Say what you like about little bars in Shanghai or Paris, I always say there's nothing like a good East End boozer. Pearly Kings, rhyming slang, warm beer, standing round the piano having a sing-song."

"It's been a while, hasn't it? Spirit of the Blitz?" she ventured.

"All those people praying, I could at least go drink with them. Looking the East End in the face sort of thing."

"And the other side? How was the beer in Munich?"

"Well, obviously." He didn't see any problem, clearly. "Love the place. I never miss Bayreuth. Best Meistersinger I ever saw, '43 was—there was an intensity to the whole thing. I know some people didn't like that production."

"Sacred German Art," he sang, in a very creditable low baritone. "Best thing about the war years was, I could go to Bayreuth without him there—I have some standards."

There was a line of questioning here that was going to lead to trouble, so Emma let it go. For the moment.

She didn't do pubs, herself, especially in the area where she lived. She ruled out the two gay bars, and the ones that had lap dancers. And the gastropubs, and the ones with quizzes and karaoke. They ended up in one of the places on Bethnal Green Road that hadn't been too obviously tarted up and turned into part of a chain.

"I've been here before," he said, looking round the place. "It was nicer then, and smelled of sweat; you people are all too damned clean these days."

He snapped his fingers and then sat down at a table; one of the angels brought over a pint and a gin and vermouth for Emma. It wasn't anything she'd ordered and it certainly wasn't a drink she liked but it wasn't going to be an issue she raised.

Jehovah raised his glass in a vague salute. "Now what's the problem, apart from the abduction of your light of love?"

Emma dithered for a second more about how she was going to broach this. She opted for saying, "Funny thing you should mention Nazis."

"I didn't."

"Well, you sort of did, Avoiding someone you didn't want to name at a Wagner opera counts as mentioning. So anyway, I met one the other day."

"What, a real one? Not just some want to be? I thought we had all the important ones stowed away in Hell."

"Well, so you did, I'm sure. Nonetheless, I got interrogated by Reinhard Heydrich only a couple of days ago. And he and his colleague Torquemada said something very interesting."

Jehovah was looking quite intense and very serious indeed. Worth knowing, she thought—there's a crease between his eyebrows that gets deep about the time that there's a flush in his cheek. Must be quite scary when he really loses it.

"They were working for some Americans who seem to have confused the difference between being a church and being a security firm, and were weaponizing bits of dead gods."

He spoke almost lightly as if he could deflect what was coming by treating it as trivial. "I'll have a word with Lucifer. If you're right, he's being very careless."

Emma coughed politely. "Actually, careless is not the word I'd use. Money was mentioned as changing hands. And this little enterprise seems to go back to the 1930s at least. Tomas mentioned the Spanish Civil War."

"Why on earth would my old and dear friend Lucifer want money? He rules Hell, that should be enough." Jehovah sounding hurt and in denial was a little too operatic to be entirely convincing. Clearly, though this was all news to him, it explained things he did already know.

"I'd imagine," Emma saw no point in avoiding malice, "he puts it in a Swiss bank account like everyone else."

Jehovah stared into his beer gloomily. "Everyone lets me down sooner or later." he grumbled. "If I'd my time over, I'd do it all myself. You can't even rely on family. I mean, there's the Son of course, but that's not the same, not really..." He caught himself, noticing a civilian was present.

Emma was quite glad she hadn't been in the firing line for some kind of theological revelation. She thought she'd better change the subject. "How do the others manage?"

"Other what?" he said, testily.

"Oh, you know. Other divine beings."

"Well, obviously if you've got yourself a good pantheon, you can delegate. Better than saints and angels, in some ways, because they don't come running every time there's some little problem. Disadvantage—well obviously, I could pick them off one at a time."

He smiled, as one with happy memories of mayhem and bribery. "Gautama, well. Amazing how he stays in business, really. No motivation. Still, what do you expect from a sheltered rich boy who found out the world wasn't built for him personally? Don't know about you, young Emma, but all this not wanting anything at all strikes me as sour grapes..."

Gods bitch about each other, she thought, of course they do.

305

"Of course," he said, "the whole thing with the Arabs was a bit worrying at first, until I realized it was me that they were worshipping, and all the unpleasantness was just a misunderstanding. The Prophet, nice enough chap once we got to know him—his wife made a good job of training him as a sales manager, and he brought all that into the biz. And once he was there to be talked at, Gabriel stopped bothering me with his literary efforts."

Emma sipped her disgusting drink, which, horrible as it was, gave her a chance to pause and put her ideas in order.

Everything else she had to say was speculation based on what she'd seen. Maybe she'd just not seen all there was to see of the magical universe, and was about to make herself look like an idiot, or maybe there was something new and nasty going on.

Two large young men with shaven heads walked up to the table.

"He bothering you?" one of them asked. He had the sort of tattoos that make you avert your gaze from all the faded blues and never quite even reds. All flags and battles.

"No, we're fine," Emma said, "just having a business meeting."

"Business, is it?" said the other in insinuating tones. "Well, we'll see about that. Can't have Pakis doing 'business' with their slappers in our local."

"Who are you calling a Paki?" Jehovah said, in a deceptively mild voice. "And Miss Jones is anything but a slapper."

The nastier of the two thugs smashed his bottle on the table, sending Emma's drink flying. Well there's always an upside, she thought, at least I don't have to drink any more of it.

She didn't have time to think about what to do next because the next thing she heard was the crack of the thug's wrist being broken, followed very speedily by the broken bottle falling to the floor and the noise of two shaven heads being knocked very firmly together.

Jehovah suddenly seemed to be about eight feet tall.

"I am the Lord thy fucking God, and I can beat up any ten men in this bar," he said, not even raising his voice very much.

All the other drinkers suddenly found something very fascinating about their beer mat, or their neighbour's tie.

The pub was very quiet while a couple of the angel minders removed the two young men. Emma did not like to think what was going to happen, nor cared especially.

"Zeus always used to say, nothing like getting down and hitting miscreants with your own two hands." Jehovah returned to his normal size and sat down again. "I always liked old Zeus. Shame about his statues. It was business, though."

He finished his pint and suddenly there was another one in front of him. Thankfully, no one replaced Emma's drink.

"I've been thinking, Emma." His tone was more avuncular even than before. "It's not a safe place out here."

"That's true. Because there's so much going on that I didn't think was possible. I thought I knew the rules. For one thing, I didn't think that the dead could walk around in tangible flesh."

"What do you mean, tangible? Of course they can't. No one comes back from the dead in the flesh. Contrary to what some people tell you. Even those few dead who rise as gods aren't really all that solid, but you're not talking gods, are you?"

"I mean, damned souls, like Tomas de Torquemada."

Jehovah knew the name well. At least he's not pretending amnesia.

"Tough call, that one, but he just liked his work too much for me to be comfortable around him, and Lucifer really wanted him. Suited his sense of justice, or so he said."

"Well, him, and Heydrich."

"Just how tangible are we talking?"

Emma ticked things off on her fingers. "He drove a Humvee and rode a bicycle. And complained about American Army rations. And could get his pocket picked."

Jehovah looked disturbed and impressed and amused, all at the same time. Emma thought she had better press her advantage. "And however he got back into some sort of flesh, Lucifer clearly knew all about it."

Jehovah looked angrier and angrier, but not with Emma, so she pressed on into areas about which she was even less sure. "Also, the dead god ate people, and it seemed like it ate them souls and all. Which I didn't think was how it worked. All that was left was dust. I mean, when Caro got eaten, her spirit was intact."

Jehovah now looked more than angry and impressed; he looked worried. "How do you know the souls are gone?" he asked, but seemed to be clutching at straws.

"Tomas said so, which might not mean anything, except that Lucifer said he was gone and gone for good, and was pretty annoyed about it."

Jehovah was so angry at this point that he wasn't even blustering, just sitting there, drinking a pint of beer that never seemed to get any emptier. He signalled to a minder, and Emma suddenly found another drink in front of her, this one yellow, with cream, a cherry and an umbrella.

"I need better help, who I can rely on, and who understands the modern world. I'll bet you can even use this Internet thing that the Son keeps going on about."

Emma didn't know how, without Caroline, she was ever going to hear from the Boss again, but loyalty and instinct and prudence all said the same thing. "As I told the Organs of the State, a couple of days ago. I Already Have A Job." There was no point in not making the position clear; he was the Lord God Almighty and she knew his record on people who didn't do what he wanted. Like Jonah.

"I wasn't giving you a choice."

"Um. Non Serviam. Is I think the usual expression."

He ignored her. "Just take a sip of that nice sweet drink you've been brought, and we'll be on our way."

Emma would never have drunk anything with an umbrella and a cherry, but thought in this context it would be a particularly bad idea.

"What if I don't?"

"Well," he was clearly being very patient with what he saw as idiotic recalcitrance, "what's in there should do the trick. Not certain, of course, because we don't know what the Solids did to you, precisely."

"Do the trick?" She wanted to hear him say it.

"Well, kill you, obviously. I'm not having live people cluttering up heaven. Sets a bad example and looks like favouritism. I'm the only living thing there, well, me and the Ghost."

Emma wondered how the only other living thing could be a ghost, but this was clearly some sort of private joke he was dying to let her in on. Or waiting for her to die to let her in on it. She did not encourage him.

"So, what if I just walk out of here?"

He looked at her tolerantly. "Of course, you could do that. And obviously I won't be protecting you anymore, which would mean you might get a hundred yards. Lots of people don't much care for you, and they are the sort of people who will know that your girlfriend has gone and that I'm not helping you either. So, either I get you delivered to me in Heaven after a lot more suffering than is in that glass. Or, maybe, which would be regrettable, from what you tell me, it's just possible that something annihilates your soul, which would be sad. Especially for your girlfriend. But useful, because I'd get to see how it happens, and take steps."

"So either I'm your slave, or your bait?"

"Don't think of it as a choice, Emma Jones." He looked horribly complacent. "Think of it as growing up and accepting how things just are."

Emma stood up. "I'll take my chances," she said, sounding a lot more arrogant and confident than she felt. But there was no way in, well, Hell, that she was going to let herself be bullied into suicide by this old conman.

"I thought you were my friend," she said.

"Yes," his voice was rich and lustrous and complacent, "but I am not a tame lion."

Seconds later, in the cold autumn night air, she almost felt she'd made a mistake.

Then she saw a number 8 pulling up to the bus stop she was already nearly at, and with a quick turn of speed was able to jump on board. Just as she noticed two men in dark glasses, who ran for the bus and missed it.

"You won't make a hundred yards?" she thought in triumph. "Lord God Almighty you may be, but you don't control Transport for London."

Then she noticed that the two men in dark glasses were easily keeping pace with the bus, somehow running alongside it, even when it was moving with nothing to slow it down, and saw that they even waited for it at the red light at Vallance Road.

The taste of gin and vermouth in her mouth had never gone away, or grown easier to tolerate. And now it was becoming gradually overwhelmed by fear.

The silver statuette flared, leaving an afterimage, but still cold to her touch, and outside the door the noise of feet running up the stairs was replaced by someone cursing in a language she did not speak, and by a gunshot, and by the noise of steel striking against steel, and of someone, several someones, or someone in several parts falling limply to the ground and then bouncing down the stairs, noisy and heavy as bowling balls. And the soft gently rasping sound that you might almost miss of steel being wiped on coarse cloth it might almost tear, but chose not to. As if someone were cleaning their sword on a dead opponent's now useless coat.

The knock at the door was almost a relief when it came. It did not sound like an announcement of doom, more like a call to awaken.

She did not move in response to open, just stood there with the statuette under her hand, waiting to see what would happen next.

The bolts and bars of the door opened, but gently, as if seduced, not as if anyone were forcing them. Outside there stood a tall woman in shining silver armour, carrying the unfeasibly large sword she had just finished wiping.

She smiled, and it was the smile of an old friend, not the sardonic grin of a triumphant enemy.

"If you're ready, Emma Jones, we should leave this place. Before more enemies come for you."

Come with me if you want to live, Emma thought. I didn't say it to Syeed and she doesn't say it to me, but it's still what everyone means. There's something so special about a rescue, you don't want to spoil it.

"Josette," Emma said, recognizing the young acolyte of the House of Art. "How nice of you to drop round."

"These days," Josette smiled with pride, "these days, Josette in Arcadia Ego, but you know me by another name too."

"Really?"

"You've been calling me Boss, for years."

Josette held out her hand, and Emma took it, holding it so tightly that she felt the other woman wince slightly in her grasp, as if Emma had accidentally pinched the scar of an old wound.

"I'll explain later," Josette said, "but we need to be gone. And then…"

"And then?" They had begun through shadow, with the shadows and lights of a London night flickering past as fast as Emma had ever experienced them.

"Then we'll go and look for Caroline."

311

## Some Things About Roz Kaveney

She has been a professional writer since her twenties but is publishing her first novel *Rhapsody of Blood – Rituals* and her first collection of poetry, *Dialectic of the Flesh*, at the age of 63. Asked why, she says, "Well, I was quite busy."

Friends say it's hard to be out with Roz in Central London and not find yourself being randomly greeted by other people she knows. Some say this happens in New York, too, on the rare occasions when she goes there. This is because Roz's circle of acquaintance includes everyone from politicians to poets, art historians to dominatrixes, at least one serial killer to at least one Poet Laureate.

She helped negotiate changes to the law that helped trans people—Roz is a proud trans woman—change their legal status; she helped block a law that would have imposed stringent sexual censorship in UK bookstores.

She once rescued a flatmate from a Chicago mob hit.

She and Neil Gaiman once sold a two-book deal on the basis of a proposal they improvised in a meeting at which the publisher had turned their original idea down.

She discovered in the British Library an unknown verse play by a major Victorian poet; later, she told this story to a leading contemporary novelist, who based an award-winning novel on it.

She knows that British Intelligence has a file on her—she's seen the letter in which an Oxford don denounced her to them as a subversive. She does not know what the don meant…

She co-founded both Feminists against Censorship and The Midnight Rose Collective. Look them up.

She's contributed to reference books that vary from *The Cambridge Guide to Women Writing in English* to *The Encyclopaedia of*

*Fantasy.*

She was deputy Chair of Liberty (The National Council for Civil Liberties), and active in the Oxford Union debating society, the Gay Liberation Front and Chain Reaction, a dyke SM disco she helped run in the 80s.

She's been on television talking about sex, alternate worlds and who should have won the Booker Prize in 1953 if it had existed then; she's been on radio talking about fan fiction and film music.

She was a contributor to the legendary Alan Moore anti-Clause 28 comic book AARGH! (Action Against Rampant Government Homophobia).

As a journalist, she's written about everything from the Alternative Miss World competition to the crimes of the Vatican.

Her acclaimed books on popular culture include *Reading The Vampire Slayer*; *From Alien To The Matrix*; *Teen Dreams*; and *Superheroes*.

"I was reared Catholic but got over it, was born male but got over it, stopped sleeping with boys about the time I stopped being one and am much happier than I was when I was younger."

She likes baroque opera, romantic string quartets, the music of Kurt Weill and Bruce Springsteen, the singing of Ella Fitzgerald, Ricki Lee Jones and Amanda Palmer.

She makes adequate chili, perfectly decent scrambled eggs, and a good cassoulet if she's got a couple of days.

She will write you a goodish sonnet in about five minutes if she's in the mood—sestinas usually take an hour.

When she grows up, she wants to be awesome.

For more about Roz, visit her Glamourous Rags website at:
glamourousrags.dymphna.net/index.html

Ingram Content Group UK Ltd.
Milton Keynes UK
UKHW010847270623
424105UK00001B/6

9